RAZZAMATAZZ

Razzamatazz

A NOVEL BY

Sandra Scoppettone

Carroll & Graf Publishers, Inc.
New York

Originally published in hardcover by Franklin
Watts in 1985, and in paperback by PaperJacks
Ltd. in 1986. This edition published by arrangement
with the author.

First Carroll & Graf edition 1995.

Carroll & Graf Publishers, Inc.
260 Fifth Avenue
New York, NY 10001

ISBN 0-7867-0230-3

Manufactured in the United States of America.

THIS ONE IS FOR
HELEN AND MARIUS
AND
RUSS TERRY,
BECAUSE HE
LOVES TO READ

Special thanks to the following people
who helped make this book possible:

Rev. Sara Campbell, Betty Dodson, Tim Gould,
Troy Gustavson, Maria Heney, Dave Horton,
Kathy Richter, Chief Robert Walden, and John Williams.

RAZZAMATAZZ

LOOKING BACK — 25 YEARS AGO

At a regular meeting of the North Fork Clergy Association, a resolution was passed unanimously as follows: "The North Fork Clergy Association records its opposition on moral grounds to the adoption of the proposition legalizing bingo in the town of Seaville."

Chapter One

Carl Gildersleeve was a jackass. He was also the mayor of Seaville, New York. And on the Saturday before the Memorial Day weekend for the past ten years he'd gathered all his friends and acquaintances at a cocktail party where, at some point in the festivities, he'd drag everyone outside to toast the opening of his Olympic-size, vinyl-lined pool. It was a foolish occasion because the pool could not be used for at least three days. That was how long it took to refill what had been drained the previous September, and for the chemicals to become effective. Still, it was an annual event in Seaville — one that almost all the guests hated.

For Colin Maguire it was a first. Mark Griffing, his old friend and boss at the *Seaville Gazette,* had told him what to expect and explained that it was not something one could say no to.

"We go," Mark had said, "and we stand around making small talk with a lot of other people who wish they were somewhere else, too. We drink a few weak gin and tonics, eat a couple of chips with a godawful dip that Grace Gildersleeve got out of some ladies' magazine, and then after the asshole opens his pool we make our exit."

Colin had said, "Mind if I give the dip a pass?"

And now he was standing on the Gildersleeves' patterned brick patio sipping a plain tonic and smoking one Marlboro after another, idly tapping a loafered foot. He couldn't help thinking that it was strange being here, at the end of the North Fork of Long Island, an area he'd never even heard of until two years before, when Mark bought the paper. Curious the places life took you to if the circumstances were right — or wrong.

He imagined what Ryan, his old boss on the *Chicago Tribune,* would say if he could see him now.

"Jesus, kid, what are you doin' on a penny-ante paper, goin' to piss-ant parties?"

But Ryan wouldn't say that because he *knew* why. Anyway, he was lucky to have this job. Fate, coincidence, call it what you want; Mark had saved Colin's ass. So now he was managing editor of the *Seaville Gazette,* making a third of what he'd made as a crime reporter on the *Tribune.*

He shook his head as if to jog an image from his mind, then looked around, his gaze settling on an attractive woman talking to Mark and Sarah. He wondered who she was because he'd never seen her before. After six weeks he thought he'd seen or met everybody worth meeting. And according to Mark, the Gildersleeve guest list would reflect only the top echelon of Seaville society. So who was this woman who looked so confident and crisp in a blue striped blouse and white skirt? She was gesturing with long thin hands as she talked, and then she laughed, her eyes almost disappearing as they crinkled at the corners. It made Colin smile. He joined Mark's group, but before he could speak he was stopped by a loud metallic sound.

Grace Gildersleeve was holding a large brass gong, which she struck again, silencing her guests. Carl cleared his throat, ran a hand over his fleshy face, then straightened the knot on his red-and-blue striped tie. It was a cloudy day, but Carl's ever-present sunglasses sat firmly on his wide nose.

"Okay, folks," he said. "This is the moment of truth. We're about to open the summer social season of Seaville. Hey, how's that for onomatopoeia, huh?"

"Jesus," Colin said under his breath and exchanged an incredulous look with Mark.

"Boys," Carl called to the two hulks standing at each side of the pool, "are you ready?"

The men nodded, and one gave Gildersleeve a salute with a beefy hand.

"'Okay, then let's go." He turned to Grace. "Hit that thing, dammit."

Grace energetically slammed the gong again, and the men began to roll back the aqua pool cover. Simultaneously, from two speakers positioned at the far end of the pool, Frankie Laine belted out "I Go Where the Wild Goose Goes."

Colin almost choked on a slug of tonic. "You devil, you," he said to Mark, "keeping the best part a secret."

"I didn't want to spoil it for you, pal."

"Can you believe it?" Sarah asked, her hand covering her mouth.

Mark said, "Let me introduce you. Colin Maguire, Annie Winters."

The woman in the blue striped blouse offered her hand, and Colin started to say something when there was a sound like a huge intake of breath. In fact, he realized, it *was* an intake of breath: a collective gasp. People were staring at the pool.

The cover had been rolled back a quarter of the way, and sticking out from beneath it were two feet, wrinkled and purplish.

"Christ almighty," Mark said.

Gildersleeve's face had drained of color, his cheeks two quivering pouches.

The pool men, T-shirts drenched with sweat, were staring stupidly at the water-logged feet. The bigger of the two called to Gildersleeve.

"You want we should go on, Mayor?"

Gildersleeve bit at his lower lip, chewing the flesh as if it were gum. For a moment Colin thought the man might cry. But then he pulled himself together. "I think we should clear the area first, the women and children into the house."

"Not on your life," Sarah said quietly.

Annie Winters said nothing but she didn't move.

The mayor went on, "Grace, take them into the house. And fast."

Grace Gildersleeve's chin trembled as she fought tears and, like a dazed sheepdog, began herding women and children toward the sliding glass doors at the back of the house.

It took only a few minutes before the women, Sarah and

Annie excepted, were banished to Grace's kitchen. Then Gildersleeve gave the pool men a signal with a quaking hand.

Everyone moved closer to the edges of the pool. Standing between Mark and Annie, Colin felt weak and silently prayed that he would get through this all right.

The men began to turn back the cover and with each roll exposed a little more of the ugly, swollen body: calves, knees, thighs, and then the groin. The woman's pubic hair looked white against the purplish-blue color of her skin. The exposure continued, revealing a distended belly, and waist, bloated breasts, arms at her sides, fingers curled. With a final wrench of the cover the woman's face appeared, distorted and inflated, the long hair floating behind her like a grotesque halo.

When Colin saw her eyes, open and staring, a look of horror burned into them forever, he dropped the glass from his hand and crumpled to the brick patio. It was Chicago all over again, and he was passing out.

LOOKING BACK — 50 YEARS AGO

A small boy who was unable to visit his
mother, who was in the maternity ward at
the Long Island Hospital in Seaville,
found a novel way to get around the rules.
The staff was greatly amused as the 12-
year-old climbed a tree near the window
of the room in which his mother was in
bed, and sitting on a limb just outside the
window, held a lengthy conversation with
his mother.

Chapter Two

When Colin came to he saw the face of the blond. Her blue eyes were open now, concerned and not smiling.

"Are you all right?" Annie asked.

He felt chagrined, taking a dive like that. How many bodies had he seen in his life? One hundred? Two, three? But it was different now. Still, he couldn't explain that to this woman he didn't know.

"Colin?" she said.

"Hey, pal, speak," Mark ordered.

Colin turned his head away from the woman, and looked into Mark's handsome face, the prematurely gray hair disheveled.

"Should I ask where I am?" he said, trying to joke.

"Why not?"

"Where am I?"

Mark said, "At the scene of a crime, so get your ass up."

"Easy now." It was Sarah.

Colin sat up slowly, his shoulder aching from the fall. He saw that the other men were still standing around, most of them staring at the body in the pool, but a few were looking at him, making him feel worse.

"Are you sure you're all right?" Annie asked.

Colin wondered why she cared, but was glad she did. "Yeah, sure, I'm okay."

Annie smiled. "Too much dip."

"I wasn't drinking," he said defensively. He got to his knees, then to his feet, wavering a second.

Mark grabbed his arm. "Hey, take it easy."

"I was just kidding," Annie said.

He ignored her.

"Don't look at the floater again if you don't want to," Mark said quietly.

"No, it's okay, I just . . . I just . . ."

"Skip it."

Their eyes locked in understanding. In Seaville only Mark and Sarah knew about it. He wanted things to stay that way.

"Maybe you should go home," Sarah suggested.

"No. I'm fine now."

Colin and Mark walked to the edge of the pool. She was still floating there like something from one of those lagoons in horror films. But it didn't get to him now. He made himself detach, like the good newspaperman he was.

A siren wailed in the distance. Colin wondered if it would be a patrolman or the chief himself. He liked Chief Hallock. They'd taken instantly to each other, and that was valuable to Colin. Mark had no rapport with the man, couldn't reach him. Colin knew it burned Mark that he'd won Waldo Hallock the first week on the job, but Mark was fair and smart, knew it was good for the paper, so he kept his ruffled feelings tamped down.

The siren died in front of the house. Patrolman Albert Wiggins was first through the gate, hatless, his short-sleeved blue shirt showing big wet patches under the arms. The chief followed, white shirt immaculate, his hat set at a jaunty angle, back farther than regulation.

Waldo Hallock was forty-eight and he'd been chief for twenty years. During his third year on the force all policemen were required to take a civil service test. Hallock was the only one of five men who passed, and he was immediately promoted to chief, replacing the current one, Charles Gildersleeve. And now his son, Carl, detested Waldo.

Gildersleeve hurried over to him, clutching a handkerchief, which he used to wipe his sweating neck and face.

"Don't know how this happened, Slats," he said to the chief, calling him by his high-school nickname. "I never saw this woman before. I don't know what's going on here. This is a mess."

Hallock tilted his head to one side, took off his hat — exposing his full head of black hair, not a gray one in the bunch — reached out a long arm and gently but firmly pushed Gildersleeve to one side. "'Scuse me, Stinky," he said, using Carl's high-school nickname, and walked to the edge of the pool.

The chief returned his hat to his head and Colin wondered if he'd taken it off just to show that thick thatch of black to white-haired, balding Gildersleeve.

"Got to get her out," Hallock said to Wiggins. "Call the M.E."

"Right." Wiggins walked away.

"You guys want to help?" Hallock asked.

Colin felt his stomach flip-flop. He couldn't touch the body. Never again. But what could he say?

"You don't have to, you know." It was Annie, behind him.

Mark called to Doug Corwin and Ray Chute to give a hand. He stepped in front of Colin, making it impossible for him to get near the pool. The chief didn't seem to notice, and in a minute Wiggins was back, so there were five, pulling and lifting.

Colin looked down at his feet. He wanted to get the hell out of there. But it was humiliating enough without running like some chickenshit. And he had to stop being rude to this Annie Winters who was only trying to be nice and helpful. He turned to speak to her but she wasn't there.

Then he heard the flumping sound of the body dropping onto the patio, and he forgot about Annie. The men drew back, creating a space, and Colin was suddenly part of the group staring down at the dead woman.

Light-colored hair hung in long hanks around the swollen face and over shoulders that looked like they might explode. Colin avoided looking at her eyes. A piece of material was knotted around her throat like a ragged jabot. His gaze drifted to her chest, where cuts ran from the bottom of her neck over her breasts and down to her navel.

"Anybody recognize her?" Albert Wiggins asked.

There was nervous laughter.

"You must be joshin', Al," Ray Chute said.

"Just thought I'd ask."

"Carl," the chief called. "C'mere."

Gildersleeve, handkerchief still working overtime, scurried across the patio. He'd removed his sunglasses and they hung against his chest, one bow hooked over the edge of the pocket of his pink linen jacket. The two men stared at one another, their mutual lack of admiration evident.

"You know this woman, Carl?" Hallock asked.

Gildersleeve's face flushed in anger. "I told you I didn't. Don't try an' pin this thing on me." He turned toward Mark. "And don't you go writin' this up in the paper, Griffing."

Mark looked surprised. "Now, Mayor, you know I have to report the news."

"I mean, don't go writin' it like I have somethin' to do with it. You fellas have a way of slantin' the truth."

"All the news that's fit to print," Mark parried.

Gildersleeve turned back to Hallock. "This here is somebody's idea of a joke."

Hallock looked at Gildersleeve as if he were smelling something bad, then pulled on the bridge of his long nose. "You're serious, aren't you, Carl?"

"Well, what else is it? What's it look like to you, huh? Everybody knows I give this party every year. Everybody looks forward to it, waits all year for it. So some cocksucker I didn't invite goes and does a thing like this to get at me. It's clear as the nose on your face, Waldo."

Hallock blinked, and Colin wondered whether the last remark was an intentional slur on the Chief's big nose or whether it was just one more example of Gildersleeve's foot-in-mouth disease.

"You got a list of all your guests, Carl?" Hallock asked.

"A list?"

"You know who your guests are?"

"That's my whole point. I don't let just anybody in here, Waldo. My guests are the cream of the crop."

"What crop's that?" It had not escaped Hallock all these years that he'd never been invited to the Gildersleeve house, thereby making him less than cream.

"You know what I mean," Gildersleeve said.

"So you got a list?"

He nodded, looking grim.

"Then tell them all to go. I want everybody out of here. *Now*."

Gildersleeve told Doug Corwin to carry out the chief's order, and Corwin scudded across the patio and into the house. Then Gildersleeve raised his voice to the other men standing around in groups of twos and threes and told them what the chief had said. He also offered his apologies for the ruination of his party.

Mark told Sarah to take the car; he'd find a way home later.

Sarah saw the alarm in Colin's eyes. "You can't go with Colin," she whispered.

"Oh, yeah, right," Mark said.

Colin heard them and felt even lousier than he had. He was looking bad today, as if all of his problems were flashing in neon.

"I'll wait outside," Sarah said.

"It might be awhile."

"That's okay." She kissed him lightly, then kissed Colin. "Want to eat with us tonight?"

He wanted to, but he'd had dinner with them twice already this week. "No, that's okay, Sarah."

"What's that mean?"

Colin glanced at Annie and wondered if she would be at the Griffings' for dinner.

Sarah picked up on his thought. She was good at that. "Come on, why don't you and Annie both have dinner with us? We'll go out."

Annie looked startled. "Well, I don't know, I'm not ready for tomorrow."

Sarah said, "You never are and you always get it done."

"I'm really way behind."

"Well, both of you think about it. Come on, Annie, we're not wanted around here. See you soon."

Colin watched the two women leave, noting Annie's long slim legs. Tomorrow was Sunday. What did she have to get ready for a Sunday?

"So what's them marks?" Wiggins asked.

Colin moved away from the woman's head and stood near her feet. He wanted to be away from those eyes.

"They're cuts." Hallock squatted down and looked over the shoulders, his eyes tracing the jagged lines to her navel.

Colin stared. About two inches below her breasts he noticed a faint horizontal cut crossing the two vertical ones.

Hallock said, "They aren't deep. She couldn't have bled much from them. Superficial wounds."

"Before or after death?" Mark asked.

"M.E.'ll have to tell us that, but I'd guess after. *Why* is what I want to know," Hallock said thoughtfully.

"Never mind any damn cuts," Gildersleeve snarled. "Who put her in my pool and why?" He looked afraid. "You think it's a warning, Waldo?"

Colin watched the chief take this in, conquer a smile, then press his advantage. "Could be. Yeah, just might be that."

Gildersleeve passed his twisted handkerchief across his face like a windshield wiper. "Jesus God Almighty. What am I gonna do?"

The chief looked back at the body, ignoring Gildersleeve. "Wonder if it's supposed to mean something — these cuts. Can't figure it."

Colin looked again. It was suddenly as clear to him as if the last piece of a puzzle had fallen into place. "I think I know," he said.

"Yeah? What?"

"Come around here," Colin suggested. "I think maybe you're looking at it the wrong way."

The chief and the others moved down to the feet. No one said anything for a moment; then Hallock made a sound like *cheeez*. "I see it. It's an A. It's a goddamn A."

"Like Hester Prynne?" Mark said.

"Who's she?" Gildersleeve asked.

"In the *Scarlet Letter*. A for Adulteress."

Hallock said, "Or A for number one."

LOOKING BACK — 75 YEARS AGO

Last Friday afternoon the Jolly Dozen was entertained by Miss Florence Syer. At the opportune moment the girls were invited to partake of a red and white luncheon, after which Miss Syer entertained with a treat of classical music. Then the married members realized that time was flying, and husbands would soon be clamoring for something more substantial than a red and white luncheon and classical music. So the meeting was adjourned.

Chapter Three

Colin explained that he wanted to write the story while it was still fresh in his mind.

Mark said, "You have to eat, and it's not like we put the paper to bed tonight. Join us after you write the story."

The four of them were standing in front of Gildersleeve's house, and Colin knew he had to get out of it. This wasn't the night to make new friends. "I'll see, Mark, okay?"

Sarah said, "What'll you do, Colin, grab a slice of pizza or something?"

That was exactly what he'd do. Pizza Heaven was almost as good as their local place in Chicago. Shit. He had Chicago on the brain tonight. "I have stuff at home," he lied.

"I think I'd better go," Annie said.

The gate opened. Two men in white carried her out in a green body bag. Colin felt woozy again and reached out to touch the hood of the car for support. When he glanced at Annie he knew she'd seen. It pissed him off. Quickly, they each turned back to the body bag entering the ambulance. The door slapped shut.

Annie touched Colin's arm. "I don't mean to be a pest, but if you're feeling shaky or anything, well, I could drive you home. You could get your car later or —"

"No," he snapped.

She backed away as if he'd hit her.

Jesus, he kept making it worse. "Sorry. I didn't mean to .

it's just that . . . ." Just that what? How the hell could he tell her he couldn't ride in a car with anyone?

"It's okay, don't worry." She smiled faintly. "Sarah, Mark, I won't say it's been fun. See you soon. It was nice to meet you," she said to Colin.

He nodded, wanting to say something but unable to. And then she was gone, walking across the street to her blue Ford Escort.

Mark said, "You sure have a way with women, pal."

"Yeah, don't I? Talk about getting off on the wrong foot." He ran his thumb and forefinger down his black Zapata mustache.

"Oh, Annie's not going to think anything of it, Colin. After all, it wasn't exactly an ordinary day."

Colin felt it incumbent upon him to say something about what had happened to him. "Listen, I'm sorry about taking a dive like that."

Mark put a hand on his shoulder. "No sweat, pal."

"We understand, Colin. As long as you're all right now."

"I'm fine." It was obvious they didn't want to discuss it. He couldn't blame them.

"So how about dinner?"

The Griffings got in their car.

"No. I want to write the story, grab something, get some sleep."

"Leave him alone, Mark."

"Nice big juicy steak you're gonna miss."

"Thanks anyway."

"See you Monday."

Sarah said, "If you get lonely, come on over tomorrow."

He thanked her, started for his station wagon, stopped. "Hey," he called, "who is she, anyway?"

"Annie?" Mark asked. "She's the minister of the Unitarian Universalist Church. So long, pal."

They pulled away, leaving him standing by his car, mouth open in surprise.

———————

Colin liked being in his office at night, one light on in the whole place. Some people might have found it creepy. To him it was cozy, safe.

At the *Chicago Tribune* he was never alone, no matter the time. But he'd loved it. God, he'd been young and green when he started! Right out of the University of Michigan. That's when he'd grown the mustache to make himself look older. He hadn't fooled his editor.

Ryan had said, "Kid, you can grow all the garbage you want on your face, but it don't mean kaka to me if you don't produce. Get it?"

He got it. Still, he kept the mustache. It gave him confidence. Then it became a habit. Without it he'd feel naked; it was as much a part of him as his cleft chin.

For four years they shuffled him around, and he covered obits, the courts, the suburbs, high school sports, the weather. It was mean. But he hung in and it paid off — he got the crime beat. Squalid and seamy as it sometimes was, he loved it. The excitement, the cops, the rhythm. He never understood why it spoke to him. Maybe it was the possibility of danger, an illusion of living on the edge. He didn't know. But he stayed in it for nine years until everything came down on him, until everything was over.

Colin rubbed his eyes as though he were trying to wipe them clean. Maybe he was. He lit a Marlboro and blew a ring in front of him. He didn't want to think about that now, start it all up again. Jesus, couldn't he have just *one* free night? But this night was more unlikely to be absent of ghosts than any he'd had for a long time. Don't pick up the first thought, Dr. Safier had told him. It was good advice. So try it for once, goddammit!

He turned away from his desk to his typing table, stuck a piece of paper in his old Royal. Mark kept making noises about getting computers, but meanwhile both of them used manual machines. He hit the keys.

BODY FOUND IN MAYOR'S POOL

Colin knew there wasn't a single person in Seaville or any of the towns on the North Fork who'd give that headline a pass. He also knew Gildersleeve was going to have a coronary. Too bad.

He stared at the head, his two hunt-and-peck fingers poised on the keys. Nothing came to him. The trouble was, he kept thinking of Annie Winters. He kept seeing her smile and hearing her say his name. And thinking, too, of what an asshole he'd been.

Reaching down into his bottom drawer he pulled out the phone book, flipped to the back, and ran his fingers down the W's. He found it right away.

Winters, A., Rev.

Could he just call up a reverend and ask for a pardon? Lifting the receiver, he punched out the number, then hung up. He did it again but this time let it ring.

She answered on the third.

"Hello," he said, "it's Colin Maguire."

"Oh. Hello," she said, sounding surprised.

"I just wanted to apologize. I acted very badly. I'm sorry."

"Thank you, that's nice."

He smiled. Most people would've said, "No need, it's okay, don't bother." She hadn't. He liked that.

She said, "Are you feeling better?"

"Yes, thanks. I hope next time we meet it'll be under better circumstances."

"It's bound to be," she said.

"Well, listen, I just wanted to say that to you. You were awfully kind."

She didn't say anything.

"Have you eaten dinner?" he asked impulsively.

She laughed. "Yes, have you?"

"Not yet."

"Don't let Sarah know that — I think she wants to mother you."

Smiling, he said, "I think you're right. Would you like to meet for a drink or something?" He was astonished, as if a ventriloquist were operating him. Jesus, what if she was married? He tried to remember if there'd been a ring but couldn't.

"I'd like that," she said, "but I don't have my sermon written for tomorrow."

He'd almost forgotten: *Reverend* Winters.

"Another time?" she asked.

"Sure. Why not?"

A second of silence. "Thanks for calling, Colin."

He said goodbye and they broke the connection.

Slamming his hand down on the phone book he said, "Shit." Why did he have to say "Sure, why not?" like some teenager? Well, it had been a long, long time since he'd tried to date a woman. The few women he'd had contact with in the last three years were almost strangers. Casual sex. Not very satisfactory. But this woman was different.

At least he knew one thing: she wasn't married. She wouldn't have said she'd have a drink with him if she was. On the other hand, maybe she'd have a drink and try to convert him. What a joke if the old altar boy became a Unitarian Universalist — whatever the hell that was.

No, Annie Winters wasn't married. So why not? Hadn't met the right guy? Or maybe she was divorced. Could ministers get divorced? He squashed out his cigarette in his metal ashtray. Enough.

As he turned back to his typewriter he heard the light sound of a woman's footsteps coming down the hall.

"Hello, Maguire." It was Babe Parkinson, feature writer for the paper.

Colin figured Babe called him by his last name because she thought it made her sound more like a real newspaperwoman. Too many Roz Russell movies. He didn't feel like seeing Babe. "What brings you here in the dark of night?"

"Murder," she said, an unnatural flush to her face as if the word excited her.

"You heard?"

"Everybody's heard. Sorry I missed it."

"Yeah, it was great fun." He lit another Marlboro, coughed.

"I didn't mean it like that. Mind if I sit down?"

He gestured with an open palm. Babe sat in the wooden armchair across from him as Colin assessed her. There was no question about it, Babe was a stunning woman: a tall, cool redhead. She wore her hair in a French braid, and Colin found himself wondering what she'd look like with it loose.

He watched as she alternately fussed with a plastic bag and the hem of her dress, pretending to try and pull it over her knees. She reached into the bag, took out a bottle of white wine, two glasses, and a corkscrew.

"Celebrating something?" he asked.

"I thought you might like it after what went on this afternoon."

"How'd you know I was here?"

"I saw your car." She handed him the bottle and corkscrew.

He didn't like that much. Couldn't she open a dinky bottle of wine? She was far from helpless if what he'd observed in the last six weeks was true. His analysis of Babe Parkinson was that she was shrewd, calculating, aggressive, and on the make. For him as well as his job. Or maybe more. Maybe she wanted to be publisher. Nancy would've said he was thinking like a chauvinist pig. Oh, God.

He opened the wine, poured two glasses, and slid one across the desk.

"Should we drink to something?" she asked.

He shrugged.

"How about to Gloria Danowski?"

"Who?"

"Gloria Danowski, may she rest in peace."

Colin was beginning to get the idea that this wasn't just a social visit. "Do you want to tell me about it or are we going to play twenty questions?"

Babe smiled, a glint in her green eyes. "Gloria Danowski, age thirty-one, married to Hank Danowski, mother of Patti, age six, and Danny, age four. Home, One Twenty One Randolph Avenue, East Hampton. Last seen four weeks ago when she left home for a class at Southampton College. Only she wasn't registered for any class. Found today in Mayor Gildersleeve's Olympic-sized pool." She raised her glass, gestured toward Colin as if they might clink glasses, then took a long sip.

Colin stared, not drinking. "East Hampton?"

She took a pack of Kents from her purse and lit one with a silver Dunhill lighter. "East Hampton."

"What's she doing over here?"

"I don't know. Maybe she liked our pools better."

"It's not funny, Babe. It's not a goddamn bit funny. This was a woman, a wife and mother. Have you thought about that?"

"Oh, vicious, vicious," she said.

"You're talking about a human being, not a statistic or a good story."

"You mean it's not a good story?"

"That's not the point. Forget it. So how'd you find this out? Who identified her?"

"I did."

"*You* did?" He was furious. Trying to calm himself, he took a sip of the wine.

"In my trusty file cabinet," she tapped her head with a ringed finger. "I found a story about a missing woman."

"We didn't print it, did we?"

"Nope. *Newsline*. I remembered the husband was stunned, no explanation. Friends said Gloria was happy, loved hubby and kiddies, and would never ever have run away. Don't ask me how I made the connection, Maguire, because I don't know. Just dumb luck, I guess."

Colin toyed with saying that nothing was dumb luck with her, then thought better of it. "Go on."

"I called Danowski in East Hampton, asked if wifey had returned, he said no, so I told him about the floater. I met him at the morgue and he identified her. Simple."

"Simple," Colin said, disgusted.

Babe said, "You know, you're going to have to get a thicker skin, my friend. How'd you manage in the Windy City with that attitude?"

"I managed," he said. "Does Hallock know?"

"About Danowski? Yeah, I told him. Now I'm telling you. Too bad this is a weekly, you'd have a scoop."

"Me? It's your baby, you dug it up."

"It's yours, Maguire, I'm just the feature writer. Interviewing octogenarians who've lived here all their lives, writing pieces about local merchants who hand-dip candles and create art from shells, doing in-depth stories on the couple who turn the old church or schoolhouse into a showplace home. Babe Parkinson, girl grind."

"If you hate it so much, why do it?"

"I don't hate it, I love it. It's much better than sitting home baking cakes for some wimp who wants to play King For A Lifetime."

"You really think a lot of men, don't you?"

She smiled, her eyes going to halfmast. "I think a lot *about* them. Especially some in particular." Her implication was clear.

Colin said, "Did the M.E. have anything to say about Danowski?"

"He hadn't worked on her yet." She sipped her wine. "You're not drinking, Maguire."

"I'm not thirsty." He stood up. "I'm leaving."

"It's early."

He walked to the door. "If you're staying, turn out the light when you go."

"I'm not staying." Babe left the glasses and grabbed the bottle by the neck. She snapped off the light and followed Colin down the hall.

On the sidewalk she stood very near him while he locked the door. "Any chance the husband did it?" he asked.

"He seemed broken up. But maybe he's a good actor. I guess they'll question him."

"Whose jurisdiction will this be, East Hampton or ours?"

"Ours. But there'll be cooperation." She moved closer to him, looked up into his eyes. "Speaking of cooperation."

"Goodnight, Babe," he said and started walking toward his car.

"You're a shit," she called after him.

In his car he wondered if he *was* a shit. From the beginning he'd made it clear he wasn't interested. No, what he'd done was nothing. No encouragement but no discouragement either. Maybe he *was* a shit.

Starting the car, he thought of Gloria Danowski. And then of her husband. What was he feeling tonight? Remembering, Colin thought he knew. But at least Danowski had his kids.

LOOKING BACK — 25 YEARS AGO

An extended period of amnesty through June 30th has been granted to authorized gun holders, to permit them to turn them over to the police department, it was announced this week by Police Chief Charles Gildersleeve. Chief Gildersleeve urges that persons wishing to avail themselves of the amnesty period get in touch with the police department.

Chapter Four

They'd found her. Just the way he'd planned. It served that asshole Gildersleeve right. Putting her in his pool had been a perfect touch. It was like killing two birds with one stone. There was only one sour note. He wished Gloria's parents had been forced to identify her instead of the husband. After all, Danowski had nothing to do with it. It was the parents he wanted to suffer. And they would. They'd see her — in the coffin. He could picture the mother whining and crying, sniveling and wringing her hands, calling for her baby Gloria. The father would keep it all in, tough it out. But inside, his guts would be aching, like his own had ached all those years. Still ached.

Should he go to the funeral? he wondered. Better not. But he could imagine it. He smiled. When they lowered the coffin into the ground and Gloria's parents watched, that was the part he would be sorry to miss. Sorry to miss the dirt falling on top of the casket, shovelful by shovelful.

He could still hear it even though it was all those years ago — that plopping sound, just as real now as it was then. So maybe Gloria Danowski's parents would dream about it long as they lived, like he did. Plop, plop, plop.

And the kids, too. Why should they have it easy? Now they won't. They'll miss their Mommy. Good. He missed his Mommy, even now. And Daddy, too. His missed his Daddy. He missed his Mommy. I ain't had any satisfaction.

Tears coursed over his cheeks and dripped from his face onto the desk. He put his head down. Thinking of Mommy and Daddy. Crying. Lonely. Little boy. All alone. Crying. Calling for Mommy. Calling for Daddy.

Nobody came.

LOOKING BACK — 50 YEARS AGO

At a late hour Saturday night, the quiet village of Seaville was awakened by the commotion caused by Fred Karenewski, who put up a stiff battle and resisted arrest after his erratic driving had caused him to collide with several other motor cars, driving motorists off the road and finally ending up by crashing through the grape arbor of his own residence.

Chapter Five

Standing on Richter's dock, looking out over the boats in the bay at six-thirty Sunday morning, Waldo Hallock felt as if he were at a turning point in his life. There'd been other turning points in his forty-eight years, but he hadn't had one in a long time.

In the twenty years that he'd been chief, there had only been two murders in Seaville and both had been solved immediately. One was a transient who'd killed an old lady for a tin can that held twenty-six dollars and forty-two cents, and the other was a guy who'd murdered his wife in a jealous rage.

A cool breeze came in off the bay and a dozen gulls squawked overhead. Hallock sniffed the air. Nothing else was quite like salt-water air. He'd smelled it all his life. Seaville was home; he wanted it to stay that way. And he wanted to remain chief of police.

Hallock watched the ferry from Shelter Island as it made its way toward the Seaville dock. He could see there were only two cars aboard, and only one car waited to take the ferry back. It was a far cry from what it would be like when the season started. By mid-July cars would be backed up for blocks waiting to make the trip to the island, where they'd cross to a second ferry taking them to Sag Harbor and the Hamptons.

Turning his back to the water, his gaze took in the buildings at the foot of Center Street. Most of those on the south side had been built before the turn of the century, clapboard buildings with Victorian arches. Once they'd been homes but now they housed shops, restaurants, and the police station. On the north side of the street, a fire five years before had destroyed all but one or two buildings, and the new ones of brick and wood always jarred him. It was the same with the beach houses people were building now. They looked out of place with their modern angles and walls of glass, like girls at a formal dance wearing miniskirts.

It wasn't that he was against progress, not a bit. But lots of people in Seaville were. There was always some kind of squabble going on at Town Hall about developers wanting to put up condos. One side claimed development would tax local services, drain the water supply, and jeopardize the preservation of open space. The other side invariably pushed the notion of more jobs for the locals. And if that was true, it was a good thing; there were never enough jobs. Especially for the young people who graduated high school or college and left the Fork as fast as they could. No, he wasn't against progress. What bothered him about condos was the way they looked. Dull. Like the bank.

Four years before, the Seaville Bank & Trust, which was housed in the old Gillespie home, was torn down and replaced by a low brick job, characterless and cold. And it was happening more and more all over the North Fork. The new pushing out the old. That was something you expected on the South Fork, where the so-called Beautiful People congregated, but not here.

Thinking of the South Fork brought his mind around to Gloria Danowski. Now he had this damn murder on his hands and the victim wasn't even somebody from town. Memorial Day weekend was six days away. Murder in Seaville could hurt the local merchants. That meant pressure. Who the hell wants to come to a resort town where there's been a murder? An unsolved murder. And goddamn, he knew Gildersleeve would be on his ass.

He smiled in spite of himself, thinking about the mayor huffing and puffing over the woman in his pool. If it hadn't been so serious, he might have had a good laugh about it.

The thing was, Hallock didn't believe that the murderer had chosen Gildersleeve's pool by chance. And that made him believe the perpetrator was a local. As Fran had said before they went to sleep last night, "It looks like this thing is going to be in your lap no matter what, hon."

He'd taken her hand. They always went to sleep that way. "Don't worry," she said, "we'll get through it."

And they would, too. Like they got through everything. Fran would support him the way she had all those years when he'd been chief over Charles Gildersleeve, Bob Phillips, and Pete Shaw who'd been demoted and stayed status quo because they couldn't pass the damn civil service test. They'd made his life one long misery and there'd been times, plenty of them, when he'd wanted to quit, but Fran had helped him go on.

He'd say, "You don't know what it's like going to work every day with three men who hate your guts."

She'd say, "Waldo Hallock, you weren't made chief of police at twenty-eight because you won a popularity contest. You got that job because you were smarter than anybody else, so don't be dumb now. Anyway, I didn't plot and plan to marry a quitter, did I?"

"Poor guy, never had a chance," Hallock kidded about himself.

It was a game they played. Fran and Waldo were the same age, had gone all through school together, but when he went into the Navy after high school he never gave her a thought. Not so with Fran. She'd always loved him, refused two proposals while she waited for him to come back. She knew someday she'd marry Waldo. And it was she who got in touch with him by inviting him to a party she was giving for a friend. The only reason for the party was so she could invite him. And that began a three-year courtship. It was only after they were married a few years that Fran admitted how she'd schemed to get him. So that was why he always said he'd never had a chance. But he adored Fran; never slept with, or even looked at, another woman since the party twenty-seven years ago.

Now they were up against something once more. At least things at the station were okay. It was five years since the last of the old regime at work had gone. His men liked him now, all good guys.

But even so, last night when he'd held her hand he'd prayed for a break in this case. An unsolved murder wasn't good for anybody: not the town and not him. Fran read his mind, as usual, and told him they'd get through.

And they would. Maybe.

The thing was he could never be sure Fran wouldn't get all involved in one of her *causes*, leaving little room for him and the kids. Since Cynthia, the youngest of their three, had gone to junior high, Fran had thrown herself into one cause, one march, one protest after another. At first he didn't mind, because he knew Fran was bored at home and needed something. But then she seemed to get obsessive about it, and everything else, like housework and cooking dinner, went all to hell.

When he'd finally said something Fran got furious and called him a chauvinist, telling him to make his own damn dinner. And then the name-calling accelerated, and it turned into one of the worst fights they'd ever had. But that was nothing compared to the time she was arrested protesting the nuclear plant in Shoreham.

Hell, he didn't think the damn thing should be there either, but a police chief couldn't go around expressing his private views and neither should a police chief's wife. And he'd told her that.

She'd said, "Then maybe I just won't be a police chief's wife."

He'd said, "What the hell's that supposed to mean?"

"You don't understand English, Waldo?"

"What I understand is that you're making my life a misery."

"Is that so?"

"Yeah, it is."

"You can leave any time you want, you know. If you're so miserable, why don't you just move out?"

He had actually felt frightened. Fran had never said anything like that before. Even so he couldn't stop himself from saying, "Maybe I will."

"Fine. When?"

"Now." He'd stood there, unable to move or say anything more.

Then she said, "So? What are you waiting for?"

He'd marched upstairs then, pulled a suitcase from the top of the closet, knocking a bunch of boxes on the floor, slammed it on the bed, and depressed the catches. Shaking with rage and maybe a little fear, he was standing over the open empty suitcase when she came up behind him and put her arms around his waist.

"This is dumb," she said.

He'd felt so relieved that he'd immediately turned around and grabbed her in his arms. They'd made love then, long and luxuriously, and ended up feeling even closer than they'd felt before the Shoreham deal. Neither of them had mentioned the incident again until the following Thursday.

Thursday was the day the *Seaville Gazette* came out. And there she was, smack on the front page, being hauled away by two bulls toward a paddy wagon. The fight started all over again, but this time no one spoke of moving out. It had taken almost three weeks for things to cool down between them, and finally Fran promised she wouldn't do anything again that might embarrass him. And she hadn't.

Mark Griffing was another story. It seemed to Hallock that whenever he could, Griffing printed anything that would put Hallock in a bad light. The antagonism between them had begun almost from the first month Griffing had owned the paper.

Hallock had gone to see Griffing to ask him not to print the victims' names in items he culled from the police blotter. The previous owners had agreed with that policy. Griffing had insisted Hallock was trying to impose censorship and he'd have none of it; he wasn't going to be under anybody's thumb. Hallock tried to point out that printing the names of burglary victims might encourage potential thieves. But Griffing wouldn't budge. From then on it had been open warfare between them. He expected Griffing to have a field day with this murder.

"Hey there, Chief."

Hallock turned to see his detective. "Hey there, Charlie."

Charlie Copin was a good man. He was thirty-five years old and had been with Hallock seven years. Four inches shorter than Hallock's six feet, he weighed about twenty pounds more. Copin wore a lightweight tan suit, white shirt, brown tie and brown oxfords. He was a pleasant-looking guy who smiled a lot and made you feel he was content, easy.

"Taking the air?" Copin asked.

"Yeah. And thinking."

"'Bout the Danowski woman?"

Hallock nodded.

Copin said, "I been thinking, too. I been thinking maybe she was screwing somebody over here, ya know, and Danowski found out. Or maybe the somebody over here got tired of her. But whatever, Seaville's connected somehow. I mean, think about it. Who's gonna kill a woman in East Hampton, then take an hour driving to Seaville, 'cause sure as shit he didn't take no ferries over here with a body in the car, then risk everything putting that body in a pool. I mean, what for? 'Less you got a good reason, ya know? 'Less that pool has some significance."

"I've been thinking along the same lines, Charlie."

"Ya think it's possible Gildersleeve was banging this woman?"

"Can't feature him doing it with anyone, but who knows? Still, he wouldn't put her in his own pool, would he?"

"You mean because it would incriminate him?"

"Right."

"But, see, that's just it. That's what he'd count on, that we'd think that. See, who wouldn't say, why should a man kill a woman, then put her in his own pool? He'd just be counting on that. See what I'm trying to bring out, Chief?"

"I do, Charlie. But I don't know. Gildersleeve's a mean son of a bitch but he's not dumb. He'd know we'd think of that sooner or later, and look how soon you thought of it. But how about this? The Danowski woman's sleeping with Gildersleeve and Danowski finds out, kills her, and dumps her in the pool."

"I thought of that. It's a possibility. Wanna have a coffee?"

"Sure."

The two men walked off the dock, crossed the wide parking area, and went down the sidewalk past the police station, Roseanne's Dress Shop, and Alberton's Hardware, to the corner of Center and Main and the Paradise Luncheonette.

The Paradise had been built fifty years before and hadn't been touched since, except for an occasional paint job. The style was art deco, with wooden booths and silvered mirrors. The same man built the movie theater.

Copin and Hallock said hello to almost everybody in the place and took a booth near the back so they could keep talking in private. Vivian, the waitress, brought them each a coffee and Danish without waiting for their order. Hallock's coffee was black, Copin's light.

Hallock said, "Then again, it might be somebody else who was banging the Danowski woman and had a grudge against Gildersleeve," just as though there'd been no break in the conversation.

"But who?"

"That's where you got to do some work, Charlie."

Copin smiled because Hallock was always kidding him about being lazy, even though he didn't really believe it.

"Well, if I have to, Chief," he said, putting on a face.

Hallock said, "It's those cuts that worry me, Charlie."

"I know what ya mean. Think it *is* an A?"

Hallock nodded. "Sure looks like it."

"So what's it mean? A for Adulteress or A for Number One?" Copin bit off a piece of Danish.

"Or something else we got no way of knowing. Haven't had a whole lot of experience with murderers, but I've done some reading, just in case, you know, in case of the eventuality. There's practically no way to know what's in a killer's mind, the way he thinks. Maybe a psychiatrist could, but not us. So those cuts could mean almost anything."

"I see what you mean. But let's just say, for the hell of it, let's just say that it *is* an A and it means Number One. Then we maybe got a serial murderer on our hands, right?" Copin lit a cigarette and blew out the match with a puff of smoke.

"Could be. And unless we get him now, we got real trouble. But let's not jump to conclusions, okay?"

"Right."

"I want you to get over to East Hampton and run this thing down, Charlie. You got to talk to Gloria Danowski's parents and neighbors, find out who her girlfriends were, see what you can get about a boyfriend. Push Danowski a little. Not too hard, 'cause if the guy's innocent he's grieving."

Copin nodded. Only Hallock would think of that. No other cop would care if the guy was grieving or not. He finished his coffee. "Guess I'll get going."

They walked to the cash register, where Hallock paid. It was his turn.

Outside on Main Street the village was beginning to come alive. Next to the Paradise, George de Walter was sweeping the sidewalk in front of his bar and grill, while just past him Elbert Palmer's barber pole was spinning endlessly. Across the street, Harry Townsend was dusting off the wooden Indian in front of his candy and newspaper store and Jake Hicks, the mailman, was walking past Gould's Spirit Shop on his way to buy the Sunday paper. Jake waved a hand at the two men, who waved back.

Under his breath, Copin said, "Looks like Jake's put on a couple of pounds again."

"Does it every winter," Hallock replied.

Hallock and Copin parted company, and Hallock walked back along Center to the police station. Usually Sunday was his one day off but today was different. He'd miss Sunday dinner with Fran and the kids. He hated that. They always had his favorite meal on Sunday — roast beef, mashed potatoes, tomato aspic, green beans, and lemon meringue pie for dessert. Well, it couldn't be helped.

Inside, behind the high desk, Frank Tuthill was ending the midnight-to-eight shift. Tuthill was twenty-eight, single, and eager. Hallock thought he had a hungry look, like a bird of prey, but he liked the man, trusted him.

Tuthill said, "Telephone's going crazy, Chief. Seems like everybody and his brother's heard about the murder and knows who did it."

Hallock raised an eyebrow. "Yeah? Any good leads?"

"Nada."

"Got to follow them up anyway, Frank."

"I know. I got 'em all down here for Richie and Al," he said, tapping his pencil against a yellow lined pad.

Richard Clark and Al Wiggins worked the eight-to-four shift, and Kathy Booth was the radio operator.

Hallock went on into the back where his office was. It was a good-size room with two gray metal desks and one battered wooden one. The walls had been painted a light green ten years before, and the only other touch of color was some orange plastic chairs. Everything else was gray metal.

He sat at his desk, took off his hat, and looked at the gold badge on it that said Chief. How long could he stay chief if he didn't solve this damn murder? Gildersleeve would use it, for sure. But why was he thinking so negatively? The hell with that. He was going to solve it and that was all there was to it.

———————

At nine o'clock, Colin Maguire sat across the desk from Hallock writing in his notebook. Hallock liked Maguire. There was something about him that spoke to the chief. He even liked the way Maguire looked, dressed. The droopy mustache was the only thing that was kind of off-putting, but Hallock suspected the man wore it to give some maturity to his boyish face. Still, he wondered what he'd look like without it, and planned to say something about the mustache when he got to know Maguire a little better.

Colin said, "So the M.E. says no rape, huh?"

"Hard to tell after all this time in the water, but there was no tearing or bruising there."

"No semen either?"

"No. But it doesn't mean she didn't have intercourse before. Just too much time has passed. And the water."

"How long's she been dead?"

"About a month. Cool weather kept her from really going bad."

Colin nodded and tried to blank out the image. Quickly he asked, "What about the thing around her neck?"

"Part of a sheet. The forensic boys will check that out."

"And the cuts?"

"Made with a sharp knife, serrated edge. Knife probably held in a fist, pulling downward and across. Done after death."

"Do you have any more ideas about what the A means?"

"The thing is, Maguire, to you and me it looked like an A, but maybe it wasn't that at all."

"True."

"Could be anything."

"But *you* think it's an A, don't you, Chief?"

"Might be."

Colin smiled, stuck the end of his pen in his cleft.

"That how you got that thing?" Hallock asked.

"Huh?"

"The hole in your chin."

He laughed.

"Reason I say that is, my mother used to tell us boys a story about how she spent months twirling the eraser on the end of a pencil in her chin, trying to get a dimple there like Jean Harlow."

"Did it work?"

"Nope."

"How about that A, Chief?" Colin asked, refusing to be distracted.

"No kidding, Maguire, we *don't* know if it's an A or not."

"So when will we know, when somebody turns up with a B?"

Hallock frowned. "Not funny. And I mean what I say. Don't go writing that it was an A."

"I can give an opinion, can't I?"

"Guess so. But we don't want pandemonium around here. If you think about B, so is every bozo out there going to. It's bad enough what's going on." He cocked his head toward the outside office and the ringing phone.

"You needn't worry, Chief. I'm not practicing to get a job on the *Enquirer*. I'll stick to the facts, play down anything else."

"Thanks."

"You'll keep me posted?"

"Sure thing."

The moment Colin left the phone buzzed on Hallock's desk. He picked it up. "Yes, Kathy?"

She said, "Jim Drew's out here to see you, Chief."

"Send him in."

A moment later Drew came shuffling into the office looking rumpled and bedraggled as always.

"H'lo, Jim. Sit down."

"Thanks, Chief."

Jim was thirty-one, a Vietnam vet, and new to Seaville three years ago. He ran a junk and antique business up on the North Road in an old barn.

"What can I do for you, Jim?"

"I came in to confess."

"'Bout what?"

"The woman they found in the pool. I killed her."

LOOKING BACK — 75 YEARS AGO

The summer girl has a new fad, that of tattooing herself by aid of the sun's rays. At the bathing hour it has become a common thing to see girls with bits of black paper pasted on their arms and neck, sprinkled about with salt water, sitting where they get the full force of the sun. In this way girls are decorating themselves with initials of their friends, fraternity pins, and fancy designs.

Chapter Six

When Annie Winters finished her sermon on the Idea of Home the congregation stood to sing a final hymn. She looked out over the small group and wondered if she was getting anywhere. But where did she want to get? She knew she reached these people; there just weren't many of them.

She'd had the opportunity for a larger congregation. A sizable parish in Wisconsin had been offered to her, another large one in California, and this one. She'd told herself she'd chosen this small one because she wanted to be near her mother, who had bouts of incapacitating depression, and that the few months she'd spent in Seaville as a child were her happiest. But there was another reason, one she tried not to admit to herself. A small parish would be less likely to present romantic possibilities. And that was the way it had been — the way she wished it to remain.

So then what was her problem? There was only one: Steve Cornwell. And there he sat in the front row, staring at her. No. Glaring. Why did he bother to come, feeling the way he did? Meanness, she guessed.

The hymn ended and Annie made her closing remarks. Then, as Burton Kelly played "Whispering" on the organ, one of his usual whimsical choices, the congregation began filing out. Most of them would join her in the parish hall behind the church for refreshments. She hoped Steve Cornwell wouldn't bother.

Some of the parishioners, both men and women, had laid the table with homemade coffee cake, cookies, cheeses, crackers, and fruit. Coffee being brewed in the kitchen filled the hall with a wonderful aroma. Annie was dying for a cup, but she was kept from the other side of the room by one after another of her congregation congratulating her on her sermon. From the corner of her eye she saw Steve Cornwell, still glaring. Perhaps she should speak to him. The truth was, he frightened her. A gigantic man, he towered over her, hulking and sour. But why talk with him? She knew winning him over was impossible. He was set: Women were not ministers. So there was nothing she could do that was right.

"I understand you were there yesterday, Annie." It was Madge Johnson, warm and caring.

"You mean at the mayor's?"

Madge nodded and put a hand on Annie's arm. "It must have been awful for you."

"It was. I've seen death before but nothing like that." Not even Bob's death had been so ugly.

"Are you talking about the murder?" said Carolyn Dobbs, a member of the church for twenty-seven years, also a bully and a gossip. Annie had tried, but she just couldn't like Carolyn.

Madge said, "No, Carolyn, we were talking about the summer fair. Are you going to take a booth this year?"

Carolyn eyed them both curiously. "I was sure I heard something. Well, never mind. You were there, weren't you, Annie?"

"Yes."

"I hear she was from the other side, East Hampton." She rolled her eyes as if to say, You know how *they* are.

"A wife and mother," Madge said defensively.

Carolyn persisted, "What do you suppose she was doing in Gildersleeve's pool?" She laughed. "What an opening for a crack. What I mean is, who put her there? Do you think Carl did it?"

Annie sighed. She knew trying to stop the speculation would be impossible, and Carolyn's obvious relish for the murder was predictable. "No one knows anything at this point, Carolyn."

"You saw the body, didn't you?" she barreled on.

Annie said, "I think I need some coffee. How about you?"

Ignoring the offer, Carolyn whispered, "I hear she was raped."

Annie knew that couldn't be the official word; there hadn't been time. "I need coffee," said said, refusing to worry if Carolyn thought she was rude. "Excuse me."

As she walked away she heard Carolyn say to Madge, "She's a prude, but what can you expect?" She didn't hear Madge's reply, but Annie knew it would put Carolyn in her place.

Ruth Cooper stopped her. "It was a wonderful sermon, Annie. I don't know where you get your ideas."

Russ, her husband, said, "That's a trade secret, isn't that right, Annie?"

She smiled enigmatically.

"You know I had this grand idea myself," Ruth went on. "I thought a sermon on the birds and bees might be nice. The *real* birds and bees," she amended, giving her husband a curious glance. "Would you like to do one on that, Annie?"

"Why don't you do it yourself, Ruth? Any third Sunday in the month." Once a month a parishioner conducted the service while Annie sat out front.

"Oh, I couldn't," she demurred.

"Sure you could, Ruthie," Russ said proudly. "You'd be real good at it, too."

"No, I don't think so."

"From reading your column, Ruth, I think Russ is right." Ruth Cooper wrote the Bayview News column for the *Gazette*. The other women who did the columns for the various towns on the Fork reported straight news, but Ruth always started hers with a paragraph devoted to nature observations. Annie recalled that last week's column had begun: "Lacy curtains of dew cloaked the grass and shimmered in the May sunshine." Some laughed at Ruth's efforts but Annie, while she didn't think the woman had a literary career ahead, admired her intentions. "Give it some thought," she added, and patted Ruth's arm.

"I will," she said, beaming. "I seriously will."

"Good," Annie smiled and moved away.

Burton Kelly almost tripped her. "Sorry, Annie."

"That's all right."

"I was bringing you some coffee. Black, no sugar, right?"

"Right. Thanks." Burton was an odd person, she thought. He was always helpful, always offering his services, but she knew practically nothing about him except that he worked for Seaville Water & Light. Tall and thin, his sandy hair was parted low on the right side, then combed over to the left in an effort to disguise his balding head. She wondered why men did that — it drew so much more attention to the condition than if they'd left it alone.

Burton said, "I saw Carolyn flapping her mouth at you and thought you'd need some strong coffee."

She diplomatically refrained from commenting, sipping the coffee instead. Her friend, Peg Moffat, swore Burton had a crush on Annie, so she tried never to encourage him. But lately she thought it was possible that he was working up to asking her for a date. Her next thought was Colin Maguire. Inwardly, she laughed at the connection. Did she want to date Colin? Ridiculous. She didn't even know him. Yet she thought that if she'd had her sermon written last night, she might have met him for that drink. It puzzled and intrigued her.

"You okay, today, Annie?" Burton inquired.

"Sure. Why?"

He shrugged. "Well, I heard."

"Oh. Yes, I'm fine." Quickly, she changed the subject. "You sounded great this morning, Burton."

"Thanks," he said, shuffling and spilling a few drops of coffee on his shoes.

Annie pretended she didn't notice and looked past Burton at Peg Moffat, who was talking to a group across the room. Their eyes met and they smiled.

Annie said, "Will you excuse me? Thanks for the coffee."

She threaded her way through some people to join Peg, who broke away from her group and met Annie halfway.

"Good sermon, Annie. You never fail to give me something to chew on all week."

"Thanks."

Peg was Annie's age, thirty-three, and married to Tim Moffat who had his own small advertising firm. They had two children Karen, ten, Beth, three. Sunday mornings Tim stayed home with the girls. Annie and Peg had been friends from the start, discovering they both liked Mahler and the Rolling Stones. Physically they were opposites. Where Annie was tall, thin, and blond, Peg was short, chunky, and dark. But otherwise they were similar, liked the same people, books, movies, music. Food, too. Sometimes they'd drive down the island together and pig out at a Friendly's Ice Cream Shop. Peg loved butterscotch sundaes; Annie, Swiss chocolate almond. Once they'd each had two and groaned all the way home.

"Feeling better today?"

Annie nodded. She'd called Peg the night before, told her what had happened.

Peg said, "That's all anybody can talk about today."

"I know."

"What really burns me are the innuendos."

"Meaning?"

"Oh, you know, the usual 'she asked for it' bullshit."

"Not really?"

"Yes, really."

"I guess some things never change," Annie said. "Can you stay for awhile?" Often, on Sundays after the others left, Peg stayed and they had a half hour or so before she had to get home and Annie had to go to dinner at one parishioner's or another.

"I can't. Tim's mother's coming to dinner. In fact, I better make tracks. Where are you going today?"

"The Smiths'."

"Oh, that's not bad."

"Roast chicken, mushroom stuffing, white asparagus, roast potatoes, cranberry sauce, apple pie." She smiled, blue eyes almost disappearing.

"Every time?"

"Yup. But it's good."

"Well, enjoy. Talk to you tomorrow."

They kissed cheeks and Annie watched her go. She was unusually sorry that Peg couldn't stay, and wondered why as she said goodbye to the others while making her way to the back door. She didn't have to stay until the bitter end.

Crossing the lawn to the parsonage, she felt her mood alter, the euphoria she experienced after delivering a good sermon receding. It was always the same, this half hour or so between the gathering in the parish hall and when she left for Sunday dinner. This was the time she missed Bob the most. It was crazy because they'd never shared this time. He'd died before she was ordained.

But she'd fantasized what Sundays would be like, and it was this time she'd imagined sitting with Bob in some rectory, reviewing her sermon, sharing anecdotes about parishioners, sipping a sherry, laughing, holding hands.

A flash of anger rushed through her. She was surprised, believing that the rage she'd felt about Bob's dying was over; it had been five years. But maybe it never left you.

Opening the back door she went into the kitchen and immediately loneliness, like something alive, engulfed her. Her eyes misted and the fury came back again, stronger. In the dining room she went to the sideboard her mother had given them as a wedding present. The decanter of sherry stood on a crystal tray — another wedding present, she forgot from whom.

Annie poured herself a small glass and took it with her to the living room. Bob would have loved the room — oak woodwork, high ceilings, two rose wing chairs, and a comfortable gray velvet couch, good for napping. And the old ice chest with the brass fixtures, a wide oak coffee table, flowered curtains. It was Bob's kind of room; hers, too. Oh, damn him.

She took a sip of the sherry, wondering what her congregation would think if they saw her drinking alone. What did *she* think? Well, hell, it was hardly a big deal, a thimbleful of sherry before lunch. The Smiths didn't drink, so there'd be no more.

Jumping up, she went back in the kitchen and reached for the phone. She had a sudden desire to speak to her mother. Her father answered.

"Hello, Dad, how are you?"

"Annie? I was just thinking about you," he said. Harrison Winters always said the same thing to her.

"What were you thinking?"

He cleared his throat. "Nothing very important, honey. Just wondering how you were."

"I'm fine," she dissembled. "How about you?"

"Just fine, sweetie. We heard from Jason last night."

"How is he?" Annie suspected her younger brother had a cocaine habit, but she'd never said this to either parent.

"He moved again. He's living in Santa Monica now."

"Is he still with Holly?"

"I guess. He says he had almost all the money to start his picture."

She'd heard this line from Jason for almost three years. "Good. How are Rebecca and Ken and the kids?"

Harrison chuckled. "Linda's taking ballet classes and Jeff lost both front teeth. Some kind of kids, they are."

"Are you working, Dad?" Her father was a trumpet player, and now that he was older jobs didn't come his way that often.

"I'm playing a bar mitzvah next week."

For a man who'd played with Dorsey, she knew this was painful for him. "Good, Dad. Is Mother there?"

There was a long silence, and Annie felt her knees grow weak. Surely she would've been called had her mother made another suicide attempt. "Dad?"

"Yes, honey. She's here but she's sleeping now."

"Sleeping?" It wasn't a good sign. "Is anything wrong?"

"Of course not. It's just the old gray mare ain't what she used to be, you know," Harrison laughed falsely.

Annie knew he denied his wife's problems because he felt responsible for them — all those years of leaving her alone for months at a time when he'd be out on the road.

"Should I tell her to call you when she wakes up?" he asked.

"It's nothing important. I just wanted to say hello."

"I'll tell her, honey."

"Okay, Dad."

"Glad you called, sweetie."

"Me, too."

They hung up and Annie leaned against the kitchen counter, sipped her sherry. She'd be damned if she'd ever be dependent on a man the way her mother had been with her father. Oh, who was she kidding? Wasn't that *exactly* how she'd been with Bob? That was why she'd been thrown so terribly by his death, practically going under herself. She was her mother's daughter, all right.

She wished Peg were here. Was it her parents she wanted to talk about? No, it was Colin Maguire. So what? But it was nuts. Why should she want to talk about this guy who was rude to her, passed out at the sight of a dead body, and obviously couldn't drive a car with anyone else in it! Something was definitely wrong with him. On the other hand, his passing out didn't bother her at all. But his rudeness was another matter. Still, she suspected he didn't mean or want to be rude. After all, he'd apologized. Would he call again? she wondered. Oh, honestly, she was being like some silly school-girl. Besides, there was no room in her life for a romantic involvement. She wasn't about to trust some man who'd just . . . just what? Die? Never mind.

She finished her sherry, put the glass in the sink, took a check in the mirror by the door, ran a brush through her hair, and left the house and thoughts of Colin Maguire behind.

"So just what the fuck is going on?" Colin said.

"Tell me again," Mark answered.

He lit a cigarette, paced the Griffing living room, wondering if he was going nuts. "Didn't you hear me?"

"Calm down, Colin, okay? I'm just trying to get a mental picture. You want a drink, coffee, or something?"

"No. I want you to listen, to do something."

"I will, I will." Mark wasn't annoyed exactly, but he hated being interrupted when he was listening to Pink Floyd. Colin had come bursting in right in the middle of "Brain Damage." The guy hadn't cared a damn about rock when they were in college together and didn't care now. "Take it from the top, all right."

Colin blew smoke from his nostrils. "I'm leaving Hallock's office and I stop to say hello to Kathy, the radio operator, you know her. I always shoot the breeze with her, nice kid. So Kathy's on the phone and then hangs up, tells this guy to go in. I stand and talk to Kathy, we laugh about something, then there's this silence right after us laughing, you know how that is?"

A few squawks from Mark's big police radio in the corner distracted Colin for a moment, but then he went on. "So during that silence I hear the guy who goes into Hallock's office say: 'The woman they found in the pool. I killed her.'"

"And what does Hallock say?"

"He tells him to sit down but Kathy starts talking again, telling me this long story about her sister and some boyfriend, and so I don't hear anything else. Besides, I couldn't act like I was listening. Friendly as Kathy is, she's all rules and regulations. Okay. I go out and sit in my car across the street, figuring Hallock's going to come out with this guy in cuffs, take him over to the jail or drive him over to East Hampton jail, but no. Fifteen minutes later this bimbo comes out alone. No cuffs, no nothing. He walks."

"So?"

"So? What do you mean, so? A guy confesses and Hallock lets him walk? I don't get it."

"Colin, obviously the guy didn't do it. Describe him."

"You've got to be kidding."

"Let's hear your powers of observation."

Colin mashed out his cigarette in a large ashtray that said Stork Club on it. He felt like twisting the fucking alligator off Mark's blue shirt. "Okay. He was on the short side, about your height." He knew this would bug Mark, who hated being reminded of his size. "No, maybe a little taller. About five ten, eleven. Medium build. Dark hair, dark beard, scraggly looking. Wearing Levi's, leather belt, work shirt over a brown polo, work boots."

Mark, smiling, said, "Dirty nails?"

"I didn't notice. What is this? Why the stupid grin?"

"You just described a nut case. Jim Drew. Every time anything happens around here, burglary, vandalism, it doesn't matter what, Drew confesses. He's got a guilt complex or something. Didn't I brief you about him?"

"No."

"Sorry, pal. I should have."

"So what you're telling me, Mark, is that this guy heard about it somewhere, confessed to the murder, but didn't do it."

"You got it."

"Jesus." He flopped down in an easy chair, legs outstretched. "How long's he been doing that, confessing to stuff?"

"Let's see, he came here about three years ago. He wasn't here a month before he made his first confession. A burglary. The paper listed it; then Drew goes into Hallock and confesses. Hallock books him. The next day another guy's caught burglarizing a house and confesses to the first one. Hallock confronts Drew but he sticks to it. So Hallock asks him about a detail only the real burglar could know. Like, 'Will the real burglar please stand up?'" Mark laughed.

Colin didn't.

"Anyway, Drew gets it wrong and Hallock lets him go. He doesn't figure it, until two weeks later Drew comes in to confess about a hit-and-run of a dog that's already been solved. Then Hallock realizes the guy is some kind of wacko. Harmless, but wacko in this area. Vietnam veteran. He runs an antique and junk shop. A loner. Probably he killed some innocent people in Vietnam or something and has this need to confess."

"Spare me the amateur psychology."

Mark shrugged. "You wanted to know, pal."

"Yeah." Colin pushed himself up out of the chair.

"Where're you going?"

"The office. I didn't get to writing the story last night."

"Write it tomorrow. Stay. The Mets and the Phillies are playing this afternoon."

"Maybe I'll come back."

"Don't feel too bad about the Drew thing."

"Yeah. See you."

Driving to the office he wondered why the hell he didn't just ask Kathy who the sucker was? Slipping? Or was it circumstances? There was no denying that the discovery of the body in Gildersleeve's pool had given him a jolt. And maybe his attraction to Annie Winters had thrown him too. He looked at his watch, wondering when she did her church thing. Then he glanced in his rearview and saw a car close behind. He realized it had been there since he'd left Mark's. The driver was a man but that was all he knew.

Pressing down on the pedal, he watched the car behind him speed up, too. When Colin turned a corner, so did the other car. Obviously he wasn't worried about being spotted. Colin slowed, turned from Fielding into Center, then coasted to the *Gazette* building, where he stopped. The other car pulled up behind him. Colin waited. The man got out of the car and came up to Colin's window. Colin recognized Phil Nagle, a local insurance broker. He'd met the guy twice and didn't like him much.

Nagle bent, eye level with Colin. "I want to talk to you."

"What about?"

"Gloria Danowski."

LOOKING BACK — 25 YEARS AGO

On Saturday May 30, there will be a special dance for teens at the popular American Legion Hall in Seaville. The wonderful Moonlovers will be featured and two other singing and instrumental groups will be on hand: The Divebombers and The Persuaders, featuring vocalist Gary Bell. Dancing will be strictly for teenagers only, from 8 to 11 P.M.

Chapter Seven

Sundays after church Ruth Cooper always went to her linen store, even though it wasn't open for business. In Seaville they stayed open on Sundays but not in Bayview. Although the towns were adjacent to one another, they couldn't have been more different. As Ruth saw it, Seaville was a working-class town and Bayview was chic, elite. She was proud she lived and worked in Bayview.

The reason she came down to her store on Sundays was because it was quiet and she could review stock, place new orders, and go over the books in peace. During the week it was impossible to get that sort of work done. Too much chattering between the clerks and customers, too much gossiping and fussing. Another reason Ruth liked to come to the store on Sunday was so she could get away from Russ.

Still excited by Annie's suggestion, Ruth put her key in the lock — made in the shape of a heart — let herself in, and locked the door behind her. Blissful quiet. No annoying sounds from a television, and most of all, no annoying hands trying to paw her.

What was wrong with Russ anyway? Married twenty-nine years, and all of a sudden he was chasing her around like she was a dog in heat.

She flipped on a light and pulled down the ruffled pink shade on the door. Looking around she took a deep breath, sighed. Ruth loved the look of the colorful towels stacked on the shelves, the printed sheets, the napkins, tablecloths. And in the center of the room were the decorative doorpulls, soap dishes, toothbrush holders, gold, silver, and porcelain light switches.

She walked down an aisle, let her hand trail across the stacks of Cannon and Fieldcrest towels, thinking maybe Russ was getting senile or something. But that was ridiculous, he was only fifty-six. They both were. So what was going on, then? He hadn't touched her for eight years and all of a sudden it was sex, sex, sex every minute. Maybe it was all those girls on the television with the big bazooms that were getting him crazy. Whatever, he was getting *her* crazy. It was so peaceful those eight years, and now he had to start up.

She went down three steps into the back room where she kept curtains and bedspreads, and snapped on another light. Off this room was her office, small but efficient. She opened the door and screamed.

"What are you doing here?" she said, heart knocking against her chest.

The last thing Ruth Cooper saw before he slit her throat was a glint of metal and his smile.

LOOKING BACK — 50 YEARS AGO

The body of Dr. Peter Tuthill, the 68-year-old eccentric "corn doctor," was found on Saturday in a lonely wooded road near Mattituck. The beaten, bullet-ridden body was discovered in his antiquated old coupé. The old doctor was known to carry large sums of money on his person due to his distrust of banks. When found the body was stripped of $10,000 in cash, and the five revolvers which he carried were missing.

Chapter Eight

Phillip Nagle was a slight, dark man in his late thirties. A pointed nose and chin gave him a pinched look, as if he were in pain. His hair was thin and drifted over his forehead in separate strands. The glasses he wore were the aviator type, rose-tinted. Usually he dressed in finely tailored sports jackets and slacks, but on this day he was in worn jeans and a faded Ralph Lauren polo shirt. On his feet were worn Topsiders with no socks. He had a fairly successful insurance agency and had gotten himself elected to the Village Board the year before. Many people in Seaville called him a sleazeball behind his back.

Colin sat across from the man, thinking he looked like a murderer and wondering why he'd never seen it before. Nagle hadn't said a word yet, but Colin was sure the guy was here to confess. He offered him a cigarette. Nagle took one with a shaking hand.

Colin settled back in his chair. "So what about Gloria Danowski?"

"This is off the record, right?"

"Right."

"I don't know how to start."

"Did you kill her?"

Nagle's eyes widened behind the glasses. He looked like an owl. "No. Hey, no. That's why I'm here. I don't want anybody thinking I did. I mean . . . see . . . shit!" He looked at his cigarette as if he didn't know how it had gotten into his hand, and put it in the black ashtray. "Mind if I smoke a joint?"

"Yes."

"Huh?"

"I mind if you smoke a joint."

"How come?"

"I'm an old-fashioned guy. I don't like people smoking joints at my place of business."

"What if I said I wanted a drink? You newspaper guys all drink. You wouldn't care if I wanted a drink, would you?"

"Yes."

"No, you wouldn't, and it's the same thing."

"Did you come here to debate the marijuana-liquor issue or do you want to tell me about Gloria Danowski?"

"Yeah, Gloria," Nagle said, picking up the cigarette.

"Did you know her?"

Nagle nodded. "I was fucking her."

Colin knew Nagle was married and had three kids. "Tell me about it."

Nagle grinned stupidly. "She gave good head."

"Jesus. I didn't mean the sex, Nagle. I don't give a shit about that." Colin pulled at his mustache, worked an end between his fingers. "Tell me what you came in here to tell me, for Christ's sake."

"Okay, okay. I thought you meant . . . I met her at Southampton College last fall. We were both taking a course in Advanced Accounting — she was thinking about going back to work. Anyway, we, you know, got to talking before and after class. I took her for a drink one night. She was a good-looking broad. Nice jugs."

Colin hated guys who talked about women that way. "Spare me the details, okay?" He wanted to bust Nagle in his weasel face.

"What's the matter, don't you like cunt?"

"I'm losing my patience, Nagle. Maybe you want me to call Chief Hallock, huh?"

"All right, all right." He took a long drag of the cigarette, blew a stream of smoke in front of him. "In the second semester we both pretend we're going to some class, but we don't. We start this thing. Every Tuesday night. I'd meet her in the parking lot, she'd leave her car, we'd go to a motel, fuck our brains out, then I'd take her back to her car. She'd go home, I'd go home. So everything goes along as usual, then about four weeks ago I read in the paper she disappeared. See, it was the night I'd seen her. The last I know I take her back to the car, we say goodnight. That's it. But sooner or later somebody's gonna remember we were real friendly in that class and maybe put two and two together, see?"

"What two and two?"

"That I knew her. That maybe I knew her pretty well. And then they're gonna be on my ass."

"Did you see her drive off that night?"

"No. I saw her get in her car, but I left before she did. They found the car in the lot."

"What do you think happened to her?"

"Beats me."

"Did she ever mention anything to you about somebody hating her or wanting to kill her?"

"No."

"How about her husband?"

"What about him?"

"What'd she say about him?"

"Not much. Just that he was a drag and couldn't get it up."

"Did she ever say that her husband might suspect?"

"No."

"Do you think he did?"

"How should I know?"

"Do you think he killed her?"

Nagle took some time, thinking what he should say. Colin knew the guy was weighing whether or not to put the finger on the husband.

"I don't know," Nagle said.

"Did Gloria ever say that Danowski was violent?"

"No."

"Did she have any other boyfriends?"

"She didn't need any," he gloated.

"But did she *have* any?"

"No."

"Not that you know of."

"Right."

"How about before you?"

"No. I was the first."

"Are you sure?"

"That's what she said."

"Okay. So what do you want from me?"

He shrugged. "Advice. What do you think I should do?"

"Tell Chief Hallock."

"Are you crazy?"

"That's my advice. Tell him before he tells you. If you're innocent, you have nothing to worry about."

"I'm innocent. But what if it gets out? I mean, I'm telling you this off the record, but I can't keep Hallock from spreading the word. I've got a wife and three kids."

"And you're a member of the board." Colin knew which was more important to Phil Nagle.

"Yeah, that, too."

"You don't have a choice. You have to tell Hallock. If you're innocent, he won't spread it around about you. He's not like that."

"Listen, you've only been in town what, five, six weeks? You don't know what shits people can be."

"Why'd you come to me if there's so much I don't know?"

"I'm beginning to wonder myself. I thought you looked like a decent guy."

When you start getting compliments from a sleazeball, Colin thought, it's time to worry.

"What are you going to do with what I told you?" Nagle said.

"Nothing. I don't have to. The connections will be made soon enough. Then you'll really look suspicious, Nagle. Can you prove you didn't kill her?"

"Of course not. I thought I was innocent until proven guilty."

"Where'd you hear that?" Colin stubbed out his cigarette, lit another. "And if I remember correctly, you're not exactly a Gildersleeve fan, are you?"

"He's an asshole."

"That's what I mean. If you keep this information to yourself, when they finally get onto you it's going to be more than putting two and two together. More like two and three. Do you think Hallock doesn't know how you feel about Gildersleeve?"

"Fuck. I don't know."

"Well, what did you think I'd tell you to do?"

"I don't know. I guess I thought you'd say I had nothing to worry about. I don't know." He took off his glasses, wiped them with the bottom of his shirt.

"Hallock might give you a hard time for awhile, until he's sure you didn't do it, but he's not going to book you. On the other hand, if you don't go to him on your own, if you wait until he has to pick you up, then he's going to make you wish you'd been in that pool instead of Gloria. Me, too."

"What's that mean?"

"It means if he arrests you on his own, then you're fair game."

"Shit."

"Up to your neck."

Nagle put back his glasses. "Okay. I'll do it."

"Good."

"See you," he said and started to leave.

"Hey, Nagle?"

"Yeah?"

"What do you feel about Gloria Danowski being murdered?"

"Feel?"

"Right, *feel.*"

"I don't know. I feel bad, I guess. She was a good lay."

Colin was glad Nagle left quickly; he wanted to clobber him. He had always hated fighting, even though he was pretty good at it. The first real fistfight he'd had was in grade school when the public school kids picked on the Catholics. He'd knocked Freddy Martin's two front teeth out, and Colin's father had had to pay for Freddy's bridge. In junior high he was always getting into fights, but in high school he managed to stay clear of them, using up his aggression on the football field. In college he never fought anyone. He talked his way out of things because he just didn't have the heart for fighting. By then he knew it was pointless. After college it never came up — except that once — but he couldn't remember it and didn't even know if he'd won or not.

Still, guys like Nagle made him remember and understand the pleasure of smashing a fist into a face, feeling knuckles against teeth, splitting lips open. He hoped Hallock gave Nagle a bad time, hoped he scared the shit out of him.

Colin smiled thinking about Nagle: knees knocking together, hands too shaky to hold a butt. He deserved anything he got. But he believed Nagle was innocent. So, who did it then? The husband could've found out about his wife's affair and killed her, but it wasn't likely. With that kind of murder, he would've broken down by now if he'd done it. Nobody knew that better than Colin did. Jesus. Everything always came back to that. He turned to his typewriter, stared at the piece of paper still there from the night before.

BODY FOUND IN MAYOR'S POOL

It hadn't changed, hadn't written itself. And it wasn't going to get written now, either. He reached for the bound volume of the *Gazette* seventy-five years before for the week of May 26th. One of his duties was to do the "Looking Back" column. At first when Mark gave him the job, he was insulted, feeling this was some rinky-dink thing one of the others could do, not the managing editor, for Christ's sake. But that was the way it was on a small weekly: You did all kinds of stuff no matter what your title was. Anyway, he'd come to like it, found it fun going through the old issues, pulling things from seventy-five, fifty, and twenty-five years before. Sometimes he lost himself in the papers, hours passing before he'd pull just the right excerpts.

Colin knew it was something you could do in half an hour, but he liked reading all the ads, the sports and the real estate section. It knocked him out seeing things like:

FOR SALE:

WATERVIEW–10 RMS, FIREPLACES, ICEBOX, PORCH, 1 ACRE, PRIVATE BEACH. $3000.00

Today that same property would be worth about half a million.

So he got lost in the past, and when the phone rang and he glanced at his watch he was stunned to see it was almost three. Mark said, "We have another one, pal."

"Another what?"

"Murder."

"Where?"

"Bayview. Cooper's Linen Shop. Ruth Cooper."

"Christ."

"Get over there."

"Right."

Getting into his car, Colin wondered what he'd do if any murders happened past Riverhead. He wasn't sure he'd be able to go. The truth was even Riverhead was alien to him. Since he'd been on the North Fork he hadn't gone past Mattituck. That was twenty miles from Seaville. Riverhead was twenty-five, and his panic attacks weren't getting any better. But it was useless to worry about that now. Now there was another murder.

Starting the car, he wondered if a B was carved into Ruth Cooper's chest.

LOOKING BACK — 75 YEARS AGO

Some miserable wretch, without a grain of self-respect or an atom of conscience, stole the hospital collection box in the post office some days ago. If the guilty person has really enjoyed the loose change which had been deposited therein for the purpose of charity, he has sold every speck of honor he ever had, if he ever had any. The box was torn from the writing desk in the office, to which it had been attached.

Chapter Nine

When Ruth Cooper did not come home for Sunday dinner, Russell Cooper, who had prepared roast pork, potatoes, asparagus au gratin, and a salad, became worried. He called the store, but there was no answer. So he turned off everything on the stove, sick that the dinner was going to be ruined, and got into his new silver Toyota Tercel and drove down to the shop. The door was locked. He knocked. There was no answer. Ruth's car was parked in front of the store, which alarmed Russ further, thinking she'd had a heart attack. He shouted Ruth's name, but nothing happened. Officer Dan Reeves of the Bayview police was driving by, saw Russ and came to his aid. Reeves gave the front door a flat-footed kick, and it broke open like a cracked egg.

One minute after they were in they found her — throat slit from ear to ear, blood everywhere. Her blouse had been torn open exposing her chest, which displayed long bloody slashes. It took Colin to tell them what it was.

"It's an A. Like the other one."

"What other one?" Bayview Chief of Police Ed Webb hadn't been informed by Chief Hallock of the details on Saturday's homicide.

Colin, fighting nausea and dizziness, explained.

Webb said to Officer Reeves, "See if you can get Chief Hallock here."

Although Bayview's police department was autonomous,

technically they were under the authority of Seaville Township, and Colin could see that Webb was already thinking about dumping this mess into Hallock's lap.

"What do you think, Chief?" Colin asked.

"I dunno. Maybe a Ten-Three. She probably surprised him. The window in the back was open."

Colin knew it was no Ten-Three. "Don't you think the A on her chest means it was something other than a burglary?" he asked gently, not wanting to offend.

"All I got is you saying these cuts are an A. How the hell do I know what's what when I get no official word? *A*, he tells me." Webb walked away, watched the fingerprint men sprinkling powder on the window ledge.

"Hey, Chief," Reeves said, "I couldn't get Hallock, but they said he's on his way."

Webb snarled, "*Chief* Hallock."

"Yeah, Chief Hallock," he repeated, not understanding.

Colin walked into the other room, away from the body, to where a white-faced Russell Cooper was sitting. The man was in shock, Colin could tell — could remember. A good newspaperman would interview him; *he* would have before, but not now. He couldn't do it, intrude like that. Maybe he'd have to find some other work. Jesus, who thought there were going to be murders out here in the sticks? It was the whole point in coming, and now it was getting to be like some nightmare.

Hallock and Charlie Copin arrived looking serious. When they saw the A they would know they had a serial murderer on their hands. Colin followed them to the back, keeping far enough away so he didn't have to see her again, saying nothing, listening.

"Ed."

"Waldo."

"What've we got?"

"A Ten-Five."

"I know that. Lemme see." Hallock bent down, knees cracking. "Christ. Look at this, Charlie."

Copin leaned over. "Same fucking thing."

Webb asked, "What's that?"

"An A. See." Hallock traced the line of the A in the air, above Ruth Cooper's chest.

"Maybe," Ed said.

Hallock said, "It's no maybe, Ed. That's an A, all right." He turned to Colin. "What did Griffing say the A might be?"

"A for Adulteress."

"I dunno," Hallock said, standing up. "What do you think, Charlie?"

"Could mean anything, Chief. Well, one thing we know, he ain't gonna go through the alphabet." Charlie grinned.

"Swell. Just twenty-six A's, huh?"

"I didn't think of that," Charlie admitted soberly.

"Where the hell's the M.E.?" Hallock asked.

Ed said, "We called him. Didn't you, Reeves?"

"Who, me?"

"Jesus fucking Christ! Get on that phone and call him now, you shit-for-brains moron!" Webb yelled.

Reeves said defensively, "I got the I.B. boys here."

"You want a medal?"

"No, I just . . . ah, shit."

Colin blinked as a flashbulb went off. He didn't know any of the men from the identification bureau and stayed out of their way. He wondered what more he could learn by hanging around, knew he didn't dare leave. But the smell of blood was getting to him. Making him think of Nancy. He wished he could recall the perfume she wore instead, but he never could. It was the smell of blood he would forever identify with her, not Je Reviens.

Casually, he sat on the top step of three that went down to the back room. His head was throbbing; his eyes ached. He wrote some details in his notebook.

Fifteen minutes later, Dr. Hubbard, the M.E., came in and went past Colin down to where the body was. Another fifteen minutes passed before he heard the ambulance pull up. When the men came in with the gurney, Colin got up from his spot on the steps, making room. It was awhile before they took her out, but when they did Russell Cooper spoke to Colin.

"Should I go with them? Is that what I'm supposed to do?"

Colin felt for him, put a hand on his arm. "No. They're taking her to the morgue. There'll be an autopsy."

"Autopsy?"

"Yeah." He knew that Cooper was wondering why. It was clear how she died. Colin remembered wondering that himself. "They have to. It's the law."

Hallock came over to them. Copin behind him, stood to the side, his notebook and pencil ready.

Hallock said, "I'd like to ask you a couple of questions, Russ."

"Okay."

"Have you or Ruth received any threatening letters or telephone calls in the last month or so?"

Cooper ran his tongue over his dry lips. "No. Nothing like that."

"Would any of the girls who worked for Ruth have anything against her? Maybe one of them wanted a raise, and Ruth wouldn't give it to her? Anything like that?"

"I don't think so. Ruth would've mentioned it if there'd been any trouble. Wait a minute. Sondra Segal wanted to take her vacation the same time Jane Williams wanted to take hers. Ruth had approved Jane's time way back, so Sondra lost out."

"Was she mad about that?"

"Who?"

Hallock turned to Copin. Copin consulted his notes. "Segal. Sondra Segal."

Russ answered. "More annoyed than mad, I think."

Hallock gave Copin a look as if to say, check her out anyway. "Anybody else besides those two work for your wife?"

"No. That's all."

"Okay. I understand Ruth always came to the store on Sundays, is that right?"

"Right after church."

"Who knew about that?"

"Just about everybody, I guess. It wasn't a secret or anything," Russ explained.

"You mean, everybody at your church knew?"

"I guess. Other people too. Other friends."

"Could you make up a list of all the people who knew about Ruth coming to the store on Sundays, Russ?"

He nodded, shoulders drooping as if even the thought of the task was too much for him.

Copin asked, "You or your wife owe anybody money?"

"We never borrowed. Ruthie doesn't — didn't — believe in buying things you couldn't pay for." He coughed, and passed a hand over his face trying to disguise his watery eyes.

Hallock said, "Okay, that's all, thanks very much. Get that list to us soon as you can." He squeezed Cooper's shoulder. "Sorry about this, Russ."

Hallock and Copin walked away, leaving Colin alone with Cooper.

"What should I do now?" Russ asked Colin, tears springing to his eyes.

"Why don't you go home, Mr. Cooper. Or to a friend's. Is there somebody I can call for you?"

"I don't know." He rubbed his temples as if an answer would appear, like in a crystal ball. "Maybe Annie."

"Annie?"

"My minister. Yes, Annie. Could you call her?"

Colin hesitated for only a moment. "Do you know her number?"

After a few false starts, Cooper gave it to him. Colin told him to sit down, and went across the street to the public phone in the parking lot. It rang four times before she answered.

Colin identified himself, then said, "This isn't a social call."

"Okay," she said.

"You know Ruth and Russell Cooper?"

"Yes."

He didn't know how to tell her gently. "Ruth's been murdered. In her store. He's there now and asked me to call you. I . . ."

"I'll be right there." She hung up.

Colin slowly walked back across the street. A few people were standing around rubbernecking. He'd been so intent on making his call to Annie Walters he hadn't noticed them before.

A man stopped him. "What's going on, son?"

"I can't help you. Sorry," Colin responded.

Back inside, he went over to Cooper and told him Annie was on her way.

Cooper said, "Why would anyone want to kill Ruthie?"

Jesus, Colin wondered, did every survivor say the same thing about their murdered loved one? How many times had he heard it? He'd even said it himself. "I don't know, Mr. Cooper," he said, "The police will find out, though."

"Will they?"

"They'll try."

"Was it a burglary?"

"I don't know." Colin knew it wasn't. He tried desperately to think of something else to say to Cooper but couldn't. His mind was on Gloria Danowski and Ruth Cooper. What did they have in common? Gloria was thirty-one, Ruth must have been in her fifties. "How old was your wife?" he asked.

"Fifty-six. Same as me. She just celebrated her birthday last week. I won't be fifty-six till Friday. I always kidded her, saying she robbed the cradle." His mouth twisted to the right and then he was sobbing, his face in his hands. Cooper's shoulders heaved and he let out a bellow. Colin couldn't help thinking he sounded like a wounded animal. He wondered if that was how he'd sounded. At a loss as to how to comfort Cooper, he decided to give him privacy. He went over to Hallock and Copin.

"Got a statement, Chief?"

"We don't want to panic the people, Maguire. You know what I mean?"

"I do."

"Good." He ran thumb and forefinger over his long nose. "Let's say it was a suspected burglary."

"But it wasn't?"

"No way. Nothing's gone, not even looked through. Ruth Cooper came here every Sunday after church, somebody knew that. This thing was planned. Got in through the window in back, probably waited for her in her office. Motive? Who the hell knows? Who the hell ever knows with a psycho?"

"You think that's what he is, a psycho?"

"Don't you?"

"It looks that way. You know, Chief, it's one thing not to panic people and another to try and make them cautious."

"You can do one without the other. We don't know enough yet to make any judgments about anything."

"Don't you think you have a serial murderer on your hands?"

Hallock said, "Two killings don't make a mass murderer, Maguire."

"What about the A?"

"What about it?"

"Any ideas?"

"Frankly, no."

"She wasn't raped, was she?" He'd noticed the lower half of Ruth Cooper's clothing hadn't seem disturbed.

"Offhand I'd say no. We'll have to wait for the M.E.'s report to be definite on that."

"What do you think about the M.O. being different?"

"You mean the fact that Danowski was strangled and Cooper's throat was cut?"

Colin nodded.

"Don't know. Got to be the same perpetrator though. The A."

"Could be a copycat killer," Colin offered.

"Maybe. But I don't think so. Too early for that."

The front door opened and Reeves stuck his head in. "Annie Winters is here, says Mister Cooper called her."

"That's right," Colin responded.

Reeves opened the door wider and Annie came in, went right to Cooper, and put an arm around him.

"So you'll be careful what you say, Maguire, okay?" Hallock emphasized.

"Don't worry." He was looking at Annie, watching her tending Cooper. He like what he saw.

Hallock and Copin left. Colin thought there was nothing more for him to do, but he wanted to speak to Annie. She was helping Cooper up, leading him toward the door. Colin got to it first and opened it for them.

Annie glanced at him. "Thanks," she said.

"Anything I can do?" he asked.

"I don't think so. I'm taking Russ back to the parsonage with me now if anyone needs him."

He watched them go across the street to Annie's Escort, waiting until they drove off before he got into his own car. What he should do now was to interview the Cooper neighbors, get a line on Mrs. Cooper. Maybe she was sleeping with somebody, too. Maybe the A *was* for Adulteress. Or maybe A stood for the killer's mother's name. Or his wife's. Or any goddamn thing. Hallock was right: When you were dealing with a psycho there was nothing logical to go after.

But it was all absolutely logical to the murderer. Colin knew that whoever he was, cutting an A in his victim's chest made perfect sense to him. At this point the only thing they could rule out was that A stood for one. A. What else could it mean?

And then a stupid ditty from grade school was running through his head. The girls bouncing a ball in time to the words: "A, my name is Alice, my husband's name is Al. We come from Alabama, and we sell apples." It was funny thinking of that after all these years. There was something sad about it, he observed, something making him feel terrible.

He started his car knowing he wasn't going to interview the Coopers' neighbors or write his story; he was going up to the Sound, to sit and think.

He took a left off Bayview's main street, drove up to the north road, and headed back to Seaville. There were several farms along the way. Most of them grew cauliflower and potatoes, he'd been told. The road was four lanes here, and you couldn't see the water until it narrowed. He noticed a barn set back from the highway. A sign for Antiques and Junque swung in the breeze at the entry road. He wondered if this was Jim Drew's place. It was funny he'd never taken it in before. He'd have to concentrate on improving his powers of observation.

The north road became a double lane, and the houses more expensive. Some were old, turn of the century; others, big modern structures. Lilacs were abundant, their lavender blooms splashing color indiscriminately along the way. The purples, pinks, and whites of azalea bushes bordered paths and porches. Finally Colin left the greens of grass and hedges behind as sand became the front lawns of the beach houses.

Flashes of blue caught his eye as the water became visible. Soon he passed the public beach, empty except for a lone fisherman. He crossed the invisible line between Bayview and Seaville, and the houses immediately became less opulent. A few minutes later, Colin slowed near Orlowski's, the big farm stand, and turned left onto Pointy Rock Road.

At the end of the street, he parked his car. Sarah Griffing had shown him Snapper Cove a few days after he'd arrived in Seaville. She'd taken him to various spots, driving her own car with Colin following in his. It was amazing how understanding she was about his problem. But women were like that. It was men who couldn't deal with it, didn't want to talk about it. Like Mark. "No need to go into a bunch of details," he'd said when Colin tried to explain, then looked away as if he might catch something if his eyes met Colin's.

Snapper Cove was in East Haven, the town on the other side of Seaville. Nobody lived on the cove, it was just a high point on the Fork where you could park and look at the view. Looking down at the big boulders on the pebbly beach gave him the feeling he was gazing at the Mediterranean. The water had a greenish cast to it, and the wind created small waves.

There were no other cars today. Sarah had told him that he'd never be alone there or anywhere else once the season started. More than twenty thousand people swelled the Fork from Memorial Day to Labor Day. Colin didn't look forward to it.

"A, my name is Annie..." The child's ditty started again. "A, my name is Annie, my husband's name is . . ." He'd meant to ask Mark what her status was, but had forgotten. The sadness he'd felt earlier pushed up into his chest. What was it? And then he remembered.

The schoolyard of Our Lady of Sorrows, and Sister Mary

Agnes grabbing him by the collar, pulling him away from Patti Ellen Fagan, whom he'd been teasing mercilessly because she couldn't get past "A, my name is Audrey, my husband's name is Arthur." She couldn't think of a place starting with A because Patti Ellen Fagan wasn't your brightest and all the kids knew it.

"All right, Colin Maguire, that's enough now. You leave Patti Ellen alone."

"I was just foolin', Sister."

"You were just a fool, is what you mean. Oh, Colin, I don't know what's gonna become of you. Some day if I read in the paper that you've been arrested for murder I won't be surprised."

Jesus, he thought, what a thing to say to a kid. He remembered feeling terrible when she'd said that to him, and he felt terrible now. Funny how you could feel the same thing twenty-seven years later, just from recalling a ditty, not even knowing the connection right away.

But he knew it wasn't childhood rhymes, or Patti Ellen Fagan, or demented nuns that were bothering him. It was the murders, ugly and unsolved. He was wondering again.

What if someone here, other than the Griffings, found out? What would happen then? But no one was going to rake up the whole thing and bring it to the attention of the people in Seaville. As long as he kept his cool, didn't pass out every time a body turned up, he'd be all right. No one would ever have to know that his wife and two children had been murdered and their killer never found. No one ever had to know that.

Chapter Ten

Colin was twenty-six when he met Nancy Michelle. She was twenty-four and studying for her Ph.D. in mathematics at the University of Chicago. Colin had been on the crime beat for a year. At first, each of them had thought the other was just another date. He had always been attracted to tall, slim blondes, and Nancy was short and dark. But he liked her and asked her out again.

They dated for over a year before they realized that they were in love. Another year passed before they married. By then Nancy was teaching at the university, and their combined salaries made them feel rich. And then Todd was born and Nancy left her job. Money got a little tighter, but. they managed. Nancy wanted to be at home with her child and said she would go back to work when Todd went to school. But Alicia was born two years later, and Colin and Nancy could see that it would be another five years before she'd be working again. It was rough, money-wise. Still, they loved each other and the children, had a good life — most of the time.

The fights about money were frequent. It was almost impossible for Nancy to budget. She'd grown up in a wealthy family and worrying about money was new to her. She tried, but if she wanted steak for dinner she'd buy it, or a new sweater, or some trinket for the kids, a book for Colin. She'd forget that these things weren't on the budget and give in to impulse.

It had been one of those impulses that had started the fight that last night.

Colin said, "Jesus Christ, Nan, you just don't get it, do you?"

"I thought you'd like it," she said, hurt.

"Like it or not liking it is beside the point. We can't afford it."

"Well, why don't you ask for a raise, then?"

This pissed him off. He knew asking for a raise was a matter of timing and the time was not right. "I'll ask for a raise when I think it's right."

"Oh, the hell you will."

"What's that supposed to mean?"

"Nothing."

"No, come on, what's that mean, *the hell I will*?"

"I think you're afraid to, that's all."

Colin stared at her, wanting to slap her silly. He'd never touched Nancy in anger, never even felt like it before. But this really made him mad. It was the first time she'd accused him of being cowardly. Usually she'd just hold him up against her father. He wondered when that would come, how long would she take before throwing Alex Michelle in his face. He decided not to wait. "Not like dear old Dad, huh?"

"Leave my father out of this."

"Why? You never do."

"Well, why should I? When he and Mother were our ages they already owned a house and had plenty in the bank."

"Your fucking father was not a newspaperman, Nancy. He was a *business* man. There's a difference."

"You bet there is," she shot back.

"Oh, that's terrific. Just great. I suppose you think I should give up writing and join the great Square C Company of Philadelphia, huh?"

"You've always acted as if my father offering you a good job in his company was some kind of insult."

"It was. I'm a writer, goddammit. You don't go offering a writer a job selling spark plugs or whatever the fuck he makes."

"A writer, a writer," she mocked. "You'd think you were Hemingway or something."

"Hemingway or some*one*," he corrected.

"Oh, who cares?"

"*I* care."

"Well, hell, Colin, maybe you should start caring about other things besides proper English."

"Like what?"

"Like providing for your family."

"Since when haven't I provided for my family?"

"Since always. I haven't been able to buy a new dress for myself without a fight since I quit working. Do you know how damn guilty I feel if I buy the kids a toy or myself a new lipstick?"

"I haven't noticed your guilt stopping you." He picked up the record she'd presented to him minutes ago. "It didn't stop you from buying this."

"You love Judy Collins. I thought you'd be pleased." She started to cry.

"Oh, shit, don't start that."

"I can't help it. I'm stuck home here with two kids and a husband who's a goddamn gutless wonder and can't even ask for a raise."

That did it. He'd snapped, and suddenly his open hand was connecting with her cheek. She screamed, and first Alicia woke crying, then Todd. And the gutless wonder couldn't face it, none of it. He'd grabbed his jacket and slammed out, Nancy yelling behind him not to come back, he shouting don't worry.

Downstairs, in front of the apartment house, shaking with rage, he wondered what to do, where to go. He combed his pockets for a cigarette and found nothing. At the end of the block was Maxie's, a bar he'd never been in. He knew it was a local hangout, seedy, for hard-core drinkers, and when he started toward it the only thing in his mind was to buy a pack of Marlboros.

Once inside, the idea of having a drink suddenly appealed to him. He'd never been much of a drinker, a few beers with the guys on the paper, but it didn't interest him. He liked feeling straight, hated losing control. But tonight anything that might change the awful feelings he had about having slapped Nancy, he was eager to try.

With his open pack of cigarettes he took a stool at the end of the bar. Several men occupied places near him, and they were all joking around, razzing the bartender, yelling things at the baseball game on the fuzzy black-and-white television above them. Something about the atmosphere, the camaraderie of the men, made him feel good, comfortable, and he heard himself ordering a boilermaker, a drink he'd never had but remembered his uncles drinking.

It wasn't long before he was in conversation with the others and then they were all leaving, going to a strip joint on South State Street, Colin among them.

He remembered the place: lots of smoke, girls with tassels, more boilermakers. He remembered going to the men's room. But that was it.

When he awoke in his car he was stunned. It was six-thirty in the morning and the sun was beating in through the windshield. The taste in his mouth was sour, like old socks. He'd been crumpled up under the steering wheel and when he tried to straighten, everything hurt, as if he'd been in a fight. It was then that he saw the blood. The front of his shirt was stained and there was some on his pants. In the rearview mirror he saw that although he looked like hell, there were no cuts or scrapes. So he must have been in a fight, and the blood was from the other guy. But what other guy? He couldn't remember. The last thing he could clearly recall was going into that men's room at the strip joint.

He got out of the car, pulled his jacket closed over the bloodstains and made his way home. Nancy would be up with the kids. He didn't know what he was going to say, hoped she'd forgive him, felt pretty sure she would. When he got to the apartment and put his key in the door he found that it was unlocked. For a moment he was alarmed, then figured Nancy might have been afraid he'd forgotten his keys, left it open for him. It gave him some courage. But when he stepped inside his courage fled, leaving only fear in its stead.

He could see immediately that the place had been ransacked. Lamps were knocked over, drawers pulled out, things strewn about the floor. He yelled for Nancy. There was no answer. Cautiously moving into the room, he called for her again. Then for Todd. No one answered. And then he saw her. Across the room partially under an upended table. He shouted her name and ran to her, pushing the table aside. She was on her stomach, and when he turned her over he almost vomited. Alicia was under her. They were covered in blood, dead. He'd seen enough dead people to know. He shouted for Todd, then raced madly through the rooms, falling, bumping into things, continuing to call for his son. He found him in his bed. Dead. Blood everywhere. Falling on the bed, he picked up the boy and held him, crying, rocking. Time passed, and then he lay Todd down and stumbled back to the living room, to his wife and daughter. He crumpled to the floor and held Nancy in his arms, Alicia too. Over and over he said their names. He didn't know how long he stayed with the bodies, holding them, rocking them, talking to them, but eventually he realized he had to do something. Gently he placed Nancy and Alicia on the rug and slowly got to his feet. When he found the phone under the couch, he saw that it had been pulled from the wall. Something about that pushed him over the edge and he began to scream, baying almost. He left the apartment, went into the street, and shouted for help.

People ran from him. He was covered in blood — face, hands, shirt, jacket, pants, even shoes. No one would help him. And then he was attacked, wrestled to the ground, handcuffed. He tried to tell them, but no one would listen. It was only later, in the police station, that they understood what he'd been attempting to tell them about Nancy and the children.

Colin was arrested for the murders. Unidentified fingerprints were found in the apartment and unidentified blood on Colin's clothes. He couldn't prove where he was after midnight, but the blood helped his story of being in a fight. The murder weapon, a large knife of some sort, was never found. Colin was let go for lack of evidence, and the murders went unsolved.

But in the back of Colin's mind, some days, some nights was the nagging question he would live with forever. Would they have died if he'd been at home?

Most of the time he knew he couldn't have saved them, probably would have been murdered himself. And the year after the murders that he'd spent living with his mother, talking to a therapist, had helped him to lessen his guilt. Still — sometimes when he woke in the night, covered in sweat, having dreamed of his family, mutilated and bloody — he wondered and wept.

LOOKING BACK — 25 YEARS AGO

The controversy over the proposed plan to turn Terry's old oyster factory, at the foot of Sixth Street in Seaville, into a nightclub, continued at last night's Town Meeting. Residents of Sixth Street claim there is no room to park the cars of all the patrons to a night club in that vicinity. There is also the question of noise and possible rowdiness. Ralph Heaney, the prospective owner of the club, said that he will blacktop a large enough area for cars to park.

Chapter Eleven

On Monday morning Carl Gildersleeve, sunglasses low on the bridge of his nose, stood over Chief Hallock, his hands gripping the edge of the desk. "Well, what the hell've you got?"

"On what?"

"Don't bullshit me, Waldo, you know damn well what!"

"You mean the murders?"

"What else would I mean?"

"You wanna know what I got? I got nothing. A big fat zero, if you mean a suspect."

"I mean a suspect. And more to the point, an arrest."

Hallock laughed. "No suspect, no arrest."

"You think this is funny?"

"Nope. But I think you're ridiculous."

The mayor's face flushed, turning brick red. "You'd better watch your mouth, Waldo, and I mean it. You can't talk to me like that."

"I'm telling you I got nothing and you're pushing me. So I find that pretty ridiculous."

"I can't believe you haven't got one damn shred of — of anythin', not one suspect."

Hallock pushed his cap back on his head, ran a big hand over his chin, and felt a patch of stubble he missed that morning. "Okay. This is what I got. I got a confession."

Gildersleeve stared at Hallock with cold eyes. "What's that bullshit?"

"No bullshit. I got a confession. To both murders. Jim Drew's confession."

"You mean that loony-tunes peckerhead who confesses to everything from being a peepin' tom to armed robbery?"

"The very same."

"What the fuck good is that?"

"So who said it was good? I told you I didn't have diddly-squat."

Gildersleeve was silent for a moment, sat down in an orange chair, and played with his flowered tie. "Wait a minute, wait a minute. Lemme think."

"Be my guest."

"Drew confessed, huh? To both murders?"

"I was waiting for him. Took him five hours before he confessed to Ruth Cooper's murder."

"So arrest him," Gildersleeve ordered.

"I'm dying laughing."

"I'm serious." Gildersleeve moved forward in his chair, his tie end resting on the desk. "Listen. We make an arrest now, get an indictment, and if it doesn't hold up three, four months from now, nobody gives two farts in the wind. You see what I mean?"

"No. I don't see. It wouldn't hold up for two minutes, let alone months. Nobody's gonna indict that bedbug. Like you said, Carl, he confesses to every misdemeanor comes down the pike."

"We need an arrest."

"What's the *we* stuff, huh?" Hallock leaned forward, stared into Gildersleeve's eyes. "I make the arrest, I take the heat when the DA goes to indict and sees he's got snow in August. But before that the paper nails me like a piece of . . ."

"What paper? That rag? What do they know?"

"They'll squeeze my balls till they bust if I go arresting Drew. They know he's a loon."

"Listen, Waldo, the guy confessed, right? So give him what he wants, and give the public what they want. Everybody wants to sleep easy."

Hallock walked around the side of the desk and stood over Gildersleeve. "I don't think you understand what we got here. Two murders in two days."

"The first one was over a month ago. Bastard, puttin' her in my pool."

"Okay, so it happened a month ago. The point is, there's been a second one. And maybe there's gonna be a third. So let's say I got Drew locked up nice an' cosy, and the real killer bumps off another woman and writes another A on her chest. Then what, huh? It's my ass in a sling, not yours."

Gildersleeve fanned the idea away with his hand. "Nobody's gonna blame you if a guy confesses."

Leaning over, his face level with Gildersleeve's, Hallock said, "But look who the guy is, Carl. He confesses but he doesn't know dick about the murders. I say to him, 'Where'd you get the silk stocking you tied around Gloria Danowski's neck?' and he says to me, 'I bought it at Van Duzer's department store.'"

"So what's wrong with that?"

"Jesus, Carl, you saw her. It was a piece of sheet around her neck. And when I ask him where the gun was that he used to shoot Ruth Cooper, you wanna guess what he says?"

"He threw it away, doesn't remember where?"

Standing straight again he said, "Now you're getting smart."

"And it wasn't a gun, right?"

"Right. Look I want this thing put away as much as you, but sending Jim Drew up to bat isn't gonna do the trick."

"Okay, okay. Forget Drew. You got anything else?"

"Nothing." Hallock wasn't going to tell him about Phil Nagle. There was no point; the man was innocent.

"It's a maniac, isn't it?"

Hallock shrugged. "I don't think he's your picture of health."

"And I don't think it's anybody from around here."

Hallock walked past the filing cabinets, ran a hand over the edge. "No? What makes you say that?"

"I just don't think we got those kind of people around here. I mean, we got some lulus but not cold-blooded killers."

"It's hard to know about that. A cold-blooded killer could be walking around just like you and me, nobody noticing anything. Besides, Carl, I think you're forgetting something."

"What's that?"

Hallock tried not to smile. "Whoever did it dumped the first one in your pool."

Gildersleeve jumped up. "Just what in hell's that supposed to mean?"

"It means I don't think that was an accident. I don't think that was some stranger killing a woman, then picking out some unknown pool and dropping her in there, that's what it means."

"You think somebody's got it in for me, Waldo?" Gildersleeve was sweating.

"I'd definitely say somebody doesn't like you."

"You ought to give us a guard then, twenty-four hour guard."

"Don't have the manpower."

"But maybe Grace'll be next."

Hallock wondered if what he saw in Carl's eyes was fear or hope.

"We have to protect Grace."

"I personally think what's gonna be done to you has already been done."

"But you don't know that, do you, Waldo? You can't guarantee it because by your own admission you don't know anythin'. Well, I'm gonna tell you somethin' right now. You better make an arrest soon, because what we have here is a resort town which has a season which officially opens this Friday. That's four days from now, Waldo. If we don't have this thing under control in four days nobody's gonna come here, and if nobody comes here then nobody who lives here is gonna make any money, and if nobody makes any money then this town goes down the fuckin' tubes. So you better arrest somebody quick. I don't give a shit who, just do it."

"I can't just arrest any old person, Carl."

"I'm tellin' you, you'd better do somethin'. And you wanna know why? I'll tell you that, too. You've been chief a good long time, had a great run, right? Youngest police chief in the state an' all that crap, but it can disappear just like that." He snapped his fingers. "No benefits, no pension. Know what I mean? So make an arrest, Slats, and make it in the next forty-eight hours." Gildersleeve pushed past Hallock and walked out.

"Fuck you," Hallock said softly.

At lunch Hallock sat across from Fran at the kitchen table. "So that's what he said, make an arrest, doesn't matter who."

"What're you gonna do, hon'?"

"I don't know." He reached out a hand and Fran took it, squeezed hard. She was still a damned good-looking woman, he thought. Clear blue eyes, small nose, Cupid's bow mouth: pretty. "The thing is, Fran, I want to catch this guy myself. I don't want the state troopers in here, know what I mean?"

"Do you think that'll happen?"

"Could. Sure could. If I don't do something fast Carl'll call them in himself. Maybe even have the Village Board on my back. Main thing though, is to keep this quiet as we can. Don't want a panic, big city papers coming out here to do stories and stuff."

"How're you gonna keep a thing like this quiet?"

"I gotta pay a visit to Mark Griffing. Maguire's okay. We're friends and I know I can make him see my position. But Griffing — I don't know about him. See, the thing is, much as I think Gildersleeve's an asshole, he's got a point. This thing gets out, the town's in real trouble. If the tourists don't come nobody makes money, and who do you think they're gonna blame? Gildersleeve? Griffing? The killer? No. It's me they're gonna blame." Hallock picked up the second half of his egg-salad sandwich and took a bite, mayonnaise streaking his lips.

Fran handed him a napkin. "You got a plan?"

"Nope, no plan. Only thing I know now is I got to spend more time on the job."

These were not the words Fran longed to hear. As it was, she hardly ever saw him. Even Sundays were messed up when something big was going on. Still, this was no time to nag him about staying home with her and the kids more. Anyway, she knew he would if he could. Waldo Hallock loved his family. "You've got to do what you think's best."

"Don't wanna lose my job," he said solemnly.

She tented her hands beneath her chin. "Carl can't do much without the Board, Waldo. And I can't believe anybody'd criticize you for not nailing this thing down right off. People know you've been a good police chief, and honest as the day is long."

"My honesty isn't at stake here, Fran."

"Well, you know what I mean. People love you in this town."

"People might love me, but if they're afraid for their lives they're gonna view me differently."

"How can Carl, or anyone else, expect you to solve a murder in a minute when you don't have experience with that kind of thing?" she said angrily.

"Ah, Fran, you just don't get it." He wiped his mouth and crushed the napkin into a ball, dropped it on the table.

"Sorry about that," she said sharply.

Hallock saw that her eyes were the color of cobalt: she was hurt. He walked around the table and knelt in front of her. "Listen, Fran, I don't mean to be impatient, but I don't think you're understanding the situation here. Nobody gives a rat's ass whether I got experience or not. All anybody wants is for their chief of police to keep them safe. And they got a right to expect that."

"I know. You're right. I just get like a mother bear with her cub when you get attacked."

"Some cub."

She laughed. He stood, pulled her up with him.

"I wish I could help," she said.

He wanted to tell her the best way she could help now was to not do anything conspicuous, anything that might reflect on him.

"You're thinking about Shoreham, aren't you?"

"Kind of, How'd you know?"

She shook her head. "Waldo, after all these years how can you ask me that? Don't you think I know you?"

"I guess."

"You guess! You know it. Well, what about Shoreham?"

"I wasn't really thinking about that. Just . . ."

"Just that you hope I'll behave myself and not go marching or writing letters or anything else right now."

He nodded.

"Well, don't worry, hon'. The only think I've got scheduled for the next two weeks is collecting clothes for the poor and a very quiet NOW meeting."

"Good. I have to be getting back." He put a big hand on either shoulder. "I'll probably be late tonight. You and the kids better eat without me."

She walked him to the door. "I'm just making meatloaf. You can have a sandwich when you get home."

He loved meatloaf sandwiches with plenty of ketchup. "Sounds good." Hallock kissed her forehead, then her lips. It started out friendly, then developed into something more.

"Wish you didn't have to go back," she said, smiling.

"Me, too."

"It's been a long time since we had a matinee."

He laughed. "A matinee? Where'd you get that?"

"I don't know. Read it, I guess."

"A matinee," he said again, shaking his head. "How about a late show?"

"Okay with me."

He kissed her again, then hurried down the front steps.

She called, 'Was that a real invitation?"

"'Course it was."

"Okay, then."

He opened the door to the cruiser. "Okay, what?"

She looked up and down the street, thinking of the neighbors, then stepped back into the doorway, gave a little bump and grind, and shut the door.

Hallock sat in the car laughing. He was pleased Fran wasn't going to be doing anything public or all-consuming for awhile. He needed her. And when she got deeply involved in one of her causes, she vanished emotionally. And that was especially hard on him because it reminded him of his mother. Marion Hallock had always been distant, like a governess, not a mother.

Well, hell, he didn't want to start thinking about his mother now. He started the car and backed out of the driveway. He couldn't think about his mother *or* Fran. He had to get his mind on this case. First thing he had to do was see Mark Griffing and make him understand that he had to downplay the murders. Fat chance.

LOOKING BACK — 50 YEARS AGO

———————

A certain young local businessman hates to get up in the morning and go down to his store. How he does love his sleep. His friends claim he sleeps better in the morning after the sun comes up. One morning this week it was about 10 o'clock when he reached his store. Hanging on the door was a large wreath made of yellow crepe paper, seaweed, and onion tops, with the words: "Not dead but sleeping." He tore the wreath off the door and threw it in the gutter, then saw a number of his friends laughing heartily across the street. In a moment he joined in the merriment, saying: "Well, the joke's on me."

Chapter Twelve

Colin had decided to wait until after lunch to tackle the story. Now it was after lunch. The story was no closer to being written than it was *before* lunch. He lit a cigarette. It was his second pack of the day. Mark had told him he wanted the story by three. The clock said ten after one. There was plenty of time. Plenty of time, if he could write it at all.

For the third time that day he considered telling Mark he couldn't write stories about murder — they made him sick. But would he understand? Or would that get Mark thinking, wondering if there was more to it than just a man losing his wife and children through murder, wondering if maybe Colin had done it after all. And why not? He was sure even his mother had had a moment. The year that he'd spent with her, he'd caught her looking at him a number of times, a strange expression on her face. He'd interpreted that look to mean that she was wondering had he or hadn't he? She'd never asked of course. Not Betsy Maguire. No, she'd most likely go to confession and tell the priest she'd had unkind thoughts about her youngest son, then say a bunch of Hail Marys and maybe the Act of Contrition. One time when he'd caught her looking at him that way he asked what she'd been thinking.

Disconcerted, she said, "Just how much you look like your father."

He knew it was a lie but he'd let it ride.

Christ. This wasn't getting him anywhere. Either he was

going to write the goddamn story or he was going to tell Mark he couldn't do it. But if he begged off, it might make Mark think he had something to do with the murders here. No, Mark would never think that. Colin knew what he had to do was detach himself, the way he'd been taught, and write the sucker.

"Some guys got real tough jobs," Hallock said.

Colin was startled. "Hey, you scared me, creeping up like that."

"Didn't creep. I walked. You were in a dream world, buddy."

"Yeah, I guess."

"Who is she?"

"Hmmm?"

"Man's dreaming like that, it's gotta be a woman."

"Matter of fact, it wasn't. I was just wondering how to write this story about the murders."

"Funny thing. That's why I'm here."

Colin waited for him to go on.

"We need to play it down."

"I can't do that, Chief. I mean, I have to tell it like it is. A murder's a murder. Especially two. How can I play that down?"

"You know what I mean. Is it going on the front page?"

"Probably." He knew it was.

"See, that's just what I'm talking about. Why do you have to feature it?"

"I think you'd better talk to Mark."

"Will you come with me?"

"If that's what you want."

"That's what I want. I don't expect to win this one, but I've gotta try."

"Okay." Colin buzzed Mark, told him they were coming up.

Hallock followed Colin past the offices and front desk to the stairs. Griffing's office was on the second floor. When they came in Mark shook Hallock's hand.

"Nice to see you. Sit down, make yourself comfortable." He crossed to his tape deck and turned off David Bowie.

The room looked more like a living room than an office.

There was a fireplace, two blue easy chairs facing it, and a gray denim couch with colorful throw pillows on the right wall. Griffing's desk was a white parsons table, his chair soft tan leather. He sat on the couch while Colin and Hallock took the chairs.

"What can I do for you, Chief?"

Colin watched Hallock pull on his long nose, stalling. It wouldn't be so easy to tell Mark he wanted to downplay the story.

"Well, the thing of it is, Friday's the start of Memorial Day weekend, and I don't have to tell you what that means."

Griffing looked at him blankly. "Maybe you do, Chief."

Hallock glanced at Colin as if he were asking for advice. Colin felt for him but didn't know how to help.

Hallock continued. "It's the start of the season. Our merchants got twelve weeks to make enough to carry them through the year."

Griffing nodded.

"The real estate people, too," Hallock amplified.

"And?"

"Well, hell, what I'm trying to bring out is that if you go splashing those murders all over the front page on Thursday, it's gonna hurt this town. Real bad."

Griffing ran a hand over his gray hair, then lit a Camel as he assessed Hallock. Colin noted something cold in Mark's brown eyes.

"I'm not saying you should suppress it or anything. I know you can't do that. Just don't make a big deal out of it," Hallock suggested.

Griffing laughed mirthlessly. "But it is a big deal, Chief. You of all people should know that."

"'Course it is. That's not what I meant."

"So what *did* you mean?" he asked, an edge to his voice.

Hallock pressed his lips together. An aureole of white appeared around his mouth.

"The chief doesn't want it to get front-page coverage," Colin explained.

Mark shifted his gaze to Colin, the baleful look still present. "Really?"

"That's right," Hallock said.

Eyes still on Colin, Griffing inquired drily, "And you agree with this?"

"I didn't say that."

"Well, do you?" The tone was frosty.

As Colin had noticed many times, there was almost a feminine quality to Mark's good looks. The features were small, delicate. But when he was angry or challenged his face took on a hard edge, making him almost ugly. "You know I don't," he answered. For a moment he felt guilty, as though he were betraying Hallock. But he was a newspaperman and certain values were ingrained. You didn't bury a hot story because someone outside the paper wanted you to.

"Thanks, pal," Griffing said sarcastically. He turned back to Hallock. "Two people have been found murdered, Chief. We're not talking about somebody catching a big fish, or winning the annual foot race, or giving some money to the hospital. We're talking about murder. That gets the front page and no two ways about it."

Hallock had begun to sweat. He pulled a handkerchief from his back pocket, wiped his neck and forehead. "I don't think you understand what kind of repercussions that story's gonna have."

"Like you losing your job?" Griffing asked.

Colin didn't like the small smile that played around Mark's mouth.

"Me losing my job is only a drop in the bucket. It's everybody. You want to see a ghost town, you print your story up big and bold, you'll see what happens."

Griffing leaned forward. "I have no desire to screw up the merchants of Seaville, Chief, but I have a duty to report the news. *Newsline* has already printed a story, so how would it look if I skipped it or buried it on page fifteen? I don't think you understand that this is out of my hands. I really don't have a choice."

"I don't think *you* understand that if you put that story on page fifteen, nobody in Seaville would bat an eye. They'd be grateful to you."

"I'll live without their gratitude."

Hallock stood suddenly, as if he were snapping to attention. "Ah, hell, what do you care? This isn't your town."

"Oh, shit," Griffing said, "now we're going to get the outsider routine." Even if you lived in the town for fifty years you were still considered an alien of sorts. To be accepted you had to be born in Seaville. "No matter what you think, Chief, I feel that Seaville *is* my town, and I have a moral obligation to tell the truth. What you're asking me to do is *im*moral."

Colin could see that Hallock was shaking, hands at his sides in fists.

"I'm asking you to think of the town, is all."

"You're asking me to bury an important story."

"Why do you keep saying it like that?"

"Like what?"

"Burying it."

"Because that's what it would be. If I put that story anyplace besides the front page, where it belongs, then I'm burying it. And that's immoral."

Hallock stiffened; a vein in his temple throbbed. "You calling me immoral, you preppy twerp?"

Griffing stood up. "I think we've said everything we need to say to each other."

"Hey, come on, guys," Colin pleaded.

Griffing whirled on him. "You stay out of this!" Then back to Hallock. "And maybe if you got down to the business of finding the murderer instead of trying to get me to compromise my ethics, maybe then the town would be grateful to *you*."

Hallock stretched his lips tight across his teeth. A sound came out, like a horse neighing. Then he pushed past Colin, and fuming, left the room.

"Waldo, wait," Colin called.

"Let the prick go."

"Jesus, Mark."

"What?" he asked innocently.

"Did you have to imply that he was immoral? Don't you know what kind of a man he is?"

"Listen, Colin, don't try to lay a guilt trip on me because you're in bed with Waldo Hallock. The man was trying to get me to suppress a story. You heard him."

"What I heard was a frightened man who was trying to get you to downplay a story, not suppress it."

"Same thing."

"No, it isn't," Colin contradicted. "It really isn't."

"Well, fuck it. Who cares?"

"I do. You *should*. We need the chief of police on our side."

"Before you got here I managed very well without the chief of police on my side."

Was he jealous? Colin wondered.

"So where's the story?" Griffing asked suddenly.

"I was working on it when Waldo came in."

Griffing looked at his watch. "You'll have it by three?"

"I think you should apologize to the chief."

"You've gotta be kidding, pal."

"I'm not. You maligned his character. He's not going to forget that so easily."

Griffing sat behind his desk and picked up his pen. "I want the story by three."

"Mark, don't you realize what you've done? We've got murder cases here, and you've cut off our best source of information for the future."

"You sound like there's going to be more murders, pal." He smiled wryly. "Do you know something I don't know?"

Colin stepped back as if he'd been shot. "What's that supposed to mean?"

"Take it the way you want." He shuffled the papers on his desk. "The story, Colin. By three."

Colin felt his limbs beginning to tremble. He wanted to know what Mark had meant but he needed to get away more. He couldn't afford a full-blown panic attack in front of Mark. Quickly he moved to the door and hurried down the stairs. Judy Ulick, the bookkeeper, called to him as he rushed by her.

"Not now," he snapped and ran for his office. Slamming the door shut, he hurled himself into a chair. His mouth was dry, as if he'd been in the sun for hours, but his body was clammy with cold sweat. The noise in the room was deafening. He realized then that it was his own shallow breathing coming in quick gulps.

He closed his eyes, afraid to see the walls crumbling, the floor buckling, as he had so many times before. Desperately, he tried to remember what Dr. Safier had told him to do, but no constructive thoughts would come. Only the sickening, ruinous ones: He was going to vomit, become insane, die.

It's not really happening, he told himself. I only *think* I feel these things. I won't go insane. I won't die. He tried to open his eyes. Hundred-pound weights pressed down on his lids. He was alone, lost, a minute particle swirling in the universe, growing smaller and smaller, ready to disappear, evaporate.

A roll of nausea eddied through him, and he dropped his head between his knees. When that had passed he sat up slowly, only to have dizziness overtake him. His mind whirled round and round like a dancer gone mad. Then the pains began. First in his elbows, sharp and piercing, then moving on down his arms, jumping to his thighs, knees, calves, shooting through his feet, exiting from his toes.

It was subsiding. His breathing slowed, began to come more regularly. The dizziness had narrowed, the nausea gone. He had to open his eyes, see that he existed. Slowly he pushed up his lids, the long lashes forming a scrim. He opened them further, until his eyes took in the room. His desk, chair, typewriter were all in place. The walls were straight.

Holding out his hand, he saw that there was only a slight tremor now. He felt as if the attack had gone on for hours, but experience told him this wasn't true. Looking at his watch he saw that only seven minutes had elapsed. Mark had never witnessed one of his panic attacks, and Colin was grateful he'd been able to get out of his office before it was too late.

In comparison to others, this attack had been fairly mild. He'd had the first one when he was twenty-seven, following his father's hideous death. Edward Maguire had been a doctor. At the age of fifty-two, when he developed cancer, he refused treatment. Instead, he stayed at home and slowly disintegrated.

Both Colin and his brother, Brian, had been summoned home for the last week of their father's life. It had been a nightmare. Edward's screams precluded sleep. They tried to get him into a hospital, but he refused. None of them dared defy him, even in his weakened, pitiful state.

"It's my punishment," he'd said. "God's punishment."

But when Colin tried to pursue it, Edward looked at him with glazed eyes and declined to answer. After he was dead, Colin asked his mother what his father had meant.

"Ask Robin," she'd advised.

Colin did ask her. Robin Wise had been his father's nurse for twenty years and his mistress for seventeen.

It was after the funeral and he'd spoken to Robin that he'd had his first attack. Although it frightened him, he thought it was understandable considering the strain of that final week and the revelation of his father's affair. He dismissed it from his mind. Nothing like it happened again until after the murders of his family. Then the attacks became constant and relentless. When he'd finally faced that he couldn't go on that way, he'd left Chicago and gone to live with his mother. It was there he'd found Dr. Safier. The first six months he had his sessions on the telephone, afraid to leave his mother's house for fear of an attack. Eventually he was able to travel to Safier's office by car.

Here in Seaville he felt safe almost anywhere. If panic seized him he could always leave a room, a restaurant, a party. He was able to travel up and down the Fork, but the fear of becoming hysterical and causing a scene kept him from riding in a car with another person. Safier was in New Jersey, so he was back to having phone sessions; fortunately, he had one tonight.

But before that he had to write the goddamn story. The goddamn fucking story about murder.

He had forty-seven minutes.

LOOKING BACK — 75 YEARS AGO

Jimmie Hand of Seaville and a young lady — it wouldn't be nice to mention her name — were thrown from their carriage while driving one night this week, by being run into by another vehicle. If the young man had looked after the ribbons instead of the waist, things might have been different. But then maybe it was worth it.

Chapter Thirteen

He couldn't believe how stupid and gullible they were. Or how easy this whole thing was going to be. He had nine more to go in this grouping. Then he'd start again.

He remembered all those years when he'd been planning it; he'd been scared. Now it just made him laugh. What the hell had he been afraid of, anyway? There was nothing to fear. *I'm a steamroller, baby.* And speaking of babies — that was a good one. He couldn't stop laughing. Laugh and laugh and laugh. It felt good to laugh. Some people didn't think so. Some people punished you if you laughed too much. Or too loud. Some damn people hit you if you laughed. But not Mommy and Daddy. They never hit.

So two down, nine to go! What a holiday weekend he was going to give them. One they wouldn't forget, for sure, for sure.

Damn fucks. Always asking him what he was thinking. Which ones were the worst? Maybe the ones when he was twelve. Always bugging him. Questions, questions, questions. They didn't even know how smart he was. Nobody knew that. It was hard to be so smart. Hard to have friends when you're so smart. People get jealous. Jealousy is the worst sin. Worse than anything, they told him. Told him that. Told him. You're just jealous, they said. Stupid. They were the ones who were jealous because he was so smart.

But you'd have to be smart to work this thing out. He'd been planning forever, it seemed. Planning and planning. Diagrams and names. Taking his time. *But time is on my side cause this is the right time of year.* Years and years of careful study. You can pull the wool over anybody's eyes if you have patience and cunning. Cunning. He'd heard that one, all right. What a cunning little boy he is.

So cunning they beat the shit out of him. Scars to prove it, buster. You'd better believe it. Right. Yo. All right. Cat-o'-nine-tails. Fists. Belts. Razor strops. You name it, he'd had it. Didn't faze him. Not him. Wouldn't cry. Planned instead. Resolve. He resolved to do it. Do it. Kill them. Every last stinking one of them. He didn't know it would be such easy work. Such enjoyable work. Not like work at all. More like play. Fun. *And I'll have fun, fun, fun.*

Enough. Get down to work, you. Fooling around, all the time, all the time. Got to plan it out right. Friday night. Music soothes the savage beast. Ha. Music is his name. Musical accompaniment. Music to kill by. Shit, don't start the fucking laughing again. How can he help it when he's so goddamn funny? Keep a civil tongue in your head, boy. Get out the diagrams, the charts. See who's next. He knows who's next.

This one is really going to get them. Really get them. Blow them out of their socks. Blow them from here to kingdom come. Blow, Gabriel, blow. Who did it? they'll ask. Who could do such a thing? they'll say. Who? What beast? What maniac? What brilliant mind could conceive such a thing?

And I'm the last one. The last chance, the last rose of summer, the last Mohican, the last supper, the last killer, the last suspect. I'm the last one they'd ever suspect. Perfect. That's me.

LOOKING BACK — 25 YEARS AGO

At about the mystic hour of midnight on Monday, a woman bit a cop instead of biting a dog, and in addition the fracas occurred in front of the Seaville police station. Patrolmen Bob Phillips and Pete Shaw were just relieving each other when they heard a terrific crash in the municipal parking site as a motor car backed into a parked truck. A woman driver refused to get out of the car and was abusive to the officers. The woman then fell out of the car. As Patrolman Phillips endeavored to help her up she turned and bit him in the right thigh so severely that he was attended by a physician.

Chapter Fourteen

Chuck Higbee was almost overwhelmed by his sense of well-being. You just don't always feel this good, he thought. And then he wondered if he was going to have to pay. It was stupid but that's the way his mind went. You get something good, you have to pay for it. Maybe with a disease, or could be you lose your wallet. He'd been given a raise that morning, twenty dollars more a week. Sally'd been real pleased, rubbed up against him in the kitchen, promising more to come later.

So now he and Sal and the kids were walking down Main Street toward the bank parking lot where the first band concert of the season was being held. They always went to the first one, some of the others, and always the last. The band wasn't great, but it was fun sitting there with friends taking in the night air, listening to renditions of "Oklahoma!" or "Yankee Doodle Dandy" and ushering in the Memorial Day weekend. Still, Chuck couldn't shake the feeling that he was going to have to pay somehow. It was a dumb superstition, but he guessed he didn't lick it off the ground; his parents talked about paying for what you get in this world all the time.

Of course their big example was the fire. Ed Higbee had just gotten a bank loan for the farm, so he and Rosie went out celebrating, dancing at the new club in town, and the damn place caught fire. There was panic and, although his parents had gotten out, Ed had third-degree burns on his right arm and part of his back. So they were always talking about how they had had to pay a lot more than interest on that farm loan.

And what about his own life? The same day he'd gotten his job with the bank he and Sal had found out that their six-month-old, Mary Beth, was hydrocephalic. How's that for paying dues? Sure, it turned out okay, she had the shunt operation and it was successful, but there were some hairy days in there.

Chuck looked down at Mary Beth, five now, and as cute a little girl as he'd ever seen. She looked like her mom, big brown eyes, and yellow curls the color of buttercups, and just as healthy as she could be. He squeezed the little hand in his.

"What, Daddy?" Mary Beth asked.

"Hi, cutie," he said.

"Hi."

"Love you."

"Love you, too."

Katie, his older daughter, peeked at him from the other side of Sally.

"Love you, too, Katie-did."

She grinned, showing the gap in her teeth where she'd lost a front one last week. Chuck couldn't believe how big she was getting. Eight next month.

Funny, but he never thought he liked kids. Now the sun rose and set on his two girls. His three girls. Sal, too. If anything happened to any of them he just didn't know what he'd do. Aunt Addy's ass, he was depressing. Here he gets a raise they desperately needed, and all he can do is think morbid stuff. Well, maybe it was the murders getting to him. He'd forbidden Sally to go out alone at night. They'd had a big fight about it, too. Finally they compromised, and he'd driven her and Ann Shepp to their exercise class and Dan Shepp brought them home. Yeah, it was probably the murders making him so morbid and creepy.

"What's wrong, Chuck?" Sally asked. "You got a funny look on your face."

"It's just my regular ugly puss, Sal, nothing new."

"Some ugly puss," she said, and gave him a wink.

Chuck knew Sally thought he was a looker — like Burt Reynolds, she was always saying. It made him feel good even if it wasn't true.

As they turned into Center Street they saw people heading toward the parking lot and could hear the musicians tuning up. Hell, Chuck thought, I'm going to cut this bullshit and just have a good time. I got a raise I deserved and nothing bad is going to happen, nothing at all.

———————

Colin sat on the cement wall on the right of the parking lot. The band was playing "In the Good Old Summertime" and the whole thing made him feel good, better than he had in awhile. He guessed it reminded him of when he was a kid, and they had concerts like this behind Our Lady of Sorrows school. He and Brian and his mother always went to them, and afterwards she'd take them both to Grunning's for an ice-cream cone. He always had black raspberry.

Looking around he saw a lot of kids with their parents. Phil Nagle and his family; the Higbees and their two girls; Jake, his mailman, and a couple of boys who looked just like him. The place was loaded with kids. Mark and Sarah were there too, sitting in the center section with Kristen and Brent. Colin had forgotten to bring his own chair, the way you were supposed to, so he couldn't sit with the Griffings. They'd meet up afterwards and go to the Paradise, get cones for the kids. Colin wondered if the Paradise had black raspberry. Mark had told him the band was nothing to write home about, but that he always went to the opener for support and he liked his staff to turn out as well. So here he was banging his heels against a cement wall in time to "Has Anybody Seen My Gal?" He'd been surprised at how many people showed up. There must have been about two hundred. Mostly couples with little kids, a few teenagers, and a lot of senior citizens.

Colin spotted Tug Wilson, head of the historical society, and there was that guy who confessed to everything. Carl Gildersleeve was here with Grace. And the veterinarian; Steve Cornwell, the real estate agent who'd gotten him his house; the owner of Van Duzer's and his wife; the barber; Betty Mills, the librarian; Doug Corwin and Elaine; Ray Chute; and Pete Volinski from Rotary. And who was that waving to him? Oh, yeah, Burton Kelly from the electric company. It made Colin feel good to recognize so many people, as if he really belonged. Another reason he was feeling good was because Mark had finally apologized to him. Of course, the other thing he'd told him hadn't made him feel so hot. Still, the apology was welcome.

It had been a lousy week at the paper, with him and Mark only speaking when necessary. He'd written the story about the murders and he knew it was damn good. Mark hadn't said a word until this morning when he came into Colin's office.

"Good story you wrote, pal."

"Thanks."

"Really good. Gritty. You know what I mean?"

"I think so."

"I got about thirty calls complaining about it."

"I had twenty-six," Colin said.

"Fifty-six calls, that has to mean it's a good story."

They both laughed.

"Susan Harrison said she thought it was outrageous that we'd print such a graphic story because what if her four-year-old got hold of it? I asked her could her four-year-old read? She said no but what if he could?"

They laughed again, and as if it were a sign of forgiveness, Mark sat down.

"Hey, Colin," he said soberly, "this is nuts, you know. I mean the way we've been this week. I know these murders, writing the story, must've been tough for you. I'm really sorry."

"It's okay."

"No, don't. I was an asshole." Mark ran both palms over his hair, front to back, then let his hands linger on his shoulders as though he were holding onto himself. "I was in a shitty mood that day and, I don't know, I guess I just took it out on you."

"I understand."

"No, you don't, pal. I mean, we've known each other for what, eighteen, nineteen years?"

"Twenty."

"Okay, twenty. That's a helluva long time. Longer than I've known my wife. Longer than I've known practically anybody who isn't a member of my family."

"Okay, okay. So what's up? I know you're not just doing a riff here on the beauties of friendship."

Mark's brown eyes deepened in color, as if sadness were changing their hue. "No," he said somberly, "no, I'm not."

"So what is it?"

"Oh, shit." He pulled a crumpled pack of Camels from his shirt pocket and lit up. "Last year I had an affair. Sarah found out. It was a mess. I stopped seeing Amy because I didn't want to lose Sarah. Amy called me right before you and the chief came up the other day. I hadn't had any contact with her for about six, seven months. I was off the wall because of it. The call, I mean. I took it out on you."

"And Hallock."

"And Hallock," Mark confirmed.

Colin thought of Nancy. He'd never strayed, not even in fantasy. "Why?" he asked.

"Why did I have the affair?"

"Yes."

"Look, Colin, I love Sarah, I think you know that. But, well, when we first took over the paper it was fucking hard, know what I mean? We hardly had a pot to piss in. So there was all this stress and Amy was there and, shit, I don't know, it just happened."

Colin thought, *just happened,* like the way he'd happened to leave his house that night, gotten drunk — lost his family. *Just happened.* "How are things between you and Sarah now?"

"Tricky."

"Are you going to see this woman again?"

"Amy? I don't know. If I do and Sarah finds out, that's going to be it. I don't want to lose my family."

"So why risk it?"

Mark hissed out a stream of smoke. "It's sex."

"What about it?"

"Sarah's always been, well, reticent, sort of inhibited."

"And Amy's not?"

"Right."

Colin thought of his sex life with Nancy. They'd both enjoyed it, often trying new things, never letting more than a few days go by without making love.

"Have you talked to Sarah about it?"

"Not really."

"What's not really mean?"

"I don't want to hurt her, Colin."

"Seems like you already have."

"Come on, pal, that's hitting below the belt."

"I'm not saying anything you don't already know. What I'm getting at, Mark, is that you owe it to Sarah to try and work the problems out."

"What if she can't do anything about them?"

"You can at least try."

Mark stood up, signaling an end to the conversation. "I just wanted you to know why I was such a shitheel the other day."

"Thanks, I appreciate that." Colin thought of telling Mark that he could talk to him any time but decided against it. He didn't want to know if he started seeing Amy again. He liked Sarah too much.

Before he left the room Mark said, "The trouble is, I miss her."

Remembering the look on Mark's face, Colin glanced across the parking lot and tried to see the Griffings. Mark had his arm across the back of Sarah's chair, fingers touching her shoulder. To the uninformed eye they looked like any happily married couple. But they did love each other, he reminded himself. He hoped Mark would resist temptation. It wasn't worth it — nothing could be worth losing your family.

The band finished a rendition of "The Blue Danube" and he found himself clapping along with the others and desperately missing Nancy.

————

"Where's Mary Beth, Katie?"

"I thought she was with you."

"You mean you let her come back here by herself?"

Katie's chin trembled. "She said she'd come right back."

"She's five years old, for God's sake," Chuck snapped.

Sally said, "Let's not get all steamed up, she's got to be here someplace. Where'd you leave her, honey?"

"Over there." Katie pointed to a spot near the drive-in-teller road. "I said, 'Now go right back over to Mommy and Daddy,' and she said she would."

"Didn't you even watch?" Chuck asked.

Katie's face twisted into a grimace and tears filled her eyes. "I started to, then . . . then . . ."

"Oh, never mind. C'mon, Sally, let's look for her."

"Chuck, calm down, she couldn't have gone very far. She'd never leave the lot or cross a street or anything."

"What's wrong with you, Sally? She's a five-year-old kid." Chuck ran off in the direction Katie had pointed.

Katie was sobbing and Sally hugged her. "It's okay, honey, we'll find her. Daddy's just strung out tonight. C'mon, we'll go the other way." As they hurried off, Sally called her daughter's name.

But there was no answer.

It was intermission and Colin was standing with the Griffings when they heard the screams. It was a man's voice, and Colin thought something about it was familiar. And then he remembered that night in Chicago when he'd found his family. He'd screamed like that. Oh, Christ, he thought. Oh, sweet Jesus.

LOOKING BACK — 50 YEARS AGO

New Paradise Coffee Shoppe to open for
Memorial Day weekend. This new brick,
fireproof building is the most complete
business place of its kind on Eastern Long
Island. Not only will the new store have all
modern appliances that are usually found
in an ice-cream parlor, but it will also be
equipped with the latest machinery for the
manufacture of ice cream, for the cold
storage of meats and vegetables for the
restaurant, and an efficiently equipped
kitchen. A Japanese chef has been engaged.

Chapter Fifteen

It was no longer believed by anyone that the A carved on the victims' chests meant Adulteress. After all, how could a five-year-old commit adultery? Waldo Hallock was convinced that the A stood for the killer's name, first or last. The anger he'd experienced at the two previous murders now turned into a full-blown rage. Part of the fury was because of the victim's age — Hallock was sure he could never survive the death of one of his children — and part was because the state police had been brought into the case. Special Agent William Schufeldt, twenty-nine years old, was now calling the shots. For the first time in his career Hallock had some sympathy for old Charles Gildersleeve. Funny how things came full circle. But Schufeldt or not, the chief had plans of his own.

On Sunday morning Colin found himself in the Unitarian Universalist Church. It was strange for a number of reasons — he hadn't planned it, he hadn't been inside a church since his wedding, and he was in a new place and not feeling particularly panicky. Still, he'd protected himself by sitting in the last row opposite the door.

The service, he'd read on the notice board outside, began at eleven, the Reverend Ann Winters presiding. It had not escaped Colin's attention that the Reverend Ann Winters might be the reason he was here. Even so, he was sure it wasn't the sole reason. Or was it the soul reason? He smiled at his own joke.

The need to be in a church came from spending the weekend thinking nonstop about Nancy and the kids, plus the murders here in Seaville. It was difficult for Colin to talk to anyone about the latest killing. The murder of Mary Beth Higbee reminded him too much of the murders of his own children. The same question that had haunted him at the time of his own tragedy baffled him now: What kind of monster could kill an innocent child? He had no answer. He never would. And once again he was faced with writing the story; he wasn't sure if he could do it.

Colin looked around at the congregation. It was small, perhaps forty or fifty people. Quite different from Our Lady of Sorrows. Or the Catholic church at the end of Fifth street, where he lived now. Those churches were always packed.

A middle-aged man and woman sat down in the pew in front of him. When they were settled they turned around.

"Good morning," the man said, holding out his hand for Colin to shake.

"Good morning," the woman said.

"Good morning," Colin repeated, shaking the large hand, nodding to the woman.

The man said, "Glad to see you here."

"Thank you," Colin answered, slightly nonplussed by the friendliness of these two. After the couple turned back he noticed people all over the church shaking hands, smiling, talking to each other in a normal tone of voice. He thought back to his Sunday mornings as a teenager, lolling around in front of the church with his friends, smoking that last cigarette, exchanging notes about their Saturday night dates. But when they entered the church there was no more talking, no laughter. Church was a solemn affair. And no one ever looked glad to be there. It was different here. He could feel it.

The organist began to play, and Annie Winters appeared from a side door to the left of the altar. She crossed behind the pulpit, sat down in an ornately carved wooden armchair, and looked out at her congregation.

Colin felt something stir inside him when he saw her. She was dressed in a tan suit, red silk blouse, and brown pumps. Her wavy blonde hair shimmered in the sunlight coming through the windows. He wished now he'd been able to sit up front, see her better.

When the Prelude ended Annie walked to the pulpit. "Good morning," she said.

"Good morning," the congregation replied.

"Although it's a beautiful day," she said, "I'm sure that none of us is particularly joyful in light of recent events. In my sermon this morning, as you've probably noticed in your program, I will try to deal with sudden death and its repercussions.

"Now I would like to welcome any new people and invite you to join us after the service in the parish hall for refreshments and conversation. Please sign the guest book, which is on the piano, if you haven't done so before. And if you have any questions, please feel free to ask me or any member of the congregation.

"Today Deborah Bard will light the Chalice."

Annie returned to her chair as a young woman with one long braid rose from the front row and went up on the altar. On the railing was a large metal plate with a candle in the center. Deborah struck a match and lit the candle on the first try.

But Colin wasn't looking at Deborah Bard; his eyes were on Annie. Technically she wasn't a beautiful woman — not the kind who makes you turn around on the street or take a deep breath when you first lay eyes on her — but she was damned attractive and especially so up there behind the pulpit as Reverend Ann Winters.

Annie announced the hymn they were to sing, and with the rest Colin rose, opened the book, and began singing "The Morning Hangs a Signal."

How long had it been since he'd sung anything? He'd always enjoyed singing. He had a good rich baritone and sang with the glee club at Ann Arbor. But that was fifteen years ago. Then he remembered standing around the piano at Christmas with the Myrons, the Stimpsons, and the Lanes, singing carols. That had been his last Christmas with Nancy. By the end of the hymn he was feeling depressed, but when Burton Kelly, the organist, played "Brother, Can You Spare a Dime?" while the collection was taken up, he was somewhat cheered.

In the course of the silent meditation and prayer he found himself thinking of Mary Beth Higbee, Ruth Cooper, and Gloria Danowski, and wondering who would be next. He had no doubt that it would happen again and no faith that the state trooper was going to crack the case.

The chorus, ten men and women, sang "Movin' On," and then Annie came to the pulpit to give her sermon. Colin was enthralled. It was not only *what* she was saying but *how* she was saying it. She had a mellifluous voice and it washed over him, making him feel peaceful. Her ideas were original and fresh. By the end of the sermon there were tears in his eyes. He wiped them away with forefinger and thumb.

After the final hymn the congregation began filing out from the pews and going up toward the altar, where Annie waited to greet them. Colin was torn. He wanted very much to shake her hand, tell her how much the sermon meant to him, but he wasn't sure he wanted to join the others in the hall. He stayed in his place, staring down at his shoes, deliberating. And when he looked up again, the church was empty except for Annie.

"I'm glad you joined us today, Colin," she said. "How about some coffee?"

He rose slowly, like an old man, then found himself walking briskly down the aisle toward her.

"Thank you for a wonderful sermon," he said. She offered her hand and he shook it, holding it a moment longer than he should have.

In the hall Annie was immediately approached by a man and woman, and he was left standing to one side. But Burton Kelly rescued him and took him first to the large table that was laden with food, and then to the coffee maker.

A number of people he knew by sight came over to welcome him and engaged him in conversation. Colin thought these people were interesting — mavericks, independent thinkers. Now he understood why Mark and Sarah came to this church from time to time; he knew he'd be coming back, and not just to see Annie. He liked the atmosphere here, felt right at home.

By the time he'd finished his second cup of coffee, and a heated discussion about nuclear war, most of the people had left. He put down his empty cup and walked toward Annie who was saying good-bye to two young women. When they left she turned to him.

Colin said, "I just wanted to thank you again."

"I'm glad that you enjoyed it," she said. "Would you like to come to the parsonage for a glass of sherry?"

Colin could see that her words surprised her as well as him. "Thanks. That would be nice." He felt a kind of thrill, as if he were a boy getting to see the inside of a teacher's house.

"Great." As Annie started toward the door, Burton Kelly appeared from the kitchen and stepped in front of her. His high forehead was dotted with sweat. He was wearing a blue shirt, the collar out over his light tan jacket, a pen clipped to the breast pocket. "Going home?" he asked timidly.

"Yes."

"I wonder if I could talk with you?"

"Sorry, not today, Burton. Do you two know each other?"

"Yes, we do," Colin said.

"Tomorrow, then?" Burton sniffed.

She thought a moment. "How about Wednesday? Tomorrow's a holiday and Tuesday's my day off."

"Work," he said gloomily.

"Wednesday after work?"

"Five-thirty?" He adjusted his steel-rimmed glasses, wiped away some beads of sweat from his long upper lip.

"That'll be fine."

"The parsonage or your office?"

Colin bet he'd prefer the parsonage.

"Office," Annie said.

Kelly's countenance fell like a failed facelift. "See you Wednesday," he said, and walked away.

"Goodbye, Burton."

He answered with a wave over his shoulder.

Colin said, "I'd say that's a disappointed man."

"He's very sensitive."

Colin thought it was more than that, like having the hots for his preacher.

This time they made it out of the parish hall and crossed to the parsonage. Colin stood on the steps while Annie unlocked the door. Looking out at the street, he saw Kelly sitting in his car across the way. When he realized Colin had seen him he started the car and drove off. Colin decided he didn't much like the guy.

Inside the parsonage Annie showed him to the living room. He found it warm and cheerful, a reflection of her. She handed him a sherry, then sat across from him. They looked at each other for a moment that seemed like hours. Colin heard his heartbeat and wondered if she heard hers.

"Is there any news about the murders?" she asked.

"Nothing. The state police have come in, though."

"How does Waldo feel about that?"

"I haven't talked to him, but I'd guess he's not too happy. On the other hand, he's a decent man and I'd bet his first concern is getting this thing solved."

"Yes, I'm sure that's true. I feel so terrible for the Higbees. I wish there was something I could do. There can't be anything worse than losing a child."

Except maybe losing two and your wife, he thought, then nodded in agreement. "You never had any?"

"No."

Quickly he added, "Sarah told me you'd been married. Your husband died?"

"Yes."

She looked sad. He could have kicked himself for getting into this. Aside from making her unhappy, she was bound to ask him now.

"And you?" she asked, on cue.

He could feel his breathing coming faster, prayed he wouldn't have an attack. "My wife is dead, too. An automobile accident."

"I'm sorry. Bob had a heart attack. He was only thirty."

Colin wondered if in some mystical way he was only capable of feeling for people who'd had a loss. Annie, Gloria Danowski's husband, Russ Cooper, the Higbees? "Nancy was thirty-two," he said, hoping she wouldn't ask about children.

She didn't, just nodded, understanding.

"It's hard, isn't it?" she said.

"Yes. Very hard. How long has it been for you?"

"Five years. And you?"

"Three, almost. Does it get easier?"

"I suppose so. Time dulls those sharp edges."

It was different for him, but he couldn't say that. He wanted to get off this subject.

"Of course, there are times when it's as fresh as if it had happened yesterday," she went on.

He knew all about those times.

They were silent, he examining his shoes, she intent on her glass of sherry.

Then Annie said, "How do you like it on the North Fork?"

"It seems like a nice place." He shook his head as if to dismiss what he'd said. "I guess we're back at the murders. I mean, a nice place besides that."

"It is a nice place. I lived here for awhile when I was a kid. That's one of the reasons I chose this parish. I remembered being happy here."

"What's the other reason?"

"The other parishes were in the Midwest and the West. I wanted to be near my parents. My mother, especially. She suffers from depression. They live in Brooklyn Heights. Are your parents living?"

"My mother."

For the next fifteen minutes they exchanged background information as if they were submitting résumés to each other.

Siblings, schools, jobs. He discovered that Annie had a younger sister and brother, that she'd gone to Bennington, worked for CBS as a casting associate for two years, then became casting director on a soap. She was married at twenty-five to Robert Lockridge (Winters was her maiden name), lived in Greenwich Village for two years and, although she was ecstatically happy in her marriage, she felt something about her life was unfulfilled. It was then that she and Bob started going to a U.U. church.

"After about six months something happened. I guess the only way I can put it is to say everything I was doing then seemed frivolous. My job, the kind of life we were leading, our friends. I mean, there was nothing wrong with our friends, they were all nice people, but they were operating on a superficial level, as we were. I knew I needed something more. I needed to be in touch spiritually. I know that sounds corny."

"Not at all."

She smiled.

He felt it.

"I told Bob I wanted to be a minister. He was very encouraging and urged me to apply to divinity school. The only one I wanted to go to was Harvard and I was lucky enough to be accepted. We moved to Boston and seven months later he was dead. We'd been married two-and-a-half years."

They were back to death again, Colin thought. "What did you do then?"

"I took a leave of absence for the rest of the year. Then I sat in my apartment for six months and stared at the walls, cried, and felt sorry for myself. Bob left me a lot of insurance money, so I didn't have to worry about that. It probably would have been better if I'd had to. Anyway, one night I had this dream that Bob found me sitting in our apartment in my dirty robe, hair uncombed, cigarette butts in the ashtray, you get the picture?"

"I do."

"Well, I was this mess in the dream — in life, too. And Bob came to me and said, 'What's wrong with you, Annie? You've got work to do. Get off your butt and do it.' That was it.

When I woke up I felt better. I knew I had to show up for life again."

"I can understand your grief but I'm surprised that you couldn't handle it differently. Didn't you think he was in a better place?"

"You mean an afterlife?"

":Yes."

"I don't believe in an afterlife."

"I didn't know you people didn't believe in that."

"I said, *I* didn't believe. Many U.U.'s do."

"You mean you can believe what you want?"

"Just about."

"But you must stand for something."

She smiled. "We have a saying: "Unitarian Universalists don't stand for anything. We move.'"

Colin liked that, liked her. "Listen, would you mind if I smoked?"

"Go ahead." She opened a drawer in an end table and took out a brown-and-white ashtray.

When she handed it to him their hands touched. For Colin it was electric. Wondering if she felt it too, he said, "So after the dream you went back to school and then what?"

"I graduated and came here almost two years ago."

"Don't you ever miss the beat of a big city?"

"I thought I might, but I'm so busy here I don't have time to think about it. What about you?"

"I guess I'd have to say the same. But I've only been here a short time. I can imagine missing certain options, though."

"Like what?"

"Oh, theater, concerts — even movies. It's pretty bleak when something like *Conan thé Barbarian* is your only choice."

She laughed and he felt himself respond, smiling at her.

He said, "Did you know that the guy who wrote the book *Conan the Barbarian* lived with his mother until he died?"

"You know," she said, "this will probably shock you, but I *didn't* know that."

Now *he* laughed.

Annie said, "I won't deny that the North Fork is often a cultural desert, but we try to rectify that as much as possible. We have music programs, poetry readings, even some theater."

"I thought the biggest form of entertainment around here was yard sales."

"Sometimes it feels like that. Thank God for the library. Have you tried it?"

Colin shook his head. He'd assumed the Seaville library stacks were loaded with romances and how-to junk.

"Last year we got a new, smart librarian and the whole place has changed. Betty'll get you any book you want." Annie cocked her head to one side. "Assuming you read, of course."

"I've been known to crack a book now and then."

They were smiling at each other again, eyes meeting. Colin felt it in his toes. And then they were exchanging names of authors they liked. He experienced a kind of excitement he hadn't felt for a long time — that magic when you discover someone you like has the same taste as you. They had just started on movies when Annie realized the time.

"I'm sorry, Colin, I have to go. I'm late already."

They both rose.

He knew it was none of his business, but he asked anyway. "Where are you going."

She was clearly surprised by his question. "Sunday dinner with parishioners."

"Have it with me," he said recklessly, "I'm a parishioner."

"Are you?" she asked softly.

"Yes."

"I'm glad."

They looked at each other for several moments before she picked up their empty glasses.

In the kitchen Colin asked, "Do you always have Sunday dinner with a parishioner?"

"Almost always."

They were standing very close and he wanted to kiss her.

"How about Saturday night dinners?" he said instead.

"That depends."

"On what?"

"The kindness of strangers."

"I'm a stranger."

"I thought you were a parishioner."

"A strange parishioner."

"Yes," she said.

"Yes, I'm strange or yes, you'll have dinner Saturday night?"

"Both."

"Good."

They left the house together, and he walked her to her car. Bending down, he spoke to her through the open window. "It's going to be a long week."

She smiled. The engine turned over and she put the car in gear.

Colin watched as the Escort pulled out onto the main street and turned left toward Bayview. He stood watching until it was out of sight.

In his own car he sat for awhile and smoked a cigarette. He felt odd, as if he'd done something terrible. Was this what Dr. Safier tried to warn him about? The feeling of betraying Nancy? He had no doubt that what he was experiencing was guilt. Why should he feel guilt just from making a date with a woman? But that was rational. Feelings weren't rational. So what was he feeling? Guilt and anxiety. And lust. Don't forget good old lust.

He flipped his cigarette out the window, started the car, and sat waiting to pull out while two cars went by. The second was Burton Kelly's. Kelly looked straight ahead as he drove past. Colin couldn't help wondering what the man was doing around there again; then decided he was making something out of nothing. After all, it was the only road into town. Still, something about it bothered him. Maybe the intense way Kelly had been driving, hands gripping the top of the wheel, eyes glued to the road. He waited until four more cars went by. Each driver looked his way, checking for a car that might pull out. It was a reflex, natural and predictable. Only Burton Kelly had kept his eyes straight ahead. Colin surmised that Kelly didn't wish to be seen driving by the church again, driving by Annie's.

As he turned into the road he thought that unless Burton Kelly was guilty about something, like spying on his minister, he would most certainly have looked at Colin's car, even waved. A prickle of fear danced across the back of Colin's neck. And then he told himself to forget it and get on with his day. He turned on the radio to WNEW. Peggy Lee was singing "Day by Day" and he found himself joining her and thinking of Annie.

LOOKING BACK — 75 YEARS AGO

Miss Olive Sheraton, of Seaville, had a strange mishap one night last week. She dreamed she was bathing and dived through a window screen to the ground 12 feet below, striking on her face. After an examination it was found that she had broken her nose and badly bruised her face.

Chapter Sixteen

On Tuesday morning Special Agent William Schufeldt sat behind the only wooden desk in the squad room, facing Chief Hallock. Schufeldt was a beefy man, at first giving the appearance of someone who still had to lose his baby fat. But there was no fat on him. Schufeldt was like a well-trimmed roast. His eyes were small and blue, and when he leveled his gaze they were hard, like shooting marbles.

Hallock looked into those eyes and felt a wintry chill even though the thermometer was registering a comfortable seventy. He didn't like Schufeldt, and not just because he'd come in on the case, acting like he ran the place, treating Hallock like an inferior, generally hot-dogging all over; he didn't like him because the guy wasn't likable. There was something missing. Hallock thought. An important ingredient, maybe soul. Whatever it was, Hallock couldn't warm up to him and didn't want to.

"Let's take it from the top," Schufeldt said. "Danowski, Gloria."

Hallock tried not to show his irritation. This was the fifth time Schufeldt wanted to review the cases. Nothing new had developed since the first time they went over them, inch by inch, word by word. The chief opened the folder on his desk, picked out the autopsy report. "Why don't you just read it?" he asked evenly.

Schufeldt cocked his head to one side, an arrogant smile threatening to bloom. "I wouldn't have to be here if that's all I was going to do, Waldo."

It angered Hallock that this guy called him by his first name. He knew it was an interrogating technique designed to make the suspect feel inferior. Besides, he could be Schufeldt's father. In turn, Hallock never called him anything. "It seems pointless for me to read it aloud to you."

"Nothing I do is pointless, Waldo. There are things I hear when someone reads to me that I don't pick up when I read to myself. You understand, Waldo?"

There was no way he was going to answer. Hallock's eyes locked with Schufeldt's; the younger man's gaze, steady and chilly, was set for eternity. Hallock looked away. Angry with himself, he began to read aloud.

Schufeldt scratched at yellow lined paper from time to time. When Hallock finished the autopsy report, Schufeldt lit a cigar and leaned back in his chair, springs creaking. "Husband's statement," he ordered.

It went that way all morning until Hallock had finished what they had on Mary Beth Higbee, which wasn't much.

Schufeldt said, "Do you have a list of sex offenders, Waldo?"

"Yeah."

"Let's pull 'em in."

"What for? These aren't sex crimes."

"Some guys get their jollies funny ways, Waldo. I heard about a guy likes to be put in a coffin, just lies there while the broad stands next to the casket. He gets off that way. It takes all kinds, Waldo. There's another guy beats his meat while some girl pisses on his feet. I could tell you plenty, Waldo."

Hallock ignored the invitation. "I don't see what sex offenders have to do with these murderers. None of them were raped."

"You're not listening, Waldo. Some turkeys don't have to rape to get off. Maybe slitting the Cooper broad's throat was what did it for our boy. Or strangling Danowski. Then there's pederasts can only do it with kids. But maybe this scumbag needs to *kill* kids to get off."

"There's no evidence to support that theory," Hallock said stiffly.

"Schufeldt let out a cackling laugh. "You grow up out here, Waldo? I mean, you're from the North Fork, right?"

Hallock knew Schufeldt wanted him to feel ashamed of that fact. He wasn't. "Born and raised," he said proudly.

"I knew it. There's more to life than what goes on in this finger of land, ya know. People out here are cut off from the real world. You're like children believing in Santa Claus and that."

Hallock wanted to knock him on his ass. Instead he ignored Schufeldt's deprecations and went back to the original point. "None of the sex offenders we know have any M.O. that would link them up to our killer."

"How d'you know? Let's say a guy usually takes a girl behind some bushes to cop a feel suddenly gets a new idea. Maybe seen a X-rated movie or read one of these porno books are all over now, you can buy 'em in your local drugstore. Maybe another guy that flashes year in year out gets bored, needs bigger thrills. Chills an' thrills, Waldo, that's what it's about for some of 'em. What I'm trying to bring out, Waldo, is there could be an escalation. Bigger and better, more and more. In other words, a guy can go from pinching asses to slitting throats overnight. There's no knowing. So we gotta investigate. See what I mean, Waldo?"

"You want to interview all sex offenders, is that it?"

A razor-slit smile cracked his face. "That's it."

Hallock went to a file cabinet. "A waste of time."

"Remains to be seen, Waldo."

As he went through the files he told himself to cool it, but when he threw the folder onto Schufeldt's desk the contents spilled, fanning out like a deck of cards. "Sorry," he murmured grudgingly, but went back to his chair instead of trying to straighten out the papers.

"What're you giving me this for?" Schufeldt asked, feigning innocence.

He could feel his blood pumping hard. "You said you wanted the sex offender file. That's it."

"No, you don't listen, Waldo. I said we should pull in the sex offenders. I didn't say nothing about wanting to read the file. What good's that gonna do me? When the creeps come in, that's when I read their sheets and that. *You* know these guys, *you* pull 'em in. Me, I'm goin' to lunch now." Standing, he stretched, arms spanning the length of the desk, then adjusted himself in his polyester brown pants. A tan sport shirt hung loosely outside them concealing his .38. "Where's a good place to eat, Waldo? That Paradise joint you sent me yesterday sucked. Had a burger tasted like shit."

"Try Whitey's down on the dock," he told him perversely. Everybody knew Whitey's was a sucker joint for tourists and the food all tasted like it came out of a microwave, which it did.

"Thanks, I will. Be back around two, take a stab at these sex offenders. See ya, Waldo."

When Schufeldt came back from Whitey's, Hallock knew there'd be hell to pay but he didn't give a damn. The satisfaction he felt thinking about the man eating one of Whitey's expensive cardboard meals was worth it.

Hallock straightened out the papers and brought the file back to his own desk. Then he picked up the receiver on his Portacom and told Al Wiggins, who was out on patrol, to come on in. There were thirteen known sex offenders on the North Fork, and two of them were over seventy and hadn't done a thing in two decades. He'd be damned if he'd bring in either of them. Talk about getting off! He'd stake his career that Schufeldt wanted the sex offenders brought in because that was how *he* got off. Damned hotshot going at this thing ass-backwards. Bullshit, the whole goddamned thing was bullshit. Well, he wasn't going to sit still and twiddle his thumbs while the boy wonder was interrogating a bunch of sex nuts. He was going to take some action on his own. And what Special Agent William Schufeldt didn't know wouldn't hurt him.

———————

Hallock met Fran in the bookstore. They had a date for lunch. Fran knew last-minute things came up for Waldo, so she always met him where she didn't mind waiting.

Martha Terry, who owned the shop, greeted Hallock when he came in. "'Lo there, Chief. Any news?"

He knew she meant the murders. Feeling sheepish, he shook his head. As always he was taken aback by Martha's face. Years before she'd had an attack of Bell's palsy that left her with a droopy eye and mouth on her right side. She looked like two different people if you saw her first in one profile, then the other. "Fran here?"

"In Used." She pointed to the rear of the store, where there were shelves and shelves of secondhand books.

He thanked Martha, and made his way to the used book section. Fran had her back to him, head bent over a book. Hallock quietly stood behind her, whispered. "How about a quickie, lady?"

She jumped. "Sex in the stacks?"

"Why not? Give old Martha a show."

Fran laughed, her blue eyes luminous. "You're wicked, Waldo."

"That's me, Wicked Waldo!" He grinned at her, pushed his hat back. "What've you got there?"

She glanced down at the book. "Oh, this is an old one by Shirley Ann Grau. *The Keepers of the House.*"

"How-to book?"

"Oh, honestly, hon'. It's a novel. Sometimes I think I'm married to an illiterate."

"Well, not all of us went to college."

"Junior college," she said disparagingly.

"So? Still more education than I got."

"You're self-educated," she said, touched his cheek.

"Yup, a self-educated illiterate." He smiled. "Come on, I'm hungry."

"Me, too."

At the counter Fran waited to pay for the book while Hallock stood near the door. A woman and child were ahead of her.

The woman said to Martha, "Well, this was some lousy holiday weekend, wasn't it?"

"How's that?"

"I don't know about you, Martha, but I'm scared stiff all the time. I won't let Paulie out of my sight." She put a protective arm around the boy. "I don't know what kind of police we got here. Seems like they're just sitting around on their duffs."

Martha glanced uncomfortably toward Hallock, then back to the bill she was writing. "That'll be four-eleven, Mrs. Rowland."

She opened her purse, rummaged around. "Maybe we should just impeach the chief or something, I don't know. It makes you feel so helpless. Arthur says these local police don't know diddly-squat about catching a murderer. Arthur says —"

Hallock didn't wait to hear what else Arthur said. He left the store, walked down the block and stopped in front of Rita's Jean Shop. His hands were clenched at his sides and he'd begun to sweat.

Fran came out of the bookstore, saw where he was, and ran to him. "Oh, Waldo, don't let her get to you."

"It's not her. I mean, not her alone. What I'm trying to say is, if she thinks that way then there must be others — lots of them."

"Even if there are, you know you're doing the best you can."

"Maybe my best isn't good enough."

"Your best is *always* good enough."

"I don't know," he said sadly. He thought of Schufeldt. He didn't want to tell Fran about him, but knew he would. "C'mon, let's go. Where's your book?"

"I left it."

"Ah, hell."

"It doesn't matter, hon'. I'll get it another time."

"Sorry."

"it's okay. Where are we going?"

"Out of Seaville, that's for sure. Let's drive down to Mattituck, go to Crawford's, have a steak."

"Sounds good."

"Where's your car?"

"Round the corner." She put her arm through his, held her chin up, proud to be with the chief of police.

———

The lunch crowd at Crawford's had thinned out by the time they got there. The place had a rustic look — cedar-shingled walls and hunting trophies. Tables were covered in brown-and-white checked cloths, salt and pepper shakers were in the shape of bears and deer.

Hallock wished he wasn't in uniform. He got a few stares. Some hostile ones, he thought. Fran said he was paranoid. He would have liked a martini, but didn't dare. That's all he'd need, Schufeldt smelling liquor on his breath, making a fuss.

"Stop eying my drink," Fran said.

"I'm not."

"The hell you're not. Oh, have something, Waldo. Never mind about that twerp."

"I have to mind, Fran. One false move and Schufeldt would be happier than a pig in shit to tell Carl Gildersleeve."

"I hate that expression." She wrinkled her nose.

"Well, it's true. He would."

"Never mind about him. Tell me about your plan."

Hallock took a sip of his club soda, and decided it tasted better than those fancy carbonated waters costing three times as much. He knew he was stalling. The plan involved Fran, and it meant her sacrificing a lot of time. He didn't know if she'd go for it, but he had to give it a try. "I guess I told you I think the A stands for either the killer's last name or first."

She nodded.

"Well, I was thinking we could go through the phone book and list all the A names, both first and last, then call those people with a questionnaire we make up that'll sort them out. You know, find out which ones are women if it's an initial, which ones are old, housebound, crippled, etcetera. Narrow them down, get them into categories by age, jobs, stuff like that. I think we'd have something, Fran. It'd be a start anyway."

"That's a swell idea, hon', but you can't spare any of the men for that kind of thing, can you?"

"I wasn't —"

"Two steaks, one plain, very rare; one marinated, medium," the waitress interrupted, putting the rare one in front of Fran. "Will there be anything else? Another drink?"

They shook their heads.

"What were you going to say before she brought our steaks?"

"Boy, this looks great," Hallock said.

"I can't help feeling guilty having steak for lunch."

"Why? Don't you think you deserve it?"

"We shouldn't be spending the money, Waldo. I mean with Cynthia needing all that dental work."

Hallock reached across the table, put a large hand over her smaller one. "Tell me this: If we were here for dinner instead of lunch, would you be feeling this way?"

"Maybe not. It's just that having a drink and a big steak for lunch seems decadent somehow."

"You're just like your mother."

"What's that mean?"

"Rules and regulations. Don't wear white till after Memorial Day, always put the toilet seat down after you go, only have steak for dinner."

Fran laughed. "I see what you mean."

"Good." He patted her hand. Hallock knew how much Fran loved to eat and marveled that she never gained an ounce. "Now dig in."

They both attacked their steaks in silence for a few minutes. Then Fran said, "So go on about your plan. You were telling me about the phone book thing."

He kept his eyes on his plate, fiddled with his baked potato.

"Waldo? What's up?"

He raised his head, the brown eyes with their downward slant appearing sad.

"Stop looking like a cur, Waldo."

"I'm not looking like a cur. Christ!"

"I know a cur when I see one. What I don't know is why you're behaving like one. You have something up your sleeve, don't you? Something you don't want to tell me."

"I want to tell you, I just don't know how."

She put down her fork. "You're going to do something dangerous, aren't you?"

"No, no, nothing like that."

"You sure?"

"Positive. I swear." He crossed his heart with his forefinger.

"Well, what then? You're making me crazy."

Hallock put down his utensils, ran his hand over his chin as if he were feeling for stubble. "Fran, the thing is, about those names in the phone book — I mean, well, you said it yourself."

"Am I supposed to know what you're talking about? I'd need a decoder ring for that one."

"Hold on, hold on. You said I couldn't spare anyone for that kind of work and you were right, I can't. But it needs to be done, the stuff with the phone book and —"

"I think I'm getting it," she said despondently. "*Me*. You want *me* to do it."

"You and some of your friends." He smiled crookedly.

"You have to be kidding, Waldo."

"I'm not. It wouldn't be so bad. Get the girls over, make a contest out of it."

"Oh, that's nice, that's real nice put that way. Like we're a bunch of ninnies who need to play games or something."

"Ah, no, Fran, I didn't mean it like that."

"And this lunch," she said, eyeing him suspiciously, "this damn lunch was to butter me up, wasn't it?"

"Not a bit. I just wanted to have lunch with my wife. Is that a crime?"

"Waldo Hallock, you'd better own up, because if you don't I'm walking right out of here and leaving you to get back to Seaville on your own."

He knew the jig was up. "Okay, I'll admit it. I brought you here to get you in the mood for my proposal, but I also just wanted to have lunch with you. Because I like having lunch with you. Fran, listen, we've got nothing to go on. Not one goddamn clue. Except for the letter A."

"How do you even know it's an A? Maybe it just *looks* like an A."

"I've thought of that. But seeing it as an A is the best thing I've got. I'll admit it's a long shot, but I've got to try it."

"You mean *I've* got to try it."

"You and your friends. I don't expect you to tackle the phone book alone."

"Which friends?"

"Well, the ones you go marching with. Seems to me something like this would be right up their alley."

"Waldo, in case you don't get it, my marching friends are interested in human rights, not solving crimes."

"This is human rights. It's a human right not to be murdered."

"That's not even funny."

"Didn't mean it to be funny. Look, there's about twenty-five thousand names in the local book. If five of you took five thousand names each, you'd get the A's out of it in about a day or two. You should end up with maybe three hundred A-related names each. I'll have four new phone lines put in, and it probably wouldn't take more than three or four days to get through them with the questionnaire we'll make up. Then you'd have to sort them, get them into categories. After that, well, I'm not sure exactly how we'd approach it from there, but I'll figure it out."

"What you're saying, Waldo, is you want five women, me included, to give up a week of our time to try out a scheme you're not even sure will work."

"Dammit, Fran, you give up your time for stuff a lot less important than this."

"Like what?"

"Like every damn cause that comes down the pike, that's what! Save the whales, drunk drivers, nuclear plants, save the wetlands, planned parenthood, right to abortion —"

"You just wait a minute, Waldo. Are you saying those things are less important than running down some names in a phone book so you can *maybe* find some nut?"

"Some nut who's a killer, Fran, just don't forget that little point. I mean, you spend hours every week on stuff like getting sex education in the schools, which I could add is a little bit embarrassing to me, and when I ask you to do me, your husband and public servant, a favor, you go bananas."

"You call *this* going bananas? Oh, hon', you ain't seen nothin' yet."

The whole point of this lunch was slipping through his fingers. He had to calm down, do something quick. "Okay, okay. Let's not get all hot under the collar. I won't attack you, you don't attack me. Here's the deal. I'm asking you to do me a favor. You and some friends. I'm sure you can find some willing to help. I'm asking a favor of a wife for her husband. In other words, a love gift for a husband, and service to the community."

"That is out-and-out blackmail."

"I guess it is. Even so, that's what I'm asking." He grinned boyishly.

Fran stared at him not smiling. "I'll think about it."

"Time is of the essence."

"I need to think about it."

"Two hours?"

"Three."

"Right."

She picked up her knife and fork, cut a good-size piece of steak, popped it into her mouth, chewed, swallowed. "Not going to let this go to waste."

He'd be damned if she wouldn't sit down to a five-course meal after a nuclear attack warning. Nothing could put Fran off her feed. A nice slice of Crawford's cheesecake ought to clinch the deal. Ten-to-one by tomorrow morning Fran and her friends would be making their lists.

LOOKING BACK — 25 YEARS AGO

Miss Harriet Laine, who had previously appeared before the board to register complaints about the dogs roaming the village, presented a petition signed by many residents and non-residents. Mayor Nichols said there was reason to believe an item might be placed in the town budget providing for a well-equipped dog-catcher. The board was not unanimous that the problem had been solved.

Chapter Seventeen

Colin hadn't slept well the night before. He'd had bad dreams — Nancy begging him to save her, calling him a traitor. Once awake, thoughts of Annie kept him from going back to sleep. Now, as he went over the material for an article about Seaville Hospital's deficits, his eyes kept closing.

Picking up his coffee cup, he left his office. He stopped at David Wenshaw's desk. "All ready to cover the big meeting tonight?"

Wenshaw gave an exaggerated yawn. "Ready as I'll ever be. I don't even need to go. I could write that shit in my sleep. Same damn stuff every time."

"Think of it as experience, Dave."

"Experience for what?"

"Maybe it'll make its way into your novel."

Wenshaw gave a weak smile. The novel was a sensitive subject and he wasn't sure if Colin was making fun of him.

Colin picked up on Wenshaw's expression. "I'm serious. You never know what might be material."

"Believe me, I know. Whether we're going to have condos at the end of Fourth Street or not is never going to make it into any novel *I* write."

"You promise?"

"I promise."

He gave Dave a friendly slap on the shoulder and continued toward the front. The coffee machine was near the receptionist's desk. Sarah was filling in for the regular, who was out sick.

Colin poured himself a cup. "I can't stay awake today."

"Did you have a bad night?" Sarah asked.

"Yeah." He ran his fingers down his mustache.

"Mark told me about you not wanting to do the story. I don't blame you, Colin."

He'd finally gone to Mark, said he couldn't write the Mary Beth Higbee story. He'd keep on with the rest, follow-ups, anything new. Mark had said okay. "I just couldn't hack it," he said to Sarah.

"That's understandable."

He nodded, feeling lousy.

"I hear you went to church yesterday. How'd you like it?"

"Annie told you?" he asked, slightly annoyed.

"Everyone but. People saw your car. Or you. You can't do anything in secret here."

"Except kill people."

"I guess," she sighed.

"Church was interesting. A lot different from what I grew up with. I never heard a woman preacher before. She's good."

"The best."

"Is she seeing anyone?"

"You mean dating?"

He nodded.

"No. I think she's still getting over her husband's death. A few men have asked her out but she hasn't been interested."

"She seems nice."

Sarah smiled. "She *is* nice, Colin. And so are you."

"Matchmaker." He smiled.

"Sorry."

"It's okay. See you later." At the typesetter's room he stuck his head in the door. "Sparky, let me know when you have Page Three set."

"Yo," Sparky answered.

In his office Colin pushed aside the hospital material and began shuffling through items for the back of the book, but he still couldn't concentrate. He kept thinking about Annie and —

Nancy. Dr. Safier had warned him about this. It was inevitable, he'd said, that when Colin met a woman whom he found appealing, he would compare her to Nancy.

Colin couldn't believe he was doing it already. There really was nothing to compare. He'd spent forty-five minutes alone with Annie. But even in that short time he'd found he liked her. She was smart and funny, interesting and attractive. So had Nancy been. Fuck it.

He switched over to the bound issue of the *Seaville Gazette* of twenty-five years before, opened it up and ran his finger over the columns until he came to one that looked interesting.

> Due to numerous complaints regarding the speeding of motorcars and the disturbance caused by blaring car radios and exhaust cutouts by teenaged motorists, the Seaville Police Department started a drive this week against teenaged motorists who create disturbances late at night.

As they said in his youth, Colin thought, rots of ruck! Twenty-five years later they still had the same problem in Seaville. It was just like the dog-leash law. According to Mark, an article on that subject had been in the paper every year at the beginning of summer for the last thirty years. He decided to use the teenage-motorists piece and marked the place with an index card. As he was opening the book for fifty years before, Babe Parkinson came into his office.

"You're looking mighty dour," she said.

"Am I?"

"Mmmm. Rough weekend?" She wiggled her eyebrows suggestively.

"A rough weekend for everybody."

"Ah, yes, *that*. Terrible. You were on the scene again, I hear."

Had he heard an incriminating hint in what she said or was he just imagining it? "Me and about two hundred other people," he responded.

She touched a hand to the back of her hair, patted her braid. "Don't get testy, sport."

"I'm not. It's just that your lack of sensitivity boggles the mind."

"Really? Well, *my* mind's boggled by your lack of ambition."

"What's that mean?"

"Mark's given me the Higbee kid story to write. How come?"

He played with a paper clip. "I guess he thinks you'd do a good job. Why look a gift horse —"

"Puleeze, Maguire, don't treat me like some asshole just 'cause I was born and bred here. I've been to the big city, you know."

He felt uneasy, under fire. And he was pissed off at Mark; he'd thought he'd write the story himself, not draw attention to Colin's abdication. "I didn't want to write it."

Babe said, "Clearly. The question is, why not?"

"I don't think I have to answer to you, Babe."

She leveled her green eyes at him. "You can't blame me for wondering, can you?"

He couldn't. Had it been reversed he would have had the same questions. Still, he didn't know what reason to give her, so he remained silent.

She said, "No, Babe, can't say that I blame you. Good, Maguire, I'm glad you see it my way. Sure thing, Babe. So, Maguire, how about answering why you gave up a super story, something that doesn't come around too often in the career of a small-town journalist? Well, Babe, its like this —" she gestured toward him, palm up, indicating he was on.

"Give me a break," he said softly.

"No, you have it backwards. It's you who's given me a break. And I appreciate it, I do. But what's the catch?"

"No catch."

"You just didn't feel like writing this story. You'd rather do something fascinating like covering the zoning board meeting or maybe another little piece on how Temik is polluting our water? Sure, that makes perfect sense."

"It's really none of your business why I don't want to do the story, but I'll tell you anyway." He took a deep breath, having no idea what he was going to say. "Something happened when I was a kid, to my sister," he lied. "I'm not going into it. Suffice it to say I have a hard time writing things — bad things — about kids. Okay? can we leave it at that?"

"Sure. I'm sorry."

She didn't look sorry, Colin noted.

"Want to have lunch?" she asked.

"Can't. I have too much work."

"You have to eat."

"Not today."

She stretched, giving him an eyeful of her breasts. "Catch you later."

He watched her walk away, ass swinging. Now he found himself comparing Annie to Babe. Feature by feature maybe Babe was better looking but Annie had class, sweetness, and strength. Babe was strong but had no vulnerability. What bothered him most about Babe was her ruthlessness. There were reporters like that in Chicago and he'd never liked any of them. When his family was murdered there were two of them who'd taken advantage of their relationship with him, he'd expected it from one but the other surprised him. And it had hurt. At least Babe could never hurt him; he knew exactly what to expect.

In a moment Annie was back in his mind. Then it hit him. How the hell was he going to explain why he had to meet her at the restaurant instead of picking her up? And what about after dinner? Would she invite him back to her house even though they were in separate cars? Maybe he should forget the whole damn thing. But that wasn't acceptable. Besides, she undoubtedly knew about his problem from the way he'd behaved the first day they met.

Recalling her laugh, her eyes, her mouth, he decided that nothing was going to stop him from seeing her Saturday night. Not nerves, panic attacks, revelations, or comparisons. Nothing.

At the counter of the Paradise, Babe Parkinson stared down at her scoop of tuna on a leaf of worn lettuce. She kept going over her little chat with Colin. About the sister. Why couldn't he tell her what had happened? Babe could only think of two reasons: Either the sister had died some terrible way and Colin was responsible for it, or he was lying and there was a whole other reason he couldn't write the Higbee story. She didn't know why but she favored the second.

Then she got an idea and smiled, thinking if somebody was drawing this they'd put a light bulb over her head. She reached inside her red Sportsac bag and pulled out a battered address book, turned to R, and ran her finger down the page. There it was: Susan Rice, her old journalism school chum. She hadn't talked to her in a dog's age, but so what? They were good enough friends for that not to matter. Susan lived in Chicago and worked for the *Sun-Times*. Why hadn't she thought of this sooner? By tomorrow night she'd know everything there was to know about Colin Maguire. Babe paid her check, leaving her tuna uneaten. She wanted to get to a phone in a hurry.

There were three cars ahead of him at the Drive-Thru window when Hallock stopped at the bank on his way back to the station. Crawford's, like everything else, had gotten more expensive than the last time. It was a dumb thing to do when every cent counted, Stephanie being one year away from college. Still, he'd achieved what he'd set out to do: Fran was going to help him. Even though she had the appetite of a truck driver, he didn't believe the steak had done the trick, but it hadn't hurt. Crummy business bribing your own wife. Crummy business being a cop, the things you sometimes had to do, all in the name of law and order.

He moved up one car, looked at his watch. He was late. Damn! Late for what? Late for Schufeldt? Christ Almighty! Since when did he have to answer to some snotty twenty-eight-year-old kid? Gildersleeve had called the bastard in and told Hallock Schufeldt was to be given every cooperation. Did that mean the kid was in charge? Not in his book. Checking the time again, he decided to skip the bank, but when he glanced in his rearview he saw that there were two cars behind him and he couldn't move out of the line. Naturally he could pull rank, order the cars to back up, pretend something important was going on, but he didn't want to play that game — not with a triple murder worrying everybody.

What if his phone book plan didn't work? he wondered. He'd told Fran the job would take about five days, but he thought it'd be more like ten. And just what the hell was that questionnaire going to be? Maybe he could get Maguire to help him with it on the QT.

The car in front of him pulled out, and Hallock eased his cruiser into place at the window. Debbie Van Tuyl was on duty.

"Morning, Chief," she said through her microphone.

"*Afternoon,* Debbie."

She looked startled, then giggled. "I'm just all discombobulated today."

He placed his check in the drawer she'd pushed open. "Must be in love." He'd known Debbie all her life, delivered her on the way to the hospital in the back seat of Henry Van Tuyl's Ford.

"How'd you know, Chief?"

"There's nothing goes on that Chief Hallock doesn't know," he said, then immediately was embarrassed seeing her smile fade. They were both aware that he didn't know a damn thing about three murders. Quickly he got back to the love subject. "Anybody I know, this fella you're in love with?"

"Well, you probably do," she answered, counting out his money. "Joe Carroll."

"Ted Carroll's son?"

She nodded, held up her left hand, and showed him an engagement ring with a small diamond.

Hallock admired it, thinking about Ted, wondering if he'd stopped boozing and if Debbie was going to like being married to an undertaker. She pushed out the drawer again and Hallock picked up the envelope with his money.

"'Course, Dad's having fits 'cause he doesn't care for Joe's profession. He says I'll be depressed all the time but I can't see it. I mean, *I'm* not going to be hanging around with dead bodies, after all." She pulled the drawer back in.

"Well, Debbie, you got to lead your own life. Henry'll come around, you'll see."

"I hope so."

He put the cruiser in gear. "He will. See you. And congratulations."

"Thanks, Chief. Have a good day."

He was past her window by then, so she couldn't see the irritation that settled on his craggy face. If there was one thing Hallock hated it was people telling him to have a good day. He would or he wouldn't, and so far it had been mixed. Waiting for the light to change, he figured the rest wasn't going to be too bright since he had to spend it with Schufeldt and the sex offenders.

As the light turned to green Hallock waved to Tug Wilson and his cronies standing in front of Wilson's stationery store. OTB coming in hadn't changed anything in Seaville. The boys still made their bets with Tug and all of them, including himself, pretended innocence to the offense. What the hell, nobody was getting hurt. It was just easier than driving the twenty-five miles down to Riverhead and besides, if they were going to lose, they'd rather lose to Tug than to OTB. Keeping it in the family, so to speak.

Hallock pulled up in front of the station. Inside he was confronted with six men standing around the small front room. Al Wiggins was with them.

"This everybody?" Hallock asked.

"Two've already been in," he motioned to the rear door with his head, "one's in there now, and I couldn't locate two."

"Hey, Chief, what this all about, huh?"

"Don't worry about it, Willie, it's just routine."

Willie Smith didn't look relieved. "This guy pull me outta work. I gonna get dock now 'cause you peoples got you routine."

Hallock said, "If you didn't have a routine of your own you wouldn't be here now."

The other men laughed.

"Ah, shit, Chief. I knowed that what it was. I'm clean, ain't touched nobody. You peoples like elephants, never forget nothin'."

"That's right, we forget nothing."

"But I been good, jus' ax my old lady, she tell you I been good."

"So if you've been good, Willie, then you've got nothing to worry about. Just relax."

Willie's brown face tightened. The other men began mumbling among themselves, and Hallock told them all to shut up.

Schufeldt was sitting at Hallock's desk, feet up on the edge. In front of him was Fred "Barbecue" Riley. He got his nickname because he'd been in a fire and had third-degree burns on his back and legs. Barbecue was a flasher, last offense two months before.

"Have a good *long* lunch, Chief?" Schufeldt asked.

"Good, long, and delicious. How about yours?"

"Short and lousy. You got taste up the ass."

Hallock bit the inside of his cheek to keep from responding. It wouldn't do to let Barbecue see any animosity between himself and Schufeldt. Word would spread like butter on toast. But it was damn hard not to say anything about Schufeldt sitting at his desk, dirty shoes on his papers.

Barbecue said, "I ain't done nothin', Chief."

"Anybody say you have?"

"Well, no." He was a small man, but muscular. His ginger hair was lank, looking like it hadn't been washed in a long time. He had grubby hands, too, the nails black.

Schufeldt said, "Let's get on with this, okay?" He glared at Hallock who sat on a chair facing the back, arms akimbo on top. "Okay. Where were we before we were interrupted?" he asked Barbecue.

"Beats me, Officer."

Schufeldt's face tensed. "Special Agent. How many times I got to tell ya? Special Agent."

"You want me to say, 'beats me, Special Agent'?" Barbecue shook his head. "That sounds dumb. Don't it sound dumb,

Chief? Beats me, Special Agent. Don't it just make you wanna laugh, Chief?"

Hallock couldn't agree more. "Just do what the special agent asks, Barbecue."

Schufeldt cleared his throat. "Let's get on with it. So where were you the night of May twenty-ninth?"

"Me?"

"Yeah, you, who the hell you think I'm askin', Donald Duck?"

"Huh?"

"Just answer the question, Fred."

"Could you repeat the question?"

"You cocksucker, did you burn your brains in that fuckin' fire?"

"No, sir, Special Agent." He looked over at Hallock. "Now that sounds dumb, don't it, Chief?"

Schufeldt spoke before Hallock could respond. "Just shut up, Riley. Okay? Just shut up."

"Okay."

"Now. Where were you the night of May twenty-ninth?"

Barbecue stared at Schufeldt, his eyes dead-looking, as if he were on drugs.

"You hear me, Riley?" Schufeldt yelled. "You deaf or what?"

Barbecue shook his head.

"What? You're not deaf or you didn't hear me?"

"Neither."

"So why don't you answer the question?"

"You tol' me to shut up."

Schufeldt dropped his feet to the floor, came forward, and slammed his fist on the desk, papers flying. "Goddamn you, you turd, you knew what I meant."

Barbecue didn't flinch. "Huh?"

Schufeldt whirled around, facing Hallock. "This man was doing fine till you came in."

"What's that supposed to mean, Special Agent?" Hallock needled.

Schufeldt snapped to his feet. "Okay, that's it. Go on, get out of here, Riley."

"I can go?"

"That's what I just said, didn't I?" His face was turning the color of June strawberries, a vein throbbing in his temple.

"Yeah, that's what you said, Special Agent."

"Get out!"

"I'm goin'." Saluting Schufeldt and Hallock, he made his exit.

Schufeldt, his hands hanging at his sides like two ham hunks, towered over the chief, who remained sitting. "You're supposed to cooperate with me, Hallock, not thwart me."

"Thwart you? I wasn't thwarting you, Special Agent."

"That's just what I mean, you fuckin' asshole," he screamed.

"I don't understand. I did what I could to get the suspect to answer you," he said innocently, pressing his nails into his palms to keep from laughing.

Schufeldt stuck a finger in Hallock's face. "You better cut it out, Hallock. I'll get you for interfering in an investigation. Now I'm goin' out for a walk, give you time to think this over, get yourself together. And when I come back we're gonna question those men out there, understand?"

"Perfectly."

Schufeldt slammed out.

And then Hallock started to laugh and kept on laughing until there were pains in his sides and tears running down his cheeks. He was having a good day, after all.

LOOKING BACK — 50 YEARS AGO

The Seaville Fire Department is to be modernized in keeping with other departments on the Island. A delegation representing the Fire Department requested that the Trustees replace the present chemical and hose apparatus with a modern piece of motor fire apparatus. Also, that they be equipped with new wheels and pneumatic tires, replacing the present solid rubber tires, and that a suitable piece of racing apparatus be purchased for the use of the Department.

Chapter Eighteen

The Higbees were Catholics, and the funeral was held on Wednesday morning at the church on Colin's corner, the Blessed Sacrament. It had been delayed because of the holiday and the mandatory autopsy.

News of a small child's murder could not be contained within the district. Reporters from *Newsline, The New York Times, The New York Post,* and The *Daily News* were all present, as were reporters from the major television networks.

Colin watched as Connie Collins from NBC taped her lead-in. Again he was hurtled back in time, to Chicago and the murders of his family. He inhaled deeply.

"You okay?" Sarah asked.

"Yeah. I guess I really hate the whole circus atmosphere."

"Just doing their jobs, pal," Mark said.

Babe was covering the funeral, so Colin wondered if the remark had been pointed.

"Let's go in," Sarah said.

For Colin it was the first time he'd been in a Catholic church in years. There was a period, home from college on vacation, when he would go to Mass with his mother. But when he graduated, he considered himself an adult with ideas of his own and stopped attending.

Then, the past year, when he'd been living with his mother, she'd gotten on his back about going. They'd had a blowup over it and said things to each other they were sorry for later.

He said, "I haven't gone in years, why should I go now?"

She said, "To pray for the souls of your dead family."

He said, "You expect me to believe in a God that allowed two innocent children and an innocent woman to be slaughtered?"

She said, "Maybe if you'd been going to church in the first place it wouldn't have happened."

He said, "Go to hell, you goddamn bitch."

Later he'd apologized to her, and she'd mumbled something which he'd taken for an apology. She never asked him to go to church again.

The Higbees hadn't come in yet. Colin knew they would enter by a side door after everyone else had been seated. He thought it was a strange practice, the family entering last as if they were the stars of a show. But the star of the show was already there. Her small, beautifully appointed casket rested on a gurney just below the altar. Colin felt a surge of grief, like the swelling of a wave. Two small caskets and one large were suddenly as real to him now as they'd been three years before. For a moment he felt dizzy, sure he was going to have an attack. Then it passed and he was left with the feeling of sorrow he'd known intimately since that terrible morning in Chicago.

Maybe he shouldn't have come. But he'd felt it was important to support the Higbees, especially Chuck. All through the weekend he'd thought of calling the man, stopping by his house. But Higbee didn't even know him. And what would he say, unless he told the truth about his own family? So in the end he'd done nothing. This was his only way of showing he cared, understood. It didn't matter that Higbee wouldn't note his presence.

Sarah gently tucked her hand in his. Tears sprang to his eyes. He didn't want to cry, fearful that once started he wouldn't be able to stop. For diversion he concentrated on the church, the other people. The Blessed Sacrament was small but pretty: the usual stained glass windows and mahogany pews. Wood carvings and brass ornaments decorated the altar.

The pews were almost filled. Chief Hallock and Charlie Copin sat near the back, one on each side of the aisle. Down a few pews was Fran Hallock with both daughters and one son. In front of them was Burton Kelly. Colin imagined Kelly as a teenager — awkward and painfully thin, keeping close to the wall when he walked through the school halls, his books held as a shield against attacks from bullies. The only difference now was Kelly knew how to hide it better. Colin had learned he worked for Seaville Water & Light as a clerk, and had lived with his mother until she died, two years before. He and Mark had speculated on whether Kelly could be the killer. They decided he wouldn't have the nerve or imagination. Still, Colin couldn't dismiss the idea altogether, and he wondered if his reason for that had anything to do with Annie.

Gazing around at the rest of the crowd he spied a lot of familiar faces — Carl and Grace Gildersleeve; his mailman; Babe, her red hair neat in its french braid. He watched her arm make short, palsied movements, then realized she was taking notes. Disgusted by what his profession forced people to do, he looked away from her, across the aisle to Steve Cornwell. Even sitting, he towered over the man beside him. In the next pew were Tug Wilson, Raymond Chute, Debbie Van Tuyl from the bank, the Klipps who lived across from him, the — he stopped, thinking this was exactly what he was doing when Mary Beth Higbee was being murdered. It made him feel sick. A spate of coughing and rustling drew his attention.

The Higbees were filing in. The mother first, then the daughter, and behind her the father. Colin's throat tightened. The immediate family was followed by others; grandparents, aunts, uncles, cousins. Father Dominick and three altar boys appeared from a door at the back and the Mass began.

When it was over the pallbearers carrying the casket filed out first, the family next, and then the others. On the sidewalk Colin watched as the reporter from *Newsline* and the man from ABC jostled each other trying to get a statement from Chuck Higbee. For a moment Higbee looked at the reporters blankly, his chest swelling as he gasped for air. Colin thought Higbee might lash out, but his wife put a hand on his arm and helped him into the waiting limousine.

People formed small groups, talking softly. Joe Carroll slammed the back door of the hearse, the sound recalling memories Colin had tried to forget.

Neither he nor the Griffings were going to the cemetery, but he couldn't bring himself to leave. The hearse pulled away. Cars followed, yellow flags attached to their aerials designating their right to be in the procession. When the first car passed, Colin got a glimpse of Higbee, his head on his wife's shoulder, tears streaming down his cheeks.

A man next to Colin said to a woman, "You'd think the father would have a little dignity. Besides, he should be taking care of his wife, it's harder on her."

Colin wanted to tell him he was wrong. It hurt the father just as much, perhaps more, because he felt responsible. Wasn't he supposed to guard his children against such eventualities? He admired Higbee not giving a damn what people thought, experiencing his grief now instead of later like Colin had.

When the cars were gone the small groups began breaking up, dribbling away. Hallock and Copin stood on either side of the church, watching. Colin knew they were hoping to get an idea, a clue. He started toward Hallock but was stopped by a furious expression crossing the man's face. Then Colin saw the scruffy figure of Jim Drew approaching the chief.

"Get the hell away from me, Drew," Hallock spat.

"But, Chief," Drew pleaded, "I gotta talk to ya. Gotta tell ya about it."

Frantically, Hallock glanced around, then relaxed some, seeing that the reporters had left. He motioned to Colin with a nod of his head.

Colin took Drew by the arm. "Come on, Jim, let's go."

"But I gotta talk to the chief. It's important. I gotta tell him about the little girl."

"Yeah, yeah, we know. Let's go for a walk, you tell *me* about it, okay?"

"I . . . I guess."

Colin and Drew started down Main Street toward the town. Colin looked back at Hallock. A muscle was jumping in his cheek.

Mark said, "Everybody's got a breaking point. I guess Hallock just couldn't hear a fake confession about the murder of a little girl."

Colin wondered what Hallock would think of his story, the murders of his children and wife. He wished he could tell him but knew that was a Pandora's box he'd better leave closed.

———

Wednesday afternoon Annie said to Sarah, "I'm having dinner with Colin on Saturday night."

"I think that's great," Sarah said.

They were sitting in Annie's office in the basement of the parish hall. The room was small and comfortable, with a new couch, flowered curtains, an oak desk and chair.

"Is it?"

"What do you mean?" She wished she could have a cigarette but the Please Don't Smoke sign was staring her right in the face.

"I guess I mean, is it really great to be going out with Colin Maguire? Is there something I should know about him?"

"Know about him?" Sarah fussed with her hair, twirling a curl.

"He's intelligent and very nice but there seems to be, oh, I don't know, something odd about him. No, that's not right. It's not that he's odd or weird, he's — guarded."

"Guarded?"

"Sarah, why are you repeating everything I say?"

"Repeating everything you say?"

"See? You're doing it again. And please don't say, 'doing it again.'"

Sarah laughed. "I'm sorry. I guess I'm distracted," she lied.

"Is it Mark?"

"No."

"Is everything okay between you?"

"Fine."

"Why don't I believe you?"

Sarah shrugged. "I'm dying for a cigarette, that's what you're picking up."

"If you'd give up the vile things then you wouldn't be distracted when you come here."

"True. But I'm not giving them up, so lay off," she gently chided. "And Mark and I are okay. It's tough sometimes. I wonder if he's thinking about her, missing her."

Annie nodded and thought of Bob. What would she have done if Bob had had an affair? It was impossible to imagine.

"He says he loves me and that he doesn't miss her or anything. Still, I can't help wondering from time to time. Trusting him again is going to take awhile."

"It's bound to."

"And he understands that." She smiled dreamily, thinking back. "Sometimes Mark's so sweet and thoughtful. He sends me love cards in the mail. You know the kind I mean?"

"Yes." Bob had sent her cards like that. She recalled one that had said 'Life is just a chair of bowlies.' There was a picture of an overstuffed chair with hundreds of bowls in it. Inside he'd written, "For my darling. I can't tell you how much I admire what you're doing. I long to be the preacher's husband. Love you forever." But forever had turned out to be never.

"What is it?" Sarah asked.

"Nothing."

"You were thinking of Bob, weren't you?"

"Yes."

"Oh, Annie," she said sympathetically. "I feel like a dope worrying about Mark and Amy. I should be grateful I still have him."

"Just because my husband died doesn't mean you don't have a right to feel insecure, Sarah."

"I know."

"No, you don't."

"No, I don't."

They laughed, reached out and squeezed a hand.

Sarah said, "You were talking about Colin." She didn't really want to go back to that subject, but Annie was her friend and didn't often ask for anything.

"I was just wondering what it was I detected in him, as if he had a secret or something. Dumb, I know."

Sarah wanted to tell her that it wasn't dumb, in fact, was perceptive, but her loyalty had to be with Colin on this. If he wanted to tell Annie about Nancy and the children that was fine. It wasn't her place to tell her. Still, she had to say something. "He has a few problems. Nothing serious."

"Like not being able to ride in a car with anyone?"

"Yes."

"What's that about?"

"Why don't you ask him, Annie?"

"I will."

"He's a terrific guy. We've known him for ages. He and Mark went to the University of Michigan together."

"Did you know his wife?"

Sarah was startled. What had Colin told her? She nodded, hoping Annie would clue her in.

"Was Colin driving the car?"

Obviously he'd said Nancy had died in an automobile accident. But what should she say now? "Maybe you'd better ask him."

"So that's why he can't be in a car with someone else." It was said more to herself than to Sarah. "What was she like?"

"Nancy? I don't know. I liked her, but I didn't know her that well. They lived in Chicago and we only saw them a few times a year. But when we did we had a lot of fun. And our kids liked their kids and . . ."

A look of surprise had come over Annie's face.

"Oh, shit. He didn't tell you about the kids, did he?"

"No. How many?" Annie asked quietly.

"Two."

"They died with Nancy?"

"Yes." At least that much was true.

"Oh, poor Colin."

"He's suffered terribly." After a moment Sarah said, "I think it's great you're going out with him. For both of you."

"Thanks. I have to admit I feel slightly nervous. It's been a long time since I dated. I've even found myself worrying about what I should wear." She laughed. "High-school time."

"I don't blame you. I always hated dating, didn't you?"

"Loathed it."

A knock at the door made Annie look at her watch. "Just a minute," she called. "It must be Mrs. Ludwig, a little early."

"I have to run anyway. If I don't speak to you before, have a good time Saturday. He's really an awfully nice person."

It was not Mrs. Ludwig waiting in the hall; it was Burton Kelly. "Burton, what are you doing here this time of day?"

He glanced at Sarah, then back to Annie, obviously not wishing to answer the question in front of Sarah.

"Never mind, come on in."

Annie and Sarah said their good-byes. Inside her office, Annie told Burton she had a two o'clock appointment and asked him what she could do for him.

"I'm going to come right out with it, Annie, I like you very much and I always enjoy talking with you. Some of our talks have been very edifying. You're an amazing woman."

"Thank you." She felt extremely uncomfortable, wished she could deflect him somehow, but didn't see a way.

"I'm not just saying all this to flatter you." Kelly's sandy hair lay in neat strands across his large head. "I'm only trying to throw a little light on the subject. You know, of course, that I've never married?"

She nodded.

"People around here think it's because of my mother. Because I lived with and took care of her until she died." He laughed, but it sounded like a snarl. "Well, it's not true. I haven't married because I've never found anyone suitable to marry."

Uh-oh, Annie thought.

"As you well know, the rate of divorce in this country is extremely high. I have no intentions of becoming one more statistic. Marriage is a very serious proposition. And I would never enter into it unless I was totally sure about the woman and my feelings for her."

She had to say something. "I think that's very wise, Burton."

A thin film of sweat covered his forehead like a veil.

"Is it too hot in here?" she asked. "Should I open a window?"

"Yes. Yes, that would be nice. But let me do it."

Annie watched him move stiffly across the small room as if he were a robot. How could she keep him from saying what seemed inevitable? She felt helpless, out of control, and prayed Karen Ludwig would arrive.

"There," Kelly said, "much better." His mouth twitched several times and he tried to pass it off as a smile. "All right, where was I? May I sit down?"

"As I said, I have a two o'clock appointment. She's late but she should be here any second. Maybe you should come back later, as we planned."

"I'd like to go on now. I'll come right to the point. I would be greatly honored if you'd have dinner with me on Saturday night."

Annie was so relieved she almost sighed audibly. Then she realized that even though it was a dinner invitation instead of a proposal of marriage, she still had to reject him. "That's very nice of you, Burton, but I'm afraid I can't."

"Why?" he demanded, eyes growing cold.

"I have other plans." Immediately she was sorry she hadn't made another excuse. This way would only allow him to ask for another time.

He smiled, showing small uneven teeth. "Then Friday?"

"No. Sorry." Before he could ask again she added, "I don't think it would be a good idea, Burton."

"What do you mean?"

She felt she must be forthright. "I gather you mean to invite me to dinner in a — a romantic way. If I accepted, it would be unfair."

"Is there someone else?"

Colin, she thought. Stupid. "No, not really."

"I never know what 'not really' means," he said acidly.

"There's no man in my life at present." That should be direct enough, she thought.

"Then why can't you have dinner with *me*?"

"Because I don't want to give you the wrong idea. I like you, but I'm not interested in you as anything but a friend."

"How do you know?"

"I don't feel I have to go into all my reasons. I think you should accept my answer like a gentleman."

His face folded, cheeks sucked in as if she'd slapped him. "I see." He moved past her to the door, stood with his back to her. "Is it something I've said or done?"

For a moment she wanted to comfort him, but knew it might seem patronizing. "No, it's not you," she lied. She couldn't bear to hurt him further.

"Thank you," he whispered, and left.

She felt terrible. In divinity school they'd talked about this sort of thing happening and how to handle it, but it was much different in reality. Burton Kelly was a living, breathing human being and she'd rejected him. She only hoped his fragile ego was left intact with her inference that the failure was on her part, not his.

Damn you, Bob, she thought. If you'd lived, this sort of thing wouldn't come up. I wouldn't have pathetic Burton Kelly asking me out. Then she thought, I wouldn't be having dinner with Colin Maguire either. For the first time since he'd asked her she knew she really wanted to go. The knowledge surprised her. And pleased her, too.

LOOKING BACK — 75 YEARS AGO

One of the best and most successful conventions ever held by the W.C. T.U. of Suffolk County met in Seaville last Monday. The churches, the schools, and the members and friends of the local Union extended a most cordial welcome to the delegates. The sincerity of this welcome was proven on every hand by the open churches, the tasteful decorations, the generous hospitality, and the beautiful music.

Chapter Nineteen

As planned, the women arrived before Hallock left for the station. There were four. Julia Dorman was the youngest at twenty-nine. Divorced for a year, she was tall, angular, and blond. At fifteen she'd had a botched abortion in the back room of a bar and now couldn't have children. Hallock thought it accounted for the downward turn of Julia's mouth.

Anne Hulse was the oldest of the five. Born in Poland, she immigrated to America at nineteen, married Bob Hulse at twenty, and lived in New York City most of her married life, while summering in Seaville. Three years before, they'd moved to Seaville full-time. Anne's sweet smile and tender gaze gave her a beatific look. Her only child was married to a black man. Although Anne was far from being racist, she admitted that Mary's life had been made difficult because of the interracial marriage.

Florence Barker was middle-aged. Her delicate features were framed by copper-colored hair, and when she smiled she was almost pretty. But she seldom smiled; her mother-in-law lived with Florence and her husband, and the situation was barely tolerable.

Sandy Roach, thirty-seven, married to a science teacher at Seaville High, was like the group mascot. She was small and feisty and always urging the women on to one more cause, one more meeting. Hallock thought of her as a perennial cheer-leader, with her short, yellow curly hair, pink cheeks, cherry-red mouth. Her indefatigable nature made her a champion of more causes than any of the others. She would be invaluable in this cause.

In fact, they all would. Hallock was pleased that Fran had been able to enlist these particular women and had told her so the night before.

Four new telephone lines had been installed. The phones were all touch-tone, all black.

Hallock stood near the door of the living room watching the women settling themselves, taking from their purses cigarettes, cough drops, tissues, combs. Then he cleared his throat.

"First of all, I want to thank you for helping us out. I know you're all busy gals, and sparing me this time is really appreciated." He thought he sounded stupid. He'd never been good with bunches of women, so why'd he expect this to be any different? "I guess Fran's told you a little bit about what we're going to try and do."

"She gave us a sketchy idea," Sandy said.

Julia said, "Is it true you don't have a clue to the identity of this killer, Chief?"

Hallock bit the inside of his cheek. How could he pretend he had an idea, a suspect, when he was asking them to help him in this way? "That's right, Julia. Hate to admit it, but it's the truth. That's why I need you gals so badly."

"Do you think you could stop calling us *gals,* Waldo?" Julia said tersely.

"Huh?"

"*Gals.* We don't like being called gals."

"Why not?" he asked innocently.

Julia waved a dismissive hand in his direction. "It's too long to go into now." She turned to Fran. "Haven't you taught him any better?"

"Let's get on with it, okay?" Fran said, keeping her voice as even as she could.

"Fine by me," Julia responded.

Hallock continued to gnaw at his cheek. This was worse than addressing the Rotary. "Sorry if I offended."

Anne said, "Waldo, please go on. We wish to hear what you have to say."

He smiled at her, feeling a little better. "As you probably know each victim has been found with an A . . ." Having to say it aloud to these women made him feel really lousy. "Found with an A cut into their — bodies."

Florence said, "How'd you know it was an A?"

"It looked like one. We think this A is a very important clue. It could be the killer's initial. But we don't know if it's the first or the last initial."

"Or if it's an initial at all," Julia put in.

"That's right," he mumbled.

"So," she said, "to coin a phrase, we're shooting in the dark."

"Yes."

"You know, Julia," Sandy said, "you don't have to do this if you don't want to."

"I just want to know the facts, that's all. Is it so terrible to get the lay of the land, so to speak?"

"Julia's right. I want you to know everything. And I intend to tell you everything in due time," he said pointedly. "I have no idea if this will work, but I want to try it." From a side table, he picked up five copies of the Yellow Book, the community directory, and passed one out to each of them. "There are about one hundred ninety-two pages that we have to cover in here. The last names starting with A's will be easy. One of you can just go through with a yellow marker." He got these from the drawer of the table. "Highlight everything that isn't a store or business of some kind.

"That leaves twenty-five letters, five for each of you. You can divide them up any way you want. Now, it's not just the first initial that's important. A middle initial is just as good."

"Because some people are called by their middle name even though they list their first name in the book. Right, Waldo?" said Sandy.

"That's right," he smiled. He took Fran's book, flipped it open, ran a finger down a page. "See, like this: Goodridge, Robert A."

"Do we run the marker over those?" Anne asked.

"Yes. There are about twenty-five thousand names you'll have to go through, five thousand each. Don't rush it. The one you miss could be the one we want most."

"I don't understand," Julia said obstinately. "What good is this going to do?"

"In a couple of hours I'll be back and tell you the rest," he stalled. He was meeting with Maguire in fifteen minutes to work on the questionnaire. "So, are there any more questions?" He prayed there weren't, avoiding Julia's eyes.

Florence said, "Are we going to be calling these people, the ones we're underlining?"

"What do you think all these phones are for, Florrie?" Julia said.

"I guess," she said meekly.

Hallock felt sorry for Florence. "Later on you'll be calling the people you've underlined, yes."

"What will we say to them?" Sandy asked.

"That's what I'm going to tell you later. Okay, ga — ladies, I —"

"Just as bad, Waldo," Julia interrupted.

"Oh, Julia," Anne said, "don't."

Julia said, "He needs his consciousness raised."

"I'll walk you out," Fran said.

"Thanks, all," he said, playing it safe. "See you later."

On the front stoop Hallock said through his teeth, "What the hell am I supposed to call them?"

"Women."

"*Women?*"

She nodded.

"I'm supposed to say, thank you, *women*?"

"Forget it, hon'."

"Thank you, women," he said again, puzzled.

"Thanks, *all*, was just super, Waldo."

"I think it's stupid," he sulked. "'Thank you, women.'" He felt like Barbecue with Schufeldt.

"Look, I don't want to start World War Three, but you'd say, thank you, men, wouldn't you?"

"It's different."

"It's not."

"Is."

"Isn't."

"Is."

"Waldo, what's stupid is this."

"You're right. I got to go, check in with Schufeldt, meet Maguire." He kissed her on the cheek.

"Come here," she said, pulling his head toward her, kissing him on the lips.

"Nice," he said. "You're some kinda ladygal."

She laughed. "So long gentlemanguy."

"Oh, you're a hoot, you are," he said, going down the steps.

"Waldo?" she called.

"Yeah?"

"Don't let Schufeldt get to you."

"I won't." Famous last words, he thought.

———————

Colin sat in a back booth at the Paradise nursing a cup of black coffee. Hallock was late. Colin wondered what the chief wanted. He hadn't indicated on the phone, just said he needed his help. It was bound to be about the three murders, but how could he help?

He shouldn't have told Mark he was going out to meet Hallock, but he couldn't have predicted Mark's reaction.

"What do you mean he wants your help?"

"Just that. I don't know what it's about."

"Are you slipping or what?"

There it was again, the soft edge of criticism — a feeling that Mark was trying to undermine him. "Slipping?" He tried to sound casual.

"You didn't *ask* Hallock?" Mark said acrimoniously.

"I asked, he didn't answer. He said he didn't want to talk about it over the phone."

"I think he's getting flaky. He's never had a murder to solve before, now he has three of them."

"I don't know, he doesn't seem flaky to me. Just cautious."

"Cautious, hell. Behind the eight ball is what he is."

"Maybe, but he's got some kind of plan."

Mark laughed derisively. "Waldo Hallock's never had a plan in his life. You don't really know this guy, Colin."

"No, not well, but —"

"Not well? Not at all."

There was no use in arguing the point.

"Suppose I say you can't go?" Mark said.

"Come on, what's this all about?"

"It's about wasting time, Colin, that's what it's about."

"If you don't want me to go, I won't go. But I don't know what you're afraid of."

"Don't be an asshole. What do I have to be afraid of?"

"You tell me."

"Go on, big-time crime reporter, get the hell out of here. But when you come back with egg on your face don't blame me."

Annoyed, Colin left. Walking toward the Paradise, Mark caught up to him.

"Hey, pal, listen," he said, a hand on Colin's shoulder, turning him around. "I'm sorry. I don't know what's wrong with me . . . yeah, I do."

Colin waited.

"I spoke to Amy this morning. It screwed me up. You know how it is."

In fact, Colin *didn't* know how it was.

"Forget everything I said, okay, pal?"

"Consider it forgotten," he answered grudgingly.

Sitting in the Paradise, Colin hadn't forgotten any of it. He didn't believe Mark but he didn't know why. Maybe he *had* talked to Amy, maybe it had even upset him, but Colin didn't think for a moment that Mark's attack had anything to do with Amy. There was only one reason Mark behaved the way he had: He was in a jealous rage. He couldn't stand Colin's good relationship with Hallock. Although it was nothing new, and Mark had previously said he was glad Colin got on with Hallock, something about this was out of sync and it nagged at him.

Hallock, mouth set in a grim line, approached the booth. "Son of a goddamn bitch!"

"What's up, Chief?"

"Son of a frigging bitch!" He sat down and slammed the table hard. "That ass-backwards moron! Christ Almighty!" His mouth was tight, shoulders in a dispirited droop.

Colin waited, lit a Marlboro.

"Schufeldt," he hissed, sounding like a steam engine.

One look at the macho wonder boy and he'd known there'd be friction between him and Hallock, so he wasn't surprised at the chief's outburst. "What happened?"

"The fucker's decided the mark's not an A."

"Yeah? What is it?"

"You ready? It's a cult marking."

"A what?"

"A cult marking. You know, the mark of some loony-tunes group like Hare Krishnas or Moonies or some damn thing."

Colin thought maybe Schufeldt might be onto something.

"What's that look in your eye, Maguire?"

"No look."

"Bull."

"Tell me why he thinks that?"

"Who the fuck knows? You think he lets *me* in on his thought processes? Doesn't even let *himself* in on them. Coupla days ago he's dragging in all the sex offenders, even though I point out to him that's not our guy's M.O. So now he wants to bring in any weirdos. Eighty percent of the Fork are weirdos, I tell him." Hallock laughed.

"What'd he say?"

"Nothing. Just gives me this look supposed to be hardass or some such. The bastard thinks he's Clint Eastwood."

Colin smiled. "I wish you knew why he thinks it's a cult marking."

"What the hell difference does it make?"

"Maybe he's got something."

"You kidding me? Forget about it."

Colin shrugged. "You never know, Chief."

"*I* know." He jabbed a thick thumb at his chest.

Colin could see this was not a line of inquiry to pursue. Still, you never knew. Maybe he should investigate this on his own. "So why're you so bugged about it?"

Hallock leaned forward, lowered his voice. "Because the stupid bastard is rounding up whoever he thinks is weird, going to bring 'em in, grill 'em. I mean, shit, Maguire, we don't do stuff like that around here. Thing is, he wanted me to go out, round the loons up. No way, José, I tell him."

"What'd he say?"

"Said if I didn't he was going to report me."

"Who to?"

"I don't know. Gildersleeve, I guess. Town board."

"Did you say again you wouldn't do it?"

"I said nada. Just walked out. Came here." He took off his cap, dropped it on the seat beside him and ran a crumpled handkerchief over his sweaty brow.

"Hey, Chief," Vivian said, "I didn't see ya come in."

"'S'okay, Viv."

"Want a coffee an' Danish?"

"Just coffee."

"Refill for you?"

"Yes, thanks."

"Comin' up."

Colin said, "So what are you going to do?"

"Nothing. I mean, I'm not cruising around looking for what he calls weirdos."

"What *does* he call weirdos?"

Vivian placed a cup of coffee in front of Hallock and filled Colin's cup.

When she was gone Hallock said, "He says, 'You got any homos around here? Well, Jesus, Maguire, this is a resort town a hundred miles from New York City, it's like asking you got any Jews in Israel.'"

Colin laughed. "A quarter of the businesses are run by gays, from what I've seen."

"You'd better believe it. You think I'm going to pull them in for questioning? I mean, for instance, can you feature me dragging in Harriet and Ginny from the card shop, giving them the third?"

Colin shook his head.

"Let the bastard make a federal case against me, I'm not wasting my time with his bullshit. Not going to embarrass a lot of nice folks 'cause this little prick's a Falwell follower or whatever. You start pulling in what he calls weirdos, next thing you have him arresting all the Democrats, or all the blonds with blue eyes, if you see what I mean." Hallock took a large swallow of coffee. "Ah, hell, Maguire, it's a dog's life."

He stifled his laughter. "C'mon, Chief, it's not that bad."

"No? I'll tell you, it's pretty bad, bringing in this hotshot from the troopers, telling me how to run an investigation when he doesn't know his dick from his elbow. Not my fault this killer's some smart Joe. Jesus, Maguire, not a goddamn clue in three murders. No prints, no hair samples, no blood samples, not a goddamn thing." His body slumped in the booth as if the puppeteer had dropped his strings.

Colin thought Hallock looked old. 'It's tough, Chief, I know. But what about your plan?"

"Oh, yeah, the plan," he said unenthusiastically.

"You sounded excited about it on the phone."

"I don't know, it seems like a million-to-one shot now."

"Tell me anyway."

Hallock outlined the plan for Colin, filling him in on his early morning meeting with the women, ending with his idea of the questionnaire.

"What kind of questionnaire?"

"That's where you come in. I want something that sounds like a survey, not too long, but meaningful, give us an idea of the person. See who we can rule out. Narrow it down."

"You realize the killer may not have a phone?"

"Yeah, I know. Might not have a phone; might not be an A; if it is an A, might not be the initial of a name. Yeah, I know. But I got to do something. Maguire. I got to try."

"Okay, let's think about the questionnaire."

They sat in the Paradise for more than an hour, trying

hundreds of ideas, rejecting most. In the end they came up with ten questions. Colin read them out to Hallock.

"One. Ask if respondent is the person listed in the phone book. (If yes go to Two. If no ask to speak to that person. If not at home find out when he will be home. Thank respondent hang up. If the respondent is the one listed and a woman go to Two and Three.)

"Two. Were you watching TV Friday night, May twenty-ninth? (If yes go to Three. If no go to Four.)

"Three. What program? (When they tell you, thank them and hang up.)

"Four. Were you at home on that night? (If yes continue. If no go to Eight.)

"Five. Were you home alone or with friends? If alone go to Six. If with friends go to Seven.)

"Six. What were you doing?

"Seven. What were you and friends doing?

"Eight. Were you at a movie, out to dinner, with friends other? (If respondent was with friends somewhere other than band concert go to Ten. If at band concert go to Nine.)

"Nine. Did you enjoy the concert?

"Ten. Will you be watching TV tonight? Thank respondent, say good-bye."

"That's not half bad," Hallock said.

"You ought to get something out of that."

"It's worth a shot. Don't know how to thank you, Maguire."

"Forget it."

"This was off the record, right? I mean, you won't print this."

"No."

"Or tell anybody about it?"

"Not even Mark?"

"'Specially not him. He's not in my cheering section, if you know what I mean."

"I'll try, Chief, that's all I can promise. He *is* my boss."

"Do the best you can."

"I will."

Outside, Colin and Hallock stood in front of the Paradise feeling the quiet of the town.

"It's like a frigging morgue," Hallock observed. "Usually starts jumping by this time of year. I gotta get this bastard."

"I'm sure you will, Chief," Colin said.

But he wasn't sure at all.

LOOKING BACK — 25 YEARS AGO

Early in January Roy Chute advertised in *The Seaville Gazette* for a valuable camera he had lost. The months went by with no response. Mr. Chute, who thoroughly believes in the fundamental honesty of the average individual, refused to give up hope for the safe return of the camera. One day last week he and his wife were out. Upon their return they found the missing camera on the table in the living room. Where the camera had been for five months or who returned it he had no idea. But his belief in the honesty of human nature was verified.

Chapter Twenty

It was one of those days Joe Carroll hated more than life itself. No Thank God It's Friday for him. And if this morning's breakfast was an example of how the day was going to go, he was screwed.

"Mom, how many years have I been asking you to make me four-minute eggs, huh?" The hardened yolk fell with a thunk into his bowl.

"Look, Joey, I got a lot on my mind, okay? Your stupid eggs aren't the only thing I gotta worry about, all right? I got Billy with crusts I gotta trim, and Tommy with Sugarboats he hates and —"

"What's Sugarboats?"

"Cereal. And Lana with pimples so she's crying her eyes out and —"

"Why do you give the kid a cereal he hates?"

"Last week it was his favorite. This week he'd rather be dead than look at it," Mary explained.

"What pimples? I didn't see any pimples."

"On her chin. She's got two pimples on her chin."

"And she's crying about that?" He loaded salt on the egg, pointedly used his knife to cut through it.

"She's got a date with some big wheel at school and thinks she can't go now."

"'Cause she's got two pimples? That's stupid."

"Not everybody's got peaches-and-cream complexions so they never have to worry, you know."

Joe knew she was talking about Debbie. It ticked him off that his mother didn't like her, never had. She said the Van Tuyl family thought they were too good for Seaville and looked down their big noses at the Carrolls. "You don't have to say it like it's a crime or something."

"So have a little sympathy for your sister." She slammed down a plate with two pieces of overdone toast. "Don't say anything, Joey, I'm warning you."

"I'm saying nothing." He eyed the toast with distaste, then began scraping, black bits falling on his napkin. Hell, he shouldn't be so hard on his mother; he knew what was wrong with her this morning and it wasn't trimming Billy's toast or Tommy's Sugarboats or Lana's pimples. It was his father. He'd come in last night drunk as a skunk again. He'd broken a couple of dishes and kept the whole house awake screaming at his mother, telling her she was stupid, the next thing to a moron, and that he should have married Sis Terry instead of her. It was a routine he did at least once a month, like he was a goddamn werewolf or something.

Joe remembered the three years his father had been on the wagon. Those were Joe's last three years in high school, and they were great. He and his father had even become friends, going camping together like in some television program. Then the old man fell off — no, crashed off — the wagon and it had been hell ever since. At least he'd gotten away from it for a while when he was at school. But now, Chrissake, it was like living in a war zone. Even when the old man didn't go out on his whopper drunks he was always squiffed, mean and cruel, and never did a goddamn bit of work.

And that was the worst part. Joe had never wanted to be a mortician to begin with, but his mother had begged him, said the business would be lost if he didn't go into it, and then where would the family be? So now he was a goddamn undertaker wearing a black suit and tie two, three times a week, and when he wasn't officiating at funerals he was draining blood out of bodies and pumping them full of chemicals, rouging up their pasty faces, and combing their hair. Yeah, it was a great life hanging around a lot of stiffs.

Like today.

"What's wrong?" Mary asked.

Joey looked at the deep circles, like small sacks, under his mother's eyes, the two deep furrows from nose to mouth, the sallow complexion, and he wanted to weep for her. "Why don't you leave him?" he heard himself saying, a question he'd thought many times but never dared ask.

"Leave who?"

He almost laughed, understanding why he hadn't asked this sooner. "Nobody. Skip it." Giving her a kiss on the cheek, he left the house.

The mortuary was next door to the Carroll home, so Joe had only to cross the lawn to go to work. It was a beautiful June morning, sun in the sky, warm breeze tickling his arms. Boy, would he have liked going on a picnic with Debbie, maybe taking the ferries over to the Hamptons, getting a six-pack, some ham-and-cheese sandwiches, a bag of chips. But no dice.

He unlocked the front door and went inside. The first floor held the viewing rooms and a small chapel. Today Ostrowski was in Room One, better known as the Blue Room, and Miller in Two, known as the Rose Room. Nobody was in Three yet, the Gold Room, but Turner, the stiff he had to work on, would be there by afternoon.

Joe walked along the dark hallway. There was no need to throw the light switch, as he knew the walk by heart. He was grateful that the body he had to embalm today wasn't a kid. Like Mary Beth Higbee. That was a bitch. It really tore him up to do kids. And then the funerals themselves, the parents practically going nuts, falling on the caskets, wanting to jump in the graves.

But Mary Beth Higbee was the worst he'd ever had to do. Besides being a kid she was his first murder victim, that goddamn A carved in her little chest. Afterwards, he'd had nightmares for two nights running.

He opened the door to the prep room and hit the light. It was small but big enough for the job. Big enough to house the electric lift, the sink, and the embalming pump. The damn thing looked like a watercooler!

Turner was on the table under the sheet. God, how he hated doing ones he knew. Sure, it was easier 'cause you knew what the guy looked like, but it was harder on the old emotions. A lot of people thought undertakers didn't have any feelings, but it wasn't true. He switched on his little gray Sony. Some rock group were singing their guts out. Joe saw that the station had been changed from the one he usually listened to. He wondered who'd done that. Turning the dial, he found his favorite station; Frank Sinatra was singing "My Way." Debbie and all his friends laughed at him for liking such square music but what the hell? Could he help it if rock left him cold?

Next to the radio was his pair of yellow rubber gloves. He looked them over carefully, checking for cuts or holes. His father was always yelling at him for going through gloves like Kleenex, the cheap bastard. He wished the old man would do a little more work and less complaining. Besides, could he help it if he nicked a glove now and then? Those instruments were sharp. He pulled on the gloves and walked to the table. Standing next to the body, he took a deep breath. The moment of pulling back the sheet, seeing a corspe that might have passed though rigor mortis but still looked very dead, always got to him. Much as he knew, much as he'd done it maybe four hundred times, it still gave him the creeps. Ah, shit, just do it.

With a flick of his wrist he pulled back the sheet. The body sat up and Joe screamed, stumbled backward, eyes wide and staring, mouth hanging open. "What . . . you . . . doing here? Oh, shit, no . . ."

The killer sprang from the table, and Joe felt the knife plunge through his sweater, shirt, skin. It burned and he fell to his knees, his hands grabbing at the hilt of the knife, wanting to pull it out, struggling in vain against the force of the killer.

Tears trickled from the corners of Joe's eyes as he looked into the face of his killer. "Why?" he whispered.

"It's your birthright," came the answer.

I couldn't have heard right, he thought. He couldn't have said *birthright*. He'd ask again. Later. But now he had to lie down, now he had to sleep. Slowly, Joe fell sideways, grateful for the cool of the tiled floor. Gazing at the man above him he tried to speak, ask why again. Words wouldn't come. Later, much later. He closed his eyes. The very last thought Joe Carroll had was: See you later, alligator, and he wanted to laugh but he couldn't.

———————

The first thing that morning Colin had put in a call to Mike Rosler at *The New York Times*. Mike wasn't there and he hadn't called back yet. He thought Mike might help him with information on cults, their symbols and signs. They'd gone to college together and Mike, Colin, and Mark had been great buddies, all of them determined to write for *The Times*. Only Mike had made it. Although writing for the *Chicago Tribune* wasn't kid stuff, it still wasn't the same as writing for *The Times*. Mark was the only one who'd never written for a big paper. He'd gone from one small weekly to another until he finally owned one himself. Colin wondered if Mark ever felt insecure about his writing history. When Colin had asked Mark why he no longer saw Mike, he'd said that Mike bored him, that he'd gotten too big for his britches. Although Colin had only seen Mike two or three times over the last five years since he'd been writing for *The Times,* he hadn't detected any egomania in him. And he'd been a damn good friend during the year that followed the murders of Colin's family. He hated to admit it, but he couldn't help thinking that Mark was jealous of Mike.

There was a pile of mail to be opened and it wasn't getting done by ruminating on Mark and Mike. He slipped the silver letter opener his father had given him for his twenty-third birthday under the sealed flap of a letter addressed, in a large, slanting hand, to *The Editor*. It was for Mark.

Dear Mr. Griffing,
I had always thought we were kindred spirits until I read
your column last week. I assumed that you were a dyed-
in-the-wool preppy like me with tasseled loafers, chino
pants, and all the rest. And then, to my horror, I find out
you went to a public high school in Pennsylvania. Who
ever heard of a real preppy coming from there? No,
Mr. G., you don't qualify and as far as I'm concerned,
you might as well be a Yippy!

An ex-fan

Colin laughed, picked up the phone and buzzed Mark. The
were always getting letters criticizing one or the other of them
and for reasons just as absurd as this. He and Mark had a
running contest as to who'd get the worst letter. He pushed the
buzzer again. It was nine-twenty, and Mark was usually in by
eight-thirty. He buzzed Penny at the front desk. "Pen, do you
know where Mark is?"

"He hasn't come in yet."

"Is he still at home?"

"I don't know. He hasn't called in."

"And he didn't tell you about an appointment or anything?"

"Nope. Want me to ring his house for you?"

"No, that's okay. Thanks."

He'd never known Mark to be this late if he didn't have an
appointment. He even got pissed off if Colin came in late by
fifteen minutes. The phone rang, interrupting his thoughts. It
was Sarah, asking if Colin knew where Mark was.

"He had an appointment." Colin wasn't sure why he was
lying but felt he should.

"I guess he forgot to tell me," she said. "He was gone by the
time I got up."

Colin was alarmed, knowing Sarah usually arose at six-
thirty. "It was a breakfast appointment," he said quickly.

"Who with?"

"Gildersleeve, about the murders." Colin swiveled his chair
around and looked out on a small backyard. A few yellow and
white flowers grew near a birdbath. "Sarah?"

"Yes?" Her voice was soft, almost breathless.

"Are you okay?"

"Colin," she asked gingerly, "you wouldn't lie to me, would you?"

"About what?"

"About where Mark is?"

"Of course not, Sarah." He felt like a shit.

"I never heard of breakfast appointments at six o'clock."

"Well, he came in here first; you know how he is."

"You were in the office by six?" she asked facetiously.

"No, Sarah, I have to admit, I was happily snoozing at six." He forced a false-sounding chuckle.

"Then how do you know he came into the office at six?" she pressed.

"I don't *know*, I'm just assuming." He didn't want to say, "Where else would he go?" because he thought he knew.

Sarah said crisply, "All right, Colin, just have him call me when he gets in."

"Okay, Sarah, but don't —" He heard the click breaking the connection. Christ, he thought, if Mark was fooling around with Amy again, all hell was going to break loose. He was sure that this time, Sarah would leave him. But maybe he wasn't with Amy; maybe he *did* have an appointment.

Colin walked down the hall, past the bank where Susan and Consuelo were pasting copy, and up the stairs to Mark's office. At the desk he turned the calendar page from Thursday to Friday. There was nothing written down before eleven. He knew Mark had another calendar, a leather-bound book. Hurriedly he searched through the papers on the desk but found nothing. Feeling like a louse, he opened the top right-hand drawer and began examining the contents.

"Can I help you, pal?"

Colin jumped. "Jesus, Mark!"

Mark's eyes were hard, like chipped glass. "What are you looking for, Colin?"

"Your calendar."

"Yeah? How come?"

"Sarah called and said you'd left the house by six, and she

didn't know where you were. I told her you had a meeting with Gildersleeve about the murders. She didn't believe me, she said she never heard of a breakfast meeting starting at six. I said you probably came into the office first. She hung up on me. She said you should call when you came in."

Mark tapped a sneakered foot. "So why're you looking for my calendar?"

"I wanted to see if you *did* have an appointment."

"What business is it of yours?"

"Come on, Mark, don't be a shit. I had to lie to your wife for, God's sake."

"So? Are you some fucking Boy Scout suddenly? Or are you bucking for the George Washington award?"

Colin slammed the drawer and started for the door. Mark stopped him, his fingers pressing into Colin's shoulder, his eyes looking cold, devoid of any emotion.

"What the heil's wrong with you lately?" Colin asked.

"*Me?* What about you?"

Colin remembered this technique from college days; Mark would always turn things around so that the questioner was on the defensive. He pulled out of his grip. "Let's just forget it. You'd better call Sarah."

"I was with Amy," Mark said.

"You're a schmuck, you know that?"

"Yeah, I know. I couldn't help it, Colin. She called me yesterday and said she was going to kill herself if I didn't come see her. I mean, what the fuck else could I do?"

"For one thing you could have lied to Sarah instead of just disappearing. Do you think Sarah's a dope or something?"

Mark slumped down into the gray denim couch and put his head in his hands.

Funny, Colin thought, you know a man for years, think you understand him, and then in a flash you realize you don't know a damn thing. He would have bet twenty to one that Mark wouldn't jeopardize his marriage again.

"It's none of my business," Colin said, "but what are you going to do now?"

"I don't know, that's the trouble," he said gloomily. "She's such a kid, Amy. Such a mixed-up kid."

Colin wanted to ask him why a thirty-eight-year-old man had gotten involved with a kid in the first place, but he knew that was beside the point.

Mark said, "I'm afraid she'll do it, Colin, I really am."

"Does she want you to leave Sarah?"

"Yes."

"You don't want to leave Sarah and the kids, do you?"

"I'm so screwed up," he lamented. "You don't know, Colin, you just don't know how screwed up I am." He ran both hands through his gray hair.

The words chilled Colin and he didn't know why. "Maybe you should see a shrink."

"Like who?"

"I don't know. Aren't there any out here?"

"Yeah, I guess but —"

The phone rang, sounding shrill and assaultive.

"Want me to get it?" Colin asked.

"No, I will." He plodded to his desk and picked up the white phone. "Yeah? When?" Mark looked ashen, as if he'd been drained of blood. "Oh, shit. Okay, yeah, right away. Thanks."

"What is it?" Colin asked.

"Another one."

"Jesus. Who?"

"Joe Carroll, the undertaker. Do you want to go or should I try to locate Babe? *I* can go, for that matter."

"No, I'll go. I told you, it was just the kid I —"

"Yeah, sure I understand."

Colin felt a twinge of irritation that Mark had forgotten their agreement about him covering the murders. "We'll talk later, okay?"

"Right."

"Don't forget to call Sarah."

"Yeah. And thanks for covering for me."

Colin waved a hand in answer, but didn't say he wasn't going to go on lying to Sarah. Now he had to be a reporter, a goddamn *crime* reporter. Again.

LOOKING BACK — 50 YEARS AGO

On Tuesday noon a large sedan carrying four people fell into the excavation on the former R. Young property, corner of Main and Center Streets, and although the heavy sedan ended up in the deep cellar, no one was injured and the only damage to the car was a bent fender. The machine, a Buick sedan, was the property of Fred Goodwin of Seaville.

Chapter Twenty-One

A special emergency meeting of the town board was called for the afternoon of Joe Carroll's murder. Colin sat in the audience waiting for the meeting to begin, still shaken by the scene he'd encountered at the funeral parlor that morning.

By the time he'd arrived, the mortuary was packed with people. Schufeldt and Hallock were screaming at one another while the lab technicians popped their flashbulbs and made their measurements. Buzz Gormley from *Newsline* was on the scene because he'd been in the area on another assignment.

In the far wall of the prep room, a closet door hung open, grotesquely exposing the nude body of Fred Turner, who was wedged inside on an angle between floor and side wall, arms hanging forward limply like a huge inflated doll. On the table Joe Carroll lay dead, his shirt ripped open, a carving on his chest. Only this time it wasn't an A. Now there was a new symbol, more complex, more mystifying than the other.

Colin flipped the pages of his notebook and looked at the copy he'd made of what the murderer had carved into Carroll's chest. He had drawn it speedily and now he ran his pen over it, making the markings thicker, darker. And then he studied it:

Schufeldt had insisted it was a swastika, but Hallock had pointed out that although it resembled a swastika it was not one: the characters were backwards. A loud argument had ensued, then escalated into a shoving match, Hallock and Schufeldt having to be separated by Charlie Copin and himself.

The way Colin saw it, it could either be a swastika drawn by someone who didn't know what one looked like, or it could be an arcane symbol. But whatever it was it had completely blown Hallock's theory about the A being an initial of a name and had made the women's two-and-a-half-days' work totally useless.

The Town Hall was a new building. The meeting room was large, with orange and yellow plastic chairs, tan drapes, and an orange carpet of indoor-outdoor material. Fluorescent lighting was recessed into an Armstrong ceiling and spilled out in a depressing glow. In the right-hand corner of the room was a large American flag and on the nearby wall a photograph of the president of the United States. At the front of the room was a platform supporting a long, desk-type piece of furniture where the mayor and board members presided.

Word about this emergency session had leaked and now a number of townspeople were filing in. Hallock and Schufeldt sat in front, ten seats separating them.

A few board members, Phil Nagle one of them, had already taken their seats when Jill Townsend, town clerk and the only woman on the board, joined them. Colin watched Gildersleeve as he climbed the four steps to the platform and assumed his place in the middle. He removed his sunglasses and surveyed the room, his small mouth tightly closed in an unyielding line. He wore a seersucker suit, white shirt, red striped tie. A handkerchief in a breast pocket showed three neat points.

The room was filling up. Colin was surprised to see Fran Hallock seated in the back with about eight other women. She looked tired. Burton Kelly came through the main double doors. Colin slid down in his seat, not wanting to talk to Kelly.

The last councilman arrived just as somebody tapped Colin on the shoulder. He felt a rush when he saw her. "What are you doing here?" he asked.

"I'm a citizen," Annie said smiling, eyes crinkling shut.

"Sorry. I didn't mean — I don't know what I meant," he laughed. "Why don't you sit here?" He indicated the chair next to him.

They brushed shoulders as she sat, and Colin felt as if he'd touched a live wire. She was wearing a lavender button-down collar oxford shirt, and a khaki shirt. He thought she looked marvelous.

"What do you think will happen?" Annie asked.

"I think we're going to see a lynching, figuratively speaking."

"Waldo?"

"Between Gildersleeve and the state trooper, old Waldo doesn't have a chance. But the people will do it for them, you'll see."

"I can understand how they feel. Four murders in two weeks is a lot of people to deal with, Colin."

He liked it when she said his name. "That's not Waldo's fault."

"No, of course not, but he's in the office of chief to protect the people of Seaville."

"And he's not doing a very good job, is that what you're saying?" The last thing he wanted was to fight with her.

"*I'm* not saying that, but it's what the people are saying. I had a lot of calls today after word got out about Joe Carroll."

"What kind of calls?"

"Angry calls, scared calls. Everybody feels very vulnerable, and they are," she said thoughtfully.

"I can't argue with that but Waldo's doing the best he can, Annie. He's got practically nothing to work with. Whoever's doing this is very smart, very cagey."

The gavel sounded and Gildersleeve rose. "We'll begin this special meetin' of the town board, as usual, with the salutin' of the flag."

Everyone faced the flag and placed their hands over their hearts. When they'd finished the pledge and resumed their seats, Gildersleeve banged the gavel once more.

"Councilmen, members of the audience, this special meetin'

has been called to determine what action the town of Seaville should take in relationship to these unsolved murders. As you all know, there have been four terrible killin's since Saturday, May Twenty-third. That is to say, the discovery of one murder," he coughed and scratched an ear, "and then the brutal killin's of three of our own citizenry. One of them a darlin' little girl, Mary Beth Higbee."

Along with the rest of the audience, Colin followed Gildersleeve's mournful gaze and found himself looking at the broad back of Chuck Higbee. The man's shoulders heaved and Sally Higbee leaned closer to her husband, a hand sliding up his arm. Colin felt disgusted by Gildersleeve's theatrics. He wondered if Russ Cooper was in the audience, then spotted him two rows from the back. None of the Carrolls was present.

". . . and so," Gildersleeve was saying, "we intend to take action today. There will be no more so-called privileged information. Every citizen in this township will know everything he or she wants to know about these killin's."

Colin shook his head. "What an idiot," he whispered to Annie.

"Don't the police purposely hold back information to trap the killer?" she asked.

"Exactly."

". . . it is our duty. We will now hear from Councilman Philip Nagle."

"Terrific," Colin said sarcastically.

Nagle pulled his microphone closer and adjusted his aviator glasses. He was wearing a light blue linen jacket, gray creaseless trousers, a white shirt, and a dark blue tie. When he bent his head to read his prepared statement, the light shone on his thinning hair, revealing a pink scalp.

"This guy is the pits," Colin said. "Do you know him?"

"I've seen him around."

"He was Gloria Danowski's lover."

"No kidding?"

"But he's innocent."

". . . and members of the Council. I am here today to propose the immediate dismissal of Chief Waldo Hallock. In the past weeks, Chief Hallock has failed to uncover one shred of evidence, not to mention that not one suspect has been detained. Why? Because Chief Hallock has not been able to come up with a suspect. Why? Because Chief Waldo Hallock is incompetent and ill-suited for the responsible and difficult job of chief of the Seaville Police. I urge you, Council members, to vote for removal of Waldo Hallock from his present position. Thank you."

Colin made some notes on his pad. "He probably thinks *he* should be chief, the creep."

Annie said, "I'm getting the feeling you don't like him."

"Hey, you're one sharp woman," he kidded.

"You have to get up early to get something past me, fella." Colin laughed.

Gildersleeve wiped his face with a handkerchief and leaned toward his microphone. "Thank you, Councilman Nagle. We will now hear from Special Agent William Schufeldt."

Schufeldt, his broad shoulders straining the jacket of his green leisure suit, looked around for the standing microphone. It was in the aisle, near Colin. When Colin made no move to bring him the microphone, Schufeldt's fleshy face began to turn the color of raw beef.

Colin heard the scrape of a chair and footsteps behind him, then saw Burton Kelly carry the mike to the front. Coming back to his seat, Kelly gave Colin a dismissive glance.

Schufeldt adjusted the mike. "Mayor Gildersleeve, and Councilmen, I thank you for this opportunity to put my problems before you. Since I have come on this case four days ago I have had no cooperation whatsoever from your chief of police, Waldo Hallock. I would have to say that he has gone out of his way to be obstructive. Time after time when I asked him to give me certain information he refused."

Colin looked at Hallock, saw the muscle jumping in his cheek.

"Each new line of inquiry I wished to pursue was met with disapproval and insubordination. I am not familiar, as you can imagine, with this township. Therefore, I needed the help of the chief to clue me in to the various criminals, their records, and that. On several occasions he told me that that was unnecessary, and even went so far as to steer me wrong about things."

Hallock's head snapped up. He wore an expression of puzzlement that quickly turned to understanding, then finally faded into a bemused smile.

"And last but not least," Schufeldt went on, "I happen to know he pursued lines of inquiry that he did not make me privy to. There is no way that I can work with this man and bring this case to a swift conclusion. I urge the Council to dismiss Chief Hallock from his present position. Thank you." Schufeldt sat in his chair with a thud.

"Schufeldt's right up there with Nagle for the sleazeball of the year award," Colin whispered.

"I'm glad I don't have to choose between them," Annie said.

"Thank you, Special Agent Schufeldt. Now, would you like to make a statement, Chief Hallock?"

"No, thank you. No, wait. Yes, I would." Hallock, in his summer uniform of short-sleeved white shirt and lightweight dark blue trousers, gun holstered on his right hip, walked slowly past Schufeldt, eyes straight ahead, shoulders squared. He bent down, not bothering to adjust the mike.

"Mr. Mayor, Miss Townsend, Councilmen. I wish to respond to the charge *Special Agent* Schufeldt made against me of deliberately steering him wrong. I am guilty of that charge."

There were murmurs in the audience.

"I willfully and deliberately steered *Special Agent* Schufeldt to Whitey's Dockside Restaurant with full knowledge that the food is lousy and the prices exorbitant. Thank you." He walked back to his seat.

A burst of laughter filled the room and Gildersleeve rapped the gavel. Colin could see that Hallock was trying not to smile and almost losing the battle.

Gildersleeve hammered the desk, his small eyes shrinking with anger. "Quiet. Quiet, people!" Slowly the laughter subsided and Gildersleeve resumed control. "This is not a laughin' matter, there's not one thing funny about this."

A male voice from the back called out, "Whitey Barnes ain't gonna find it funny, that's for sure."

This time there was a trickling of laughter, but the sound of the gavel sliced through it, cutting it off before it could build.

"We are here today to discuss serious business, and I'm shocked to see that our own chief of police would intentionally try to reduce these precedin's to such a trivial level. I think that action speaks for itself. The forum is now open. If any of you would like to say anythin' before the Council takes a vote, this is the time." He nodded his head for emphasis, his jowls wobbling. "The chair recognizes Rita Sherr."

She was a tall woman who had long dark hair streaked with gray. Near the front, she had only to walk a few steps to the microphone. "I've been in business here for six years. By Memorial Day my jeans shop is packed and it doesn't let up till after Labor Day. But not this year. So far, this year has been a disaster. I say, why? A. The economy is in better shape than it's been for a long time. B. This area was written up last year in *The New York Times* as a swell place to vacation. So why is my business off by over half?" She shrugged and stretched out her hands as if waiting for the answers to fall into her palms.

"I'll tell you why. Because nobody wants to come to a place where they might get murdered. And I say, who can blame them? The thing of it is, and I'm sorry to say this, if the chief of police can't do his job then we got to be ruthless. We got to put somebody in charge who can."

The audience applauded enthusiastically.

Gildersleeve said, "The chair recognizes Elbert Palmer."

"I had to let go the boy I hired for the summer," the barber said. "Couldn't afford to pay him no more. I still got my usual customers but nobody new 'cause there ain't nobody new around here. Leastways, I ain't see no new heads."

Jake Hicks was next. "This kind of thing don't hurt the mail — rain or shine, you know. But what it's doing to me and my family is making us stay home nights. Feels like it's February and I can tell you, me and the wife've got cabin fever."

"It's a disgrace," said Carolyn Dobbs. "This should have

been stopped right in the beginning. You don't let a thing like this get out of hand. I say Chief Hallock's had long enough to show his mettle, and he just isn't up to snuff,"

"The chair recognizes Reverend Ann Winters."

"I've never been close to a murder case before, but I can't believe that Chief Hallock isn't doing everything possible. If you don't have anything to work with, you can't simply make up clues or arrest people without reason. I feel we should stick by the chief and give him all the support we can."

There was a smattering of applause, but the boos and hisses drowned it out. Annie sat down, shoulders sagging.

Colin said, "Good for you."

"I don't think it helped much."

"It'll mean something to him."

After Annie there were six more speakers, five against Hallock, one for. And then Gildersleeve recognized Julia Dorman.

The microphone was hustled up the aisle by a youngish man Colin didn't recognize and placed in front of the cool blond who had risen from a seat next to Fran Hallock.

"Thank you, Mayor. I believe what I have to say refers to the lines of inquiry Special Agent Schufeldt was kept in the dark about. Three days ago, I and four other women were enlisted to help Chief Hallock pursue an idea he had pertaining to the murderer."

Colin saw Fran's face fall. She reached out a hand toward Julia Dorman as if to stop her, then let the arm drop back to her lap.

"We were all glad to help because we, as you can understand, wished the murderer to be apprehended as soon as possible, and if we could do anything to help gain that end, well, then we were more than willing to give our time. However, in light of the murder this morning and a certain fact that has come to our attention, we now feel that Chief Hallock has not only wasted our time but his own as well, thereby slowing down an investigation that needs to move rapidly forward."

"Could you please tell the Council what Chief Hallock asked you gals to do?"

Julia Dorman's mouth twitched. "Certainly. Chief Hallock believed that the A that seemed to be a trademark of the killer's was either his first initial, his last, or his middle."

A bark of laughter came from near the door. Colin saw that it was Jim Drew, his hand now covering his mouth and his glance darting from person to person as if to ask for forgiveness for his inappropriate laughter.

"Go on, Mrs. Dorman."

"Well, we had to go through the local phone book, marking off any names that fell into that category. And then we began phoning these people, asking a series of questions meant to narrow down a list of suspects."

"Hey, I got one of them calls," a woman cried out.

"Me, too. Got one this morning."

Others joined in, and Gildersleeve rapped the gavel for silence.

"I'm very sorry," Julia said, looking ashamed, "for anyone who was inconvenienced. We were just trying to help, not realizing what a total waste of time it was. At any rate, we women believe," she swept a hand to her right indicating Fran and the others, "that Chief Hallock has totally bungled this investigation. Thank you."

It didn't take long after that. There were a few more statements, mostly against Hallock. Colin wanted to speak for him, but as a newspaperman he could not take sides publicly. The vote was predictable and unanimous.

Gildersleeve announced, to no one's surprise, that Special Agent Schufeldt would be in charge of the case and that everyone was expected to give him their cooperation.

When the meeting was adjourned Colin and Annie approached Hallock, who immediately shook Annie's hand and thanked her for her support.

Colin said, "Sorry, Waldo. You don't deserve this."

"Maybe I do," he answered softly. "Maybe I do."

"The hell with that," Colin said. "You've done your best. That asshole Schufeldt isn't going to solve this thing."

"That's what really bothers me."

"Maybe you can still work on it," Annie suggested.

"Think so?"

"Why not? Who can stop a private citizen from doing a little investigating?"

"You might be right," he acknowledged, a dim light in his eyes.

"Let's talk, soon," Colin said.

Annie hugged Hallock.

He tried to smile and failed.

Colin saw Mark near the door. He hated board meetings, and Colin wondered what he was doing here.

"Don't look so surprised, pal. This is the biggest story of my career in Seaville. I don't want to miss anything. Hi, Annie."

"Sarah was looking for you this morning," she said.

"Yeah, I know. We got it straightened away." He turned to Colin, "So what do you think of the verdict, your guy being pushed out?"

Colin was irritated at the almost gleeful sound in Mark's voice. He didn't like Hallock being called *his* guy, either. "I think it sucks. Not to mention stupid. The only way I can see Schufeldt catching this guy is if he happens to stumble over him in the act."

"It doesn't seem like Hallock was doing much, screwing around with a lot of names, calling half the people on the Fork. What an asshole thing to get into. Did you know about it before today?"

He was not going to tell Mark he'd helped Hallock, but he couldn't totally lie. "I knew."

Mark shook his head as if to say that Colin was an asshole too.

It was an exceptionally warm day for early June. Colin took off his khaki sport jacket and threw it over his shoulder. He turned to Annie. "I'll call you tomorrow, okay?"

She nodded and said good-bye to them both.

"What's going on, pal?"

"With Annie? I'm taking her out tomorrow night."

"Great. I'm glad, Colin, no kidding."

"Let's not make too big a deal out of it, okay?"

"Hey, listen, I don't want to make you uptight. But I think it's good. Healthy."

"My car's down there. Where's yours?"

"Over there," he said, pointing in the opposite direction from Colin's. "See you back at the shop."

"Right." Walking toward his car, Colin thought he was really looking forward to seeing Annie the next night. He opened the door of the car, tossed his jacket to the passenger side, and climbed in. "Jesus!" he said, "What are *you* doing here?"

"Waiting for you," Babe said. She was slumped down in the seat, Colin's jacket slung across her.

"What do you want?" he asked, sounding harsher than he felt.

She sat up in the seat, threw his jacket in back. "I want to talk to you. *Need* to." She smiled, cocking her head to one side, trying to look cute.

"What about?"

"Had lunch?"

He hadn't. "What do you want to talk to me about, Babe?"

"I'm just longing for some moo shu pork. Let's go to the Peking Palace."

"They have lousy food," he said.

"I know but what choice do we have? Confucius say: Lousy moo shu pork is better than no moo shu pork. Come on, let's go."

"Get out of the car, Babe."

"I do believe he's cross." She batted her green eyes at him in mock fear.

"Out."

Suddenly her eyes lost their playful gleam, turning hard like two pieces of jade. "I think you'd better talk to me, Colin. I'm not kidding."

"Out," he said again, but with less conviction. He sensed danger.

She got out, then leaned back in. "I know you can't drive with me in the car, so meet me at the Peking. I want to talk to you about something very important. A murder. In fact, three murders. They happened in Chicago about three years ago."

She slammed the door.

LOOKING BACK — 75 YEARS AGO

Last week the Rev. Dr. John L. Scudder of Seaville stated that he was thinking of starting an Anti-Kissing Society. Then, with great seriousness, the progressive clergyman amplified his views on the pernicious habit of kissing. "Kissing is a pretty custom, but there is such a thing as kissing a person to death," said he. "If the kisser has tuberculosis or diphtheria, there is great danger that the disease will be communicated to the kissee. It is time to start Anti-Kissing leagues throughout America."

Chapter Twenty-Two

Perfection. That's what he strived for, always. Never managed it before. This time he was succeeding. Better than he'd imagined. Making them all crazy. What a touch of genius to put the undertaker on his own slab. Wished he could've seen the father find the son. Hearing about it was pretty good but not the same. They were saying Ted Carroll could be heard clear down to Bayview, screaming his lungs out. And the mother, later. Had to give her a shot, they said. Felt sorry for the girl, Debbie, though. Not her fault, nothing connected there. She'll find another guy.

It's merely justice that I seek. Is that so terrible? I get no justice any other way. You can't rely on the police, God knows. Not then, not now. Not ever. If you want results you must be aggressive. Assertive. Plan your plan. Make your move. Make a sad song better. But not anyone could do it. It takes insight, imagination, power. These three things have been my legacy. Three is the lucky number. If you have three you have a bonus. Bonus. Bonus is the whole bunch of them, the whole lousy town's scared. Who's next? they wonder. Who's next? So dumb. All they'd have to do is think. Put it together. Put their heads together. Think back. Look back. Yes, it's true. Simple is best. If you complicate things you get nowhere. Alphabets. Initials. What shit. What will they think of next? They cannot see the forest for the trees. They are simply — *spellbound!*

LOOKING BACK — 25 YEARS AGO

Whitey's Dockside Restaurant has received national recognition in the new edition of "Duncan Hines' Adventures in Good Eating" just of the press. It is the only restaurant in Seaville included among the 3,500 selected restaurants "Recommended by Duncan Hines," out of a total one-third million eating places in North America.

Chapter Twenty-Three

Hallock sat in the parking lot of the Seaville Nursing Home. The two most important women in his life for the last thirty years or so had been Fran and his mother. Three years before his mother had had a stroke that paralyzed her on one side. She couldn't be there for him anymore. In the last months she seemed to be slipping away, in a world of her own, talking a lot about *her* mother. It was painful and hard to watch. Still, he needed to see her today as he always did when things went wrong. Usually he went to her *after* Fran. But not today. Maybe not ever again. He didn't want to think about Fran now.

Looking down at his hat and gun on the seat beside him, he couldn't believe he'd never wear them again. Goddamn Schufeldt. Goddamn town. Who the hell was he kidding? You can't stay at the top if you're sliding toward the bottom. The fact was, he didn't have a clue to who this killer was. Maybe he'd been going at it wrong. Maybe? That was a laugh. He must've been nuts to try that scheme with the initials. But he couldn't believe he'd been publicly humiliated by that snot, Julia Dorman. The trouble with her was she'd had a husband who didn't love her, married her for her money, and everybody knew it. Including her. But Fran? Fran had a husband who adored her. So how could she have sat there like a lump and listened to that bitch pull him down? Ah, hell.

He took his gun out of the holster, rested it on his leg. How many cops had taken their .38s and just left all their troubles behind? One of the first things he'd heard as a rookie were the stories about cops "eating their guns." Mostly big-city cops, but occasionally a country cop would stick the barrel in his mouth and pull the trigger. Hallock shut his eyes. The image was terrible. No matter how bad things got he couldn't imagine doing that. He returned the gun to its holster.

Lifting his butt, he pulled his Sam Browne around his waist and buckled it in front. Technically he wasn't supposed to wear the gun any longer, but he didn't want his mother to know what had happened. More than likely she wouldn't even notice, but sometimes she was surprisingly lucid. He picked up his cap, set it on his head, checked his rearview and caught a good look at his face. Christ almighty, he thought, who the hell is that? Quickly he got out of the car.

As always when he first entered the nursing home, his sense of smell was assaulted, but by the time he left he had become used to it. As nursing homes went this one was pretty good, he was told. Still, there was no way to avoid the institutional feeling of the place, light green walls, tile floors, the hollow sound as you walked to your destination.

"Hi, Chief," June Lynch, the head nurse, called.

He hadn't the heart to tell her he was no longer the chief. "Hey there, June. How you doing?"

From under her cap yellow curls, like dandelions, framed her face. "Okay. You?"

What was she going to think when she heard? That he was a damn liar, that's what. "Doing fine. How's my mom?"

June came out from behind the desk, stuck a skinny arm through his and walked down the hall with him. "Well, Chief, she's in and out today, know what I mean?"

"Uh-huh."

"But she's been a good girl. Ate all her lunch."

"That's good."

Marion Hallock was tied in her wheel chair, staring straight ahead.

June shouted, "Look who's here, Mrs. Hallock!"

Hallock knew his mother wasn't deaf, guessed June was just in the habit of shouting at her patients.

"Your best beau," June added.

The left side of Marion's face drooped. When she spoke she looked like she was sneering. "Not my beau," she said with contempt, "he's my son. My beau's dead."

June knew Marion's husband was very much alive. "Isn't she something?" she said to Hallock, trying to make a joke out of it. "She's our Peck's bad girl sometimes."

Marion looked disgusted and turned away.

"Well, have a nice visit. See you later."

Hallock kissed his mother on the forehead. She looked up at him, pale blue eyes like bleached denim. "Woman's a horse's ass."

Hallock smiled. "Ah, Mom, she's just trying to be friendly."

"What for? Got all the friends I need. Saying you're my beau. Stupid. My beau's dead."

"Why are you saying that, Mom? Dad's not dead." He sat on the edge of the bed.

"Oh, him," she said contemptuously.

"Who else?"

The right side of her face smiled. "Never mind. Just forget it."

Hallock remembered some garbled story about his mother and Ben Davis, the Chrysler dealer in Bayview, about forty years ago. He couldn't recall the details now, the whole thing had been hazy then. "You talking about Ben Davis, Mom?" He took her good hand in his.

"He's dead," she said, not looking at him. "Died in that fire."

"What fire?"

"That damn club."

"Oh, yeah." Hallock remembered that most people had gotten out but ten or twelve had died. He'd forgotten Ben Davis was one of them. Who else? It was twenty, twenty-five years ago, he couldn't remember. "Was Ben Davis your beau?"

Marion Hallock touched a wisp of white hair that had fallen loose from her bun, then tucked it back in place. "Don't go playing chief of police with me, Waldo. I don't go for it."

"I'll never do it again," he said. "I promise." And he never would, not with her, not with anyone. Suddenly the reality of his dismissal was shattering. He wished he were small enough to sit in his mother's lap, have her stroke his hair, kiss his cheeks, tell him not to worry, it would all work out.

Marion broke through his thoughts. "Who *are* you?" she asked, pulling her hand from his. "Just who the hell *are* you?"

"Mom," he whispered.

"I'm going to ring for the nurse if you don't get yourself out of here. Policeman or no policeman."

"No policeman," he said.

"What's that?"

He bent to kiss her. She pulled back.

"Get," she commanded.

"So long, Mom. See you tomorrow."

"Don't come back here, I'll get the *real* police."

Hallock said, "Yeah, you do that." He hurried down the hall, ducked past the front desk and got outside before anyone could see the tears streaking his face.

Colin stared at the hill of fried rice on his plate, the moo shu pork, its pancake slowly unwrapping. He'd been stunned by Babe's parting shot, and dutifully followed her to the Peking Palace.

"You're not eating," Babe said.

"I told you I wasn't hungry. What do you want, Babe?" He pushed the plate to one side, lit a cigarette.

"Are you going to smoke while I eat?"

"Yes."

"That's rude, Colin."

"Tough. What do you want?" She'd been playing a game, refusing to talk until the food came. Now it was here, and she still wasn't talking. "Either you tell me what you have up your sleeve or I'm leaving."

"I don't think so," she said, a piece of rice stuck on her lower lip.

She was right, of course, she had him by the short hairs. Colin stared at the grain of rice clinging to her mouth. "I came to this goddamn place with you, so what are you waiting for? Tell me what you want, for Christ's sake."

She picked up her roll of moo shu pork. Colin grabbed her wrist, squeezed. "You're hurting me," she said.

"That's the idea." He tightened his grip and her hand opened, the filling dropping from the unfurled pancake.

"Stop it," she hissed, looking frantically around the room, fearful they'd be seen.

"Then tell me what you want."

"All right, let go."

He did. The pancake clung to her palm for a moment, then dropped with a splat onto the plate.

"You're a bastard," she said, rubbing her wrist. "You could have broken it."

"I'm waiting," he stated.

"It's simple. I know about your wife and children."

"Know what?"

"I know they were murdered."

"So?"

"I know you were a suspect."

"So?"

"I know they never found the killer."

"So?"

"It's an unsolved case."

"I'm not getting your drift, Babe."

"No? That's funny, I thought you were kind of bright. I guess you can't ever tell by appearances, can you?" She sat back in her chair, continuing to rub her wrist.

"You're not telling me anything I don't know."

"Well, how about this then: Other people in this town who don't know about it might find it very interesting, like your boss maybe?"

Colin smiled, blew a plume of smoke toward the ceiling. "He already knows."

Her face fell like a bad soufflé. "I don't believe it."

"Ask him."

She leaned toward him, her hands clutching the edge of the table. "Do the police know, too?"

"No, the police don't know. I take it you mean Schufeldt."

"Any police."

"So what's your point, Babe? Are you blackmailing me?"

She laughed like the sound of squealing tires. "Oh, I love it. I just love it. Blackmail!" she snorted.

"What then?"

She lit a cigarette, let the smoke curl out from her mouth and drift upwards while she looked at Colin from under heavy lids. And then she began to blink, eyes watering.

Colin laughed. "You don't make a good Mata Hari, Babe."

"Fuck you," she said.

"Oh, is *that* what this is about?"

She dropped the cigarette in the metal ashtray and wiped her eyes with her napkin. A trail of mascara streaked one cheek. "What this is all about," she snarled, "is that for the first time in its history, the North Fork has had a rash of unexplained killings and among its citizens is a man who, in his past, was involved in three murders. Coincidence? Maybe."

Rage worked its way up from Colin's gut to his chest. "Are you implying that I not only killed my family but I've killed the four people here as well?"

She picked up the chopsticks, caught some moo shu pork between them, popped it into her mouth, and began to chew, a slight smile playing around her lips.

"Babe, answer my question," he demanded.

"Let's put it this way, Colin: it makes a damn good story."

He was grateful that they were in a public place. He'd never felt this kind of rage before. The anger he'd experienced over his family being murdered was different. That was laced with abandonment, helplessness, the fury free-floating. But this anger was clear and pointed. "I'm going to pretend you didn't say that, Babe."

"Really? Why?"

Colin breathed deeply, trying to ward off the beginning of a panic attack. "A good story for whom?" he asked softly.

"Well, I was thinking about the *Seaville Gazette,* but since Mark knows who he's got working for him I guess that's out. But I'd bet *Newsline* wouldn't be above using it."

Under the table he could feel his legs shaking. "So why have you told me, if that's what you plan to do?"

"I thought maybe we could make a deal?"

"Like what?"

"I want your job, Colin. And I deserve your job. I've worked for Mark since the beginning. We had a tacit agreement that I'd be the next managing editor, at least I thought we had. Then you got the job. It wasn't fair."

"What is?" he interjected.

"So how about it?"

Colin's breathing was accelerating; he was beginning to feel lightheaded. "How about what?"

"Your job. Aren't you listening?"

"You expect me to hand over my job to you? Don't be stupid. Even if I were to leave, what makes you think Mark would give my job to you?"

"He would. He'd have to."

Colin laughed. "You have stuff on Mark, too?"

Her eyes were cold. "The reason Mark gave you my job was because he was an old friend, and you were having some kind of breakdown in New Jersey. He thought a job on a country paper might help you. That wasn't hard to find out. But if you left there's no doubt the job would be mine."

The shakes were beginning to crawl up his body into his arms. He had to get out of there. "And if I don't leave?"

She shrugged. "I guess I'll have to give out the story."

Colin pushed back his chair, got unsteadily to his feet. "You know what you are, Babe?"

"Before you tell me, let me say one more thing. I don't think Annie Winters would really like going out with a murder suspect, do you?"

He wanted to throttle her, instead he clutched the back of the chair.

"Steady there, big guy."

There was no use trying to hang on so he could tell her what a shit she was. He forced himself to walk through the restaurant and out. When he got to his car he grabbed the handle, wrenched open the door, and fell inside.

Leaning back, head against the seat, he tried to regulate his breathing. But the roof began to crumble and crack, the doors closing in on him. He shut his eyes. Immediately Nancy's cut and bleeding face swam round in the blackness, the sounds of his children calling for help surrounding him. He opened his eyes. Black and yellow spots danced in his line of vision. Dizziness overcame him and he gripped the wheel for support, his knuckles growing white.

A knock made him jump. He turned to see Babe bent down, her face separated from his by the window. "I'm not fooling around," she said. "If you don't quit I'm giving this story to *Newsline*. You have until noon tomorrow." She left.

Slowly Colin's breathing became regular, the car interior returning to its original shape. He felt exhausted. He had no doubts that Babe would carry out her threat and that once the story appeared he'd have to leave Seaville. Despite the murders he'd grown fond of the town and wanted to stay. Most of all he wanted to get to know Annie better. If ever he needed Mark to be there for him, he needed him now, he thought. And then he wondered why that made him uneasy.

LOOKING BACK — 75 YEARS AGO

Elisha Congdon of Seaville, who claims to have great power from the Almighty, is in the public eye again. He returned recently from Atlanta, Ga., where he went to the federal authorities in a vain attempt to secure the release of Mr. M. Silver, who is in the federal prison there, serving a term for his religious acts. Elisha says Mr. Silver is all right except for a dent in his forehead.

Chapter Twenty-Four

Fran said, "What're you doing, Waldo?" She was watching him throw socks and underwear into his beat-up old suitcase.

"I'm packing," he answered. He was wearing a green polo shirt she'd given him for his birthday, worn jeans, and high-topped Keds. His gun was on the bed next to the suitcase.

"Packing for what?"

"I'm leaving." He opened a drawer and pulled out some shirts.

"I went down to the station looking for you when you didn't come home. I wanted to be with you. I was driving around looking for you, hon'."

He slapped the shirts into the case. "We've had it, Fran."

"Meaning?" She put a hand on the suitcase lid.

Hallock glanced at her hand, went back to the bureau, grabbed a bunch of T-shirts. "It means just what it says." He wouldn't look at her.

"I don't understand. Explain."

"Ha!"

"Ha?"

"Yeah, ha! *I* should explain? That's a good one."

She slammed the suitcase shut and sat on it. "Waldo, what the hell is this? Are you leaving because of what happened today at the meeting?"

"Now you're getting smart. Get off the goddamn suitcase."

For the first time he looked at her, the grooves under his slanting, sad eyes deeper.

"Oh, Waldo, that didn't have anything to do with me."

He crossed his arms over his chest. "Then what the hell were you doing there with those gals, right in the row with Julia Dorman and the rest?"

"I came to support you, Waldo."

"Funny way of showing it."

"I had no idea Julia was going to do what she did."

"I've put up with your being on this committee and that, marching here, there, everywhere, embarrassing the bejesus out of me, but this time you've gone too far. Get off the goddamn suitcase, Fran."

"Waldo, you're not listening."

"I hear you. Get off."

"No, I won't get off, not until you listen."

Hallock suddenly had a sense of déjà vu, then remembered that fight years before when he'd threatened to leave. But this time he was serious. "What do I have to listen to, huh? More bullshit?"

"It's not bullshit. I came down to the meeting to support you, Waldo. Naturally I sat with my friends. Nobody said anything to me about speaking against you because nobody knew. Julia did that on her own, and you can bet we've had it with her."

"It's too late, Fran."

"That's just dumb." She reached out to touch his cheek and he pushed her hand away, hard. She was knocked off balance and slipped from the suitcase to the bed, then onto the floor, cracking her head against the wood.

Hallock was beside her in a second. "You okay?"

"I think so," she answered, sitting up, rubbing the side of her head.

"Jesus, Fran, I didn't mean to —"

"I know. Don't worry about it."

He helped her up. They stood close to one another.

She put her arms around his neck. "Waldo, you've been hurt bad, and you've got to take it out on somebody. Don't make me the enemy."

"Can't help it, Fran." He pulled her arms from around his neck and went back to his packing.

"Didn't you hear anything I said?"

"I heard. Doesn't much matter what you meant, it's what happened, what everybody saw."

"Since when do you care what people think?"

"I always cared about your damn causes. You don't know the crap I took about it." He removed some shirt stays and cufflinks from a hand-carved box that had been his grandfather's.

"I felt I was doing some worthwhile things, not just being a housewife and mother."

"What do you mean, *just* a housewife and mother? That's a lot."

"Sure it is. I don't mean it that way. Oh, hell, Waldo, I don't know how to explain it. But if people were giving you a hard time about it, you should've said something. It's no good keeping stuff like that inside. It has to come out, explode. Like now."

"You knew, Fran. How about that time you got thrown in the clink for picketing the nuclear plant?"

"Are you going to go into ancient history? I told you then I'd never do anything to embarrass you again and I haven't."

"Until today."

"You're not listening."

He closed the suitcase, snapped shut the catches, lifted the case from the bed. "I have to go."

"Where?"

"I dunno. Motel, I guess."

"What should I tell the kids?"

"Whatever you want."

"How long will you be gone?" She sounded frightened.

"Long as it takes."

"Long as *what* takes?"

"I don't know." He started through the door, turned around. "Make sure you lock up at night. And don't go anyplace by yourself — anyplace you're not familiar with, especially at night. Don't let the girls go off by themselves either. That sucker's still out there and nobody knows who's next. Least of all Special Agent Schufeldt." A flicker of a smile crossed his lips.

Fran said, "Don't you do anything dangerous either, okay?"

"I won't."

"Will you call me?"

"I don't know. I need some time, is all."

She nodded. "I love you, Waldo."

His eyes met hers and for a moment she thought he might stay, take her in his arms. But then he was gone.

Colin had asked Annie to meet him at seven-thirty at the Anchor Inn on the water. He'd blamed his failure to pick her up on having to work late, and she accepted what he said without question. As he drove to the restaurant he reviewed his two conversations with Mark. One on Friday, the other only a few minutes ago. Friday's conversation had been unsettling at best.

"She probably has her period or something," Mark said about Babe.

"Come on, Mark, that's absurd. Are you living in the Dark Ages?"

He shrugged. "Sarah always gets weird around her period."

"Believe me, Babe's behavior has nothing to do with anything but her goddamn twisted ambition."

"Don't you think you're being a little hard on her?"

Colin was stunned. "No. No, I don't. Are you sure you understood what I told you? She wants my job or else she's going to give the story about me to *Newsline*."

"I heard you, okay? I just don't think she'll do it. She knows I'd fire her if she did."

"Would you?"

"Of course." He looked surprised that Colin would think anything else.

"Even so I'd rather not wait and see what she does, Mark. I wish you'd tell her that now."

"Why borrow trouble, pal?"

Colin was losing his patience. "I'm not borrowing trouble.

I'm telling you what the woman is going to do, and I believe she will unless you talk to her."

"Okay. I'll talk to her.".

"When?"

"When I see her."

"When will that be?"

"She'll be in on Monday."

"Christ, Mark, she's given me until tomorrow. What the hell is wrong with you?"

"I'm sorry, I've got things on my mind."

"Don't we all."

He laid his hand on Colin's shoulder. "No, listen, I really do. Amy's —"

"Mark, this is important. Babe is going to blow my cover. I'll have to leave Seaville if this thing gets into the papers."

"You don't think this thing with Amy is important? My marriage, my whole life might go down the tubes, pal, and you don't think it's important? Fuck that." He put his head in his hands.

"Mark," he said softly, trying to pacify him. "I'm sorry. I know this thing with Amy is important, but there's not much you can do about it right now, is there?"

No answer.

"So what I'm asking you to do is to concentrate on my problem for a few minutes and —"

"Mike Rosler called you. What's up?"

"What?"

"Rosler returned your fucking call."

"I didn't see a slip about it."

"I didn't write a slip. I'm telling you instead. I got the call by accident. How come you called *him*?" His bottom lip protruded like a sulky baby's.

"I had an idea I wanted to check with him."

Suspicion clouded Mark's eyes. "What idea?"

"It's not important."

"Important enough to call a bigshot *New York Times* reporter."

Colin quickly weighed the pros and cons of telling Mark,

decided if he wanted him to take action on the Babe thing it would be smarter to let him in on his idea. "I thought Mike could tell me something about cult markings, symbols, stuff like that. I had an idea there might be some connection with the A's the killer was cutting on his victims."

"What's Rosler know about that?"

"Maybe nothing. I just thought I'd give it a shot. Mark, are you going to talk to Babe or not?"

"Yeah, sure. I'll call her."

"When?"

He looked at his watch. "She's doing a story in Riverhead now. I'll catch her later. Okay?"

He'd agreed but it hadn't felt okay at all. Then, today, Mark had been impossible to find. He'd finally reached him ten minutes before he'd left to meet Annie.

"Did you speak to Babe?" he'd asked.

"Yeah. She quit."

"What?"

"She quit the fucking paper, Colin. Now who the hell am I going to get to do the soft stuff?"

Colin wanted to ram his fist through the phone. He'd never realized how self-involved Mark was. "What about the story she was going to write?"

"She wouldn't talk about it, just said she was quitting."

And that was it. Nobody had to tell Colin that Babe was going to carry through on her threat. She probably had a job at *Newsline* already. He didn't know what to do. Should he tell Annie the truth? Get out of town before the story broke? Run like he was guilty? But there was always the chance that Babe wouldn't give the story to *Newsline*. Slim but possible.

Colin pulled into the parking lot of the Anchor Inn. Annie had said the place was very popular, the food better than most restaurants on the Fork. But by the few cars in the lot he wondered if it were really true. Annie's car was already there.

The sun, like a red beach ball, was slowly slipping below the horizon. Colin stopped for a moment and breathed in the salt air coming off the Sound. In the distance he spotted two sailboats moving across the water toward shore. Despite the murders, there was a certain sense of peace here he'd never felt elsewhere. He would hate to have to leave this place. Crossing the lot he tried to shake his gloomy mood.

The Anchor Inn had a predictably nautical theme — life preservers on the walls, surrounded by fishnets; ship's wheels for chandeliers; varnished hatch-cover tables.

She was sitting by a window, her profile to him, looking at the Sound. He thought she was lovely. Her blond hair shimmered in the last light of the day. She was wearing a red cotton dress, scooped at the neck, with three-quarter sleeves.

As he started toward her she turned, signaled him with a wave of her hand, her face breaking into a gorgeous smile. He felt giddy.

"Am I late?" He knew he wasn't.

"I was early."

He thought her blue eyes were the color of cornflowers he'd seen as a boy. Or was it a sky somewhere? "Would you like a drink?"

"I've ordered one. Isn't it a beautiful sunset?" she asked.

"Do you always arrange for them to be like this?"

She smiled. "I try."

The waitress brought her a daiquiri. He ordered a whiskey sour.

"We've practically got this place to ourselves," Colin remarked, looking around.

Only a handful of tables were occupied. "It's still early in the season," she concluded.

"Maybe. How was your day?" It had been three years since he'd asked a woman he cared about that question.

"Lousy, how was yours?"

"The same. Why was yours lousy?"

"It started off with —" Annie looked up at the man standing next to their table. "Hello, Otto."

"Annie," he said, nodding in her direction.

Otto Lein was a huge, overweight man. His thinning brown hair was cut short. A pair of tortoiseshell glasses sat low on the bridge of a bulbous nose festooned with broken veins.

Annie introduced the two men.

Otto said, "I know who he is. That's why I come over. Not that I wouldn't say hello to you, Annie, but hellos aren't what I got on my mind right now. What I got on my mind right now is my place." He swept his arm in a large arc, taking in a good portion of the room. What d'you think?" he asked, looking at Colin.

"Think?"

"Yeah, think. About my place."

"I think it's very nice." he answered.

"'Very nice'," Lein repeated sarcastically. "He thinks it's very nice."

"What is it, Otto? What's the trouble?" Annie asked warily.

"You ever seen this place like this? Empty like this? Don't bother to answer. I know you haven't, because *I* never seen it like this. Twenty-three years I been in business. Best food on the Fork, bar none. June's not my best month but it's good, better than May or April. I should be doing a hundred dinners on a Saturday night in June. You know how many I'm doing? I'm doing thirteen. You know how many I did last night, a Friday in June? Nine. It don't matter how many dinners I do or don't do, I got to pay the help anyways. And the food goes begging. Can't keep a lot of it. I lose there, too. So it's costing me, and you want to know why? Because this fuckface, pardon my French, Annie, is writing stories and scaring the pants off everybody from here to New York City."

"It's his job, Otto. He —"

"Bad enough he's keeping the tourists out of here," he went on, ignoring her, "he's keeping the regulars, the natives hiding under their beds. Everybody's afraid to go out, leave their houses, go to dinner, a movie, buy a goddamn washer in the hardware store. Everybody's hurting, not just me. All the stores, all the restaurants, everybody. Because this shithead, along with some other shitheads on that crummy paper, likes to write gory stories. So you know what? I don't need to do two more dinners, making a big total of fifteen, if you get my meaning?"

They looked at him, not completely sure they did.

Colin said, "I'm sorry your business is off but —"

"I got to spell it out? Okay. I don't want you in here, Mister Reporter. Far as I'm concerned, you're the reason for a Saturday night in June being a bust."

"Otto," Annie said, "don't you think that's a little ridiculous? You're acting like Colin killed those people, rather than just writing about it."

Colin flashed on Otto reading Babe's story and he felt sick. "It's okay, Annie, let's go." He reached for his wallet.

"Don't bother," Lein said, "I don't want your money. Just get the hell out of my restaurant."

Annie picked up her handbag. "I'm shocked at you, Otto."

"Yeah, well let me tell you something else. You're not going to do yourself no good being seen around with this guy. I like you, Annie, I'd hate to see anything happen."

"Anything happen?" Colin asked sharply. "Is that a threat?"

"Listen, pencil pusher, just scram, okay?" He made fists out of his hands and brought them slowly up in front of his waist.

Annie moved between the two men, put her arm through Colin's and started walking.

Outside Annie said, "Williams' Market's still open. Let's get some steaks and cook them at home. I have some baking potatoes, a new Boston lettuce, and I make a mean cup of coffee. Oh, Colin, I'm so sorry. Are you okay?"

"I'm fine," he lied. He felt like hell, thought maybe he should just bag the whole evening, but didn't really want to. "You sure you want to do this?"

"Why not? I'll meet you at the market, okay?"

"Okay."

"Good." She squeezed his arm then walked away.

The sun was gone. He could barely see the shoreline from his car, but he could hear the water breaking against the sand. Only twenty-five minutes had elapsed since he'd pulled into this parking lot. In that short space of time, everything had changed.

He was sure Otto Lein wasn't the only one who blamed him for their business failures. They didn't have Hallock any more, and they didn't know who the killer was. So now he was the target and by Monday morning, when Babe's story hit the stands, he'd be a walking bull's-eye.

LOOKING BACK — 25 YEARS AGO

Tom Blackwell, son of Mr. and Mrs. Henry Blackwell of Seaville, was awarded one of the prizes for scholastic excellence at the special Honors Convocation at Mount St. Mary's College, Emmitsburg, Md., on June 1st. Blackwell, who was graduated cum laude, and received his diploma from President Dwight D. Eisenhower, received the Edward T. Hogan Memorial Prize for the highest average through the pre-legal course.

Chapter Twenty-Five

"Let's have coffee in the living room," Annie said.

Colin blew out the candle nearest him and picked up his cup and saucer.

At first, dinner had been a little strained, each of them trying to shake the unpleasant encounter with Otto Lein. Eventually that passed, a new mood preempting the old, the candlelit dinner encouraging flirtation. There were long silences where they looked into each other's eyes — moments when, passing the salt or butter, their hands touched, lingered longer than necessary.

Colin hadn't desired a woman in this way since Nancy. But he was unsure of himself and thought he might be reading signals where there were none. He recalled his brother saying: "Listen, Col', if you're fantasizing about some girl, dreaming about her, wondering what she's thinking or doing, chances are damn good she's doing the same thing about you." And it proved to be true nine times out of ten. But that was a long time ago. He couldn't expect to count on that rule of thumb now. And what if Annie was the one out of ten?

Testing, he sat on the couch to see what Annie would do. She hesitated, put her coffee on the table, then sat a pillow away from him. Old Brian might have had something after all. And then he thought of Babe, the story. He should tell Annie about Nancy and the kids before she read it in the paper. Instead he said, "Good coffee."

"Thanks."

He pulled his notebook from his jacket pocket. "I wanted to show you something. Do you know what this is?" he asked, handing her the pad.

"It's a swastika. No. Wait a minute. It's not. A swastika goes the other way."

"Show me." Colin gave her a pen.

Annie said, "Like this:"

Below that was Colin's:

"So what's this one?" he asked, pointing to his own.

"Is this like the one the killer carved on poor Joe Carroll?"

"Yes."

"It's definitely not a swastika," she said evenly.

"What do you think it is then?"

"I'm not sure. I think I've seen it before, though. Let's look it up."

"Where?"

"In the dictionary. It's in my office upstairs. I'll bring it down."

Colin couldn't believe it. The dictionary! Why hadn't he thought of that? Why hadn't Mike Rosler? He'd finally made contact with Mike that afternoon. He was as stymied as Colin, but said he'd keep after it, see what he could find.

Annie came back carrying a large Random House dictionary. She opened it on her lap, riffled the pages. "See, here it is." She moved closer to him, their bodies touching, the dictionary half on her lap, half on his.

Colin struggled to ignore the warmth of her thigh against his and concentrated on the page in front of him. There were the two symbols side by side:

A. B.

He read the definition next to them: "1. a figure used as a symbol or an ornament in the Old World and in America since prehistoric times, consisting of a cross with arms of equal length, each arm having a continuation at right angles, and all our continuations extending either clockwise or counterclockwise . . . . 2. this figure with clockwise arms as the official emblem of the Nazi party and the Third Reich. Also a good luck sign." He read the caption below the two symbols. "Swastikas. A., Oriental and American Indian; B, Nazi."

"What do you think, Colin?"

"I don't know. It brings up a lot of possiblities, doesn't it?"

"Yes, I guess it does. There were plenty of Indians here at one time, you know."

"Or it could be that someone doesn't know how to make a swastika. I'll bet if you asked ten people to make swastikas at least half would draw them he way the killer did."

"You're probably right."

"Have you ever heard anything about a Nazi party here?"

"No."

"And the only Orientals I've seen own the restaurant."

"Believe me, it couldn't be any of Koi Chang's family. I know them pretty well."

"I can't back this up, but I have a feeling the one made was the one meant. I wish I could find out more about this symbol." He lifted the dictionary from their laps, placed it on the floor, and turned back to her. They were still touching; neither moved away.

"Betty Mills would problably have some information."

"The librarian," he confirmed.

She nodded.

"Could we see her?"

"The library's not open at ten-thirty on Saturday night."

"Monday, then. What time does it open?"

"Ten, I think."

"Ten," he repeated vaguely, his eyes searching hers. They were very blue, the pupils dark, the color of black olives. She'd drawn an outline around the edges, given a soft blue cast to her lids. There was a delicacy to her mouth, and he wanted to taste her lips, gently bite the lower one. He leaned toward her, she toward him. Their mouths met. He slipped an arm around her, pulled her closer. She responded, her hand behind his neck. He could feel her breasts pressing against his chest, knew just how he would touch them. When they parted he said, "I want you, Annie."

"Colin," she whispered, closed her eyes, almost imperceptibly shook her head.

But he saw it. "What?"

She opened her eyes, taking him in. "It's been so long. I'm frightened."

"Me, too." He kissed each eye. "I haven't felt like this since . . . since my wife."

"I know. I feel the same. But . . ."

"You feel guilty?"

"As if I'm cheating on Bob. I know it's foolish, but I can't help it."

"I understand."

"You're the first man I've kissed, Colin, since him." She touched his cheek with her fingertips. "It seems strange."

"I know."

"Do you feel that? Do you feel I'm strange?" she asked.

"Yes and no. You're not Nancy and that's strange. But you're Annie and I like that."

She smiled, leaned toward him. Carefully, he took her lower lip between his teeth, slid into a kiss.

Then he said, "Annie, I want to stay the night with you," his lips to her ear.

"Oh, Colin, no," she said.

"Why not?" Here come de minister, he thought.

She moved away, picked up her cup, sipped.

"Is it your religion?" he asked.

She laughed sweetly, touched his hand. "You think Unitarian Universalists don't make love?"

"I thought maybe ministers didn't, if they weren't married."

"Some do, some don't."

"And you?"

She evaded the question. "I couldn't let you spend the night, Colin. It would offend too many people."

"Who has to know?"

"Everyone would know."

"You mean my car? I'll park it somewhere else."

"No, that wouldn't work."

"Why not?"

"You'd be seen. Trust me, the people around here know everything that goes on."

"No one's spotted a killer, so what makes you think anybody's going to know I spent the night with you?"

"I can't take the chance."

"That doesn't leave us much, does it?"

"What do you mean?"

He lit a cigarette. "We're not kids, Annie."

"If we were, you'd be spending the night."

He laughed, took her hand in his, and kissed her palm.

She trembled.

"Let me ask you this. If you weren't a minister with a nosy congregation, would you let me stay?"

Hours seemed to pass before she answered but it was only seconds. "Yes," she whispered.

He put his cigarette in the ashtray, drew her toward him, traced her lips with his finger. "We could make love now and I could leave afterwards, but I don't want you that way, Annie. If we make love, we spend the night together or else we don't make love at all."

"Thank you for that." She put her arms around his neck and kissed him, long and sweet.

He couldn't take it any longer, gently disengaged himself. "I think I'd better go."

At the door he said, "Where do we go from here?"

"I don't know."

"I guess we play it by ear."

"I guess."

They kissed again, their bodies pressed hard against one another. He wanted to beg her to change her mind, but knew she wouldn't, couldn't.

"I've got to go," he said. Then he made a last-ditch effort. "How about you coming to my house?"

She smiled. "Same problem."

"I thought you'd say that." He took her face between both hands, tenderly kissed her eyes, her mouth. "We'll talk tomorrow?"

"Yes," she said.

Sitting in his car, he reflected on the past half hour. Annie was wonderful. She made him feel alive again. God, he'd wanted her. He wondered how they'd ever get together, make love. "Play it by ear," he'd said. But one thing bothered him. He hadn't told her the truth about Nancy and the kids. If there was ever to be anything meaningful between them, he'd have to tell her. Tomorrow.

He started the motor, put the Mercury into gear. And when he drove away, recalling their kisses, he failed to notice the man in the car, slouched down behind the wheel, parked across the street from Annie's house.

When Colin pulled into his driveway he saw a car in front of his house but didn't recognize it. The door opened on the driver's side and a man got out.

"Hey there, Maguire," Hallock called, coming toward him.

"Waldo. I didn't know it was you. New car?"

He ambled up the path. "Rental."

Colin wondered why he couldn't use his own car but didn't ask.

"Some beautiful night." Hallock faced the water and the tiny sparkling lights on Shelter Island.

Colin said, "Full moon."

The men looked at each other, a frisson of fear passing over each face, then laughed at their superstition.

Hallock inhaled a mouthful of air. "Ah, boy, that's good. No goddamn pollution here. Smell that air, Maguire? That's Seaville air, smelled it all my life. Can't imagine smelling any other air."

"Any reason why you'll have to?"

"Every reason." He put a hand on Colin's shoulder. "Can we go in?"

They walked up the steps. Colin opened the screen door to the porch and got out his keys.

Hallock said, "Used to be a time when nobody had to lock their doors. Gone forever."

Inside Colin snapped on a light.

"Haven't been in this house for more than thirty years. My first girlfriend lived here, Roberta Staten, Bobbie I called her. Had blond curls like ringlets all over her head. Real pretty blue eyes, the kind that make you stop and stare, know what I mean?"

Colin nodded. "What happened to her?"

"Moved away, married some pilot for one of the big airlines. Place looks different. Didn't have all this nice wallpaper then."

They walked through the living room into the large kitchen. Colin pulled the cord on the large wicker hanging lamp over the round oak table.

"Christ almighty," Hallock said, looking around. "I never saw a red kitchen before."

"Me either. You have to get used to it. Want a drink?"

"I'll take a beer." He put a stack of folders on the table.

Colin hadn't noticed them before. He handed Hallock a cold beer. "Want a glass?"

"Nope. You're not having any?"

"I had some wine earlier." He popped the tab on his can of Tab. "What's up? I have the feeling this isn't just a social call."

"You're right." Hallock sat at the table and pushed the folders to one side.

Colin joined him.

"You been with Annie Winters tonight?" He smiled knowingly and sucked on his beer.

"Have you got me under surveillance?"

"Just a lucky guess. Nice lady. I like her."

"She likes you, too." He lit a cigarette

"Thing is, I got thinking about what she said to me yesterday after the meeting. You know, about doing some investigating on my own. I mean, maybe the people have turned their backs on me, but I can't turn my back on them. It's still my town."

"Do you have something?" Colin asked, nodding toward the folders.

"Don't know. I thought maybe we could work on this together. That is, if you don't mind teaming up with the *ex*-chief of police."

"Come on."

"Well, it's a fact. Can't deny it. That's who I am. Ex-chief of police. Ex-chief of police separated from his wife."

"You're kidding."

"Fact."

"Why?" Colin was astonished. Everyone knew Fran and Waldo Hallock were crazy about each other. "It's not something to do with that Dorman woman, is it?"

"Fran was with her, Maguire. Sitting right there in the same row, listening to that gal cut me up one side, down the other. Claims she had no idea Julia was going to say that stuff."

"I don't think she did. I saw Fran's face when Dorman started talking against you. She was shocked."

"Maybe so, but she didn't do beans about it."

"What could she have done?"

"She could've got up and walked out. Or better yet, come sat with me. She did nothing. I bumped into Gildersleeve about an hour later, know what he said to me? Said, 'Well, Slats, guess you've really been pussy-whipped this time.' Nice, huh?"

"Yeah. Nice."

"And he didn't mean Julia Dorman either. Meant Fran. Ah, ell, Maguire, that's water under the bridge." He pulled the olders toward him.

Colin wondered whether to push the man to talk more about he situation with Fran. He suspected he'd said all he could. Where you staying?"

"Wood's Motel. Can't tell you how happy they were to get ne. Place is almost empty. Liz Wood, the gal who owns the oint, said business's been off by two-thirds since these murders tarted. You heard them yesterday, Maguire. Everybody's urting around here. We just got to get this bastard."

Colin made a quick decision. "I want to help, Waldo, but I ave to tell you something first."

"Shoot."

"I want to tell you about my wife and children."

"Didn't know you had a wife and kids."

"I don't. They're dead. I want to tell you how they died."

It took about twenty minutes. Sweat ran down Colin's body, is voice shook, and his hands trembled. But he did it, and was lad.

"Shit, Maguire, losing your wife and kids. I don't know what 'd do if that happened to me." He took a swig of beer.

"There's something else," Colin went on. "Babe Parkinson ound out and it looks like she's given the story to *Newsline*. When that breaks I'm going to be just as much persona non rata around here as you are. So maybe I'm not the guy you vant to team up with."

"You kidding me or what? You think what you told me nakes a difference? Hell, Maguire, what kind of schlemiel do ou think I am?"

Colin shrugged, stubbed out his cigarette. "I just thought I hould give you the out."

"Don't want it. I need a partner, somebody to bounce ideas ff, get some input, too. Charlie Copin and me used to do it hat way, but I can't jeopardize Charlie's career, ask him to penly work with me. He's got to work with Wonder Boy now. But Charlie's a good guy, he'll do what he can on the QT. He got me these," he said, pointing to the folders. "Xeroxed the originals. And he'll keep me informed much as he can."

"What are they?"

"The dossiers on the victims. I figure we've been going at this thing all wrong, Maguire. Looking for the killer before we know everything about the victims. I think the answer to who this bozo is is right here." He tapped the top folder with a long thin finger. "These people weren't picked at random. The bastard has some kind of plan. The marks, the choice of victim, the place he kills 'em, all of it. There's a design, like a blueprint, know what I mean?"

Colin told him what he'd learned about the latest symbol and said he was going to research it further.

"See," Hallock said, "that's just what I mean. The fucker's practically telling us who he is, only we aren't picking it up."

"Do you think he wants to be caught?"

"Don't they all? These kind of killers?"

"I'm not sure. I don't think Ted Bundy, Albert DeSalvo, or Albert Fish wanted to be caught."

"Who's Albert Fish?"

"He killed a lot of kids, then ate them."

"Jesus Christ almighty." He polished off the beer. "Did they leave a lot of clues around, those guys?"

"Not really. Nothing like A's or swastikas or whatever that thing is."

"I think it's good you checking that stuff out at the library, so don't get me wrong when I say this. But my instincts tell me we got to figure out what the victims got in common, then we can think like the killer. I'm going to leave these with you, Maguire. I been over them, made my notes. I want you to do the same, we'll compare tomorrow, okay?"

"Okay, but what am I looking for?"

"Similarities. Anything you can find about these people they got in common. Don't worry about it being stupid. I mean, like maybe they all have an F in their names, which they don't, or none of them have an F in their names, which is true. What I'm saying, Maguire, is that nothing is too small or too stupid to consider."

"I've got you."

Hallock pushed back his chair. "What time you get up in the morning?"

"Pretty early." He'd thought about going to Annie's church, but his priority was to look over this material. He was too tired to do it tonight.

"I'll come by around ten, see what you got."

"Okay." He walked Hallock to the door. "You know, Chief, you could stay with me if you want to. I've got three bedrooms."

"Thanks, Maguire, but I wouldn't want to crimp your style or anything."

"What style's that?"

"Oh, I don't know." He smiled and nervously pulled on his long nose. "Anyway, I need to be alone. Got to think through some stuff, figure out what I'm gonna do with the rest of my life. Besides, Liz Wood needs my business. Least I can do."

They shook hands. Colin snapped on the porch light. Halfway to his car Hallock said, "Hey, Maguire, when are you gonna get rid of that mustache?"

He was surprised. "You don't like it?"

"Puts me in mind of the outlaws in the Westerns I saw as a boy."

Colin laughed. "I'll think about it." He waited until Hallock was in his car before he turned off the light.

Back in the kitchen he checked the time. Twelve-twenty. He wanted to call Annie and say goodnight again. Lifting the receiver from the wall phone, he hestitated. Maybe she was asleep and wouldn't appreciate being awakened at this hour. On the other hand, she might like it, be glad to know that he was thinking of her. He started to dial, then replaced the phone. She had to preach the next day, it wasn't fair to wake her. He couldn't believe it — he was hung up on a preacher, for God's sake! His hand slipped from the phone and he started to walk away when it rang.

"Colin," Annie said. "I didn't wake you, did I?"

He felt himself grow light, as if all his bones had vanished. "No, I'm awake. I was just thinking about calling *you*."

"Really?"

"Really."

"That's nice," she said. "I'm calling because . . . I wanted you to know that . . . I wish you were here with me."

Her words hit him in the pit of his stomach. "Annie," he said.

"I just wanted you to know that."

"I wish I could be there, too." He didn't say he'd come back, drive ninety miles an hour to get there. He knew nothing had changed. "I'm glad you told me."

"Me, too. Goodnight, Colin."

"Goodnight, Annie."

He waited to hang up until he heard her break the connection. God, he felt good! She cared. The phone rang again. He grabbed it. "Annie?" There was no answer. "Annie? Is that you?" Again there was silence, but he could tell the line was open. "Hello? Who is this?"

No answer. And then he heard the click. Returning the receiver to the cradle, he felt an icy sweat bead on his neck, then creep down his back. He tried to tell himself it was a wrong number but he wasn't buying. Somehow he knew exactly who his caller was; he just didn't know his name.

LOOKING BACK — 50 YEARS AGO

———————

In keeping with its policy of giving its
patrons the very best in sound motion
pictures, the Seaville Theatre has installed
and has now in operation the revolution-
ary new "High Fidelity" sound reproduc-
ing system manufactured by the RCA
Victor Co. About $5000 was spent in
equipping the Seaville Theatre with this
latest development in sound reproduction.

Chapter Twenty-Six

She had given a terrible sermon, stumbling over words and phrases, having a coughing fit, losing her place, and all the time Steve Cornwell — who would give anything to see her replaced — was sitting there in the first row, grinning. The more he grinned the more mistakes Annie made. It had infuriated her, anger tripping her up further. She'd spent an inordinate amount of time on this sermon, rewriting and rewriting, and because of her date with Colin, for once she'd had it finished by two on Saturday afternoon.

And then she'd blown it. The topic was Commitment and Fidelity in all their ramifications. Was it some unconscious nonsense on her part that had made her louse it up? Some feeling of infidelity toward Bob? Or maybe it was seeing Russ Cooper in the third pew, tears on his cheeks. Or perhaps it was Burton Kelly, pouting in the fifth row, center. All those things might have added to her poor performance, but the main reason was her own fault: She had been proccupied with Colin, going over the night before, waiting for him to enter the church. She'd been so sure he'd come.

Once again she'd made herself vulnerable to another person and she'd been disappointed, hurt. On top of it all she was embarrassed about the phone call she'd made to him the night before. She truly wished she hadn't done that. Well, it was too late, the service was almost over, the final hymn just ending. Nervously, Annie gave her closing remarks, then took her place to greet the parishioners as they went into the parish hall. When they'd all gone by her she started to follow, then noticed a surly-looking Steve Cornwell standing near the back. She waited. He said nothing but continued to stare at her, hands in his trouser pockets.

Annie considered asking him what he wanted, rejected the idea, and started for the hall. As she reached the door Steve's laughter stopped her. Angry, she whirled back to face him but he was gone. For a moment she looked out into the empty church, trying to regain her calm, telling herself to forget Cornwell.

Inside, Peg Moffat, coffee in one hand, cookies in the other, was by Annie's side at once. "What's wrong, kid? You look terrible."

"Steve Cornwell," she managed to get out.

"Uh-oh. What did he say?"

"He didn't say anything. He just stared at me, then he laughed." She shuddered, running her hands over her arms as if she were cold.

"What do you suppose it meant?" Peg bit into a chocolate-chip cookie.

"I don't know."

"You didn't do anything dumb last night, did you? You want one of these? They're dynamite."

"No, thanks. If you mean did Colin spend the night, no."

"I don't know whether to be glad or not. How'd the evening go."

Annie smiled.

"That good, huh?"

She shrugged, not wanting to commit herself, even to Peg.

"When are you going to see him again?" She finished the cookie, started a new one. "You have to try one of these."

Annie held out her hand. "We said we'd talk today. But I won't be able to see him tonight. I have the Death and Dying group."

"Did he stay late?"

"Not too." She thought of telling Peg about calling him but couldn't. Absently, she took a bite of the cookie.

"Good, huh?"

"Who?"

"Not who. What. The cookie, sweetie, the cookie."

"Oh, the cookie."

"You're a goner, kid. Say, do you think Steve Cornwell saw you together?"

"I don't know. Maybe. Listen, I have to talk to some of the others. Can you stay for awhile today?"

"Sure. I'll make my way over to your house in a bit. And I expect every last detail."

Smiling, Annie watched Peg join Madge Johnson and Tug Wilson. When she turned away she saw Burton Kelly coming toward her. She didn't need this today. Fortunately, Karen Ludwig cut him off, immediately began talking about the sermon, said she liked it, and had some questions. Annie was grateful and tried to absorb herself in the conversation, but her thoughts kept sliding back to Steve Cornwell, wondering about his laughter, feeling threatened.

By the time she was able to absent herself from the crowd of parishioners she felt edgy and restless. Every encounter she'd had seemed to fizzle and die, or else they'd ended with someone miffed. Whatever she'd tried had gone wrong. She hadn't even managed to avoid a confrontation with Burton. He'd been sulky and irritating, challenging everything she said. The morning had been a mess. *She* was a mess. Was all this because she was taken with Colin? Had she been so starved for affection that a few kisses had turned her mind to mush? That possibility disturbed her. As she climbed the back stairs to her house she thought, Thank God for Peg, she'll put me straight.

"Peg," she called from the kitchen, "I'm here."

There was no reply.

And then she saw the note.

Dear Annie,
Had to leave, didn't want to come back to the Hall. Tim called, told me Beth is running a temperature. I'll catch you later. Why don't you drop by this afternoon? Sorry I couldn't stay but I still expect the gory details.

Love, Peg

Timing, she thought, is everything. If ever she wanted to talk, it was now. The phone rang and she grabbed for it, hoping it was Colin. It was only a wrong number. She thought about calling him but decided against it. The last thing she wanted to do was to appear pushy, smothering. Instead she decided to relax, have her glass of sherry before she went to the Townsends' for dinner. In the dining room she poured herself the drink, then turned toward the living room.

When she saw him she sucked in her breath, dropping the glass. "What are you doing here?" she managed to ask.

He said nothing, just smiled.

The first thing Hallock said was, "You look kind of bleary-eyed, Maguire. Didn't you get any sleep?"

"Not much. You?"

"Haven't slept yet. I tried but I couldn't. There was a paper-back somebody left in the motel, read the whole damn thing."

"What was it?"

Hallock cleared his throat. "Oh, it was just some damn thing called *Ballerina*."

Colin smiled.

"Listen," Hallock said defensively, "it got me through the night and it wasn't half bad, either."

"I didn't say anything, Chief."

"Better stop calling me Chief."

"Sorry. Want some coffee?"

"You got some made?"

"Yup."

"I wouldn't mind a cup."

Colin poured them each a mug of coffee, put a carton of milk on the table, and pushed the sugar bowl toward Hallock.

He took three teaspoons. "So what do you have?"

Colin got out his sheets of lined yellow paper and laid them on the kitchen table. Across the top of the first one he'd written the names of the victims and down the left side, fifteen categories: age, sex, color eyes, color hair, height, weight, marital status, date of birth, where born, siblings, parents, children, job, address, and financial status.

Hallock took a similar piece of paper from his pocket, unfolded and smoothed it, then placed it next to Colin's. He had an additional four categories: hobbies, friends, habits, enemies. "Two minds that work as one, huh?"

"Looks like it."

"What kind of matches did you make?"

"A few times I thought I might have something, but then the little girl, Mary Beth, would throw it off."

Hallock nodded. "Know what you mean. Let's hear it anyway."

Colin picked up his second sheet and began to read. "Two of the victims have brown eyes, two blue. Two have blond hair, two brown." He looked up from the paper. "Of course, Ruth Cooper's was dyed. She'd already turned gray but she'd been a brunette." He continued reading. "Three of them were between five feet five and five feet eleven. Mary Beth threw that one off. The weight didn't seem to mean anything," he said.

"Keep going. You're doing fine."

"Two were married, one engaged. Three were born in Seaville, one in Mattituck. They all had siblings. They all had living parents. Two had children. One was a housewife, two had jobs. Two lived in Seaville, one in Bayview, one in East Hampton. Three had a two in their address, three had fives, and three had zeros. Two had moderate incomes, one a combined income of over eighty thousand, and one none." Colin put down the paper. "I think the only significant thing is that they were all born in the North Fork. Natives."

"What's significant about that?"

"I shouldn't have said significant, that's too strong. What I mean is, it's the only common denominator."

"I agree." He held out his piece of paper, tapped the line where he'd discovered the same thing.

"So what's it mean?" Colin asked.

"I'm not sure. I just know there isn't anything else. Like you said, the only common denominator. I think we should check more on the families. Maybe it's something in the backgrounds. Grandparents, even."

"Okay. Higbee and Carroll's immediate families are here, but what about Cooper and Danowski?"

Hallock said, "Cooper's parents live in Florida. Miami Beach, I think. Got to look that up. Danowski's parents are in Bellport. If you can handle them, I can take the ones in Florida. What I mean is, I got more time on my hands than you. But you could probably take an afternoon to go down-island to Bellport, couldn't you?"

Colin took a slug of coffee, stalling for time. "Couldn't I do it by phone?"

Hallock looked surprised. "An old newspaperman like you ought to know the personal touch always works best."

"Right." He felt nauseated; too much coffee.

"What's up, Maguire? You don't look so hot."

He knew he'd have to tell him. "Waldo, I don't mean to let you down but, I . . . I can't go to Bellport. Ever since my family was murdered . . . I get these panic attacks. I can't go too far from home."

"You mean like acrophobia?"

"Agoraphobia," he corrected gently. "Sort of. But obviously I can leave my house. I just can't go too far away, and not with anybody else in the car."

"No big deal," Hallock said. "You check into Higbee and Carroll, I'll do the other two."

"Thanks."

Hallock waved his hand in dismissal. "Look, we all got problems. Anyway, sooner you can get on to those, the better."

"You really going to Florida?"

"Why the hell not?"

"When?"

"Tomorrow, maybe. I'll go down to Bellport today, see what I can find out about the . . ." He glanced down at his piece of crumpled paper. ". . . the Bennetts. Ethel and George. Think you can do some of this today?"

"Sure." He'd hoped to see Annie later, but that was tonight.

"Okay. You going to tell Griffing you're working on this with me?"

"I don't see why I should."

"Good."

Colin walked with him to the front porch. "But I don't think Mark would care."

Hallock started to say something then changed his mind.

"What?"

"Nothing."

"Come on, Waldo, that sucks."

"It'd just be better if you didn't say anything to anybody. About us working on this thing."

"Especially Mark?"

"No. Just anybody." He pushed open the screen door.

Colin thought Hallock was lying. "Okay, I'll keep it quiet."

Hallock said, "You get any leads today try me later at the motel. Room one-thirty-one."

Colin watched Hallock drive away. Some kids were coming down the street, wearing bathing suits and carrying a rubber raft. It was a beautiful day, seventy-five degrees, but Colin knew the water in the bay would still be cold. Kids never minded how cold the water was. He remembered how he and Brian would stay in the water for hours, fingertips shriveling, bodies almost blue, and still they wouldn't come out until their father or mother threatened punishment. For a moment Colin longed to be a boy again, free from problems. It was hard to believe there'd ever been such a time in his life. The last years had cast such a pall over everything he sometimes felt life had always been dark and dreary. But now there was Annie, a bright spot in an otherwise dim existence.

Back in the kitchen he lifted the phone and dialed her number, surprised as he realized he'd committed it to memory.

———

Annie's phone rang.

He said, "Don't answer that."

She was shaking from anger and fear. The phone continued

to ring and she looked toward the kitchen. "I want to answer my phone."

"No," he said, rising from the gray velvet couch and crossing the room in three long strides. Steve Cornwell towered over her, his face of oversize features like a caricature, the black hair neatly trimmed. He wore a green cotten jacket, blue polo shirt, plaid slacks with a white belt, and white loafers. "I don't want you to answer the phone because I'm here to talk. Get it?"

She nodded and backed away from him.

"Good. Sit down." He pointed to the rocking chair. She sat while he remained standing. "Why don't you give up the ghost, Mrs. Winters."

She tried to remain cool, her voice even. "It's not *Mrs.* Winters. As I've told you many times, it's *Reverend* Winters or Annie. Winters is my maiden name. What is it you want?"

The phone stopped ringing.

She looked toward the kitchen, futilely trying to will her caller to come to the house.

"Are you divorced?" he asked, ignoring her question.

"You know I'm not. My husband died. I asked you what you wanted. If you don't tell me or get out of here, I'm going to call the police."

He gave a short hoot of laughter. "So why don't you use your dead husband's name? It seems unfaithful to change it just because the poor guy's dead. You should have mentioned that in your sermon." He laughed again, showing large teeth like a mouthful of shells. "Funny you should pick fidelity for your sermon today."

Annie felt a sharp stab of guilt. "Steve," she said, trying to sound reasonable, "what's this all about?"

"I think you know."

"I *don't* know."

"I think you do," he insisted. "I've got my eye on you, Miss Winters. All the time." Cornwell pulled a pack of cigarettes from his pocket, tapped one out, and returned the pack.

"I don't like people smoking in my house."

"Don't you? That's too damn bad." He lit the cigarette, blew out the match, and dropped it on the rug.

Furious, Annie started to get up.

"Stay where you are," he commanded, eyes like two bullet holes.

"I want to get you an ashtray."

"Sit down," he ordered.

What if he's the killer? she thought. What if this is it? She knew she wasn't ready. Softly, she asked, "Just what do you want?"

"I want you out. I want you back in the kitchen where you belong."

"You're incredible." Was this really why he was here? she wondered. Was that all?

Cornwell tapped the cigarette with a long finger; ash fell to the rug.

Trying not to react, she looked at her watch. "I'm expected at dinner and I'm already late."

He went on as if she hadn't spoken. "I've put up with you as minister week after week, listened to your trite sermons, watched the others fawning over you, but now I've had it."

"I don't understand."

He smiled. "I'm going to get rid of you.

Her heart slammed in her chest.

"I might as well tell you I saw you with that reporter last night."

"So?" She could feel a small rivulet of sweat making its way between her breasts.

"So," Cornwell said, dropping more ash on the rug, "one thing leads to another. And when it does, you've had it. Just like that." He snapped his fingers, loud.

Annie flinched.

He smiled with satisfaction.

She felt a curious sense of relief. If he was the murderer, he was not going to kill her. At least not at this moment. "I'm going to dinner now."

"Good-bye."

"You are not going to stay here while I'm gone," she stated.

"No?"

"No." Annie looked into his eyes, met his hatred, and didn't turn away.

Cornwell shrugged, breaking the stare. "I don't want to stay here anyway." He dropped the cigarette on the rug, ground it out.

"You pig," she said.

He laughed. "Don't forget, I'll be watching you."

She waited until she heard the door close, ran to it and snapped the lock, rushed to the back door, locked that, then went to the living room to check the damage to the rug. Picking up the butt, she brushed away the ash. A black smudge marred the carpet. Club soda fixed the spilled sherry.

She dialed Colin. After one ring she hung up. What would she tell him? She didn't want to appear a helpless female unable to run her own life. He was the wrong one to tell. She should call the police. But she couldn't do it. There would be too many questions, and she was sure it would hurt her more than Steve Cornwell.

But what if he was the killer? She rationalized that if he was, he would already have killed her. Why bother with threats? Still, there was a nagging doubt in her mind. And as she left the house for her dinner engagement she silently prayed she wouldn't live to regret her decision.

LOOKING BACK — 75 YEARS AGO

During the electrical storm Saturday night or early Sunday morning, the barn of John Fleet of Seaville was struck by lightning and a colt owned by his son, E. D. Fleet, was killed. It was a valuable colt and thought a great deal of by his owner. The telephone in the house was also burned out.

Chapter Twenty-Seven

Driving to the Carrolls', Colin wondered about the chief's request to not tell Mark what they were doing. Was Hallock afraid Mark would purposely hinder their investigation? Or was it something Hallock wasn't about to let him in on?

Along the road Colin noticed a few yard sales. Nobody seemed to be attending them. Was this more evidence that the tourist season was off in Seaville? Perhaps if he was a businessman of the Fork or if he had a wife and children, he would have been screaming for Hallock's hide too.

Sticking a Marlboro between his lips, he shoved in the car lighter. Did Hallock think Mark knew something about the murders he wasn't telling? Suddenly Colin pulled into a side street, turned around, reentered the main road, and headed back the way he'd come. The Carrolls could wait.

By the time he crossed the causeway into Point Haven, he was beginning to have doubts, thinking maybe he was nuts. Still he didn't turn around. He realized this had been in the back on his mind since Friday, but now it jumped to the front like a page in a child's pop-up book.

Point Haven was the most exclusive town on the Fork. Old money dominated. Point Haveners were snobs and thought the rest of the Fork was tacky. The houses here were old, large, lavish. But more and more outsiders were buying land, throwing up modern houses and, according to the natives, spoiling the place.

Slowing the car, Colin started looking at street signs. Mark had told him that Amy Stauber lived on Love Lane and, winking, said how apt it was. Colin recalled that the street was near the Candymaker on the main road. He spotted it and turned. Amy had designed her own house — a rectangular shape painted pink, purple, and blue. Mark said it drove the natives wild. The house was halfway down the block, back about fifty feet from the road. The land around it was bare. He pulled in next to a green Austin. For a moment he thought he should leave. What was he going to learn here, anyway? But his curiosity smothered his doubts.

Standing next to the car he stared at the house. He'd never seen its equal. It was long and low and painted as Mark had described. Smiling, Colin couldn't help liking Amy for doing something a little different, and he was glad it drove the old-money types nuts.

At the bright pink door he used the lion's-head brass knocker. There was no response at first, but by the time he'd knocked again he heard footsteps inside.

"Who is it?" a woman asked.

"Amy?"

"Who is it, please?"

"My name's Colin Maguire. I work for Mark Griffing."

For a moment nothing stirred, then Colin heard her unsnap a lock. When the door opened he was stunned. "Are you Amy Stauber?"

"Yes." She was at least thirty-five, definitely not a kid. But she *was* beautiful. At least that much was true. She was tall and had long silver hair parted in the middle. Her hazel eyes were large. The broadcloth shirt she wore was blue with a button-down collar, and her jeans were tight, showing off a spectacular figure. On her feet were worn blue espadrilles.

"May I come in?"

"Has something happened to Mark?"

"No. He's fine. I'd just like to talk to you for a moment."

"Did Mark send you?"

"No."

"I don't understand, then. What's this about?"

"Please, this is important."

"How do I know you're who you say you are?" A thin line of sweat outlined her upper lip.

Colin realized she was frightened. Maybe she thought he was the murderer. "Don't you recognize my name from the paper?"

"I don't read the paper," she said coldly. "Do you have any identification?"

He showed her his press card.

"Okay. Come on in."

The house was pleasantly cool and smelled of cedar. Bamboo furniture from the forties filled the living room. The pillows were covered in a cotton fabric splashed with color on a black background. Plants were everywhere. A wooden fan hung from the ceiling.

Amy told him to sit. "So what's up?" she asked.

"I want to talk to you about Mark?"

"Did Sarah send you?"

"No one sent me."

"What do you mean, you want to talk about Mark?"

He wasn't sure what he meant. Part of him kept thinking if he didn't say it out loud it would go away; the other part knew it was too late for that. Still, all his reportorial skills seemed to vanish. "I know you were close once," he said awkwardly.

She laughed, a dimple dotting one cheek. "Oh, that's cute."

"I'm sorry. I don't blame you for laughing. I'm having a little trouble here. Mark's an old friend. I guess I feel disloyal."

"So why'd you come?"

"A good question. Mind if I smoke?"

"I'll get an ashtray."

He watched her cross the room and open a low bamboo cabinet. This woman was very different from Sarah. There was something fluid in Amy's movements, so opposite to Sarah's frenetic style, her constant motion. Sarah said chaos where Amy said serenity. He couldn't imagine her threatening suicide.

She handed him an ashtray. In its center in gold script was *Martha and Allen 1972*. He looked at Amy, questioning.

"I collect them. I've got about seventy-five. It's sad, isn't it?"

"Sad?"

"Well, take Martha and Allen for instance. Married in 1972, divorced when? I mean, forget it, you wouldn't give that thing away if you were still married, would you?"

He thought of his brother's wedding, the ashtrays with Brian and Maggie scripted in the center. "I think ashtrays like that are favors at the wedding reception. Everybody gets one."

"Oh. You mean it's the guests that are giving these things away, not the bride and groom?"

"Probably. Maybe the bride and groom sometimes. Like you said, when they split up." Amy looked so crestfallen he wanted to amend everything he'd said, start over. "It's still a great thing to collect."

"Yeah, well. I'm having a beer, you want one?"

"No, thanks."

He lit his cigarette, thinking maybe he should get the hell out of here and leave this woman alone.

When she came back, a Pabst can in her hand, she sat across from him. "So what about Mark?"

"First I'm going to ask you not to tell Mark that I was here. I know your loyalty is to him, not me, but our talk could be very important."

"Hey, forget it. I don't talk to Mark anymore."

Colin felt a thud to his stomach, as if he'd been punched. "What do you mean?" he asked.

She shrugged. "Just that. We don't speak. Period. Look, I don't know if you know the whole story, but as far as I'm concerned Mark Griffing is one lousy bastard. I mean, sure, it's not all his fault, it takes two to tango, but forget it, this guy's the pits. I went to work for him as a reporter and — is that what you are?"

He nodded. "And managing editor." What the hell was this woman talking about? Was she lying because she didn't want him to know the affair had started up again? Or was she telling the truth?

"So I went to him as a reporter, and he puts me on sports,

and that was okay even though I'm not a sports fan. Later I asked him to switch me over to features, the soft stuff. Forget it, he makes a pass at me instead. Look, I was lonely. I didn't know anybody here, ten months out of a bad marriage, you know how it is. Anyway, one thing led to another and we were having an affair. To tell you the truth, Colin — it's Colin, isn't it?"

"Yes."

"To tell you the truth, Colin, I fell in love with the guy. I felt lousy because of Sarah and the kids, but I know these things happen. What can you do? So after we've been sleeping together six, seven months Mark tell me he wants to divorce Sarah and marry me. I'm ecstatic. But does he ask her for the divorce? Forget it. Days and weeks and months go by, and finally I'm up to here." She held her hand under her chin.

Confused, Colin asked, "What about last Friday morning?"

"Friday morning?"

"Yes."

"What's wrong? You look strange. Are you all right?"

He felt sick. If Mark lied about where he was last Friday then . . . Colin couldn't stand to finish the thought. Still, he had to know. "This is very important, so please don't lie. I'm not going to tell anyone, not Sarah, not anyone. Please tell me the truth. Didn't Mark come to see you last Friday?"

"Mark? Come here? Forget it. Aren't you listening? I haven't talked to Mark Griffing in six months."

Ethel and George Bennett, their shoulders and thighs touching, sat on the Broyhill couch of their living room suite. The Bennetts were tiny people: he was not more than five four, she barely made five feet. They were both in their early sixties, but Hallock thought they looked much older. He wondered if they'd aged since their daughter was murdered.

George was saying, "Gloria never gave us any trouble, did she, Mother?"

"Not one minute. In fact, she was the best behaved of our children," Ethel answered.

"That's right. Now, Cheryl was a different story," George said. "Cheryl was always getting into fixes, isn't that right, Mother?"

Ethel Bennett nodded her gray permanented head. Her eyes grew smaller behind thick lenses. "It's a fact. Cheryl was boy crazy. Still is, I guess. I pity poor Leonard. That's her husband. Her second one."

George poked Ethel with his skinny elbow, signaling her not to give out too much detail to strangers. She sat up straighter, knees together.

Hallock said, "Can you think of anyone who might've been an enemy of Gloria's?"

The Bennetts turned to one another, found no answer, then looked back at Hallock.

"Can't think of a soul. Gloria was always popular. You know she was a cheerleader in high school," George said, as if he were telling Hallock his daughter was an ambassador.

Hallock nodded, smiling. He wasn't getting anywhere. "How about you folks? I don't mean to be rude, but you never know what might be important. Anything about you the police should know?" So what if he was doing a little fudging here and there about who the authorities were.

"Well," George said, "I can't speak for Ethel, I didn't know her until she was twenty, but as for myself, I'm headed for sainthood." He crackled, then looked at his wife for confirmation.

Ethel seemed disgusted and inched her body away from him. him.

"Mrs. Bennett?" Hallock asked.

"What kind of thing do you mean?"

"Anything out of the ordinary. Some event that was different than your everyday life happenings."

"Like what?" she asked.

"Maybe an argument you had thirty years ago with somebody you haven't seen since. Being stuck in an elevator with strangers. Or winning the lottery." He smiled.

"We don't buy lottery tickets," she said.

Hallock thought he was going to go crazy.

George said, "The thing of it is, Chief, we don't have unusual events happening to us. See, we're just plain people, if you know what I mean."

Hallock nodded and picked up his chief's hat from the table where he'd laid it. "Well, folks, I want to thank you for your help."

The Bennetts got up as if they were one person. George held out his hand to Hallock. "Glad to help, Chief, any time."

"Now, should you think of anything, anything at all that strikes you as something we should know, please call. You might think it's silly, but don't let that stop you. I'm going to give you a special number." He reached into his pocket for Maguire's number and handed it to George.

"A special number, huh?" He looked pleased, as if finally he'd been singled out for privilege.

"My assistant, Detective Maguire, will probably take the call. We have a special task force working on this. But it's undercover so you don't want to go telling friends about it, you understand?" He had to protect himself somehow.

"We'll be thinking on it, won't we, Mother?"

She nodded.

Hallock placed his hat on his head. "You just keep thinking. Thanks for you time."

He drove around the block before he took off his hat and laid it on the seat. The next step was to drive to the same gas station where he'd switched clothes earlier and change back to his civvies.

He couldn't help wondering if this was another futile maneuver guaranteed to make him look like a horse's ass. Glancing at his watch he saw it was three-ten. He'd booked himself on a six o'clock plane to Miami Beach. There was no reason he should hang around until tomorrow, cooling his heels. He hoped he had enough time to pick up his bag, call Maguire, and get back to Riverhead, where he'd get the limo to the airport. If he missed Maguire he could always call him from Miami.

Should he phone Fran? he wondered. He couldn't face it. But suddenly he found himself missing her terribly, wishing she was going with him. A second honeymoon, maybe. And then he recalled her sitting in the back row of the Town Hall, doing nothing while that bitch, Julia Dorman, ripped him up one side and down the other. Ah, hell, he thought, there's just something's a man's got to do alone, and going to Florida to see Ruth Cooper's folks was one of them.

———————

Colin lay on his bed smoking. Even though the blue Levolor blinds were drawn, the sun snaked its way in around them. He had plunked two pillows behind his head and put an ashtray on his stomach.

He and Annie had finally made contact around three. She'd sounded strange. He'd asked to see her later, and she'd told him no because of some group she held on Sunday nights. He found himself wondering if it was true, but she didn't seem to be the lying type. They'd made a date for the next night. She'd offered to cook dinner for him again. He hadn't refused.

Then Sarah had called, inviting him up for dinner. But he couldn't face Mark. Not yet. Maybe never.

What the hell was he going to do? When Hallock called he'd told him about his fruitless interviews with the Higbees and the Carrolls, saying nothing about Mark or Amy. But just how long could he keep it from Hallock? And what the hell did it prove anyway?

He wished he'd never gone to Amy's. But he'd had to go. His doubts had left him no choice. Still, he'd wanted Amy to confirm what Mark had told him, not the other way around. He mashed out his cigarette, took a long swig from his Tab, then lay back on the pillows.

It was impossible to think that Mark was the killer. But he'd had the opportunity in at least three cases. Colin had gone to the office after leaving Amy's and checked Mark's calendar again. The night Gloria Danowski disappeared Mark had written on his calendar "shopping in East Hampton for Sarah's birthday present." So he'd been in the area of the murder, yet said nothing. Perhaps he'd forgotten he'd written that on his calendar. Or maybe he'd put it there on purpose in case anyone saw him. Christ, this was awful.

As for Mary Beth's murder, Colin knew Mark had been at the band concert when the child was killed. He couldn't remember if he'd seen him leave his family at any point. And then there was the lie Friday morning, saying he was with Amy when Joe Carroll was killed. Why would Mark tell him that unless he had something to hide, and something desperate?

The fourth one, Ruth Cooper, happened on a Sunday morning when he'd been with Mark. Well, not exactly. The time of her death was figured at between noon and two, and Colin had left Mark at quarter to twelve. He would have had time to go to Bayview and kill Ruth Cooper and still get back to his house to wait for the police call. If he left the house at all.

Colin had to find out what Mark had done that day after he'd left, and it wasn't going to be easy. Certainly he couldn't ask Mark. Maybe he could find out from Sarah, although that wouldn't be a cinch either. It was two weeks ago, and unless he came up with something pretty clever, Sarah would get suspicious.

He lit another cigarette. Jesus, this was lousy. Mark was one of his oldest friends. Wouldn't he know if there was something off about him? And what possible motive would Mark have? But maybe you never really knew anyone.

Then he remembered his friends in Chicago. So many of them turning their backs on him, thinking he'd killed his family. He'd wondered at the time how friends could be like that. Now he was doing the same thing. Maybe he should drop it. He had no hard evidence. Still, Mark's lie about Amy bothered him. And then there was Hallock's warning not to tell Mark what they were doing. When Hallock got back he'd confront him about Mark, exchange information, and if it looked bad he'd go after Mark just the way he would if he were a complete stranger.

He had no choice.

LOOKING BACK — 25 YEARS AGO

Royal Toner, 65, one of Seaville's best known businessmen and a man who, during his busy life, did much to publicize the oyster industry, passed away May 15. Mr. Toner, one of the world's largest producers of oysters, was known in the industry as "The Voice of the Oyster." His 6,000 acre oyster beds in Peconic Bay for years been a mecca for gourmets and food writers.

Chapter Twenty-Eight

The story appeared in *Newsline* Monday morning, with Babe Parkinson's byline. The first Colin knew of it was a phone call at eight-thirty waking him from a deep sleep. When he reached for the receiver he dropped it. Leaning over the side of the bed, he picked it up by the cord. It swung freely, banging against the nightstand and the metal spring of his brass bed. He finally got it to his ear and said hello.

"Okay, buster," a deep male voice said, "we got your number now. You better get outta Seaville or else."

"Who is this?"

"Never mind who. Just know this. If the police don't put you away where you belong, the rest of us will."

Colin started to speak, then heard the click breaking the connection. He'd had a terrible night, dreaming of people chasing him, Mark laughing, then Mark swinging from a noose. Then he thought about the phone call and suddenly understood. He swung his legs over the side of the bed, reached for his robe. *Newsline* was delivered to him; he hoped it would be on time.

The second call came as he was going down the stairs. He ignored it. The paper, in its yellow wrapper, was on the lawn at the far edge of the property. Colin was convinced that the delivery guy tried his damnedest to throw the paper as far from the house as possible.

Back in the house the phone was still ringing. He picked it

up, cradling it between ear and shoulder while he unfolded the newspaper. A male voice said, "This Colin Maguire?"

"Yes."

"We don't want your kind here, Mister. Go back to Chicago where you belong. You can't go killing your wife and kids and then —"

Colin slammed down the phone. Almost immediately it began to ring again. He took it off the hook and laid it on the chair.

From the receiver came, "Colin? Colin, are you there? It's Mark."

He picked it up. "Mark?"

"You okay?"

"Yeah, I guess."

"Don't come in, Colin. I'm coming over there."

Mark hung up before Colin could tell him not to come. He pushed down the cradle and it rang again.

This time it was a woman. He didn't listen, hung it up, got a dial tone, and rang the paper. The line was busy. He broke the connection and laid the phone on the chair again. After putting on the kettle he sat at the table and opened the paper. He found it on the third page. There was a picture of him taken the day after the murders. He looked insane. The headline was CHICAGO MURDER SUSPECT IN SEAVILLE. Shaking with anger, he read the story.

> Colin Maguire, a suspect three years ago in the murders in Chicago of his wife and two children, is now residing in Seaville, New York, where four slayings have occurred in the past three weeks. The Chicago murders are still unsolved.
>
> Maguire, a former crime reporter for the Chicago Tribune and now managing editor of the Seaville Gazette, was discovered after his family's slaying running through the streets near his home covered with blood. He was unable to

account for his whereabouts the previous evening during which the murders took place. He said he had been drinking in a neighborhood bar and "blacked out" for a period of several hours. Charges against Maguire were eventually dropped for lack of evidence.

The rest of the article was a rehash of the Seaville murders. It was all innuendo. But that's all it took. The kettle whistled. He made a cup of instant coffee, lit a cigarette. In the background a man's voice told him to put his phone back on the hook. He didn't. The voice repeated the message; then there was silence.

He felt numb. He wasn't going to run, start over again. But maybe he'd have to, at least for awhile. And what was he going to do about Mark? He wished like hell that Hallock wasn't in Florida.

Loud knocking made him jump. He went to the door.

"Who is it?"

"Mark."

Unsnapping the lock, he thought Mark was the last person he wanted to see.

Wearing a red Ralph Lauren polo, chinos, and blue Adidas sneakers, his gray hair perfectly groomed, Mark took off his sunglasses and stared at Colin.

"Jesus, pal, you look like hell."

"Thanks."

In the kitchen Mark said, "I mean it, Colin. You look like you've been up all night."

Colin sat at the table and took a slug of his coffee.

Mark glanced at the paper. "What a bitch," he said.

Colin nodded, smoothed out his moustache.

"Hey, you left your phone off the — oh. Crank calls?"

"Three before I got smart."

"This sucks, Colin."

He stared at Mark, trying to imagine him slitting Ruth Cooper's throat.

"What are you going to do?"

"Nothing right now. If you want me to come in to work I will." Could Mark have cut the symbol on Joe Carroll's chest?

"Do you want to?"

"No."

"That's fine with me."

He couldn't see him killing Mary Beth Higbee.

"Do you think there'll be any more stories?" Mark asked.

Colin shrugged. "It doesn't matter. The damage is done."

"We could run something," Mark said hesitantly.

"Like what?"

"I don't know, off the top of my head."

"How are things with Amy?" Colin surprised himself as well as Mark.

"Amy?"

"Yeah, Amy. You remember her don't you?"

"I haven't seen her again," he said smoothly.

"Since when?"

"What do you mean, since when? Since Friday. What is this?"

"What's what?"

"This shit about Amy." Two spots of color, like rosebuds, appeared in Mark's cheeks.

"Is it shit?"

"Hey, pal, I don't know what the hell you're talking about."

"Amy. I'm talking about Amy."

"What about her?" Mark said sharply. "Come on. If you've got something to say, say it. We've been friends too long for this kind of crap."

"Forget it, Mark, I'm just . . . I don't know. I mean, it's not my best day."

"No, come on, you've got a bug up your ass about Amy and I want to know why. Do you think I wasn't there or something?"

Colin felt cold inside, as if all compassion had been drained from him. "Why did you ask that?"

"Wait a minute. Shit. It's Sarah, isn't it? She called you, right? Goddammit."

He said nothing.

"Christ, did she give me a hard time this weekend. She accused me of everything under the sun except committing the murders."

Colin forced himself to look at Mark, who was smiling, laughing.

"I got her calmed down, though. I just stuck to my guns about the meeting with Gildersleeve. I told her to call him up if she didn't believe me, knowing she wouldn't. But she called you, huh?"

"No."

"She didn't? So, then what's all the shit?"

"Forget it, it's nothing. I'm just crazy this morning." He couldn't go on with it. "Want some coffee?"

"No, thanks. I've got to get back."

"Have you gotten any calls about me?"

Mark waved a hand. "Don't worry about it, pal."

"A lot?"

"A few. Listen, nobody's going to tell me who I can have working on my paper, so don't sweat it."

"Who's telling you?"

"Come on, Colin, you don't need to know that."

"No, I want to know."

"Just some cranks, that's all." He started for the front door. Colin followed. "Mark, I want to know."

"Well, Gildersleeve called. You'd expect that, wouldn't you?"

"I guess. Who else?"

"Just people. Listen, pal, they're all stupid fucks and I'm not going to pay any attention to them, so don't you. Okay?" He put a hand on Colin's shoulder, squeezed. "Look, I have to get back but call me if you need anything. Do you want to come up later for dinner?"

"I'm seeing Annie." But would he? he wondered.

"Hey, terrific." He slapped Colin on the back. "If you want to drop by later give me a buzz, okay?"

"Okay. Thanks for coming over, Mark."

"No sweat. Talk to you."

Colin closed the door after him and locked it. He'd had no idea Mark was such an accomplished liar. Still, he was having a hard time believing Mark could murder anyone, let alone four people, one a child. Oh, Christ, it was all too much.

Back at the table Colin finished the last swallow of coffee. What would Mike Rosler think if he told him of his suspicions? He picked up the dead phone, pushed down the cradle, got the tone, and dialed the number of the *The New York Times*.

————

Hallock had never been to Florida before. With the exception of the heat, ninety-five in the shade, he liked the place. The sand was whiter than Seaville's, sky brighter, water bluer. And those palm trees made him smile. But he wished Fran was with him. Maybe he'd call her later, see if she'd come down. Ah, hell, what was he thinking? This wasn't some damn pleasure trip. Besides, he was supposed to be mad at Fran. And day dreaming around like this he was almost late for his appointment with the Conways.

They lived in a highrise two streets back from the beach. On the phone she'd said they'd met, mentioning a benefit party for the hospital twelve years ago. He'd lied and said he remembered it well. He told her to think back over the past, to try and remember anything about their lives that might have been unusual, or anything about Ruth Cooper's life, even when she'd been Ruth Conway. Mildred Conway had said they would. Going up in the elevator Hallock had a feeling based on nothing, that he was going to get lucky. He reached into his jacket pocket and rubbed the gold coin his father had given him forty-three years before. Even though he'd never been a superstitious man he'd always carried it. What the hell, it couldn't hurt.

————

At ten o'clock on the nose Colin pulled up in front of the Seaville Library. It was a one-story building, its facade made of fieldstone, the wooden trim painted white. Above the door was a plaque that said 1870.

Inside, the library felt cool. Betty Mills was checking something in the card catalog. She was a fairly tall woman, young, probably no more than twenty-five. Her hair was brown and she wore it long, parted on the side. She was pleasant looking, and had a sweetness to her that was immediately evident. When Colin approached her she smiled, her eyes reflecting her good humor.

"Can I help you?" she asked.

"I hope so. Annie Winters said you might be able to." He wondered if Betty had seen the story in *Newsline*.

"Well, I'm willing to give it a try."

Colin handed her his notebook with the copy of the symbol cut on Joe Carroll's chest. "I'm interested in finding out what this means."

Betty studied the drawing carefully.

Colin was startled by her fingernails. They were about an inch long, painted a carmine red. He'd never seen anything like them and wondered how she typed.

"I think I know where to find this," she said. "Just a minute."

Taking long strides she walked back into the stacks. Colin looked around. On Betty's desk he noticed a copy of *Newsline* still in its wrapper. He felt a little less nervous.

Betty returned, holding an open book. "I think this is what you're looking for." She handed it to him, the red nail of her thumb marking the place like a bloody talon. "If it's not what you want I'll look further."

"Thanks very much." He sat down at a table and began reading:

The swastika is generally considered a form of the cross whose extremities are bent back at right angles. This popular device is known by many names, probably because of its widespread distribution throughout the ancient world. From the Sanskrit word it may be freely translated into "it is well" or "so be it," implying acceptance and denoting life, movement, pleasure, happiness, and good luck.

Theories and speculation as to the origin of the

swastika are conflicting. This mystic symbol, common to both eastern and western peoples, seems to appear and reappear consisently, yet always is its significance one of happy omen.

Colin skimmed the paragraphs devoted to what the symbol meant in different countries until he came to America:

In America it is found in prehistoric burial grounds. From the earliest times this famous sign undoubtedly indicated the rotation of the heavens, expressed the power of the sun, sky, and rain gods, and symbolized all harmonious movement springing from a central source.

The many interpretations assigned to the swastika are indeed bewildering. But for the sake of brevity we may conclude by saying that in modern times it is best known as a symbol of motion, good fortune, health, and long life.

He closed the book and carried it over to Betty. "Thanks very much." On her desk *Newsline* was open to page 2. Colin wanted to get out of there before she read the article.

"When you talk to Annie, tell her I said hello," she said.

"I will. And thanks again."

At the door he glanced back over his shoulder just as Betty was turning the page of the paper. He sprinted to his car and drove away immediately.

More bewildered than ever, he wondered why a murderer would carve a symbol of good fortune and long life into the chest of his victim? Could it be that the killer meant it to be a Nazi swastika after all? Somehow he didn't think so. Then what? The answer came to him with numbing clarity. The symbol must have special meaning to the murderer, a code of some sort. A code *he'd* have to break if he wanted to stay in Seaville.

———

When Colin didn't show up or call, Annie called him. The line was busy. And it stayed busy. She asked the operator to try the number. The operator said the phone was out of order. Annie was sure it was off the hook.

It had been Burton Kelly who'd brought her the article. He was waiting for her at her office, the newspaper under his arm.

"I have something to show you," he said.

She smiled, trying to make him feel less awkward about having been rejected by her. "Come in, Burton. Aren't you working today?"

"I'm going in late."

She sat at her desk, swiveling the chair around to face him. "What can I do for you?"

His face was stony. He held out the paper. "Have you seen this?"

"No, not yet."

He handed it to her.

"What is it?"

"Read it."

She tried to decipher Burton's expression, but she couldn't glean anything from his face. Yet something made her afraid. Glancing down at the paper she saw Colin's picture. He looked terrible — gaunt, his eyes staring straight out. And then she read the headline.

When she finished the article she asked calmly, "Why are you showing this to me, Burton?"

His mouth twitched to the left. "I think that's obvious."

"Is it?"

"He's a dangerous man."

"I don't see where it says that."

"It's clear. All you have to do is read between the lines."

She stood up, slapping the paper back in his open hand.

He was startled. "I thought you'd want to know. I mean, under the circumstances."

She didn't ask him what he meant; she knew. "Is there anything else, Burton? I have a nine-fifteen appointment, so if there's nothing else I'd like to get ready for it."

He pressed his lips together, tugged at his belt, hitching up his pants. "You're playing with fire," he said.

"Burton, what I do with my personal life is no concern of yours. Now if you' ll excuse —"

"It's a concern of the board's, though."

"Is that a threat?"

"Just some friendly advice. You'd better watch your p's and q's."

"Thanks for the advice." She pointedly looked at her watch.

"All right, I'm going. But don't say I didn't warn you."

When he was gone she had immediately dialed Colin's number. It was busy.

And now it was half an hour past the time he was expected to dinner. She knew that he wasn't coming, had known it most of the day.

The shock of reading the newspaper account had lessened. She supposed the worst part of it was that he hadn't told her the truth. As she'd said to Peg when she called, "I thought we had a real rapport, that there was a basic honesty between us."

Peg said, "Give me a break, Annie. Would you have told Colin if things had been reversed?"

"I think I would have. I mean, why not? It isn't as if he was guilty."

"Annie, the murderer has never been caught. I guess there's still some suspicion about him. Or at least it was there between the lines."

She'd wanted to shout at Peg, tell her she was just as bad as Burton Kelly. But she hadn't. She got off the phone and read the article again. This time she saw that the implication was there.

But her main concern was what Colin must have suffered at the time, still suffered. She couldn't imagine anything worse. When Bob had died she'd been devastated. She tried to think what it might have been like if he'd been murdered, but couldn't. And in Colin's case there were his children. It was almost impossible to know what she would have felt in his circumstances. Surely rage. Bitterness. And frustration. She was amazed that Colin functioned as well as he did.

During the day ten people came in to show her the article and sixteen phoned to tell her about it. So it wasn't odd that Colin had taken his phone off the hook. If she'd gotten calls, he must have too. But why hadn't he phoned her? Surely he must have known she'd be on his side. Still, he might have felt embarrassed by not having told her the truth. And maybe he was trying to protect her by not appearing at her house.

Well, that was foolish. They were friends, weren't they? Were Colin anyone else she would have gone to his house and tried to comfort him. She was, after all, a minister.

The night was cool. She slipped a sweater over her shoulders and went down the back steps. Behind the wheel she faced a truth. She wasn't going to Colin as a minister, she was going to him as a woman. And it felt perfectly fine.

LOOKING BACK — 50 YEARS AGO

———————

On Wednesday of this week the Ladies'
Sewing Society of Seaville celebrated its
90th anniversary by serving a delicious
supper to nearly 150 guests, after which a
most appropiate program was rendered.
The original constitution states that its
object was to furnish and beautify the
House of God and also to promote social
and friendly intercourse in the village. The
initiation fee was 12 cents for the ladies
and 25 cents for the gentlemen.

Chapter Twenty-Nine

When Colin finally connected with Mike Rosler, telling him about the article that had appeared in *Newsline*, pretending to ask for advice, he'd found he was unable to come right out and accuse Mark of the murders. In fact, he told himself he was crazy to think Mark could do something like that. But later in the conversation, when he'd begun complaining a bit about the job, Mike offered something that made Colin suspicious all over again.

Mike said, "Tell you the truth, Colly, I don't know how you can work for the guy."

"Why do you say that?"

"I know I haven't seen Mark for a few years, but last time we had lunch all he could talk about was some chick he was balling. Christ, it was boring. It was like the guy was obsessed, you know what I'm saying?"

"Amy?"

"Huh?"

"The woman, was her name Amy?"

"Amy? Lemme think . . . no, not Amy. I can't think what it was."

"Try," Colin urged.

"Why? What difference does it make what her name was?"

"I just want to know, Mike."

"Hell, I don't know. Lemme see. It started with a G, I think.

Yeah G. An old-fashioned name, too. It wasn't Gertrude. Or Greta. Grace! Yeah, that was it, Grace."

"When was this?"

Mike said, "What's up with you? First you're calling me about some Indian symbols and now you want to know the name of some broad Mark had a couple of years ago. What the hell's going on? Hey, does this have anything to do with the murders? Mark's chick, I mean."

"No. Do you remember when this was, Mike?"

"A couple of years ago, I told you."

"Since he lived out here?"

"No, before, when they still were living in Philly."

With Colin refusing to tell Mike why he cared who Mark was having an affair with a few years ago, the rest of the conversation deteriorated quickly and they'd hung up on a somewhat sour note.

Learning about Grace further convinced Colin that he really didn't know Mark at all. Adultery and murder were two very different things, but it was Mark's deceit that was so cunning, making Colin feel that anything was possible.

After Colin had come back from the library he'd spent the day lying on his bed, looking through old magazines, smoking. It was seven o'clock when he faced the fact that he wasn't going to Annie's and he wasn't going to call. He couldn't drag her into this. If he called she'd say she wanted to see him. She was that kind of woman. It was best to do nothing, let her off the hook. So when there was a knock on his door at eight he thought it was Mark again. Still, he was cautious and asked who it was.

"Annie," she said.

He was in an old sweatsuit and socks that had holes.

"Colin? Are you there?"

There was no choice. He opened the door. "What're you doing here?"

"Say, that's a terrific opening gambit!"

He laughed, "I'm sorry."

"Are you going to let me in?"

"Of course." He locked the door behind her. "You shouldn't be here."

"Why not?"

"Aren't you the one who told me people talk, know where everybody is at any given moment?"

"It's only five after eight."

"It's not the hour I'm worried about. It's you being here at all, with me." He ran a hand through his black hair trying to finger-comb it. "Sorry I'm such a mess."

Annie said softly, "You look good to me, Colin."

He felt it in his gut. Their eyes met, held. He wondered if it was possible that she hadn't seen the article. "Annie, you know about me don't you?"

"You mean the story in *Newsline?* Yes, I know."

He put his hand on her shoulders. "And you came here anyway."

"I've missed you," she said.

He smiled, "I've missed you, too." He moved nearer and wrapped her in his arms. "You're lovely," he whispered.

"So are you."

"Especially tonight," he quipped.

"Especially." She smiled.

He brushed her eyelids with his lips, then took a step back, held her hands. "It's no good for you to be here, Annie."

"Isn't that for me to decide?"

"I don't know. I'm not sure. Maybe you think you ought to be here, the proper minister doing good works."

"I thought of that."

"And?"

"I rejected it as a motive."

"Then why?"

"I wanted to see you. I understood why you didn't show up, didn't call." She touched his cheek. "I'm so sorry about your family, Colin."

He caught her hand near his chin, kissed the fingertips. "I couldn't tell you."

"I understand. And I know you had nothing to do with it." She brought his hand to her mouth, kissed his palm.

He felt it to his toes.

She said, "I'm here because I want to be here — with you."

He placed his hands on either side of her face, met her lips with his. And then he felt her leaning into him. His hands fell away from her face as they embraced, mouths searching, exploring. When they finally broke the kiss, Colin said, "Will you come upstairs with me?"

"Yes," she said.

He led her slowly up the stairs to his room. She faced him, her back to the bed as he began to undo the buttons of her blouse. When they were both naked he gently eased her down on the bed, lay next to her, one leg across hers, his fingers tracing her nipples.

"You're beautiful," he said. "I knew you would be."

Trembling, she slid an arm around his neck.

"Are you afraid?" he asked.

"Yes."

"Listen," he said, "we don't have to."

She said, "Oh, yes, we do," and pulled him to her.

Hallock was furious. He couldn't get Colin on the phone and he couldn't get a plane out of Miami Beach. The weather, since the morning, had turned bad and planes weren't taking off. They were calling this one David. Hallock decided he liked it better when hurricanes had girls' names. He thought of Julia Dorman and laughed. That would have pissed her off. Good. Maybe he'd write her a letter to that effect, say girls too, not women.

The trip had been a bust. The meeting with the Conways had failed to turn up anything useful. And now he was going to have to spend another night in the motel. He couldn't really afford it. But what the hell, one more night wasn't going to make or break him.

He'd seen a McDonald's a few blocks away and thought he'd give it a whirl. Before he left the room he tried Maguire again. No dice. Then he found himself punching out his own number, listening to it ring.

Fran said, "Hello."

He hung up not knowing what to say. He felt like hell.

Annie lay in the crook of Colin's arm, facing him. She ran a finger down his nose, across his mustache.

"Tell me about when you lived here as a child," he said, gently biting the tip of her finger.

"What do you want to know?"

"How you happened to come here, why you left."

"My father's a musician; he plays the trumpet. He was with the Dorsey band for awhile."

"No kidding."

"Not for long. Dad had some personality problems. Still does. He has trouble with authority. Big bands didn't have to put up with that."

He kissed her earlobe. "So he played with little bands?"

"Tickles," she said, squirming, grinning at him.

"You don't like it?"

"I didn't say that." She kissed his lips.

"Go on with your story."

He played with combos, mostly. Anyway, one time when he was out of work and things were tight for us, he heard about this club out here. Musicians are very tight — they have an old boy network all their own. This combo needed a trumpet player so Dad auditioned, got the job, and we moved out to Seaville for the summer."

"And you loved it."

"I did." She took a beat, then said silkily. "I *really* loved it."

They were looking into each other's eyes.

Colin said, "Did you?"

"Yes. I loved it," she whispered.

He pulled her to him and began to make love to her again, knowing this time would be different from the first. They were too hungry then to go slow, explore each other inch by inch. But this time they would take it easy, make it last.

Hallock had picked up a paperback at an all-night drugstore. Lying on the motel bed he opened the book. It was one of Ed

McBain's 87th Precinct stories. He loved them. McBain knew his stuff, he thought. This one was called *Heat*. Fitting. Except that since the rain started it had cooled off some. It was still sticky, though.

When he turned the page he realized he hadn't absorbed a word. His mind was with Fran. It was ten-thirty. He laid the book on his belly, reached for the phone, and punched out the number. This time when she answered he said hello right away so he wouldn't hang up again.

"Where are you, Waldo?" She sounded angry.

"Florida."

"Florida? Aren't they having hurricanes and whatnot down there?"

"That's why I'm still here."

"What are you doing there in the first place?"

"I'm working on something. How are you, Fran?"

"What are you working on?"

"Can't go into it on the phone. You okay?"

"I'm okay but I'm damn mad."

"Why's that?"

"Because I didn't know how to find you. And Liz Wood didn't know where you were either."

"How'd you know I was staying at Woods'? She call you?"

"No, she didn't call me."

"So how'd you know?"

"Oh, Waldo, don't be dumb. Everybody on the Fork knows where everybody is every minute. You ought to know that better than anyone."

"What'd you want to find me for?"

"Your child got hit in the face with a baseball and needed ten stitches."

"John?"

"Cynthia."

"Cynthia? What was she doing playing baseball? I thought she hated sports."

"She does, but her boyfriend plays. She was watching a game when she got hit."

"Boyfriend? What boyfriend?"

"Oh, Waldo," she said, exasperated.

"She's only a little girl, what's she doing with a boyfriend?"

"She's fifteen and she's doing what everybody else is doing. Having fun. Something you never heard of."

He ignored her remark. "Is Cyn okay now?"

"She's fine. A little pain, that's all."

"Can I talk to her?"

"She's sleeping."

"Oh."

They were silent for a few moments.

Fran said, "You're not going to get into any trouble, are you? I mean, being in Florida?"

"No. No trouble."

"When are you coming home?"

"Soon as I can get a plane out."

"Where are you staying, in case I need you?"

He told her. He thought of saying he wished she were with him but didn't. "Everything okay in Seaville?" he asked timidly.

"If you mean has there been another murder, the answer's no. But a story broke in *Newsline* today about your friend down at the paper, Colin Maguire."

"What story?"

"I've got it here." She read it to him.

"Jesus, Mary and Joseph," he said. "Poor bastard. No wonder I couldn't get him on the phone."

Fran said, "I never did like that Babe Parkinson."

"Yeah. Fran, you think you could go over to Colin's, ask him to call me?"

"Tonight?"

"Well . . ."

"Why should I do your dirty work? You walked out, so take the consequences."

He couldn't see what his walking out had to do with this. "It's not dirty work, Fran."

"Why'd you call, Waldo?"

There it was. Why *had* he called? Because he missed her. He couldn't say so. "I just thought I'd check in."

"Thanks a bunch."

"What's wrong with that?"

"Nothing. Nothing's wrong with it, Waldo, that's not the point."

"What d'you mean?"

He heard a sigh. "If you don't know then I'm not going to tell you."

"Well, I *don't* know."

"That's a pity," she said.

He couldn't think of anything to say.

"So long, Waldo."

"Fran?" He put the phone back in the cradle, laid his head on the skimpy pillow and closed his eyes. She must be really mad at him to do that, he thought. In all their years of marriage she'd never hung up on him. He toyed with the idea of calling her back, knew it would be useless. She was too mad. He'd wait until she cooled off some. And then something she'd said made him open his eyes as if he'd been stuck with a needle.

On the Fork everybody knows where everybody is every minute. Sure they did. So why didn't anybody know where the murderer was at any given time, like right before he struck? Because maybe he was a fixture and people were used to seeing him any old place at any old time. It had to be somebody who wouldn't stick out if a person happened to see him early in the morning near Carroll's Funeral Home. Or in Bayview in the middle of a Sunday. Or at the band conert. Just there. Just there, like he always is. And so damn respectable that nobody'd think twice about him.

Hallock grabbed the phone. Maguire's number was still busy. He slammed it down. He hadn't wanted to say anything to Maguire until he was sure. But now, he thought, he should be warned. It was important he know that Mark Griffing might kill him.

———

Colin and Annie sat at the kitchen table. She was wearing his blue terrycloth robe. He was in a clean set of sweats. They were eating scrambled eggs and bacon Colin had made for them. Neither one had eaten dinner.

"Funny," she said. "I feel like I'm eating breakfast, but it's dark out."

"Nice change," he said. "You look great in that color."

She smiled.

He said, "Hey, you never finished telling me about living here when you were a kid."

"There's not much to tell. We were only here two months. We came in the middle of April and we left by mid-June."

"How come?"

"The club Dad was playing at burned down." She shook her head, looked pained. "It was awful. People panicked. Most everybody got out okay. But some were burned and twelve people died."

"Jesus. How long ago was this?"

"Let's see . . . twenty-five years ago. Right. Twenty-five years ago this month. Two of the people who died were parents of Jamie Perkins, my first boyfriend. They were trampled to death. I wonder what ever happened to Jamie? He was an only child. There weren't any other relatives. I begged my parents to adopt him but of course they couldn't. It was hard enough keeping the three of us in shoes with Dad's career always so iffy. I mean, when we left Seaville and moved back to Brooklyn Heights, we had no idea where the next dollar was going to come from."

"Where *did* it come from?"

"Oh, Dad got a job right away. He was a damn good trumpet player. Still is. I don't worry about him. But my mother's a different story."

"You said she suffers from depression."

"Yes. And sometimes she takes too many pills."

"I'm sorry."

"Me, too." She looked at her food, pushed some egg around the plate, finally put down the fork.

Colin took her hand. She smiled. He leaned toward her and she met him halfway. They kissed gently.

"Do you want to talk about it?" he asked.

"No. Not now."

"Okay." He looked at the Yale wall clock. "It's after midnight, you know."

"Do I look like I'm going to turn into a pumpkin or something?"

"Or something," he said. "Where'd you park your car?"

She looked at him quizzically. "In front."

"You're kidding?"

"No."

"Why'd you do that? You told me — "

"I know what I told you."

"Isn't it true?"

"Yes. I think it is."

"Well, then, hell, you've got to go home."

"I want to spend the night with you, Colin."

"Listen, I want to spend the night with you more than anything, but I don't think it's a smart move. I mean, people think I'm a murderer. It's riskier than ever for you to stay here."

"Why don't you come home with me? In *my* car."

He shook his head, looked embarrassed.

She said, "Colin, I know you have trouble riding with someone but maybe you could try it — just this once."

There was no way he would let her see him with a panic attack. "You don't understand."

"Then tell me."

"I . . . I can't."

"You can." She put her hand on his leg, squeezed. "You can try."

"Okay, I'll try."

Slowly he told her, describing what the attacks were like, and ended with his head in his hands.

"It's all right, Colin. It's really all right. I'll stay here."

"No," he said. "No, you can't. I won't let you. It's bad enough that you're here this late. Come on." He took her by the hand. "Let's get dressed."

"Colin, wait. What are you going to do?"

"I'm going to walk. It's not that far to your place."

"Are you sure you want to?"

He nodded.

"What about the morning?"

"I'll leave early and walk back."

After they were dressed Annie left. He watched her drive away. There didn't seem to be anyone on the street, but he couldn't be sure. He put out the porch light, closed the door, and locked it.

Inside he doused the lights one by one and made his way upstairs. In his bedroom he turned on a light. The blinds were drawn, but there was enough spill for anyone watching to see it. He waited three minutes, then turned off the light and went back down the stairs, hunkering down as he opened the back door and went out.

Keeping close to the hedges he made his way to the back of his yard, found an opening in the hedges and crossed through to his neighbor's yard. Cautiously, he crept across the lawn and came out on Sixth Street. All was still. Not a light on. He began to jog, a slow, even rhythm, down the road and out onto Main Street. If anyone was watching his house they wouldn't know he'd left. At least, he hoped they wouldn't.

LOOKING BACK — 75 YEARS AGO

Ground was broken Tuesday morning for the new *Seaville Gazette* building on Center Street, directly opposite the Auditorium and the Masonic Temple. The stone wall has been taken down in front of where the building will stand, and the land is being cut down to street level. The building will be of stucco with a two-story front and offices on the second floor. Everything will be up to date: plate glass front, electric lights, steam heat, hardwood floors, with a 50-foot basement.

Chapter Thirty

Why did everyone think they could fool him? Play games.
Tricks. He was the master, after all. Trickster. Trick or treat?
I'll have a little trick, sir. You are a little trick, dearie!

Such a peaceful weekend we've had. This town's a loser and
I'm here to win. Peace on earth, good will toward men. I know
lots of good will. Good Will Oursler, Good Will Shakespeare,
good Will James, good Will Bendix, on and on and on.

So four down, five to go. Got to make the next one a real
goody. Got to top the last one. Hard to do. Can't let down on
the perfection aspect, though. High-quality killings. Keep my
standards high. Quality is important in everything we do. Why
should it be any different killing? I'm working on my moves . . .
I'm making front page news. And then there's detail. Every last
detail must be considered. I am a stickler for detail. But that
must be evident. Surely if they thought about it they'd consider
the detail, consider the inspiration behind the detail. But no one
thinks anymore. No one knows how to put two and two
together because they are too busy dividing four into two. But,
oh, the detail. Detail, one, two, three, hup!

Look over the list. Three females gone. One male. It is true
that the females are easier. You have to really use an element of
surprise with men, have an edge. Well, surprise figures in all of
them but the females are a pushover. The kid, too. Didn't like
that one. Thought it would be easy. Almost couldn't do it.

Getting soft? Easy does it. Cool. Easy. Take it easy. Kiss the sky.

So kill the poison pen. Wordsmith. Scribbler, penman, inkslinger, scrivener, word painter, hack. Do it. Do it soon. Do it now. And that's an order, son.

Yes, sir. Right, sir. Immediately, sir.

LOOKING BACK — 25 YEARS AGO

The talk entitled "Civic Righteousness" at the Thursday noon luncheon meeting of the Seaville Rotary Club was a program in keeping with the world in which we live today. The speaker was Roger Adams, a retired Lutheran clergyman. In his opening remarks Mr. Adams stated that God had blessed America, whose cities had been spared during two World Wars. Now that we are living in an atomic age, America's hope for the future lies in its moral outlook and the moral strength of its citizens.

Chapter Thirty-One

Colin got to the *Gazette* building at six-thirty Tuesday morning. Annie had set the alarm for five-thirty. They'd had a quick cup of coffee before he set out on foot. It was a gray day. Fog was coming in from the Sound, making everything damp, the sun just a memory.

The office was cool, almost clammy. He snapped the lock on the door and left the pulled green shade in place. His heels made a clacking sound on the hardwood floor.

In his office he flipped the light switch. He dialed information for the number of Wood's Motel. When a woman answered he asked for Room 131.

"You calling for Waldo Hallock?" the woman asked.

"Yes."

"He ain't here."

"He checked out?"

"Didn't say that, did I? I said, he ain't here."

"Do you know when he'll be back?"

"Nope."

"Do you know where he is?"

"Nope."

"Did he come back from Florida yet?"

"Nope."

"Then you do know where he is."

Silence.

"Okay, never mind. Just tell him to call Colin Mguire when he gets in. The number's 777-2561."

Silence.

"Are you there?"

"I'm here."

"Did you hear me?"

"I heard."

"Thank you."

She hung up.

He sat at his desk, wondering why Hallock hadn't gotten back yet. He'd probably tried to get him yesterday but couldn't get through. Maybe Hallock had found out something. Maybe he'd cracked the damn thing, found out who the killer was, found out it wasn't Mark.

He'd managed to put thoughts of the killings, Mark, Babe's story out of his mind while he was with Annie. But he couldn't hide from it any more. Things were closing in on him; he'd have to watch Mark carefully, see what he could pick up. But Babe's story might make it impossible for him to stay on at the *Gazette*. The reality was that he didn't have any idea what was going to happen next. He'd have to play it by ear.

God, a shitload of work had piled up on his desk. The first thing to do was the Looking Back column. He'd finished the bound volumes with last week's issue and needed to get the next volumes in the series.

He walked to the back staircase and snapped on the light. The steps creaked under his weight. He hated these stairs. They were wooden and open in the back, reminding him of the stairs to the basement in his childhood home. Brian had teased him mercilessly, telling him that monsters would bite his heels as he went down the steps. Often his mother asked him to go to the cellar to get her something. Too ashamed to tell her he was afraid, he went, terrified. Then he'd fallen, breaking an arm. After that his mother never sent him down again and Brian accused him of falling on purpose. Sometimes he wondered if his brother had been right.

In the basement he crossed the cement floor to where the

books were kept. He pulled one for twenty-five, fifty, and seventy-five years ago. Each volume held papers for twelve weeks at a time. Colin laid them down on a bench, opened the one for twenty-five years ago, and flipped to the second issue.

He didn't know why he wanted to see the article about the fire Annie's father had been in. Maybe it was a way of being closer to her. After flipping through the pages, he realized he must be in the wrong issue and turned to the next one. There it was on the front page.

There were two pictures. The larger was of the building burned to the ground, with firemen standing around. The second picture showed a row of tarp-covered bodies on the ground in front of the burned-out structure. Under the first picture it said: "Firemen Ed Lacy and Jarvis Grattan, part of the team who fought a losing battle for hours, view the remains of the new, popular nightclub in Seaville." The caption underneath the second read: "The bodies of the twelve people who died in the fire." The story was on page 2. As Colin turned the page he was stopped by Mark's voice.

"Morning, pal."

"Jesus, Mark, don't creep up on a guy."

Mark smiled. "Sorry."

"What are you doin here so early?"

"Hey, it's my paper, isn't it?"

Colin didn't like Mark's answer. It seemed odd, defensive. Suddenly he felt apprehensive and wanted to get out of the basement. He closed the book he'd been looking through. "I was just getting the new volumes for the Looking Back column."

"You're not going to need them," Mark said ominously.

"Why not?"

"Don't you know?" Mark's usual good looks, almost pretty in their perfection, seemed sharp, unyielding.

"No."

Mark stared at him, his brown eyes cold. "It's all over, Colin."

"What are you talking about?"

"I was an asshole to give you this job. Christ, you really jerked me around."

Colin took a step toward Mark.

He moved back. "Listen, pal, don't try anything with me. The police are onto you. They called me an hour ago, said you weren't at your house but your car was there. I figured you'd be here. I want you to surrender."

"Surrender?"

Cut the shit, Colin."

"You think *I* committed these murders?" He almost laughed. "You've got to be kidding."

"You really had me fooled. I just couldn't believe you could kill Nancy and the kids. I guess nobody can ever believe a friend is guilty of something like that."

So this was what Mark was going to do — try to pin it all on him. "This isn't going to work, you know."

"Don't make it harder than it is, pal. They've already found her, okay?"

"Who's already found who?"

Mark smiled. "You're beautiful, you really are. Missed your calling, Colin. You should have been an actor."

Colin's mouth was dry. It clicked when he opened it. "Who did they find?" he asked. The only person he could think about was Annie. If Mark had killed her, he didn't know what he would do.

"You know who they found. Why ask me?"

"I *don't* know, Mark. Tell me."

"What I don't get are the symbols. What the hell do these swastikas mean?"

"Another one?"

"Look, Colin, you're very sick. You need help. I feel responsible bringing you here to the Fork, so the least I can do is stop you. And I will." He pulled a gun from his pocket and pointed it at Colin. "Let's go peacefully, okay?"

Colin didn't want to give Mark a reason to shoot him. Jesus, it would be so easy. If Mark killed him, he could blame all the killings on Colin and with his past, nobody would doubt it. On he other hand, if he went with Mark, let them arrest him, he might never get out. He didn't have alibis any more than Mark had. Except last night . . . unless . . . He couldn't contemplate Annie's death, but he had to know. "Mark, tell me who was killed. Humor me."

Mark shrugged, the gun still pointing at Colin's chest. "They found her body in her car this morning, swastika carved in her chest."

"Who?" he shouted.

"Babe, of course. You killed her last night, didn't you?"

Colin wanted to weep with relief. Then suddenly he realized that from the moment he'd accepted Mark's offer of a job, he'd never had a chance. It had all been carefully planned, and Babe's murder was the final nail in the coffin. After what she'd written about him, no one would believe he hadn't done it. Any more than they'd believe Mark was the killer. If only he could find a motive. In jail he wouldn't find out anything. Annie was his alibi, but he couldn't bring her into this. Her career would be destroyed.

Colin made his decision. He doubled over and slammed his head into Mark's gut, knocking him backwards. The gun fell to the floor and skidded out of sight. Colin was going for it as Mark pulled him down by his ankle. They rolled over, and Mark shot a right to the side of Colin's head. Colin kneed him and Mark let go, grunting. Colin started to get up but Mark tackled him around the calves. They fell foward, Mark on top. He grabbed Colin by the hair, pulled hard. Colin shoved both elbows up into Mark's ribs. He let go of Colin's hair, and Colin snapped over on his back. Sitting partway up, he got Mark on the chin with a right cross, then used a left hook just to make sure. Mark fell back, eyes closed.

Colin looked around for the gun. He found it under a table and scooped it up, checked Mark to make sure he was breathing, then ran for the stairs, taking them two at a time. At the top he slammed the door, threw the bolt, and ran through the empty offices to the front. He lifted an edge of the green shade. Coming down the street was a white police car, its siren silent.

The car pulled into the curb in front of the *Gazette*. Colin dropped the shade, ran back through the building, and into his office. Grabbing his windbreaker from his chair, he hastily put it on, shoved the gun in his belt, pushed up the window and keeping low, ran to the back edge of the yard.

He pushed through the hedge into the next property. Laundry was drying on a line and a cool breeze lifted a sheet that slapped him across the face, twisted around his body. He disentangled himself, made his way across that yard and into the next. He had no idea where he was going or what he was going to do. All he knew was he had to find a place to hide, to plan.

Jesus, he was pissed off Hallock hadn't come back. And then he had it. If he could just get to Wood's Motel, he would try and talk Liz Wood into letting him stay in Hallock's room until he returned. If she didn't know who he was, he had a chance. He would say he was Hallock's cousin or old friend. But getting there was not going to be easy. The motel was off the main road just outside of Seaville proper, and he couldn't take the chance of being seen. He would have to stay in the yards, then cross the main drag at a point just before the turnoff to the motel. The best way to do that was at night. Now he had to find a place to hide until sundown. And then he saw the familiar doghouse and remembered the story he'd done three weeks ago. Elsbeth Kiske's German sheperd had been killed by poisoned meat. Colin had interviewed Mrs. Kiske, who'd taken him outside, shown him where she'd found Pencil, the dog, then shown him the big doghouse her late husband had made. He remembered admiring it, saying it was big enough for a person to live in, remembered getting a wan smile out of Mrs. Kiske. And now here he was and there *it* was, the perfect hiding place.

He ducked down behind a maple. There was no sound except that of birds and insect life, a breeze rustling the leaves. It was approximately six yards from the tree to the doghouse. Colin made a dash across the yard. Dropping down on all fours, he crawled inside, hoping Mrs. Kiske hadn't gotten another dog.

———

"Shit," Hallock said, standing at the door of his room, suitcase in hand, looking at the phone as it rang. If he answered it he might be late for his plane. Glancing at his watch, he saw that he was already seven minutes behind schedule and he didn't know what he'd do if he had to spend another hour, let alone a night, in this burg. But the only person he could think of who might be calling him here was Fran. And after hanging up on him she wouldn't be calling unless something was wrong. He dropped the suitcase and crossed to the phone.

A thin, quaking voice said, "Is this the chief?"

"Yeah. Who's this?"

"Is this the chief from Seaville?"

Hallock wondered what other chief would be staying at the Breezeway Motel in Miami Beach in June. Then he recognized the voice. "Mister Conway?"

"Yessir, that's me. Ruth Cooper's daddy."

He pictured Elmer Conway, eighty-five, white-haired and stooped, his face and hands covered with age spots, and still he was Ruth Cooper's daddy. Hallock wondered if he would always be a daddy to *his* children. "What can I do for you, Mr. Conway?"

"Well sir, I did what you asked."

Hallock waited for Conway to go on, but there was nothing happening on the line but some static. "Mister Conway?"

"Yessir?"

"What is it you did?" He looked at his watch, swore silently. Now he was eight minutes behind schedule.

"Well sir, you remember when you were here?"

Hallock shifted from one foot to the other. "I remember."

"Was that yestiday?"

"That's right."

"Seems like longer ago than that, don't it?"

"Times flies," Hallock said and added to himself, when you're having fun!

"Yeah, that's the truth."

The line seemed dead.

Hallock said, "Mister Conway, are you there?"

"Yessir."

He took a deep breath, trying to control his temper. "Mister Conway, what is it I can do for you?"

"Well sir, after you left us yestiday, me and Mildred put on our thinking caps, so to speak. We did what you asked, Chief."

"You mean you thought of something that might be helpful in solving Ruth's murder?"

Elmer Conway sucked in his breath as if this were the first time he'd heard of his daughter being murdered. Hallock could have kicked himself for being so insensitive.

"Mister Conway?"

"Yessir?"

"Why don't you tell me about it?" he urged gently.

"Yessir. Well, me and Mildred spent all of yesterday and all of last night — that is, all of last night when we was up — thinking about what you said. And we come up with just one thing. You see, Ruthie was a ordinary person, just like Mildred and me. What I mean by that is she didn't go in for fancy living and business like that. She was a plain person. A good person."

Hallock heard the old man's voice break on the last word and knew he couldn't rush him. He sat on the bed and waited.

Finally Conway pulled himself together. "What I'm trying to say, Chief, is that she didn't go out a whole lot, her and Russ. But once in awhile they give themselves a treat. Maybe go to a movie, or go down-island to the Mall, do a little shopping. Sometimes they went out to dinner, maybe five, six times a year."

Hallock wondered why the old man was so intent on making his daughter's life seem so drab. He looked at his watch again, realized he wasn't going to make his plane, kicked off his shoes, and leaned back against the pillows.

Conway went on. "But there was this one time when her and Russ decided to really celebrate. Russ had got a promotion. He worked for Volinski Insurance Company. Still does. Anyways,

Russ got this promotion, and he and Ruthie decided to go all-out on a celebration. So first they go to Simpson's for some steamers and a lobster and — you remember Simpson's?"

"I do."

"You're pretty young to be remembering Simpson's. I'm talking twenty-five years ago."

"I'm not as young as you think, Mister Conway."

"Oh. Anyways, they go to Simpson's for a good meal 'cause of Russ's promotion. And then they decide to go to this nightclub over to Seaville. Now you understand they ain't the jet set or anything."

"I understand."

"Well sir, the nightclub's real crowded and somehow it caught on fire."

Hallock sat straight up.

Conway continued. "Don't think they ever found out what started that fire. Anyways, Ruthie and Russ was in there with about a hundred other people. But they got out okay. Twelve people died though. You remember that fire, Chief?"

"I remember. Look, Mister Conway, you've been real helpful. I have to hang up now and get this information to Seaville."

Conway went on as if Hallock hadn't spoken. "See, that was the only thing out of the ordinary me and Mildred could think of. It's not like a person's in a fire every other day, if you see what I mean, Chief."

"I do, and I agree with you. You've been helpful," he said again. "I have to go now, Mister Conway."

"Should we keep on thinking, Chief?"

Hallock recognized the man's reluctance to let him go, as though keeping the connection open somehow negated his daughter's death. "Yes, sure, Mister Conway. And you call me in Seaville if anything occurs to you. That's the second number I gave you."

"Yessir. I called that one but the lady said you wasn't back yet. So then I called this-here number."

"Well, I'm leaving today. Good-bye, Mister Conway, and

thank you." Hallock hung up before Conway could say anything else. Then he punched out Maguire's number. Still busy. He thought a moment, then called the *Gazette*. It rang three times before a man answered. The voice sounded familiar, but Hallock couldn't place it. He asked for Maguire.

"He's not in today," the man said. "Who's calling?"

"Who's this?" Hallock asked.

"Special Agent Schufeldt," he said. "Who's this?"

Hallock withdrew his ear from the phone as if it had been burned, then slowly replaced the receiver in the cradle. He sat on the edge of the bed wondering why Schufeldt was at the paper, answering the phone. Had something happened to Maguire? Had there been another murder? And what about Griffing? Was Schufeldt at the paper to arrest him? Had someone there remembered that fire twenty-five years ago? By some miracle had Schufeldt put it all together? He had to get back.

Quickly he stuffed his feet into his shoes and made for the door. If he missed the next plane out, he'd catch the one after that, and if he couldn't get on that one, the one after that would have to do. Because police chief or not, nothing was going to stop him from being there at the end of this one. Nothing.

LOOKING BACK — 50 YEARS AGO

———————

On Sunday of this week Professor Albert Einstein, who received world-wide notoriety a few weeks ago for his Theory of Relativity, visited Seaville. According to a well-founded rumor, Professor Einstein may become a summer resident of Seaville. While in town he made several inquiries regarding the hiring of a cottage on the waterfront during the summer.

Chapter Thirty-Two

Annie sat in the first pew of her church. The late morning light set off the large mural above the altar as if it were specially lit. She liked coming in to the church at this time of day. It was quiet and she was able to meditate. But today she couldn't concentrate. Every time she tried to focus, expand, zero in on her higher power, she thought of Colin, their night together. And it made her uncomfortable, sitting here in church, thinking of him, of their lovemaking. Not that she believed God would mind. Her God was a loving God who wanted her to be happy again. But replaying scenes of the night before made her feel embarrassed here in church. It was an old idea, an old prudishness. Still, she couldn't shake it, couldn't go beyond the ideas her mother had imparted to her: Church and sex don't mix.

Her thoughts shifted to Steve Cornwell. Did he know that Colin spent the night? If not, it wouldn't be long before he did. But Colin might leave Seaville. He hadn't said so directly, but the possibility was clear. And if he did? Was she supposed to follow him as if she had no life of her own? She smiled to herself thinking, *Who asked?*

It was crazy sitting here wondering about a life that included Colin. They'd spent one night together, something thousands, maybe millions of people did all the time, never to see one another again. But she wasn't any of those people. Making love with Colin was special, important. For her there was nothing transient about it. And that was dangerous.

She couldn't expect him to feel the same way. Most men didn't. But Colin didn't seem like most men. She felt as if she'd known him for years, perhaps always, then reminded herself that that was only a feeling, not a fact. Still, what she'd experienced the night before had been incredible, the depth of feeling overpowering.

That was what frightened her. She cared. She trusted him. And she was totally vulnerable. Enough, she told herself. Standing, she stretched, trying to remember when she last felt so tired. But what a good tired. She left the church and walked toward her office.

Peg was just coming out. "Oh, there you are. I came as soon as I heard," she said.

"Heard what?"

Peg looked stricken. "You mean you don't know?"

"Is this a game?"

"Annie," she said seriously "it's Colin."

She felt her knees give way and grabbed hold of Peg's arm. There was no way she could go through another death; it would finish her.

"Are you okay?"

She went into her office, unable to ask Peg to tell her what she meant.

"Annie," Peg called after her, "did you hear me?"

She didn't answer, just sat on the couch, waiting.

Peg said, "What is it? You look terrible. Oh, God, I'm sorry. He's not dead, if that's what you're thinking."

Annie closed her eyes, let her head fall back against the couch. "What then?" she was able to ask.

"He's disappeared. You do know about Babe Parkinson, don't you?"

"No."

Peg sat down next to her, gently put her hand on Annie's arm. "She's been murdered — one of those swastikas was carved in her chest. And Colin's run away. I can't believe no one's called you."

"I had a meeting about the summer carnival at nine which lasted two hours. I didn't take any calls, then I went over to the church. What do you mean, Colin's run away?"

"I don't know all the details and I got what I have third-hand, but it seems Mark Griffing tried to get Colin to turn himself in and Colin attacked him, locked him in the basement of the *Gazette* building. Then he just disappeared. He didn't have his car so he couldn't have gotten very far. You don't know where he is, do you, Annie?"

"No. When was Babe Parkinson murdered?"

"Some time last night, from what I've gathered."

Annie said, "Colin didn't kill her."

Peg shook her head. "You don't *know* that, Annie. You just don't know."

"I do." she said obstinately.

"Look, I know how you feel. If somebody accused Tim of killing some — "

"Peg, listen to me," she snapped.

"Okay, okay."

"Colin couldn't have killed Babe. He was with me."

"All night?"

"Yes."

"Oh."

"Who should I call?"

"What do you mean?"

"Peg, I have to help Colin. If the police think he killed Babe, they have to be told he couldn't have."

"You can't, Annie."

"Oh, yes I can." She picked up the phone.

Peg depressed the button cutting off the open line. "You just can't. Think." She took the receiver from Annie and replaced it.

"I *am* thinking."

"Look, just because you spent one night with the man doesn't mean you throw your whole career down the drain. Don't you know what's going to happen when this gets out?"

"I have a pretty fair idea. But it doesn't matter. Colin's life might be at stake."

"And so might yours," Peg pointed out.

"That's absurd."

"Is it?"

"You don't know him!" Annie exclaimed.

"And you do?"

"Yes. Yes, I do! He's gentle and sensitive and — he couldn't kill anyone."

"Don't you think it's a bit of a coincidence that this gentle, sensitive man has been invovled in murder before coming to Seaville?" Peg asked.

"Exactly. That's exactly what it is, a coincidence." She made a move toward the phone.

Peg blocked her. "Annie, please. This is just the kind of thing Steve Cornwell is waiting for."

"I can't help that, Peg. Colin's life is more important than my career in Seaville."

"It won't just be Seaville," Peg assured her.

"I'll have to take that chance."

"Can't you at least wait, see what happens?"

Annie searched Peg's eyes. "You mean wait and see if he's killed, don't you?"

"No. I . . . I didn't mean that," Peg said lamely.

She reached for the phone again. "Excuse me."

Peg moved her hand and Annie lifted the receiver. When the call was answered Annie asked for Schufeldt and was told he wasn't in. She left her name and asked that he return her call, saying it was important. Then she tried Mark at the paper. He wasn't in. She left a message that it was urgent he reach her. Next she called Sarah at home, but there was no answer there. The only thing she could do now was wait.

———

The cramp in Colin's right leg was excruciating. He clamped a hand over his mouth to keep from crying out. The other hand he used to squeeze the muscle in his calf, hoping to stop the pain. It didn't work. He tried to distract himself by naming all the teachers he'd had in grammar school. He wondered if you remembered their names all your life. The muscle was still cramping. He need to put pressure on the leg, stand on it, but the doghouse was too low. There had to be an alternative. There was. He lay down in the dirt, put his foot against one wall and pushed. Because he couldn't staighten out his leg, it took longer, hurt more. But finally the pain subsided, then vanished.

He remained on his back, legs bent, eyes studying the peaked ceiling. The number of spider webs seemed to have increased since the last time he counted. Maybe he was hallucinating.

It was almost eight-five. He'd been in the doghouse for over thirteen hours. He laughed. If anyone had ever been in the doghouse it was him. The sun should set in approximately eight to ten minutes. Then it would be another fifteen before it was totally dark and he could get the hell out of here.

His belly growled. He'd had nothing to eat since the eggs the night before. Perversely, he thought of all the foods he loved: pasta, french fries, artichokes, steak, potato chips, mocha cake, pizza. When he finished he was hungrier than he'd been. The worst part was his thirst. Coffee that morning was the last liquid he'd had. But maybe that was good. At least his bladder wasn't bursting. Still, his lips were dry and flaky, and his throat felt as if it were coated with sand.

Sitting up, he went back to thoughts of Mark. Motive was the biggest stumbling block. And the fact that Mark seemed so normal. But hadn't Ted Bundy fooled people? There was plenty of documentation supporting the so-called "normal" killer. It was just hard to believe someone you thought you knew so well could fool you so completely. Colin suspected his reluctance to see the truth about Mark was due to pride, his need to be right.

Even so, Babe's murder was the giveaway. It was as though Mark had signed his name to that one. But to everyone else the signature would be Colin's. Mark must have planned it all from the very beginning. It was the reason he'd asked Colin to work on the paper. The only reason. Still, what about motive? And then he faced the truth: Insane people didn't need a logical motive.

He pulled his sticky shirt away from his chest. It was as if he'd gone into a shower completely dressed. Earlier he'd contemplated stripping to his shorts, but was afraid he might need to make a sudden run.

Looking out the doghouse doorway he could see darkness descending. His windbreaker hung on a protruding nail. He reached for it and wrestled his arms through the sleeves. The Kiske house remained dark but lights were on in the house to the right. There were still a few minutes to wait.

Most of the day he'd thought about Annie, recalling the night before until it became to painful. There was no doubt in his mind that he cared for her, maybe loved her. She was very different from Nancy, which was good and bad. He wouldn't have wanted anyone too much like her; that would have made him uneasy. Yet having an affair with a woman so different from his wife instilled in him a feeling of betrayal, the very thing Dr. Safier warned him about.

What worried him most was not his feelings for Annie or hers for him, but the thought that Mark might harm her, hoping to incriminate Colin further. As soon as he could get to a phone he planned to warn her against Mark. He knew she would find it hard to believe, just as he had. Still, he had to convince her to leave her house, stay with a friend until this thing was over.

Night settled. The time to make his move had arrived. He picked up the gun and slowly crawled through the door into the yard. Getting to his haunches, he waited and listened. June bugs thumped against screens, and the smell of someone barbecuing made him salivate. He would have to keep low going through the yards until he came to the spot across from Wood's Motel. His legs were wobbly as he rose up to run. A dog barked somewhere, a baby cried, snippets of conversation drifted toward him, died. There was no use waiting any longer. He had to go. Now.

Hallock was booked on a six o'clock flight. The storm of the
day before had caused a tremendous backlog of people trying
to get out of Miami. He'd spent most of the day in the terminal,
reading newspapers, commiserating with strangers, making
phone calls. Maguire's phone remained off the hook. But he'd
had success with one of his calls. George Bennett confirmed his
suspicion. He and Ethel had been in the nightclub fire twenty-
five years before. And someone had killed their daughter,
Gloria. He hadn't needed to call Chuck Higbee. Hallock
remembered that Ed and Rose Higbee had been in the fire.
Poor Ed had just gotten a bank loan and was celebrating. Some
celebration

He couldn't remember whether any of the Carrolls had been
in the fire. It couldn't have been Joe, who wasn't even born at
the time, but maybe Mary and Ted were there that night. Or
their parents. Ruth Cooper had actually been in the fire herself.
The others were related somehow. Mary Beth was just an
innocent grandchild.

Hallock walked to the bank of phones against the far wall of
the terminal. He'd gotten the Carroll number through
information earlier, but no one had been home all day. He
dropped in a dime, punched out the numbers. The operator
asked him to deposit more money. He listened to the com-
puterized bells and beeps and then the distant ring. Once, twice,
three times, finally answered by Mary.

"It's Waldo Hallock," he said.

"Oh, yes. How are you?"

"I'm fine, Mary. You?"

"I'm managing," she said.

"I wanted to tell you how sorry I am, Mary. Joe was a fine
boy."

"Thank you."

He wondered how the wife of an undertaker dealt with
death. "Is Ted there by any chance?" Better to speak to the

husband, he thought, then heard Fran telling him he was being an MCP. Even so he knew it would be easier to talk to Ted, providing he wasn't drunk.

"He's not, Waldo. Do you want me to have him call you back?"

"No, thanks. Can't do that. I'm kind of unreachable at the moment." He would have to try her. "Look, Mary, I want to ask you something important."

"What's that?"

"Well, it's kind of a funny question, but I need to know. Were you and Ted or anyone else in your family involved in that nightclub fire twenty-five years ago? You know the one I mean?"

"There's only ever been one nightclub in Seaville."

"That's right. Well, were you?"

"Matter of fact, we were."

Hallock felt his heart give a thump.

Mary said, "Ted had second-degree burns on his left hand. Did you ever notice that scar he has across his palm? That's what it's from. That fire."

"Is that a fact?"

"What's this about, anyway?"

"Just something I'm trying to figure out, Mary. No need to worry about it."

"Has it got anything to do with Joe?" she asked wearily.

"To tell you the truth I don't know. It might."

"I thought you were off the case, Waldo."

"I am," he readily admitted. "Officially."

"Can't keep a good man down, I guess."

"Thanks, Mary. Listen, could you just keep this between us? I mean, my asking about the fire and all. Don't even tell Ted, okay?"

She laughed derisively. "Are you kidding? If I tell Ted, it'll be all over Seaville by the time the bars close. Don't you worry, Waldo. Mum's the word."

He thanked her and hung up. There was no question in his mind that he could trust Mary Carroll. She was definitely a woman of her word.

Hallock walked over to a coffee machine, slipped in three quarters, pushed the coffee button and then the one for milk. He watched while the cup dropped and the liquid poured in. A packet of sugar slid down the chute. He swore at this measly amount, then took his coffee over to a turquoise plastic seat.

So that was it. All four victims had a connection to that old fire. Suddenly the A's and the swastika all made sense. But the reasons for the killings were still a mystery. Or were they? Sipping his coffee, too bitter for his taste, he hazarded a guess.

Someone was systematically killing the survivors of that fire because it had somehow changed his life. And not for the better. Someone had harbored a hatred for twenty-five years; had waited and planned for just the right time. Someone whose mind was tortured and twisted. And now he was killing survivors of that terrible fire — and their relatives. The fire that totally destroyed the only nightclub Seaville had ever had: Razzamatazz.

LOOKING BACK — 75 YEARS AGO

The *Gazette* hears considerable agitation about sprinkling the village streets with oil. If this is not done, there is a likelihood of a water famine should there be a dry summer. That there is a need for the economy of water no one in authority disputes. From the present conditions it seems that it would be good judgement to consider the oiling of the streets. The village fathers have given the question some thought.

Chapter Thirty-Three

Colin waited behind a billboard advertising Alfredo's Bistro in Bayview. Rumor had it that Alfred couldn't stay away from his own food and had had to have his mouth wired shut to lose weight. The ad displayed him, looking trim and handsome, holding out a steaming plate of spaghetti. Natives knew Alfredo hadn't looked that good in twenty years.

At this moment Colin didn't care if Alfredo weighed four hundred pounds of forty, the billboard offered him a shield and that was his only concern. He'd been behind it for only a few minutes, and now the main road looked clear. Was the road always so empty on a June night, he wondered, or did the lack of traffic reflect what was happening here?

Stepping carefully around the billboard, he hunkered down, dashed to the edge of the road, looked both ways, then raced across and into the woods. As he made his way toward the motel he stayed just off the path inside the trees. He could see the lights inside the office. The rooms were behind, sixty feet or so down a path, strung one right after another, nothing but a plaster wall separating each. Hallock's room was 131, but there seemed to be no point in trying to get in unseen; he had to use the phone to warn Annie, and knew the call would register in the office. Still, he thought he'd better check to see if Hallock had returned. As he approached a man and woman came out of the end unit.

"Evening," the man said.

"Hello," said Colin

The woman looked him up and down, nodded.

He smiled at her but she averted her eyes. Did he look that bad? he wondered. He'd tried to brush himself off while he waited behind the billboard, but perhaps the damage was worse than he'd thought. Continuing across the cement walk in front of the rooms, he found 131. The room was dark. He knocked, called Hallock's name, but there was no reply.

At the office he hesitated; what if Liz Wood knew who he was, recognized him from his picture in the paper? For all he knew, there might be a warrant out for his arrest. Even so, he had to take the chance. Hallock was his only hope.

A woman sat behind the counter. Above her head, on a shelf, a black-and-white television was playing a sitcom. She watched the screen intently, a cigarette dangling from the corner of her mouth. Her copper-colored hair was wrapped around pink curlers. The light blue sweatshirt she wore said Grab a Heinie, and displayed a bottle of beer. She glanced at Colin quickly then went back to her show.

"Excuse me," said Colin.

"Yeah?" she replied, still watching the television.

"I'm a friend of Waldo Hallock's and — "

She turned, leveling a baleful gaze at him. "You the one which called before?"

"No. Are you Mrs. Wood?"

"Who wants to know?" She eyed him carefully.

Did she look at everyone this way, he wondered, or was she recalling his picture from the paper? "My name is Mike Rosler," he said. "I'm a friend of Waldo Hallock's, and he asked me to meet him in his room but he's not there. I wonder if you could let me in?"

She took the cigarette from her mouth, a bit of paper sticking to her bottom lip. "Let you in?"

"In his room. To wait."

"When'd he make this plan with you?" she asked suspiciously.

"A few days ago."

"Well, he ain't back yet."

"Yes, I know," he said patiently. "That's my point. I'd like to wait for him. In his room."

It was clear now that she didn't know who he was. He wondered what place would gain her approval, and took a gamble. "I'm from the Midwest. Omaha."

"Omaha?" She permitted herself a small, tight smile. "Had a cousin lived in Omaha. He was a drunk," she said, looking at him as if he might have the same problem. "You drink?"

"Hardly at all," he answered truthfully.

"You look a mess."

He glanced down at his clothes, saw that his trousers were wrinkled and smeared with dirt. He hoped she couldn't see the bulge under his windbreaker where he'd tucked the gun into his belt. "I've been traveling." Fruitlessly, he brushed at his pants. "That's another reason I'd like to wait in the room. I'd like to clean myself up, take a shower."

"You'd be using his towels." She raised a thin eyebrow.

"He wouldn't mind."

"Good thing you're looking for Waldo. He's about the only person you could of said you was waiting on for me to let you in, considering what's been going on around here lately."

"What's that?" He hoped nothing showed in his face.

"Never mind. What'd you say Waldo was to you? Uncle?"

"No. Just a friend."

"How do I know you're telling the truth?"

"You don't. You'll just have to trust me."

"I don't *have* to do anything, mister."

"I didn't mean it that way. I meant, I'd *like* you to trust me."

"I'll bet." She stood up and reached behind her, taking a key from a pegboard. "Master key," she said to him. "I'll have to go down with you." She cast a woeful eye toward the television screen. "Let's hop to it. I don't want to miss my nine o'clock show."

Near the door Colin spied a candy machine. He rummaged through his pockets for some change.

"You coming, or what?"

"I just want to get something," he said, pointing to the machine.

"Out of everything but Clark Bars."

"That's fine." He dropped his money into the slot and pulled the handle. The candy slid into the tray at the bottom. It took control not to rip open the paper and swallow the bar whole. He put the candy in his pocket and followed her down the path.

She seemed to slide along as if she were skating rather than walking, her blue sandals spraying dirt on either side of her. At Room 131 she turned to him before putting the key in the lock.

"Hope you aren't gonna try any funny business?"

"Funny business?"

"Don't try bringing any woman down here now. I'll know if you do."

"Mrs. Wood, I just want to wait for Waldo Hallock, that's all." And eat my goddamn candy bar, he added to himself.

"Who said I was Mrs. Wood?"

"I assumed."

"Bigshot," she muttered, put the key in the lock, and opened the door.

It was the usual motel room, one double bed with an orange spread, a plastic orange chair, a desk made of some synthetic material, two paintings on the wall of Keane-type children, and a black-and-white television in the corner.

"Now don't go messing around with Waldo's things."

Colin wondered what she was referring to as the room seemed devoid of anything personal. "I won't." He wanted her to leave so he could eat his candy.

"If you make any calls either you or Waldo's gotta pay for them."

"Yes, I know."

"Well, okay. I hope I'm doing the right thing letting you in here."

"You are. Don't worry."

"Hope so." She backed out of the room shutting the door behind her.

Colin waited a moment then snapped the lock. He pulled the candy from his windbreaker pocket, stripped the wrapper, and bit off a large hunk. He couldn't remember ever having been so hungry.

When he was finished he closed the curtain, then took the gun from his belt. Nothing of Hallock's was visible but on the night table was a paperback. It was *Ballerina*. Colin smiled. Next to the book was the phone. He dialed Annie's number. No answer. He turned off the light and lay down. A feeling of helplessness overcame him. There was nothing he could do until Hallock returned. What if he didn't come back until morning — would it be too late? If Mark was going to make a move toward Annie, it would be tonight. He couldn't afford to wait.

A swirl of lightning lit the room, then came the thunder, muted in the distance. Oh, Christ, he thought, what if Hallock's trying to get back and a goddamn storm stops him? Colin knew he couldn't deal with this thing by himself. He needed a cover, and Hallock was the only one he could trust. Lightning flashed again, the thunder closer. A splattering of rain fell on the roof. He dialed Annie again. After ten rings he gave up. He thought of his mother, who always unplugged the television set in a storm, convinced that lightning would snake through the set, killing them all.

Another streak of lightning illuminated the room and the crash of thunder that followed sounded as if it had struck the motel. It was pouring now, the drops rythmically beating against the roof. For Colin, who'd gotten little sleep in the last thirty-six hours, it was all he needed to put him out.

———

Annie forced her eyes to stay open. For once she was grateful to Carol Dobson, her voice a screechy irritant, the only thing that could keep Annie awake. The meeting of the Finance Committee felt like it had been going on for days.

None of her calls had been returned nor had she made contact with Colin or Sarah before she'd had to leave for the meeting. She'd tried Schufeldt twice more only to be told he'd call her when he could. And then, in desperation, she'd called

Waldo Hallock. His wife told her he was in Florida and she didn't know when he was returning. That news had shocked her. Somehow she couldn't quite picture Waldo lolling around on a beach when there were still unsolved murders in his town. It didn't matter that he was no longer officially involved.

"Don't you think so, Annie?" Burton Kelly asked.

Startled she answered, "Yes, yes, certainly."

Burton looked smug, arms crossed against his narrow chest.

Instinctively, Annie knew she'd made a mistake. She should have known better than to agree with Burton. There was no way to backpedal now. Whatever she'd agreed to she'd have to stick by.

"Well, I think that covers the issue then," said Steve Cornwell, glaring at Annie. "Let's take a vote. All in favor signify by raising your hand."

Annie took her cue from Burton who kept his arms crossed. She was astonished that she had no idea what they were voting about, and realized how long she must have been drifting.

"All those against."

She put up her hand with the minority. But what did it matter, she'd be leaving as soon as her night with Colin was public knowledge.

"The motion carries," Cornwell declared happily.

When the meeting adjourned Burton sidled up to Annie. "Thanks for standing by me." He put a hand on her arm. "Even though we lost it's good to go on record for what you stand for."

She forced a smile, nodded.

"How about coming back to my place for some coffee?"

Horrified, Annie realized her agreement had given Burton the impression her feelings toward him had changed. "No, thanks, Burton. I have to be getting home."

"I see. Got a late date?" he asked acidly.

She almost answered him, then changed her mind. Explaining her life to Burton Kelly wasn't required. "It's simply none of your business," she said coolly, leaving him startled and staring after her.

Saying her goodnights quickly, she fended off an inquiry from Madge, avoided Steve, and left. It had begun to pour. No one had predicted the storm, so she wasn't prepared and by the time she reached her car she was soaked.

Visibility was poor and when she turned onto the highway, her wipers doing double time, her anxiety, from lack of sleep, had reached a new height. At times she felt as if she were driving under water instead of through it. She had to go very slowly and it was maddening. All she wanted was to get home, wait, and hope that Colin would come to her. A serpentine flash of lightning lit up the sky, and the crash of thunder that immediately followed was so loud Annie jumped, swerving the car to the right, almost going off the road.

Righting the car she slowed even more, wondering if she should pull off until the storm abated. But she desperately wanted to get home, so she continued on.

Headlights appeared in her rearview mirror, the beams diffused by the rain. She stepped on the gas; whoever was behind her was too close. Another incident like the last and they could have an accident. The car stayed with her so she slowed again. There was no way she was going to try to out-distance it in this weather. Deciding to leave the highway, she turned down one of the side streets that would take her to the smaller main road.

When she completed her turn she looked in the rearview but she saw nothing. A moment later, the highbeams of another car were in her mirror again. Annie had a surge of panic. Someone was following her. Was it Steve, intent on threatening her again? Or maybe Burton, hurt and outraged.

At the end of the street she waited, trying to see if there was oncoming traffic before she made her move. The only lights visible were behind her. She flicked her signal and turned. Holding her breath she watched the rearview. At first it was dark but then the lights were there, cutting through the rain, dogging her.

She thought about going to Peg and Tim's, or to the Griffings', but she didn't want to miss Colin. Suddenly she felt joyous. Perhaps the car following her was his! The bubble burst almost immediately; he couldn't have known where she'd been.

Four blocks from her house she slowed, worried about the curving road, the pools of water that always built up in a storm. It was then that she plowed through the first one, water flying on either side of the car, splashing over the front end like miniature waves. She came out of it and almost immediately drove through the next. On the other side of that one she breathed easier. There'd be no more before she got home.

In the church parking lot she killed her lights and sat, waiting. The sound of the rain and her breathing were all she could hear. No one had followed her into the lot, she was sure. Still, she was apprehensive about getting out. But she couldn't sit there all night; she had to make a run for the house.

Looping the strap of her handbag over her head, she dropped it onto her left shoulder. It crossed her chest so the bag rested against her right hip. Slowly she opened the door and jumped from the car. The rain, coming down in torrents, soaked her. As quickly as she could she sprinted across the lawn toward her back door. And then she slipped, twisting her ankle. Pain shot up her leg. She struggled to rise, the bad ankle forcing her to put most of her weight on the other foot.

Tears sprang to her eyes. Hobbling, she reached the back stairs and hauled herself up by hanging onto the railing. She grabbed the door handle and turned. It didn't budge. "Damn," she said out loud. Ever since the episode with Steve she'd begun locking both doors. She unzipped her handbag, felt around for the keys, but couldn't find them. Frustration and pain assaulted her and she began to whimper. At last she found the keys in a side compartment.

Inside she turned the lock, and sobbing, slid down the door to the floor. Her ankle throbbed. She heard herself crying. The sound was alien, frightening. And then the phone rang.

She cried out as if she'd been stabbed. Her attempts to stand were futile so she crawled, keeping count of the rings, willing it to go on until she reached it. The seventh ring had just ended when she pulled on the cord to the receiver. It dropped to the floor. Still, crying, she reeled it in like fishing line.

"Hello, Hello!" she shouted. "Who is it?"

There was no answer.

"Hello. Colin, is that you? Please speak to me." But she knew no one would. She'd answered too late. The line was dead.

The plane had circled above Kennedy Airport for fifteen minutes before it landed. Hallock's patience was wearing thin as he waited in line at the Hertz counter. The limousine was available, but after what he'd learned, he wanted to get home in a hurry. As soon as he'd gotten off the plane he'd called Charlie Copin at home but he wasn't in. Then, hating to do it, he'd called Fran again. She wasn't in either but Cynthia was. His daughter had told him three things: Fran was at a meeting (which burned his ass), Babe Parkinson had been murdered, and the police were looking for Maguire, who was missing.

Hallock thought he knew where Maguire was, and wanted to find him before Schufeldt did. He needed Maguire to help him get to the newspaper accounts of the Razzamatazz fire. Mark Griffing's family had been summer residents in Seaville for years before Griffing bought the paper, and if his suspicions were correct, they'd find that some of Griffing's family was in that fire. But if he was wrong, if nobody connected to Griffing had been involved in the fire, then he was fucked, back to square one.

LOOKING BACK — 25 YEARS AGO

The Seaville Fire Department, despite the rainstorm, lived up to its over a century old tradition by having its annual spectacular firemen's parade of uniformed firemen and firefighting equipment. Despite the inclement weather, the streets were lined with motorcars filled with spectators, and eight visiting fire departments, together with two high school bands and three drum corps, made a colorful parade on a gloomy stormy day.

Chapter Thirty-Four

The crash of thunder that awakened Colin made him sit straight up. There was an awful moment when he didn't know where he was, and thought he was back in Chicago, waking in the car that morning. He'd been dreaming about it again.

When he got his bearings he reached for a cigarette, saw he only had four left. He hadn't noticed a machine in the office, but there must be one somewhere. Lighting up, he looked at his watch. He must have been asleep for over an hour. He tried Annie again. She answered on the first ring, sounding terrible.

"Annie, what's wrong?"

"Oh, Colin, I've been so scared, so worried about you."

"I'm okay. Are you all right?"

"I don't know. I mean, yes, yes, I am now."

"But?"

"Someone was following me tonight. From the meeting where I was."

"Are you sure?" His gut tightened and he thought of Mark.

"I'm almost positive. Whoever it was didn't come into the parking lot, but he was with me right up until I turned in."

"You didn't recognize the car?"

"I could only see headlights."

He had to tell her. "Annie, I think you'd better get out of there, go to a friend's."

"Why?"

"You might be in danger," he warned.

She was silent for a few moments, then asked, "Colin, where are you?"

"I'm at Wood's Motel, waiting for Waldo."

"I don't understand. Why are you waiting for him there?"

"This is where he's staying. He and Fran are having some trouble," he stated.

"I talked to her earlier, and she said he was in Florida and didn't know when he'd be back."

"He should be back soon."

Annie said, "Do you know about Babe?"

"Yes. Look, Annie, I want you to get out of there right away."

"You're scaring me."

"I mean to."

"Why would *I* be in danger? I don't under — oh, God!" she cried.

"What is it? Annie?"

"Someone's at the front door."

"Don't let them in," he commanded.

"But Colin, what if it's somebody in trouble? What if someone needs me?"

"The hell with that."

"I at least have to see who it is? Hold on."

"Annie? Annie, don't — " Colin paced as far as the cord would allow. Smoke from his cigarette curled past his eyes, making them water. He pulled the butt from his mouth, squashed it out in the pink plastic ashtray. A fine film of sweat covered his body, making him feel cold. Why was she taking so long? He lit another cigarette. And then he heard the phone being retrieved.

"Colin?"

"I'm here."

"Listen, everything's okay. It was Mark at the door."

"No!" he yelled. "Annie, listen carefully. You're in danger from Mark."

"That's crazy."

"No, it isn't. Now listen. Does he know you're talking to me?"

"Yes. I forgot what Peg told me this morning but I don't think I'm — "

"You're wrong. You're in great danger. Annie, you've got to get out of there. Believe me. I'm going to hang up now and try to get the police to your place. And whatever you do, don't tell him where I am. Do you understand?"

"Of course, but — "

"This is serious, Annie. Get the hell out of there. Get away from Mark. I think he's the killer."

"That's impossible."

"No, it's not. You have to trust me." His voice was calm, assured.

"All right," she said. "I wish — Colin? Colin are you there?"

Smiling, he listened to her pretending that he'd hung up, then heard her break the connection. He was just about to put his finger on the button when he heard the sound of another receiver being replaced. It could only have been Liz Wood. So now she knew who he was. He couldn't stay in the room any longer. Surely she'd call the police. But he needed to get to them first.

"Seaville Police," the voice said.

It was Frank Tuthill. Colin hoped Frank wouldn't recognize his voice. "I want to report a possible assault."

"Who is this, please?"

He ignored the question. "The address is two hundred and thirty-one Webster."

"What's your name, sir?"

"Just get there, okay?"

"Hey, is this Maguire?"

"A murder might be in progress, you moron. Now get there." He hung up. Turning out the lights, he went to the window. The rain was coming down harder than before. And the lightning and thunder hadn't diminished. There was no way he could get to Annie. He prayed she'd be able to get away from Mark. Why was he always incapacitated when the women he cared about were in danger?

Thinking of that was a waste of time. His priority now was to get out of the room and find someplace to hide. Schufeldt would probably arrive any moment. Stepping into the rain he gave the warm, dry room a longing glance, then shut the door behind him.

———————

Mark said, "What happened?"

"He hung up."

"Damn!"

Annie couldn't believe she should be afraid of Mark. He looked so harmless, water dripping from his yellow slicker, his bruised face handsome, innocent. But the same innocent face had been capable of deceiving his wife, she reminded herself.

"What happened to you?" she asked.

He touched his chin. "Colin did this. Where was he calling from?"

"I don't know," she lied. "Do you want some coffee?" She took a step and winced.

"What is it?"

"I slipped in the parking lot and turned my ankle."

He put a hand on her arm. "Let's see."

Now she felt afraid, but tried not to show it. "No, it's okay."

Mark dropped his hand. "Are you sure you don't know where Colin is? This is important, Annie."

"He didn't say."

"What was he telling you? Why did you say, 'That's impossible'?"

"I don't know. I can't remember."

He reached over and squeezed her arm. "You said it right before he hung up, try to remember."

"You're hurting me, Mark."

He let go. "I'm sorry."

Did she believe him? She tried to act natural, stalling for time. "Why don't you take off your slicker? I'll hang it in the bathroom."

He took off the wet coat and gave it to her. "Try to remember what was impossible," he urged softly.

Taking the slicker she shrugged. "I just can't think now." The ankle hurt terribly, but she made it to the bathroom, where she hung up the coat. When she turned around Mark was standing in the doorway. Startled, she drew in her breath. "I didn't know you were following me," she expained.

He looked at her coolly. "I think there's something you don't understand, Annie."

"Like what?"

"It's about Colin."

Limping, she maneuvered past him to the kitchen and turned on a burner. "I'm having some cocoa. Want some?"

"Jesus, Annie, what the hell's going on? I'm trying to tell you something and you're making cocoa like we're in some goddamn commercial or something."

"I feel like cocoa," she said lamely.

"Is he coming here, Annie? Did he tell you he was going to come here?"

"No. You want some, Mark?" She held out a mug.

He swung his hand knocking the mug to the floor, where it shattered. "Will you shut the fuck up about the cocoa?" he screamed. Then he grabbed her by both shoulders. "Colin has killed eight people, Annie. Five people in Seaville. Three in Chicago. Who knows how many others we never heard about? He's dangerous, a killer. Do you understand?"

His face was almost touching hers; she felt his breath on her cheek. "Please, Mark," she begged.

He shook her. "Listen to me. I know what I'm talking about. This morning when I confronted him he attacked me, ran away. He's been in hiding ever since. Did he tell you that? Did he?"

She didn't want to cry, swore she wouldn't. "No," she answered.

"I'll bet he didn't." He released her. "I'm telling you the truth, Annie."

What if Mark *was* telling the truth? What if Colin was the killer, not Mark? But maybe Mark was just saying that to get her to tell him where Colin was. And when she did he'd . . .

Mark said, "I know it's hard to believe. It's hard for me, too.

I've known the guy for a long time. We've been friends. I . . . I loved him. But I can't let that stand in my way, cloud my vision. And neither can you."

The kettle began to whistle.

They stared at one another. Then she limped to the stove and turned off the flame.

"Annie, I'm telling you the truth," he said again.

She leaned against the stove. "He couldn't have killed Babe Parkinson," she said flatly.

"Why not?"

"I was with him all night."

"From when to when?"

"About eight until six-thirty this morning." Was it only this morning?

"The autopsy came down just a little while ago. Babe could have been killed from any time after six P.M. He had two hours before you saw him."

His words felt like blows.

"Tell me where he is, Annie."

Looking at Mark, she realized he'd been her friend for over a year. She knew a lot about him. And there were the bruises on his face. Why had Colin attacked him if he wasn't guilty? What did she really know about Colin? She prided herself on being astute about people. Could she be so wrong about him? Had she trusted once again only to be betrayed? She had to face the facts: She knew Mark a great deal better than Colin.

"Annie," Mark pleaded, "he might kill someone else if he isn't caught. Tell me."

"All right," she said.

———————

Hallock couldn't see a goddamn thing. His wipers were virtually useless. He'd just passed the traffic circle in Riverhead. On a clear day it would take him about twenty-five minutes, but with this kind of weather it might take an hour. Caution told him he should pull off the road until it was over. But he had to get to Maguire, he couldn't afford the luxury of waiting out the storm. Besides, it didn't look like it was going to stop. He tried the radio for a weather report. There was nothing but static.

The sign warning drivers of flooding wasn't visible to him, but he knew it was there. He knew this road like he knew his own house. Slowing to five miles an hour he felt the car press through knee-high water. The backwash splashed the windows. When the deep water was behind him he accelerated, pushing the car up to fifteen.

The first place he'd go was Annie Winters'. He was sure Maguire would be there. But if he wasn't he'd have to go back to the motel, pick up his collection of keys, and try to get into the *Gazette* that way. One or another of them usually worked, and he guessed the lock on the *Gazette* building wasn't anything fancy.

Another flooding area came up fast, surprising him. He shouldn't be drifting. Although he slowed he wasn't quick enough. The car skidded out of control turning, sideways, water washing up over the hood. Hallock tried to steer into the skid but the car made a 180-degree turn, bouncing over to the shoulder, then kept going across the cinders before it came to a stop.

Hallock said, "Shit!"

Rain wasn't the worst of it, as far as Colin was concerned. It was the wind. Realizing there was really no place for him to go, and that his best bet was to stick close to the motel in case Hallock came back, he'd climbed a tree. Something he hadn't done for about twenty-five years. And it hadn't be easy.

The tree was a large maple. Standing right next to the motel, it afforded Colin a perfect view of Hallock's room. He stood in the crotch of two large branches, leaves giving him plenty of cover. His palms and fingers were scraped raw from dragging his hands over the bark as he'd tried to gain purchase.

Soaked to the skin, he wrapped both arms around a thick branch, the wind threatening to blow him out of the tree. The gun pressed painfully into his stomach but he couldn't shift it. And then he saw the rotating red light of a police car coming down the hill toward the motel. It stopped at the office for a moment, then continued on down the road. Just below him it came to a stop, and all four doors opened at once.

Colin could see them illuminated in the headlights of the car: Schufeldt, Wiggins, Copin, and Liz Wood, all in rain gear. Their voices, altered some by the wind, nevertheless drifted up to him.

"This it?" Schufeldt shouted above this storm.

"Yeah. He's probably sleeping. Looked like a wreck when I saw him. I just knew he was trouble. You can always tell."

"Is there a back way out?"

"No, only this here door and this window."

"Go ahead, Wiggins, knock."

Al Wiggins, gun in hand, standing to the right of the door, gave it three raps. "Open up, Maguire, this is the police!"

Schufeldt and Copin, guns drawn, were to the left of the door, Liz Wood behind them.

Schufeldt yelled, "We'll give you a count of three to come out, Maguire, hands on you head. One. Two. Three. Okay, we're coming in." To Liz he said, "Give me the key."

She reached in her raincoat pocket and gave it to him. He handed the key to Copin, who inserted it in the lock, then kicked open the door.

After a moment Schufeldt shouted, "Listen, Maguire, you can't get away. We've got you covered, so don't go trying anything. Come out with your hands on your head."

Colin watched, fascinated in a bizarre way, as if he were a witness to his own funeral. The three men below hovered on either side of the door, their guns ready.

"Okay, Maguire," Schufeldt said, "this is it. Let's go, boys." He stepped into the doorway, two hands on his gun, and began shooting. Charlie Copin and Al Wiggins were behind him, but only Schufeldt's gun flashed. The report of each shot spiraled upwards to where Colin, hugging the tree, observed the action in horror.

"Jesus," he said out loud. But no one heard.

"Hold your fire!" Schufeldt yelled. He reached inside the door and snapped on the overhead light. Crouching, he entered the room, the others behind him. Then they were gone from Colin's line of vision.

A strong wind swept through the tree. Colin's branch swayed, pulling him downward. He clung fiercely to the branch as it flipped back up, but his feet slipped and he slid down, crashing into the crotch, sending a jolting pain up through his body. He cried out, but the rain covered his yelp. Trying to regain his hold he tilted sideways; his gun fell from his belt down through the tree, hitting the ground with a splat.

Liz Wood heard the sound and turned. Taking a few steps toward the tree, she put a hand to her eyes under the brim of her orange rainhat. Then, seeing nothing, she moved back to the side of the door.

"The fucker's not here," Schufeldt shouted.

Liz moved into the open door. "He was *here*. I'm telling you, that man was *here*."

"Who'd you say Maguire phoned?"

"He called her Annie."

Wiggins said, "I think Maguire was seeing Annie Winters."

"Who's that?" Schufeldt asked.

"She's that lady preacher they got at that church that don't believe in Our Lord Jesus. And somebody named Mark was there," Liz added.

"Did Maguire say he was going there?"

"Nope. Just told her to leave the house. Said she should get away from this Mark person."

"Probably Mark Griffing," Charlie Copin said.

"The newspaper guy?"

"Yeah."

Wiggins said, "Frank got a call said he thought was Maguire. Called in with a possible ten-five in progress. Frank said the address was the Unitarian Church."

"That's right," Liz said, "that was the second call he made."

"Well, fuck it, why didn't somebody say so?" Schufeldt

shouted. "Let's get the hell outta here." He ran toward the car, Wiggins and Copin following.

Go, Colin wanted to shout, move it! At least they might save Annie.

Liz Wood yelled, "Hey, wait up there! You shot his room all to pieces. Who's gonna pay for that? Huh?"

The doors of the cruiser slammed shut. Wiggins backed it up and, turning around with a squeal of tires, drove up the hill.

"Hey, you bums, you wrecked this room here!" Liz continued to shout. "Somebody's gotta pay and it ain't gonna be me. Goddamn bums." She switched off the light and slapped shut the door; then, mumbling to herself, made her way up the hill toward the office.

In his tree, Colin couldn't help smiling. It served her right, he thought. When she was gone he climbed down. He found his gun, then went to Hallock's room and tried the door. It was unlocked.

Positive Liz wouldn't be back tonight, he nevertheless took a precaution and shut himself into the bathroom to wait for Hallock.

LOOKING BACK — 50 YEARS AGO

———————

John Williams, a well-known barber shop proprietor in Seaville, is very familiar with the expression "a close shave," as it is a term used by his customers. Last Saturday, while Williams was busy cutting the hair of his last customer, Louis Stauber, an employeee, attacked Mr. Williams with a hair clipper which he waved before Williams' face. Then Stauber picked up a pair of scissors and threatened to give Williams "a close shave."

Chapter Thirty-Five

Mark said, "So? Where is he?"

Annie wasn't sure what it was, perhaps the subtle change in his eyes when she'd agreed to tell him Colin's whereabouts. Or maybe the set of his shoulders. She didn't really know. But there *was* a change. It could have been as simple as Mark's competitive personality, the fact that he'd won her over. And then again it might have been because as soon as he knew — he'd kill her. She was back to believing Colin. It was absurd to think he was a killer.

"Did you hear me, Annie?" He started toward her.

"I heard." Her back was against the stove; she could feel the heat from the kettle.

"Well, then?"

"I don't know where he is," she responded.

"Bullshit!" His face contorted, anger flared in his eyes. Grabbing her by the arm, he shouted, "You'd better tell me, Annie!"

She tried to pull away, but his grip was too strong. Panicky, she wondered if these were her last moments on earth. "Is that a threat?"

He ignored her question. "You said you knew where he was. I want you to tell me. Someone's life might be at stake."

Yes mine, she thought. Not looking, she reached behind her, picked up the kettle, and swung around, crashing it into the side of Mark's head. He screamed, let go of her arm, and fell to the floor. She dropped the kettle and some of the hot water splashed on him. He screamed again.

Annie, her ankle throbbing, hurriedly limped to the kitchen door and grabbed her purse from the table. Outside the rain was hammering the ground, killing flowers. Wind roared through the trees and buffeted her as she hobbled toward the car. She began to whimper when blades of pain shot up her leg. As she opened the car door, she saw Mark stagger from the house. Throwing herself inside, she slammed the door, locked it, and reached in her bag for her keys. Unable to find them, she screamed in frustration. Then she saw them in the ignition and laughed.

The car sprang to life on the first try. There was no way to know where Mark was or how close he might be. Switching on the headlights, she saw him in front of her, his arms raised above his head, signaling for her to stop. She pressed the horn and drove directly toward him, frightened she would hit him but unwilling to stop, her only desire to get away. At the last moment he jumped to one side, and without stopping she sped into the main road, praying that no one was coming. She was lucky.

The rain crashed against her windshield, the wipers moaning like wounded cows. Her foot, aching and swollen, barely touched the accelerator. Creeping along, she thought about driving to the motel, to Colin, but was afraid Mark might follow. It was better to go to the Moffats'; Mark wouldn't dare come there. But it was almost impossible to see. How would she ever find their street?

A sense of coming apart, losing touch, overwhelmed her. If only Bob were here, she thought. She began to cry. Then, "No, dammit!" she yelled, banging the steering wheel with the side of her fist. "I don't need him, I have myself. Oh, God, please, please, help me," she cried.

And then she realized if she stayed on the main road she would eventually come to Center Street and the Seaville Police Station. It wouldn't matter if Mark followed her there. She was elated by her decision but then she felt it — something cold against the side of her neck. she sucked in air, gasping. Thoughts flew through her mind, colliding, then falling away like boulders down a mountain. Looking in the rearview mirror, she saw his face, the knife against her throat. "It's you," she cried.

"Yes. Me."

She felt a sense of guilt at what she'd done to Mark, but it was immediately diminished as she realized the irony of her situation: She'd been safe and run straight into danger. Shocked at her own calm she asked, "What do you want?"

"You," he responded.

"Why?"

"I thought you'd know."

"I don't. Tell me."

"Razzamatazz," he whispered, and then he laughed.

Hallock had gotten out and walked around the front end. Fortunately, the car had stopped just inches from the mud that would have trapped him for the night. Back in the car he'd turned the key; the motor fluttered, then died. He'd tried again and that time it caught, coughing and choking like an old man with flu. He'd eased the car off the shoulder, onto the road.

And now he was approaching the U. U. Church. When he slowed to turn he saw the police car in the lot, the red light whirling. Continuing past the church, he caught a glimpse of Mark Griffing, standing in the rain, frantically gesturing to Schufeldt. He guessed that Maguire wasn't there, maybe hadn't ever been there. He'd have to get his keys from the motel, try the *Gazette* building himself.

The floor was cool. Colin sat on it, resting his back against the toilet. His gun was in his right hand. All he could think about was how he would have been killed had he remained in the room, hiding. Schufeldt was a maniac.

Even so, he hoped the guy had gotten to Annie before Mark could do anything. By now she was either safe or . . . He couldn't let himself think about it, forcing his mind instead onto food, then cigarettes. The few he had left were lined up on the floor, drying. He touched one. Still wet. Maybe he should quit.

The sound of a key in the door brought Colin to his feet. He leaned against the doorframe, peering through the narrow opening. There was a real possibility that Mark had forced Annie to tell him where he was. His gun was ready if he needed it. He had never killed anyone, but now he had no reservations about killing Mark.

The door opened and Hallock stepped into the room. Colin waited to make sure he was alone. When the chief closed the door Colin felt his shoulders relax, as if he were deflating. So he wouldn't frighten him, he eased open the door. "Waldo," he said. "It's me, Colin."

Hallock's hand automatically went to his gun, then slid down as Colin appeared. "Jesus Christ, Maguire, what the hell you doing in there?"

"It's a long story."

Hallock looked around the damaged room. "What, for Christ's sake, happened here?"

"That's a longer story. We've got to get out of here."

"Where to?"

"Mark's got Annie."

He looked at Colin quizzically. "What do you mean, 'Mark's got Annie'?"

"I think Mark's the killer." It felt strange saying it out loud, as if someone else were speaking.

Hallock looked at him, said nothing, then took off his jacket and began unbuttoning his shirt. "I gotta get out of these wet clothes."

Colin put a hand on his arm. "We don't have time for that. Don't you understand what I'm saying? Mark's alone with Annie."

"I don't think so. I passed her place and Griffing and Schufeldt were in the parking lot."

"Doing what?"

"Talking, it looked like. I couldn't see that good with the rain and all. What makes you think Griffing's the killer?"

"Lots of things."

Hallock dropped his wet trousers to the floor and kicked them across the room. "Tell me what you've come up with."

Colin pulled the gun from under his shirt.

Hallock held up a hand, palm out like a traffic cop. "Hey, boy."

"I took this from Mark. He had it trained on me this morning." Tossing it on the bed, Colin quickly filled him in on the last twenty-fours hours. Hallock listened while he put on dry clothes.

When Colin finished Hallock said, "I think you're right. But where's your proof?"

"I don't have proof, but last Friday Mark left his house at six-thirty in the morning. Nobody knows where he was until nine-thirty. He told me he was with Amy, you know, his old girlfriend."

Hallock nodded, then pulled a brown turtleneck over his head.

"He wasn't with her, Waldo. I checked."

Hallock's head popped through the opening of the turtle-neck, his hair mashed down on either side. "So where was he?"

"I think he was killing Joe Carroll."

"Thing is, Maguire, you haven't given me a motive."

Colin threw up his hands in defeat. "I haven't got one."

"I do."

"What is it?" he asked excitedly.

"Open that drawer, get some paper out. Pencil, too." He sat down on the edge of the bed and pulled on a pair of jeans.

Colin did as Hallock asked.

"I want you to make the swastika just like our killer did."

"Why?"

"Just do it, Maguire, and stop being a goddamn pain in the butt."

"Okay, okay." He drew the swastika then held it out to Hallock.

"Now take it apart."

"I don't know what you mean."

"Just uncross the two parts. What do you get?"

Colin studied his drawing. "I don't know. One Z and maybe a weird-looking N?"

"Turn the weird-looking N around."

"I get another Z."

"Right. And the other symbols were A's, remember. Fact is, you spotted it first at Gildersleeve's that day."

"I don't get it. What's this supposed to be? Two Z's and three A's. What's that?"

"You remember how we were looking for a common denominator? I found it."

"Well, what is it?"

"About twenty-five years ago we had a bad fire here and a lot of people were — "

"Omigod!"

"What?"

"The fire. Was it a nightclub?"

"Yeah. You know about it?"

"I was reading about it this morning when Mark came in with the gun. What's this got to do with the Z's and A's?"

"I guess you didn't get very far in the story. The name of the club was Razzamatazz."

"Razzamatazz," Colin repeated, as the letters started to fall into place, one after another, like plums in a slot machine.

"Gloria Danowski's parents were in that fire. And Ruth and Russ Cooper. Mary Beth Higbee's grandparents, and Ted and Mary Carroll, too. Don't know about Babe yet."

"Jesus, Waldo, do you think the killer is planning to spell out the whole name?"

"Three A's and four Z's so far. Yeah, I think he is."

They were silent a few moments contemplating that horrible possibility. Then Hallock said, "Griffing's family were summer residents twenty-five years ago. You know anything about them?"

"He had a stepmother. His mother died when he was a kid. I

don't think he ever said how. Oh, Jesus, Waldo. Annie's father was in the band that played there when the place went up."

"He's alive?"

"Yeah."

"What's her number?"

Colin told him.

Hallock dialed, looking grim. After ten rings he replaced the receiver. "Not there."

"What should we do?" And icy sweat dotted Colin's body like measles.

"Maybe she's at a friend's."

Colin leaned against the wall trying to hide his anxiety from Hallock. "Let me think. Moffat. She has a friend named Moffat."

"Which one? There are a lot of Moffats on the Fork. Hey, you okay? You look white as a sheet?"

"I'm okay. It's Peg Moffat, I think."

"Tim Moffat's wife?"

"Yes. I think Annie said that was his name."

Hallock reached for the phone book under the night table. Finding the number, he dialed.

Colin watched and waited, his mouth dry, breathing shallow. He could *not* fall apart now, *would* not.

"Is this Peg Moffat?" Hallock asked. "Well, this is Waldo Hallock. I'm fine, thanks. Listen, Peg, I'm trying to get in touch with Annie Winters. She there, by any chance? Uh-huh. I tried her at home just a few minutes ago. You have any idea where she might be? Uh-huh. I see. Well, thanks. You, too." He hung up. "Peg said she went to a meeting, then went home. She talked to her for a minute after the meeting, and Annie told her the same story she told you about being followed. Anyplace else she might be?"

"I warned her about Mark, told her to get away from him. Maybe she did."

"Listen, maybe she's down at the station. Maybe something happened with her and Griffing and that asshole Schufeldt did something right for a change. She could have been in his car when I passed."

"How can we find out?"

"We can go there. Ask."

"I can't. Schufeldt's looking for me. That's what happened to this place. He shot it up thinking I was in here."

"You kidding me?"

"No. He stood in the doorway and blasted this room like he was at target practice."

"Jesus, what a stupid fuck. Okay, listen, I'll go down there, see what's what. Then I'll come back for you and we'll go over to the paper. I want to see if anybody in Griffing's family bought it in that fire. And then I'm going to go after the bastard." Hallock slipped into his jacket, put his gun in his belt. "You lie low here, Maguire. Don't use the phone."

"I won't. But what if it rings? What if Annie's trying to get in touch with me?"

Hallock ran his thumb down the side of his long nose. "Don't answer it. You can't trust Liz. I'll get back fast as I can."

As he went out, Hallock flipped off the lights, leaving Colin in darkness. The storm seemed stronger than ever, wind and rain rushing the room like a berserk presence. Hallock grunted as he fought to close the door.

After he'd gone, Colin carefully made his way toward the bed, felt around for his gun, shoved it in his belt, then lay down. He told himself he didn't have to go with Hallock to the paper. Dr. Safier had said over and over that he didn't have to do anything he didn't want to do. But he *wanted* to help Hallock find Annie. He closed his eyes, trying to imagine himself in the car with Hallock. Almost immediately his breathing changed to quick short takes. His eyes snapped open as he dispelled the image.

How the hell could he do it? But he had to. This time he wasn't drunk; this time he had all his faculties; this time he wasn't going to let down a woman he cared for.

What if his fear immobilized him? But the whole thing was fear of his feelings, and Safier said they couldn't kill him. He wasn't going to die from shaking or sweating or shallow breathing. What if he passed out? Would that be worst thing

that could happen? He'd tell Hallock there was that possibility
and — oh, Maguire, you tricky guy.

No, he couldn't tell Hallock, couldn't create that loophole
for himself. He'd go and he'd survive — if it was the last
goddamn thing he ever did.

LOOKING BACK — 75 YEARS AGO

The movie program to be presented Saturday night at the Seaville Opera House is said to be remarkably good. Owing to many requests that have been made to see the "Lost in the Alps" picture which was shown several months ago, the manager has secured it for Saturday night. The manager, Joe Eldredge, has been in the city this week, and his pictures are carefully selected and all who have witnessed the past exhibitions know that they are of the very best, and they tell their own story better than words can do.

Chapter Thirty-Six

He couldn't believe it. This was special. He couldn't imagine why he waited so long. Well, maybe it was like eating. Saving the best for last. No, not last. She wouldn't be the last. No way.

The best part was her being a minister. He could just imagine how crazy they'd go. Things look bad in black and white. And he could hear them: "How could he kill a minister?" "Nobody's safe if he could murder a minister." "He must be a monster!" M-O-N-S-T-E-R! Like hell. Turnabout is fair play and that's all there is to it.

Would she catch on? Or would he have to lay it out for her? Girls were dumb. Didn't matter if she was a minister or not. Where was it written that ministers weren't dumb? What the hell, he was getting off the point. Time's a wastin'. Get on up there.

He got out of Annie's car. Outside the garage he pulled the heavy wooden doors closed, walked slowly up the steps. Later he'd put her back in the car and junk it somewhere. There was still plenty of time left. Hours and hours of beautiful, dark night.

He pulled open the big door, stepped inside, then slid it back in place, locking it behind him. On his desk he flipped on the radio to his favorite rock station, turned the volume up loud. Bruce Springsteen. Yeah. Then he walked toward the room where she was waiting. The clacking of his boot heels on the wooden floor sounding like tiny drums announcing his entrance.

He stood in front of the glass door, looked in. Her back was to him, arms tied behind the chair, gag in her mouth and blindfold around her eyes. She'd never get away. Not from him. Not again. Once is enough, thank you. Ashes to ashes, windy dust.

He opened the door and went in, his long, sharp knife in his hand.

LOOKING BACK — 25 YEARS AGO

On June 10th the nightclub Razzamatazz burned to the ground in the worst fire in Seaville's history. Firemen battled the blaze from 10:30 until 3:00 in the morning. Before the club was built there was a strong debate as to whether there would be ample parking places. The club has been in operation only six weeks. Fire Chief Roger Grathwohl says the reason for the fire remains a mystery, but he would suspect faulty wiring. Twelve people lost their lives in the fire.

Chapter Thirty-Seven

"What the fuck you doing here, Waldo?" Schufeldt asked.

"Since when isn't a citizen allowed into his local police station?"

Schufeldt's cold blue eyes became slits. "So, what d'you want?"

"Information."

Laughing, Schufeldt said, "You kidding me or what?"

"Something funny about wanting some information?" Hallock knew he wasn't likely to get anything out of this creep but he had to try.

"Yeah, I guess there is something funny."

"Such as?"

"You wanting info from me. It's the other way around, Waldo."

He didn't bite.

Schufeldt's barrel chest puffed up like an inflated toy. "Just can't get it straight, can you? I'm in charge here now. You can't come trying to get information out of me. *I* do the asking. You got it, Waldo?"

Hallock tasted bile in the back of his throat. "You saying an ordinary citizen like me can't get cooperation from the officer in charge? Is that what you're saying, William?"

Blood rushed into Schufeldt's cheeks like shots of dye. "I think you better beat it."

"Where's Annie Winters?" he asked abruptly.

Schufeldt's baby face hardened. "Who wants to know? Maguire?"

"*I* want to know?"

"Are you planning on going to church or what?"

"You know where she is?"

He didn't answer.

"How about Griffing? Where's he?"

"I want to know where Maguire is, Waldo. How come he was staying in your motel room? You two queer for each other or what?"

Ignoring the question, Hallock said, "Real nice the way you shot up the room. I wonder how it would've gone down if you'd killed Maguire."

"I could get you for harboring a fugitive. We have an APB out on Maguire. Yeah, maybe I'll just book you, Waldo."

"What if I told you I didn't know Maguire was in my room?"

"I'd say you were a goddamn motherfucking liar. And then I'd book you."

"So book me, Schufeldt, go ahead," he challenged.

"Where's Maguire?"

"How the hell should I know?"

"You left your wife for him, didn't you?"

"You going to book me or tell me what I want to know?"

"Neither, cutie-pie. Too bad you're not my type." He cackled crazily.

Hallock waited for the laughter to subside. "You're a riot, Schufeldt. I'm telling you something. Anything happens to Annie Winters, I'm going to make it known that you're personally responsible. I have reason to believe she's in danger. Now if you know where she is, tell me. Otherwise — "

"Otherwise nothing, shithead. Get the hell outta here before I throw you in the slammer."

Hallock could see that Schufeldt meant it. He couldn't afford to push the moron any further. As he turned to leave, Schufeldt's voice stopped him.

"Lemme clue you in on something, Waldo."

Hallock waited but didn't turn around.

"Anything happens to Annie Winters, *I'm* gonna get *you* for being an assessory."

The words chilled him. Schufeldt had given himself away. He had no idea where Annie was. Hallock turned, gave Schufeldt a baleful gaze. "Accessory, William, accessory." He walked out before the other man could respond.

The rain was still coming down, hitting the pavement like BB pellets. Hallock wrenched open his door, saw Charlie Copin sitting in the passenger seat.

"Hey, Chief. You okay?"

"Fine."

"Couldn't help hearing what was going on in there." He shook his head as if to say he knew what an asshole Schufeldt was. "You're looking for Annie Winters, huh?"

"I'd like to know where she is," he acknowledged.

"That's just it, Chief. She took off. Mark Griffing was with her trying to find out where Maguire was, and she threw this kettle of hot water at him and ran out the door."

"Did Griffing follow her?"

"No. He says she almost ran him down. We got there about three minutes later. Griffing was kind of stumbling around the lot, holding his head. We took him over to the hospital. Needed stitches."

"He there now?"

"Don't know. That was about an hour or so ago."

"And Annie Winters?"

Copin shrugged. "Like she dropped off the face of the earth. We got an APB out right away, and Al's been patrolling since we dropped off Griffing. He hasn't seen hide nor hair of her. You think she's with Maguire someplace, Chief?"

Hallock wished he could confide in Charlie but felt it would be easier on him not to know. "Just can't say."

"You think Maguire's guilty?"

"No. Listen, Charlie, I gotta go. Thanks for the tip about Annie Winters."

"No sweat, Chief." Copin opened the car door. The rain roared. He started to get out, then looked back at Hallock. "I gotta tell you, Chief, the guys all miss you. That Schufeldt is one dumb peckerhead."

Hallock smiled. "Thanks, Charlie."

Copin gave him a three-fingered salute.

When the door was shut, Hallock started the motor. It was clear Griffing didn't have Annie an hour ago, but that didn't mean he wasn't the killer. And it didn't mean he didn't have her now. He wanted to talk to Griffing, find out how his mother died. He would go to the hospital first, then try his house. If Griffing wasn't either place, that would be the time to worry about Annie.

She felt as if she were choking. The gag, a piece of dirty sheet, was between her lips, tied at the back of her head. Annie willed herself to think of something else, anything but the gag.

Mark. Oh, why hadn't she trusted him? Okay, he was wrong about Colin, but he wasn't there to hurt her. Mark had been such a good friend, always there when she needed support, love. How could she have thought he was a killer? And her fleeting doubts about Colin. It was her basic distrust of people, Bob dying, leaving her alone. But that was over now. She had herself, and if she got out of this she was going to love again, take the risk. She simply couldn't go on the way she had. Look where mistrust had gotten her. Oh, funny, Annie really funny! She *couldn't* look: Another piece of sheet covered her eyes.

He'd taken over the wheel after ordering her to pull into Stuart Lane. The first thing he'd done was to tell her to move to the passenger side, then he carefully climbed over the seat and slipped in behind the wheel. It was then that he'd pulled out the two pieces of dirty sheet, one for the gag, the other to blindfold her. Then he'd bound her wrists with rope.

For a moment she'd considered leaping from the car. But even if she'd managed to get the door handle open, jump, what good would it do her? He'd stop the car and drag her back; she was helpless with no hands, no vision.

They'd driven for about ten minutes and then stopped. She'd

heard him get out. Then her door was opened. She'd felt his hand on her arm, heard him ordering her to get out. Rain slashed at her face. He'd told her to hurry, and guided her across the gravel driveway. She'd stumbled several times, her ankle growing more painful every moment. "We're going up some steps," he'd said.

She'd figured it was his place; she'd been there two or three times. The climb had tortured her, the ankle feeling as though it would crack. He'd opened a door, the hinges squealing, then closed it behind them. They moved along a wooden floor. Another door opened and he'd shoved her inside. Untying her wrists, he'd roughly pushed her into a chair and tied her hands behind her. Then he'd left, shutting the door.

Now she tried to move her wrists, but with each movement the rope tightened, scraping her skin. She was unable to free herself. The only possible chance she had was if he untied her. She couldn't believe that this was the way her life would end. If only he'd take the gag from her mouth so she could talk to him, she might persuade him to let her go. But that was arrogant, she thought. None of the others had succeeded; why should she?

No, this was how it was going to end. But why? What had he meant when he'd said Razzamatazz? Did he mean the club her father had played in all those years ago? Funny, she and Colin had just been talking about it.

A blast of rock music cut off her thoughts. The door opened and closed. His footsteps approached. Annie began to pray.

———————

It was hell waiting. What was taking Hallock so long? Jesus, what if Schufeldt arrested him for something? He wouldn't put it past that guy. Colin slapped his pockets looking for a cigarette he might have missed. Nothing.

If he thought he could get to his car without being seen, he'd try it. But then what? He hadn't the slightest idea where to look for Annie. Still, driving around would feel better than sitting here, helpless. Driving around. He thought about what was ahead, going in the car with Hallock. He mustn't start the fears now. What had Dr. Safier told him? Put yourself in a safe place, create an atmosphere in your mind, stay there. Colin's place was a darkened movie theater, his chair soft luxurious leather. While they drove he'd tell Hallock not to talk to him. He'd keep the panic down by going to his theater.

But that wasn't going to help him now. He paced the dark room, listening to the rain. If Hallock didn't come back in fifteen minutes he'd leave him a note and make a try for his car. He had to do something. The one thing he couldn't be was helpless. If Annie died because he hadn't given it his all, he didn't think he'd survive. He knew he wouldn't.

Hallock walked into the emergency room. A nurse was wheeling an old man down the corridor. "Excuse me, miss." When she looked up at him, Hallock saw that it was Mary Lee Larson, his neighbor. He asked about Griffing.

Mary Lee said, "He left about fifteen minutes ago."

"You know if he was driving?"

"I wouldn't know . . . no, wait a minute. Doctor asked him if he wanted someone to call his wife to pick him up and he said he had his car."

"Was he going home?"

She shrugged. "I don't think he was going out dancing. He had to have eight stitches and his cheek was burned, too. Somebody was sure mad at him."

He thanked her and ran back to his car. It took him four minutes to get to the Griffing house. There were lights on but no sign of Griffing's car. He rang the bell. Sarah came to the door. She looked odd, as though she knew something she shouldn't.

"Sorry to just drop by this way, Sarah, but I need to speak to Mark."

"He's not home," she said crisply. "Anything I can do?"

"No, 'fraid not. Know where he is?" He hated asking her, putting her on the spot. She seemed so frail.

"I don't. Sorry." She forced a smile. "He didn't come home from the paper. Have you tried there?"

"I'll go there next," he said truthfully.

"If you see him, Waldo, tell him it might be nice to call his wife." Her mouth turned down in bitterness. "No. Don't. I'm sorry, I shouldn't have said that."

He wanted to reach out, give her a hug, tell her it was going to be okay. But he, of all people, couldn't reassure her. He was trying to pin five murders on her husband. "You all right, Sarah?"

"I'm fine. Just tired."

He nodded as if to say he knew that kind of tiredness. "Well, thanks." He started to go back down the steps when she called to him.

"Please, don't . . . don't say anything to anyone, will you, Waldo?"

"Don't worry," he assured her.

"Sometimes being the wife of a newspaper publisher gets lonely. He's so busy, has so many commitments. You can't blame him for forgetting to call his wife to say he'll be late. I mean, when you think of what he has on his mind — "

"Sure, I understand," he said, cutting her off. He wanted her to stop justifying Griffing to him; it was none of his business and it was humiliating for her. "Take care, Sarah." He started toward the car, then stopped. When not ask *her?* Turning back to her he saw she was still watching him, standing in the doorway, a waiflike figure. "I wonder if you could tell me something."

"Depends what it is."

He nodded. "Mark's mother. She died a long time ago, right?"

"Yes."

"Do you know how she died?"

"Cancer," she said. "His mother died of cancer when he was ten. Why?"

Hallock felt stunned. "Oh, just something I needed to clear up in my mind." It made no sense but he wasn't going to explain it now.

Sarah didn't pursue it, just said goodnight and closed the door.

As he drove to the motel to pick up Maguire, he experienced a sense of dread, of impending doom. Something he hadn't considered was a definite possibility: Griffing wasn't the killer after all. And Annie Winters was missing. He didn't need to go back to second-grade math to figure this one out: One and one made two. The Razzamatazz killer was somebody else. And he didn't have a clue who it was.

LOOKING BACK — 50 YEARS AGO

Frank (Kid) Edwards of Seaville, an Alaskan "Sourdough," on Wednesday of this week identified Thomas P. Jensen as "Blueberry Tom," wanted for the murder of three prospectors in a battle over $9,000 worth of gold in Alaska in 1916. Edwards, who is 46 years old, has been a resident of Seaville for a number of years. He was in Alaska during the gold rush and personally knew the three murdered prospectors who were killed near Fairbanks, Alaska.

Chapter Thirty-Eight

Hallock jammed his foot on the brake. The car skidded, and this time he drove into the skid, avoiding trouble. He backed up, turned in close to the curb. Rain continued to fall, making visibility almost impossible. Still, he thought he recognized the car. Big Cherokee, black and white. Hard to miss. And he knew whose driveway it was parked in, too.

He doused the lights, left the car running, jumped out, and ran across the lawn to the side of the house. In those twenty seconds he found himself wet to the skin as if he'd just taken a swim. Streams of water ran down his face from his hair. Crouching, he slowly rose up until he was eye-level with the partially opened window.

First he saw *her*. She strode across the room. When she turned toward the window saying, "Do you want another drink?" Hallock felt a blade of fear go through him. He'd had the momentary illusion that Julia Dorman was speaking to him. A man's voice answered, "I shouldn't be drinking at all."

Hallock knew the voice at once: Mark Griffing.

Julia said, "Come over to the couch, darling." She reached out both hands.

Griffing's hands met hers and he rose up, back to Hallock, and walked across the room. When they sat on the couch, Griffing immediately stretched out and put his head in Julia's lap. A bandage spanned his head from hairline to midway down his face.

Now Hallock understood why Julia had done him in, and who was behind it. Well, he'd seen enough. As he ran back to his car, he recalled Maguire's tale of Griffing's unexplained whereabouts on the morning of Joe Carroll's murder. Hallock was sure he knew now where Griffing had been. Feeling the way he did about Julia Dorman and that bastard, Griffing, a part of him wanted to broadcast their little romance. But the other part, the part that cared for Sarah, knew he'd say nothing except to Maguire. Poor Sarah, he thought as he got into the car, poor old gal.

———————

When he took the gag out of her mouth she said, "Are you going to kill me?"

"What do you think?"

"I think you are."

He was silent.

"Are you?"

He didn't answer.

"At least tell me, okay?" Annie wondered why she wanted to know.

"What will it do for you if I tell?" he asked.

"I don't know," she said truthfully. "I just want you to tell me. And how about taking off the blindfold?"

"You want to see yourself die?"

Her stomach muscles tightened as if she'd been struck. He'd answered her after all. "Please take off the blindfold," she begged.

"No."

"Why not?"

"Because I said."

Annie felt powerless, as though she'd been made a child again. She tried a different tack. "Why are you doing this?"

"I can't believe you don't know."

"Razzamatazz?" she ventured.

"Razzamatazz. Right."

"I don't know what that means."

"The hell you don't."

She felt something sharp and cold at her neck, knew it was his knife. "What I mean," she said carefully, "is that I don't know what it has to do with me."

"But you remember?"

"Remember?"

"The club?"

"Yes." If only he would take off the blindfold she would have a better chance, she thought. As though sight would give her power.

"Your father played the trumpet in that club."

She said nothing, deciding on a strategy.

"Did you hear me?"

Frightened, she remained silent.

"Did you hear me?" he asked again.

She refused to answer, and then she felt the knife break her skin, felt blood dribble down her neck. Still she kept silent.

"What is it with you?"

"I want you to take off the blindfold."

"Why?"

"Why do I have to keep it on is more to the point."

"I'm running things here, not you."

She believed he wanted to talk to her, tell her what it was all about. It was important to make him believe the removal of the blindfold was essential to her responding to him. "I can't talk with this damn thing on."

"You don't have to see to talk."

"I do."

"You'll talk if I say so."

"No. You're going to kill me anyway, so I'll do what I choose, and I choose not to speak to you if I can't see you." It might have been the biggest gamble she'd taken in her life. And maybe the last.

After a moment he said, "Are you telling me you won't talk unless I take that thing off?"

"Yes."

"What if I say if you don't talk I'll slit your throat?"

"I just explained that. Go ahead. It makes no difference to me if I die now or later. But I'm not talking anymore with this blindfold on." These could be my last moments on earth, she told herself. It was an odd feeling, like the seconds before skiing downhill or the moment before the rollercoaster is released — suspended time, a slap in death's face.

He said nothing.

She could hear him breathing, feel the point of the knife at her throat. And then he moved. She held her breath.

"Okay," he said. "But don't get smart."

The first round was over and she had won.

Colin opened the door on the passenger side of Hallock's rented tan Camaro. He got in, didn't quite close the door.

"You okay?" Hallock asked.

"Yeah." But he wasn't. Far from it. He shut the door.

"I'm going to start the car now."

"Okay. Go ahead." There was a low roaring in his ears and then he heard Safier's voice: "You are never really trapped, Colin. There is always a way out of any situation." And it was true. At any time he could tell Hallock to stop. Get out, walk to the *Gazette* building. Sure he could! Safier hadn't counted on time being of the essence. He had had no way of knowing that his patient would one day be fighting the clock, mixed up once again in murder. Jesus, he thought, maybe it's me. Maybe I'm a jinx. "Stop being the center of the universe," Safier had said. And, "Take a positive view." What the hell could be positive about this? A second chance. He was being given a second chance. Oh, God, he thought, this time I mustn't fail.

"You tell me, Maguire, if you want me to stop or anything."

"Thanks, Waldo." His voice sounded odd, he thought, like someone with a cold.

Hallock turned the key. The motor sprang to life.

Pain shot through Colin's arms, down his legs. He'd had this before, but familiarity didn't ease his discomfort. Grabbing the leather handgrip, he squeezed, and pressed his feet against the floor.

Hallock eased the car along the road, pebbles spraying the undersides. The wipers groaned under the onslaught of rain.

Colin closed his eyes. The last time he'd driven in a car with another person had been with his family. The day before they died. Nancy'd been driving, and the kids were in the back in car seats. He saw himself turn toward Todd, his three-year-old face chocolate-spotted, dark eyes glistening with life, the lashes long, thick.

"Daddy? What's Alicia doing?" Todd always asked what everyone was doing, his way of understanding the complexities of personality.

"She's sleeping," Colin answered.

"Could I be sleeping, too?"

"Just close your eyes, honey."

"Okay."

Nancy said, "You know something, Colly, you've got a way with kids." She smiled at him, touched his knee.

"Maybe I should have more," he declared.

"Over my dead body," she said.

Colin groaned.

"Want me to stop?" Hallock asked.

"No. No, it's okay. I was just remembering something." He felt as if he couldn't breathe. "I've got to open the window."

"Go ahead."

He rolled down the window and stuck out his head. The rain pelted his face, soaking his hair. He opened his mouth, felt the drops hit his tongue.

At the end of the road Hallock put on his signal and opened his window to see. "Anything coming that way, Maguire?"

"No, go ahead."

Hallock turned onto the main road, rolled up his window.

Colin wondered why he'd never remembered that before, Nancy saying, "Over my dead body." What would Safier have made of that? The wind and rain were making it harder for him to breathe. He pulled in his head. Water rolled down his face and neck, soaking his shirt front. A touch of nausea made him gulp and swallow air.

"How you doing there, Maguire?"

"I'm hanging in," he whispered.

"Be there before you can say Jack Robinson."

"Jack Robinson," Colin said, turning to look at Hallock. "Liar."

They both laughed.

Hallock said, "No kidding, we're almost there."

"I know." To get to the *Gazette* building without becoming hysterical was all he asked. Even as he thought this, his mind swirled in dizzying circles, nausea growing.

"Another mile, Maguire, that's all."

He couldn't speak, just grunted, hoping the sound indicated that he understood. If only he could remember some of the tricks Safier had introduced him to. But everything he'd learned eluded him. His mind was as empty as if his brain had been vacuumed. Balling his hands into fists, he suddenly remembered Safier's toe-clenching trick. "If you begin to feel you are going out of control, clench and unclench your toes. Concentrate on that."

Colin obeyed his unseen doctor. He focused on his toes, clenched, unclenched, clenched, unclenched. It wasn't working. He tried something else. This is for Annie, he said to himself. This is for Annie. Over and over. Thinking of nothing else, his panic receded some, his breathing returned to an almost normal rate, the dizziness vanished.

"Here we are, Maguire." Hallock pulled into a side street, killed the motor. "Can't park in front. Even Schufeldt might think it's suspicious. You okay?"

"I'm okay." And he was. He hadn't passed out, hadn't died.

"We're going to get plenty wet between here and there. Let's head for that big tree on the corner, then we'll case the street, make sure it's empty. You ready?"

Colin nodded.

Both men opened their doors, jumped out, and made a dash for the large oak. They were drenched at once. The wind, in a relentlessly battering fury, pushed them against the trunk of the tree.

Shouting, Hallock said, "It looks all clear, nobody around. Make a run for the door."

Heading into the wind, they ran, ankle-deep water slowing their progress. Once there, Colin dug in his windbreaker pocket for his key but came up empty. "Jesus," he yelled over the storm, "the key's gone."

"What d'you mean, 'gone'?"

"It must have fallen out of my pocket when I was running," he explained.

"You sure?"

Feeling like a fool, Colin checked all his pockets. "Nothing," he said.

"I didn't bother bringing my keys since you had yours."

"Should we look?" He gestured toward the street.

"Like looking in a lake," Hallock said impatiently. Let's get off the street." He headed for the alley at the right of the building, Colin following.

In back Colin shouted over the rain, "My window. I went out that way this morning. It should still be open." He gave the window frame a shove and it slid up easily. He climbed through first, gave a hand to Hallock then shut the window.

"God almighty, I feel like I've been in the Sound. And you look like something the cat drug in," Hallock observed.

"You can see in the dark now?"

"I'm using my imagination."

"Well, use it to find our way through this place to the basement. C'mon, let's go. Take my hand." Colin shuffled forward, one hand stretched out in front of him, the other behind, clasping Hallock's.

After a few moments their eyes became accustomed to the dark and they were able to move more swiftly. Once Colin slammed into a chair left in the wrong place, and Hallock crashed a shin into something he couldn't identify.

At the top of the steps to the basement Colin dropped Hallock's hand. "There's a rail on the right."

"Got it. How the hell are we going to read anything down there?" Hallock asked.

"There should .be a flashlight somewhere."

"What d'you mean, 'somewhere'?"

"Just that."

It was darker when they reached the bottom. The windows were very small at ground level and offered no light. Carefully, Colin crossed the room toward where the bound papers were stored.

"Hey?" Hallock called. "I can't see a goddamned thing."

"Just follow my voice. Keep coming — here I am — that's right. Straight ahead. You'll make it. Good. This is where the old issues are kept. Christ, how am I going to see which is the one we need?"

"Beats me."

"We've got to find that flash."

"You don't have any idea where it is?"

"There are some shelves over on the far wall. I think maybe I saw it there."

"Where's the far wall? Can't even see that," Hallock said wearily.

"This way." He grabbed Hallock's wet jacket, pulled him along, his right hand thrust forward, protecting himself. The hand collided with something cool, smooth. He wrapped his fingers around the object, lifted if from the shelf. Bringing it close to his face he saw that it was a glass, smelled something acrid. "Okay, we're at the shelves." He reached out to replace the glass and dropped it. "Shit!"

"What was that?"

"A glass."

"What's the smell?"

"Turpentine, I think."

"Don't drop any lit matches."

"I don't have any matches. I wish I did. Come here, next to me. Feel around for the flash."

Both men felt along the shelves as if they were reading Braille. A number of things crashed to the floor, some breaking others bouncing, rolling away.

Finally Hallock said, "I got it." He snapped the button forward and a dim light appeared. "Not much life left in the batteries."

"Turn if off. Okay. Now let's go back to the books. Keep the flash off so we don't waste it."

"Right."

Again they shuffled across the cement floor like ancient men using walkers. Colin's foot caught on something and he tripped, pitched forward, falling against a crate, cracking his head. He shouted out in pain.

"Maguire. You okay, Maguire?"

"Just dandy."

"Where are you?"

"Don't move, Waldo. There's something on the floor." He sat up, scooted toward whatever had tripped him, touched it. "Over here. Give me the flash." He extended his hand, felt the cool metal slapped in his palm, clicked it on, pointed the beam toward the offending object. "It's one of the bound books," he said excitedly. "It must have fallen when Mark and I were fighting. Let me see if it's the one we need. Come here, sit down."

Hallock joined him on the floor. Colin opened the book. "Yeah, this is the one. Hold this," he said, giving him the flashlight. He turned the pages until he came to the issue he'd seen that morning. "Here it is."

The beam of light dimly illuminated the page, the bodies lying under the tarps.

"Jesus," Hallock said, "I'd forgotten how awful it was."

Colin began to read the story out loud but Hallock interrupted him. "Go to the obit page. That's what we need."

"You're right. Okay, here it is. My God." He kept turning pages. There were three devoted to obituraries. "Waldo, we don't even know what we're looking for."

"I think we'll know it when we see it. You start on the left side, I'll read the right."

Silently they read through the obits, checking names, looking for clues. And then Colin said, "Perkins."

"Who?"

"Perkins. Annie mentioned them to me."

"What d'you mean?"

"She knew them." The flashlight died. "Shit!" He clicked it off, shook it, snapped it on again. Nothing. "Now what?"

"Tear those pages out and put them under your jacket. We'll read them in the car."

Carefully, Colin ripped out the pages, folded them into as small a square as possible, shoved it into his shirt pocket, and zipped up his jacket. "Okay."

They scrabbled to their feet and stumbled toward the steps. Upstairs they made their way to the front of the building without incident. Colin unlocked the door. They stepped outside, the rain lashing their faces and bodies.

"Run for it," Hallock yelled.

Splashing through pools of water, they ran across the street, past the big oak and to the car. Inside, Colin unzipped his jacket, patted his pocket with a wet hand. "Still there," he said, relieved. "Got any rags or anything? I don't want to touch the paper with these hands."

"Look in the glove compartment."

He pushed the lock and it snapped open. There were two napkins, looking as if they'd been used.

"Not mine," Hallock said.

Colin dried his hands, dropped the napkins on the floor, and gingerly removed the folded papers from his pocket.

"Where's the light in this buggy?" Hallock asked.

Colin ran his hand over the roof. "Try your side."

"Got it." He clicked on a muted light.

Colin unfolded the sheets and handed two to Hallock. He ran his finger down the page in front of him until he came to Perkins, Evelyn and Howard.

Evelyn R. and Howard Mathew Perkins, residents of Seaville, died Saturday June 10th in the club Razzamatazz fire in Seaville. She was 35, he was 39.

Mrs. Perkins was born in Seaville, the

daughter of the late Elizabeth and Franklin Heath.

Mr. Perkins was born in Bayview, the
son of Alice and Jame Elliott Perkins. He
was an employee of Riverhead Highway
Department.

The Perkins are survived by their son,
James Drew.

"James Drew," Colin said vaguely.

"What?"

"Nothing."

Hallock looked at him, raised an eyebrow. "You find
something?"

"No, it was just a name that sounded fam...." He trailed off
his eyes glazing over.

What is it?"

"Oh, Christ! I don't believe it."

"Maguire, will you tell me what the hell you're talking
about?"

"I'm talking about a kid named James Drew Perkins. Sound
familiar?"

Hallock looked puzzled.

"Try this: Jim Drew."

"Jesus!"

"He was Annie's first boyfriend when they were eight."

Hallock snapped off the light and started the motor. "I hope
to hell we're not too late."

LOOKING BACK — 75 YEARS AGO

Some bad boy or boys without a spark of common decency or speck of manly honor have been doing various things lately that will land them in the penitentary if their identity should become known. The latest depredation occurred this week when the miscreants with heavy rocks smashed a portion of the walk and steps near the bottom of the landing of the new stairway and walks at the foot of the Sound Road. *The Seaville Gazette* will press the charge against the miscreants if their names can be learned.

Chapter Thirty-Nine

When the blindfold was removed Annie looked around. She was in his barn, a small room off the main area. Boxes were stacked along one wall, and against another was an old carousel horse painted green and red. Opposite her was a rolltop desk in the first stage of being stripped. A dining room chair with a caned seat leaned against the desk. Rock music continued to blare from the other room.

He stood above her. His hair was wet, and the shoulders and arms of his denim jacket as well. Under it he wore a red polo shirt, and when he moved the jacket flapped back exposing a worn alligator, a hole near his tail. The knife was in his right hand, a cigarette in the other.

"You don't know who I am, do you?" he asked, annoyed.

Annie stared at him, uncomprehending. "Of course I do. You're Jim Drew."

He smiled, his lips turning downward. "No, I mean who I *really* am."

Was he one of these people who believed he was Christ or Napoleon or maybe a being from another planet? Whoever he thought he was, she must be careful not to offend; try to convince him that she believed him. "Why don't you tell me who you really are?"

"Take a guess." He ran a hand over his scraggly black beard, bringing the ragged edges to a momentary point before the wiry hairs sprang back into disarray.

"It's hard to think tied up like this."

He laughed harshly and turned away from her.

"Where are you going?" she asked, panicky.

Drew picked up the cane chair, placed it in front of her backwards and sat down. Leaning his arms on the top of the frame, one hand gripping the knife, he said, "If you think I'm gonna untie you, you've got another think coming."

"My wrists hurt."

He frowned, thick black brows coming together, forming one line. "Fire hurts worse."

"What do you mean?" He still hadn't told her what his reference to the Razzamatazz fire meant.

"Next week's the anniversary. Twenty-five years."

"You mean twenty-five years since the Razzamatazz fire?"

"Boy, you're real smart," he said sarcastically. Then, switching gears, said, "How come you became a preacher?"

"It was just something I wanted to do." She couldn't help thinking how strange life was. If she hadn't become a minister she probably would never have returned to Seaville, and now her life wouldn't be hanging in the balance.

"I thought you'd be a teacher."

"What do you mean, you *thought*?"

He laughed again. "Guess."

"Guess?"

"Yeah. Guess why I thought you'd be a teacher."

"I can't."

"You'd better try," he said sharply.

"I told you I can't think with my hands tied this way."

Drew jumped up suddenly, the chair falling forward hit Annie's knees. She cried out as he lunged toward her and slapped her across the face backhanded. "Shut up. Just shut the fuck up. And don't go saying anything about being tied up again." He stood over her, his body shaking.

Her face stung where he'd hit her, knees too where the chair had struck them. She mustn't make him angry. The only hope she had was to keep him talking, win him over. But he was insane. No rules applied. Her experience with totally mad people was nonexistent.

"Jim, I'm sorry I made you so angry and — "

"I'll bet you are," he interrupted.

She went on. "I'd like to know who you *really* are. Tell me."

He looked pleased, as if he'd finally won some approval. "I'll give you a hint," he said briskly. "I wanted to be a pilot."

"A pilot," she repeated. "What do you mean, you wanted to be? When you were little?"

"Right."

The Beatles were singing "Lucy in the Sky with Diamonds." It didn't help her concentration. She felt confused. How would what he wanted to be as a child be a hint for her? "You have me stumped," she said, smiling.

"That's because I'm smarter than you."

"I'm sure it is." She hoped she sounded sincere.

His dark eyes sparked. "You'd better believe it."

"I do."

He rocked on his heels. "Anyway, I wanted to be a pilot, and you wanted to be a teacher, and we were going to get married."

She was stunned. It couldn't be. But it was. "Jamie Perkins," she said.

"Jamie *Drew* Perkins."

"I can't believe it. I was just talking about you . . . . " She trailed off. This wasn't some ordinary meeting of two old friends — a hug and kiss and talk of old times. "Oh, Jamie, why?"

"Who to?" he asked, ignoring her question. "Who've you been talking to me about me?"

"No one. I mean, no one special," she fudged.

"Who?" he demanded. He stepped toward her, menacing.

She couldn't tell him, couldn't even say it was someone other than Colin; she didn't know what he might do to the person she named. "I don't even remember."

He raised a hand to slap her.

"Please don't," she begged.

Stopping his downward swing in midair, he looked at her as if he'd seen her for the first time, a stranger suddenly in his line of vision. He dropped his arm to his side. "Oh, Annie," he said softly.

She sensed the right time had come. "Jamie, please, untie me. I won't try to get away, I promise. It just hurts so much."

He hesitated for only a moment. "You couldn't get away even if you tried."

"That's right. But I don't want to get away. We're old friends."

"Yeah, that's right. You told me you loved me, remember?"

"And I did," she admitted.

"Okay, Annie. I'm going to trust you." He walked around her chair and began to undo the rope.

She'd won a second round. Still, the battle wasn't over; she hadn't won the war. Her hands dropped when the rope was removed. As she brought her arms around to the front, pain shot through them. She rubbed her wrists, gently lowering her hands to her lap.

He came back to stand in front of her, his legs touching her knees. "You don't know what I've been through." Tears threatened to spill down his cheeks.

"Tell me, Jamie," she urged. "Tell me all about it."

He moved away from her, picked up the fallen chair, and sat down, the back no longer a barrier between them. "It's been lousy, Annie. Since they died, Mommy and Daddy."

"It must have been terrible for you." The longer he talked, the longer she stayed alive. She had to pick her moment carefully. There would only be one.

He gave her frosty look. "You wouldn't know."

"Tell me," she urged again.

From his jacket pocket he took a crumpled pack of Camels, shook one up, grabbed it with his lips, and returned the package to his pocket. Eyes still on her, he lit up, blew out the match, then dropped it on the floor. "You really want to know?"

"Yes. Very much." And she did.

"Okay, then I'll tell you," he replied, as if she'd offered a reward for information. "After it happened, after they were burned to crisps," he pointed out acidly, "my Grandma and Grandpa Perkins took me in for awhile. But that didn't work out."

"Why not?" She would ask him lots of questions, get him to expand on whatever he told her.

"They were old. My daddy was what they call a change-of-life baby. She was forty-five when she had him. Anyway, they were old — crochety. Mean, you could say. They didn't want me to move, it seemed. Every time I tried to play in the house they told me I was making too much noise, stuff like that. So I left there."

"What do you mean, 'left'?"

"They put me out," he amplified. "Sent me to a home. With nuns. My daddy was a Catholic." He sucked on his cigarette, blew long streams of smoke in the air. "They beat me up, the nuns."

"How?"

"With rulers. Metal ones. Then I went to live with some people, the Rogers. That was in New Jersey. She was real fat. He was tall and skinny. I called them Jack Sprat and wife. Remember that rhyme? Jack Sprat would eat no fat, his wife would eat no lean?"

"I remember," she said.

"They heard me one day. He beat the shit out of me."

"I'm sorry," she said, meaning it. For a moment she forgot that sitting before her was a man who'd killed at least four adults and a child. She mustn't let his story seduce her. What she had to do was look for an opening, a vulnerable moment. "Go on, Jamie."

His eyes searched hers as if within them he might find the answer to all his pain. "I like the way you say my name. Nobody's called me Jamie for a very long time."

"Because you called yourself Jim," she explained.

"I had to. You can understand that, can't you?"

"No. Tell me."

"Later." He dropped his cigarette on the floor, squashed it out with his foot. "I got sent away from Jack Sprat and wife and went to some people called Schroeder. It was the same. Every place I went, they were all the same."

"How many homes were you in?"

"Ten, twelve, I don't know. But I got out of it when I was eighteen. I enlisted," he said proudly. "I was a Marine."

"Did you go to Vietnam?"

"No. I just said that." He looked away from her, shifted uncomfortably in his chair. "They didn't like me in the Marines either, but I'm not talking about it so don't try to make me." His eyes were flat now, like slate. "I bummed around, picking up jobs here and there, and what kept me going was the same thing got me through all those places I'd lived as a kid. If I hadn't had my plan I don't think I would've made it."

"What plan?"

"My Razzamatazz plan," he grinned.

"Tell me," she said softly.

"I always knew I'd come back here. I knew I was going to make them suffer."

"Who?"

"The people who lived."

"You mean the people who survived the fire?" She remembered how shaken her father had been, how he'd talked about the panic, people being trampled.

"There were eighty-two of them."

"And you were going to kill all eighty-two?"

"You don't get it," he said angrily.

"I'm trying."

"I wanted them to suffer like I did. I wanted them to know what it was like to have people you love die. Like Mary Beth Higbee's grandparents. They were in the fire, but they got out. Knocking other people out of the way so they could save their own skins. Anyway, if I killed them they wouldn't suffer, they'd just be dead. But if I killed their grandchild, they'd suffer plenty."

She swallowed hard, feeling the full weight of this man's sickness. Suddenly she believed she would never get away. He was going to kill her no matter what she said or did. Kill her because her father had survived the fire. The will to fight leaked from her body like air from a punctured tire.

"I like things neat. Tied up, if you know what I mean. So I

thought the twenty-fifth anniversary of the fire, of my parents' dying, would be the best way to mark it. But I couldn't come back here as Jamie Perkins. Somebody might put two and two together," explained Drew. "And then there was the most important part." His eyes fired up again. "The smartest part."

"What was that?" she forced herself to ask.

"See, if I just came here as Jim Drew, the antique and junk man, and a whole series of murders started three years after I arrived, well, I'd be one of the first suspects. People here don't like outsiders, in case you've forgotten. They're suspicious of them in the best of times. But some ex-Marine, looking sort of beat-up, living in a barn off the highway, selling mostly junk? I'd be a sitting duck. But if I made them think I was a guilt-ridden nut right from the beginning, by the time the murders began I'd be the last person they'd suspect."

"So you started confessing to everything that happened."

"You got it. Well, hell, I even confessed to the murders. Nobody can say I didn't try to get arrested!" He started to laugh, rocked backwards in his chair, its front two feet raised off the ground.

Without thinking, Annie seized the moment. Arms outstretched, she jumped, flung herself forward, and pushed Drew backwards. The chair toppled over as he tumbled back, crashing to the floor.

Annie was through the doorway before Drew landed. Her ankle tortured her, she ran to the huge sliding doors and pushed. Nothing moved. Glancing back at Drew, she saw him slowly rising. There wasn't going to be time to get out of the barn. Frantically she looked around. There were boxes, furniture, curios piled everywhere. And then she saw the ladder leaning against the second story. A large iron unicorn on wheels blocked the ladder. She pushed it to the side and hobbled up the rickety steps. At the top she started to pull the ladder up after her, but Drew reached it and caught the bottom rung. She let go suddenly and the ladder fell, knocking him to the floor.

"You fucking bitch!" he screamed over the music.

A waist-high railing ran three-quarters of the way around the second story. Annie was on the long side opposite the barn doors. She could see that there were alcoves and nooks in which to hide, but there was only one way down — the way she'd come up. It was essential not to get too far from the ladder. She could hear Jim Drew scrambling around and knew she had to act quickly. He would be putting up the ladder again and she would have to knock it down. Or better still, knock him off it.

Behind her, to the right, was a rusted gasoline can. She picked it up, relieved to find it empty. The ladder thudded against the wood as Drew propped it in place. Annie moved to the right side of the opening and dropped to her knees. She heard him grunt as his boot hit the first rung. It would be stupid to throw the can before he was halfway up, but if she missed then she would have much less time to run. Still, it was a chance she must take.

Counting his steps, she calculated where the midpoint would come, the music and the thumping of her heart almost blocking out the sound of his footfalls. But as he reached eight she sprang up with all her force threw the can at the top of his head. He saw it coming and, letting go of the ladder, put up his arms to ward off the blow. The can hit his arms, bounced, and glanced off the side of his head. Balanced precariously, his arms windmilled while he tried to regain his equilibrium. A horrified expression passed over his face as Annie gave the top of the ladder a shove. It swung out, stopped upright for an instant, teetered, then finally fell backwards. Drew let go of the ladder in midair and fell to the floor with a sickening thud.

Still on her knees, Annie watched and waited. The Beatles finished their song. Immediately another record began, loud and metallic-sounding. Drew lay unmoving for several moments. For a second she was hopeful. And then he stirred, slowly sitting up. He raised his head. "I'm going to get you!" he yelled.

Annie remained where she was, watching to see what he'd do, deciding what her next move should be. She was astonished to realize that she no longer felt fear. Something more powerful had gained control of her. Perhaps the will to survive. And with it came energy, adrenalin pumping through her body.

Awkwardly, Drew got to his feet, took a step, limped. He grimaced in pain, muttering to himself. Then he glanced her way again, kicked out in anger, hitting the fallen ladder.

She smiled as he limped toward the far end of the barn. Now they were more evenly matched. Drew disappeared under the overhang of the second story. She couldn't imagine where he was going. Was there another way up? Would he suddenly appear before her, pop up as if he were a jack-in-the-box? She had to be ready for him.

Frantically, she looked around for other weapons, hoping to find a pitchfork, a spade at least. Behind her was a stall, remnants of hay littering the floor. Cartons were piled up against the far wall. She ran to them, opened the top one, peered in at books, moldy and old, earwigs crawling over the covers. She swirled around, searching for something else. And then she saw it in the corner, covered with dirt and bits of hay.

Kneeling down, she wiped away the filth with the sleeve of her blouse. The red of the cylinder began to show through. God, let it still work, she prayed. She'd never used a fire extinguisher before and had no knowledge of how it operated. She turned it around searching for directions. A chrome band circled the middle of the cylinder. There was print beneath the grime. She gave it a swipe, but the dirt was caked and needed more than a wipe with a sleeve.

She looked around the floor of the stall for something sharp to scrape off the dirt. A rusted can opener was near her foot. Perfect. She dug at the dirt on the chrome band. It seemed to take forever. While scraping away, she managed to remain alert to the sounds around her even though the rain on the tin roof and the blaring music of the Rolling Stones were almost deafening.

When she'd gotten most of the dirt removed, she brought the extinguisher closer to read the instructions. But she saw immediately that instead of instructions on how to use it, what was printed there were instructions for maintenance and recharging. Frustrated, she slammed it with the heel of her hand, cried out in pain, then slapped the hand over her mouth as she heard the squeak of a board from the far end of the upper floor.

Fear returned as Annie realized Jim Drew had gained access to the second floor. Her heart pumped overtime. She breathed, mouth open, as if somehow taking in great gulps of air would help her. Quickly, she turned the extinguisher around. She knew there had to be instructions somewhere. The front of the metal band also revealed bits of printing. She struggled with her can opener again, scraping and scratching. Slowly, a black band within the chrome one appeared. Large chrome printing spelled out, TO OPERATE: She knew she had to hurry as creaks in the distance told her Drew was moving closer.

The words were finally visible. TO OPERATE: HOLD UPRIGHT. PULL PIN. SQUEEZE LEVER. DIRECT AT BASE OF FLAME. Pin? *Pin?* She started to panic.

Then suddenly, "I'm going to get you, Annie." Drew's voice, hollow and menacing, came from nearby. "You'll never get away," he warned. "Never!"

———————

Hallock and Colin had had two close calls. The first with a trailer truck obviously heading for the ferry at Point Haven, the second with a Volkswagen bug. No one was hurt or pushed off the road in either instance, but privately each man thought that his number was up both times.

The rain had increased in the last five minutes as if they were driving under a continuous waterfall. In any other circumstances Hallock would have pulled off the road. But he couldn't do that now. Now they had to creep along the back road, both of them hanging out of the windows, trying to see, trying to keep on the right side, but not too far over.

Colin knew there was a possibility that when they made it to Drew's barn, he and Annie might not be there. He was sure that Drew had gotten to her somehow, but chances of him taking her to his barn were slim. Still, they had to check it out. He couldn't allow himself to think that Annie might already be dead; it was totally unacceptable.

There were no lights on the back road, but in the distance, on Colin's side, he could see a glow through the downpour. He pulled in his head.

"I think we're here," he said, water running down his face.

Hallock slowed to a stop. "Get out and see, will you Maguire?"

Colin opened the door, jumped out. The wind buffeted him backwards against the car, flattening him as if he were a bug. Rain stung his face. He cupped his eyes with both hands, tried to see. Something was swinging near him, its iron creakiness cutting through the storm. He pushed against the wind, moving forward until he crashed against something hard. It was the sign to Drew's antique barn. Calculating the distance to the drive from memory, he got back in the car.

"About six feet, Waldo. Six feet and turn right."

The car inched forward as both men tried to gauge six feet.

Colin pulled his head in, "Now. Turn now."

Hallock did, and they felt the wheels grip the entry road as they drove slowly forward up to the barn.

She knew he was only four or five yards away from her at best. This was no time to panic, not now. Then a new feeling of calm descended, her hands stopped shaking, her heart slowed. She read the directions on the extinguisher again, and this time she saw the pin. She pulled but the pin didn't move. There was rust around the hole. She pulled again. Nothing.

"Come on out, Annie," Drew yelled. "If you come out I'll do it quick. If you don't I'm going to take my time."

Still calm, she gave the pin a wrenching tug and it slipped out, almost making her lose her balance. Next she unhooked the black hose from its holder. Standing up, she lifted the extinguisher in her arms. It was heavy but manageable. She placed herself at the edge of the stall so that as Drew came past she could squeeze the lever, aiming the hose at him.

As she listened for his footsteps, she thought of the possibility that the extinguisher might not function. It was obviously old. And even if it did, what then? Time. It would buy her more time. She knew now there was another way down, and she would try and find it.

"Last chance," Drew called.

He sounded closer. Eight or ten feet away. She held the extinguisher in one aching arm, balancing it on her hip, and with the other hand she pointed the nozzle like a gun. She was ready.

The floor creaked as Drew came closer. Another step. She still felt in control.

And then suddenly there was a crashing sound. Louder than the music. It was coming from below. At first she didn't know what it was, but then realized it was someone hammering against the barn doors. She forced herself to block out the sound so she wouldn't be distracted as she listened for Drew's footsteps.

The second story was silent. The banging from below continued. She wondered if Drew was diverted by it. Maybe he'd gone back in the other direction, away from her. Desperately she wanted to look, to move forward just an inch so she could see. She dared not.

"YAH!" he screamed and jumped in front of her, the knife held in one upraised hand. His sudden movement sent her back a step, but she didn't lose her balance as she squeezed the lever, the nozzle pointed at Drew's face.

The foam shot out, hitting him in the eyes. He dropped the knife and reeled backwards, screaming. Annie advanced and squirted more at his face, his eyes. He kept on screaming, twisting, turning, and then he was at the open place in the railing where the ladder had been. She watched him teeter for an instant, and then he fell, screaming.

Annie dropped the extinguisher and ran to the edge just as he landed on top of the iron unicorn, its horn running through him from back to front. He hung there like a speared fish, blood staining his shirt, his eyes open wide as though he couldn't believe his rotten luck.

Dizzy, Annie grabbed the railing. She knew he was dead, knew she had killed him, but she felt no guilt. Perhaps later. The banging and yelling continued and she thought she heard her name being called, thought it sounded like Colin. Swaying for a moment, she rested her hand on the railing; then, feeling stronger, she began to limp in the direction Drew had come from. She would find the way down. The way back to life.

LOOKING BACK — 25 YEARS AGO

A memorial was held last Friday morning in the Seaville High School auditorium for the victims of the Razzamatazz fire on June 10th. Twelve people died in the blaze. The Mayor read a eulogy and various friends and family of the deceased contributed reminiscences. Grace Gildersleeve sang "Nearer, My God To Thee." It was a very moving occasion for the next of kin as well as saddened villagers. Repercussions of the fire will be with citizens of Seaville for a long time to come.

Chapter Forty

Colin held Annie in his arms. She had begun to cry and so had he. He cried for Alicia and Todd and Nancy because they were dead. And he cried for Annie, thankful she was alive.

Across the room Hallock stared down at the body of Jim Drew Perkins, still astonished by the man's elaborate scheme to avenge the deaths of his parents. He wondered what the boy would have become had there never been a fire at the Razzamatazz Club. He shook his head. There'd never be a way of measuring, toting up cause and effect. And in the end, Hallock wondered, how important was that anyway? The only thing that really mattered was that the reign of terror on the North Fork was over.

He walked across the barn to where the phone rested on a rolltop desk, picked up the receiver, and punched out a number. This first call was to the Medical Examiner, and the second would be to Gildersleeve. And then he would call Schufeldt. He grinned. Oh, how sweet it is, he thought. When all those calls were made he would phone Fran, ask her if he could come home. He realized what a fool he'd been, taking out his hurt pride, his bruised male ego, on the person who loved him unconditionally — the one person he loved more than anyone or anything. And as for her involvement in her causes, he realized that a part of him was proud of her, glad that she had principles. He wouldn't want her any other way. Somehow he would make it up to her, take her away on a vacation, make love with her four times a day. Well, two. maybe.

Colin stroked Annie's hair, kissed her cheek. "It's okay, Annie, it's okay now."

She looked up into his brown eyes, wiped a tear from his cheek. "It's so awful," she said. "The whole thing's so ugly and awful."

"I know."

"And I feel so bad about Mark."

He nodded. "Me, too." Colin knew it would never be the same between Mark and him again. Each of them had suspected the other. How would there ever be room for trust after that? Besides, after what Waldo had told him about Mark and Julia Dorman, he'd lost all respect for the man. He would have to leave the paper, move somewhere else.

As if Annie had read his mind she said, "I think I'll have to find another parish. Too much has happened here. Too many wounds." Instinctively she looked across the room at Jim Drew, shuddered, and turned away.

"Yes," Colin agreed, "we'll have to find another place."

She seemed startled, then smiled. He kissed her lips gently. Hallock cleared his throat. They broke apart.

"Listen," he said, "no reason for you kids to hang around here anymore. Tomorrow's soon enough for statements. I'll take care of the rest of it."

"Are you sure?" Colin asked.

"I'm sure. Fact is, I think you should get the hell out of here before the place starts jumping."

"What about you, Waldo? What are you going to do later?"

"I'm going home where I belong. Fran said she'd wait up for me."

"You're a lucky guy," Colin said.

"Don't I know it."

"Well, Chief," Colin put out his hand.

"Might be a little premature on that one, Maguire."

"Not a chance. I wish I could see Schufeldt's face when you're reinstated."

Hallock grinned. "I hope to have that pleasure myself. Go home now. I'll talk to you tomorrow."

Colin and Annie said goodnight, then walked to the sliding barn doors. He pushed them open. The rain had abated slightly but it was still coming down.

"Your car's in the garage underneath here," Colin informed her.

"And yours?"

"My what?"

"Your car? Where is it?"

"I came with Waldo."

She looked surprised.

"Omigod!" he said. "I didn't notice. Driving here from the paper I didn't even realize I was riding with another person. Well, what d'you think of that?"

"I think it's wonderful."

He drew her to him. "How would you like to drive a guy home?" he asked.

"I'd like to very much," she said. "Very much indeed."

FINE MYSTERY AND SUSPENSE TITLES FROM CARROLL & GRAF

☐ Allingham, Margery/THE ALLINGHAM
CASE-BOOK $3.95
☐ Allingham, Margery/MR. CAMPION'S
FARTHING $3.95
☐ Allingham, Margery/MR. CAMPION'S
QUARRY $4.50
☐ Allingham, Margery/MYSTERY MILE $3.95
☐ Allingham, Margery/NO LOVE LOST $3.95
☐ Allingham, Margery/POLICE AT THE FUNERAL $3.95
☐ Allingham, Margery/THE WHITE COTTAGE
MYSTERY $3.50
☐ Ambler, Eric/BACKGROUND TO DANGER $3.95
☐ Ambler, Eric/A COFFIN FOR DIMITRIOS $3.95
☐ Ambler, Eric/EPITAPH FOR A SPY $3.95
☐ Ambler, Eric/JOURNEY INTO FEAR $3.95
☐ Ambler, Eric/STATE OF SIEGE $3.95
☐ Ball, John/IN HEAT OF THE NIGHT $3.95
☐ Ball, John/THE KIWI TARGET $3.95
☐ Bentley, E.L./TRENT'S LAST CASE $4.95
☐ Bentley, E.C./TRENT'S OWN CASE $3.95
☐ Blake, Nicholas/A TANGLED WEB $3.50
☐ Block, Lawrence/AFTER THE FIRST DEATH $4.50
☐ Block, Lawrence/THE GIRL WITH THE
LONG GREEN HEART $3.95
☐ Block, Lawrence/MONA $3.95
☐ Block, Lawrence/THE TRIUMPH OF EVIL $3.95
☐ Brand, Christianna/DEATH IN HIGH HEELS $3.95
☐ Brand, Christianna/FOG OF DOUBT $4.95
☐ Brown, Fredric/THE LENIENT BEAST $3.50
☐ Brown Fredric/THE SCREAMING MIMI $3.50
☐ Buchan, John/JOHN MACNAB $3.95
☐ Buchan, John/WITCH WOOD $3.95
☐ Burnett, W.R./LITTLE CAESAR $3.50
☐ Butler, Gerald/KISS THE BLOOD OFF MY
HANDS $3.95
☐ Carr, John Dickson/BRIDE OF NEWGATE $4.95

☐ Gilbert, Michael/THE 92nd TIGER	$3.95
☐ Gilbert, Michael/THE QUEEN AGAINST KARL MULLEN	$4.50
☐ Graham, Winston/MARNIE	$3.95
☐ Griffiths, John/THE GOOD SPY	$4.95
☐ Homung, E.W./THE AMATEUR CRACKSMAN	$3.95
☐ Hughes, Dorothy B./THE EXPENDABLE MAN	$3.50
☐ Hughes, Dorothy B./THE FALLEN SPARROW	$3.50
☐ Hughes, Dorothy B./RIDE THE PINK HORSE	$3.95
☐ Kitchin, C. H. B./DEATH OF HIS UNCLE	$3.95
☐ Kitchin, C. H. B./DEATH OF MY AUNT	$3.50
☐ Lutz, John/BUYER BEWARE	$3.95
☐ MacDonald, Philip/THE RASP	$3.50
☐ Mason, A.E.W./AT THE VILLA ROSE	$3.50
☐ Mason, A.E.W./THE HOUSE OF THE ARROW	$3.50
☐ Mason, A.E.W./THE PRISONER IN THE OPAL	$3.95
☐ McShane, Mark/SEANCE ON A WET AFTERNOON	$3.95
☐ Masterson, Whit/TOUCH OF EVIL	$3.95
☐ Millhiser, Marlys/WILLING HOSTAGE	$4.95
☐ Muller & Pronzini/BEYOND THE GRAVE	$3.95
☐ Muller & Pronzini/THE LIGHTHOUSE	$4.50
☐ Murphy, Warren/DIGGER SMOKED OUT	$4.95
☐ Neely, Richard/THE WALTER SYNDROME	$3.95
☐ Pentecost, Hugh/THE CANNIBAL WHO OVERATE	$3.95
☐ Pronzini, Bill/DEAD RUN	$3.95
☐ Pronzini, Bill/THE JADE FIGURINE	$3.95
☐ Pronzini, Bill/SNOWBOUND	$4.95
☐ Pronzini & Wilcox/TWOSPOT	$4.95
☐ Rogers, Joel T./THE RED RIGHT HAND	$3.50
☐ 'Sapper'/BULLDOG DRUMMOND	$3.50
☐ Stevens, Shane/ANVIL CHORUS	$4.95
☐ Stevens, Shane/BY REASON OF INSANITY	$5.95
☐ Stevens, Shane/DEAD CITY	$4.95
☐ Stout, Rex/A PRIZE FOR PRINCES	$4.95
☐ Stout, Rex/UNDER THE ANDES	$4.95
☐ Symons, Julian/BOGUE'S FORTUNE	$3.95
☐ Wainwright, John/ALL ON A SUMMER'S DAY	$3.50

☐ Wallace, Edgar/THE FOUR JUST MEN	$2.95
☐ Waugh, Hillary/A DEATH IN A TOWN	$3.95
☐ Waugh, Hillary/SLEEP LONG, MY LOVE	$3.95
☐ Web, Martha G./DARLING COREY'S DEAD	$3.95
☐ Westlake, Donald E./THE MERCENARIES	$3.95
☐ Willeford, Charles/THE WOMAN CHASER	$3.95

Available from fine bookstores everywhere or use this coupon for ordering.

Carroll & Graf Publishers, Inc., 260 Fifth Avenue, N.Y., N.Y. 10001

Please send me the books I have checked above. I am enclosing $_____
(please add $1.75 per title to cover postage and handling.) Send check
or money order—no cash or C.O.D.'s please. N.Y. residents please add
8¼% sales tax.

Mr/Mrs/Ms _____

Address _____

City_____ State/Zip_____
Please allow four to six weeks for delivery.